JOAN A. CO'
MURDER OF

JOAN ALICE COWDROY was born in London in 1884, the third child of Arthur Rathbone Cowdroy and Marie Grace Aiton.

The author wrote a series of well-received romantic novels in the 1920's, but her career in crime fiction did not begin until 1930 with the publication of *The Mystery of Sett* which introduced one of her series detectives, Chief-Inspector Gorham. Her Asian detective, Mr. Moh, made his first appearance a year later and became a long-standing recurring sleuth in the author's crime fiction.

Joan A. Cowdroy, a life-long spinster, died in Sussex in 1946.

JOAN A. COWDROY MYSTERIES
Available from Dean Street Press

Death Has No Tongue
Murder of Lydia

JOAN A. COWDROY

MURDER OF LYDIA

With an introduction by Curtis Evans

DEAN STREET PRESS

Published by Dean Street Press 2019

Copyright © 1933 Joan A. Cowdroy

Introduction Copyright © 2019 Curtis Evans

All Rights Reserved

First published in 1933 by Hutchinson

Cover by DSP

ISBN 978 1 912574 85 8

www.deanstreetpress.co.uk

INTRODUCTION

ON JANUARY 9, 1923 Edith Thompson was executed, along with her younger lover Frederick Bywaters, for the brutal murder of her husband Percy, in what today is generally considered one of the most notorious of British miscarriages of justice. Tellingly, the executioner at Thompson's ghastly botched hanging, haunted by the grisly details of her death, resigned from his position the next year and later committed suicide. Yet Edith Thompson received no sympathy from prominent English educational theorist and anti-feminist polemicist Charlotte Cowdroy (1864-1932), headmistress of the Crouch End High School for Girls, who branded the undoubted adulteress and supposed murderess an "abnormal woman" because she worked outside the home, earned more money than her husband and did not desire to have any children. Throughout the 1920s up to her death in 1932 (and, indeed, beyond it, with the publication of her posthumously published 1933 jeremiad *Wasted Womanhood*), Cowdroy, who ironically was herself both single and gainfully employed, passionately denounced women's suffrage and female employment in the nation's workforce as detrimental to the public welfare. She strenuously urged her sisters in the "weaker sex" to eschew personal and financial independence and take what she deemed their natural place in society as submissive wives and mothers. Such sentiments unsurprisingly have generally not endeared Charlotte Cowdroy to modern readers. At the Stuck in a Book blog, for example, Simon Thomas chose *Wasted Womanhood* as his "vilest" read of 2011, adding that Cowdroy's virulent Thirties screed castigating "single, childless woman" as public menaces made him "want to go back in time and thwack her around her unkind head with her unkind book."

Happily for vintage mystery fans, such prominent single, childless Golden Age women mystery writers as Gladys Mitchell, Lucy Beatice Malleson, Edith Caroline Rivett (E.C.R. Lorac/ Carol Carnac) and Molly Thynne (reprinted by Dean Street Press) declined to follow Charlotte Cowdroy's advice and modestly put down their pens (even as Charlotte kept a firm grip on her own until grim death ungently pried it from her cold dead fingers). Another Englishwoman crime writer who declined Charlotte Cowdroy's nostrums was Charlotte's second cousin (once removed), Joan Alice Cowdroy (1884-1946). During her adult life Cowdroy remained single, supporting herself by producing a steady succession of both mainstream and detective novels, six of the latter of which detail the sleuthing exploits of Li Moh, presumably the first Asian detective created by a British mystery writer. (It was an American, Earl Derr Biggers, who gave us Charlie Chan.) Today, nearly eighty years after the last appearance in print of canny Mr. Moh, Joan Cowdroy's mysteries are being reprinted by Dean Street Press.

Like Ianthe Jerrold, who likewise has been reprinted by Dean Street Press, Joan Cowdroy was a Twenties mainstream novelist who began penning mystery stories near the end of the decade. Both women were descended from noted journalists, though Joan Cowdroy more distantly so than Jerrold. Joan's great-great grandfather, William Cowdroy, Sr. (1752-1814), founded the *Manchester Gazette*, the first radical nonconformist newspaper to service the population of the rapidly developing north England industrial city of Manchester. William trained all four of his sons--William, Jr., Thomas, Benjamin and youngest Citizen Howarth (born in 1795, his first name was inspired by the establishment in 1792 of the First Republic in France)--as printers on his paper, which after his death sadly was put out of business by the tremendous success of the *Manchester Guardian*. Citizen Cowdroy, who married Martha Rathbone of the prominent Rathbone shipping family of Liverpool (from whom cinema's greatest Sherlock Holmes, Basil Rathbone, likewise is descended), attempted to carry on the family journalism tradition, starting the *Manchester Courier* in 1817, but he died when he was only thirty-three years old, in 1828.

Citizen's son John Rathbone Cowdroy became a minister and served for many years as curate of Oxton Parish, near Liverpool, but John's son Arthur Rathbone Cowdroy (1851-1899) at a young age moved to Hammersmith, West London, where in 1876 he married native Scotswoman Marie Grace Aiton. There as well the couple's third child, Joan Alice Cowdroy, was born on September 16,

1884. Arthur, who served from the age of eighteen as a clerk and later head librarian for the Royal Society of Arts, died tragically at the age of 48 in 1899, when Joan was but fourteen years of age, from locomotor ataxia, a degeneration of the dorsal column of the spinal cord, which frequently is a symptom of tertiary syphilis.

In 1911, 26-year-old Joan Alice resided with her widowed mother, an elder sister, Dora Marion (who worked as a private secretary to a doctor), and a maid at a small villa at 23 Shalimar Gardens in Acton, West London, listing, in contrast with her sister, no occupation. It would take another eleven years--after Dora had married and her brother, Gerald Aiton Rathbone Cowdroy, had become a successful rubber planter out in British Malaya (in 1915 he wed, appropriately for a scion of a band of English newspapermen, Flora Still, the daughter of the editor of the Singapore *Straits-Times*)--for Joan, nearing the age of forty, to see Sampson, Low (future publishers of mystery writers E.C.R. Lorac and Moray Dalton) publish her first novel, *Brothers in Love* (1922). That this novel about "the devotion of one man to another" doubtlessly was inspired by the tragic lingering disability and painful death of Joan's father, this review from the *Straits-Times* makes sufficiently clear:

> We were half inclined to head this notice "A Study in Pain." The central figure in Joan A. Cowdroy's novel, a first, we believe, is a young man doomed by an accident before his birth to agonizing sufferings and to personal disfigurement which makes him almost repulsive to sensitive people, even while they willingly extend to him their pity. But, truly, it is rather the study of a beautiful soul prisoned in a racked and misshapen body, of a man capable of exquisite feeling, great tenderness, and almost superhuman courage and self-sacrifice.[1]

1. The reviewer in the *Spectator* was far less sympathetic to the subject matter Cowdroy had chosen for her first novel, complaining that *Brothers in Love* "is concerned entirely with the physical condition of the principal character. People who like reading about sickrooms will doubtless enjoy the book; but it is decidedly morbid in tone."

JOAN A. COWDROY

"Miss Cowdroy is a wonderful artist," the moved reviewer concluded, and Joan's next several novels--*The Inscrutable Secretary* (1924), *A Virtuous Fool* (1925) and *A King of Space* (1925)--received similarly favorable notices. After publishing four additional mainstream novels in the Twenties, the author in 1930 produced her first detective novel, *The Mystery of Sett*, which introduced her series policeman Chief-Inspector Gorham. This book was followed the next year by the debut of her amateur sleuth Li Moh, who works in tandem with Gorham, in *Watch Mr. Moh!* (published as *The Flying Dagger Murder* in the US); and with that Joan Cowdroy was well launched on her criminous way. Between 1933 and her death in 1946, she would publish ten more novels, seven of them mysteries: *Murder of Lydia* (1933), *Disappearance* (1934), *Murder Unsuspected* (1936), *Framed Evidence* (1936), *Death Has No Tongue* (1938), *Nine Green Bottles* (1939) and *Murder out of Court* (1944). Most of these were headlined by Mr. Moh and Chief-Inspector Gorham, though in the remainder Gorham performed solo. I assume, though I do not know, that Joan derived her inspiration for Mr. Moh from trips to the Far East to visit her brother, who at his death in 1939 had risen to the post of Assistant Superintendent of the Rubber Control Office in Singapore. Until the death of her mother in 1935, Joan Cowdroy resided at a small villa on Essex Road in Ealing, West London, but by 1939 she was living with three women servants in the town of Newton Abbot, Devon, where, presumably, she spent the war years. Joan Cowdroy "spinster," passed away at the age of 62 on November 16, 1946 at Hopes Rest in the village of Great Holland, Sussex, having recently completed her twentieth novel in the space of twenty-four years. That Joan's work is again in print today, courtesy of Dean Street Press, is a testament not only to the enduring appeal of vintage detective fiction, but to a womanhood that was not wasted but rather lived in fulfillment of what mystery fans will know is a worthy and admirable purpose, entertaining readers, in defiance of the zealous dictates of her kinswoman and her scolding kind.

Curtis Evans

CHAPTER I

WHITESANDS BAY reflected on its rippled surface the cool sunlight of early morning which filtered through from skies veiled as yet in haze that promised heat.

Mr. Moh sat on the end of a wooden groyne and surveyed the scene, shining waters, and smooth, unsullied sand uncovered by the tide, which had magnanimously washed away all traces of careless humanity in a spirit of deep content.

The trim little town of Whitesands lay half a mile to his left behind its screen of hotels and boarding establishments, its bandstand gardens and parade, from the centre of which jutted the grey stone breakwater which served the double purpose of pier and harbour wall. Beyond the breakwater, sheltered by a detached mole, lay the harbour in which a few fishing-boats rode at anchor, and the wide, safe strip of the bathing beach, with its gaily painted rows of machines and boats, the chief resort of the gregarious multitude.

But here, on the southern curve of the Bay where the shore shelved abruptly to a steep drop, and beyond the solitary house behind the next groyne the beach dwindled to nothingness beneath the rocky spurs of the sharply rising heights of the promontory, which thrust its final point deep into a sea that broke against its sheer cliffs in a tumble of white foam, was solitude unspoilt.

The content of Mr. Moh was twofold.

He was definitely glad to be alone here on this clean stretch of newly washed sand divided from the open pastures above sea-level by a narrow strip of shingle and a grassy bank in the freshness of early morning with the edge of the tide forming a transparent ripple at his feet, and a morning breeze in his face.

He was equally glad to be away from the stuffy atmosphere, comprised in differing degrees of the ghostly odour of uncountable meals, unaired clothing and furniture, and a synthetic compound of smells which penetrated from the ironmongery shop, of which the ironmongery element was the least displeasing, of the house of his wife's cousin in the High Street.

Yet this conglomeration of odours which he had breathed for a week oppressed the soul of Mr. Moh less heavily than the mental atmosphere diffused by the respectable Edward Clarke and his wife Ruby. He was aware that when Mary was penniless and wretched as a girl in London, they had ignored her existence and left to another, now dead, and to Mr. Moh himself to achieve her final rescue from a life of struggle and poverty. But Mary, with the large forgiveness of her nature, had felt only deep gratification at this invitation from her kinsfolk to spend a month at Whitesands, and imperturbably good-humoured as he ever was where she was concerned, he had consented to accompany her, because her pleasure and that of his small daughter in "the seaside" would have been ruined without him.

Cheerfully therefore he bore with the companionship of Edward and Mrs. Edward, since inexplicably it made his Mary happy. Edward was tall and drooping, his narrow shoulders describing the curve of a fritillary, but without its grace. His wife was shapeless and fat, and her self-complacency was jovial while that of her husband was tinged by dyspeptic melancholy. They both pitied poor Mary for having married a foreigner and having a half-foreign child, who actually heathenly chattered to her father in Chinese, but they had become accustomed to his silent and obliging presence in their midst, and if he talked to his poor little daughter in Chinese, he paid his weekly bill for his family's board in good English money.

Mrs. Edward had kept house for twenty years and still could not cook a decent dinner.

The remembrance of the meals to which he had sat down at her table during the past week, raw mutton, sodden potatoes, brackish gravy, burnt porridge for breakfast—a meal to which Ruby came down in a soiled wrapper and hair-net, and Edward unshaved—but which he had learned to escape after the first experience of it by slipping from the house at dawn, enhanced the contentment of Mr. Moh with the circumstances of his position on the groyne. He was, so far as visible witness went, alone with sea and earth, the latter represented simply from the lower level of the sands as a bank topped by a shimmering fringe of tall grasses set against all-comprehending skies.

The only house visible was the pink-washed residence of Colonel Rouncey, Melita Villa, whose lower storey was masked by the sloping line of the next groyne, and whose roofs and chimneys were back against the green-clad heights of the Rock.

The water under the overhanging cliffs of the headland was highly dangerous to the unwary swimmer through the drag of strong undercurrents, and out near the point where the rock-bed shelved to abnormal depths a small warning buoy had been placed.

But no one used the south beach for bathing except the two young women from the Villa, Colonel Rouncey's nieces; and they, who from constant, lazy practice were both expert swimmers, and during hot summer months lived an almost amphibious existence in the sea that Jay below their back garden gate, needed no guidance in avoiding the quite well-defined and limited danger zone.

Twice Mr. Moh had seen one of the Torrington girls—the plump elder one who had fair hair and wore a green bathing-dress and cap—slip down from her home and swim away leisurely, taking a wide circuit, right round the point of the promontory. Today also she had gone, later than usual, in the same direction, but it was not with any girl that he was concerned, but with James Bond. The Torrington girls had had this southern stretch of the Bay to themselves in the early morning till, six months before, James Bond, a junior policeman in the County Constabulary, had been transferred from an inland district to Whitesands. Now he lived with his mother in a trim cottage on the other side of the road which the screen of grasses hid, and every morning, when his hours of duty permitted, he dashed down across the road and beach in an ancient pair of flannel trousers topped by an equally ancient mackintosh, which failed to cover more than half his large and vigorous form, for a plunge out to the breakwater, from which he practised diving.

Mr. Moh felt a brotherly affection for all policemen, since his own best years had been passed as a detective in San Francisco, and his most deeply cherished friend in England was Chief Inspector John Gorham of the C.I.D. in London, whose coadjutor he had been in a late notorious criminal case. And it had become the chief recreation of his bored days in Whitesands, since he had made Jimmy Bond's acquaintance, to trot down to the shore and watch for the young man's emergence from the waves.

Apart from the liking he had conceived for the young man's society, and he was a very likable as well as good-looking young man, the sight of his vigorous grace, perfectly proportioned limbs and body supple with exercise filled him with a pleasure that was the complement of the calm enjoyment he drew from the beauty of sea and sky.

But today the spell of his aesthetic pleasure was roughly broken. He waved friendly greeting as, after a steady swim from the breakwater across quarter of a mile of shining water, the close-cropped, fair head approached the shore, and Jimmy, as his feet found bottom, stood up, knee-high in the transparent ripples, a statue of perfect manhood, white and glistening, grinning cheerfully to wave back.

But suddenly his cheerful grin faded. He pointed madly with a dripping hand, and emitted a yell of anguished horror.

"My bags, Mr. Moh! For the Lord's sake see what's happening to my bags!"

Mr. Moh turned swiftly in the direction of his pointing finger. Under the impulse of some force invisible, he beheld the tail end of Jimmy's raincoat vanishing from the further groyne.

Stimulated to sudden activity by this frenzied appeal from his bereaved young friend, he raced across to peer over the fence. A large, rough-coated brown dog had got a corner of the coat gripped between firm teeth and, head held stiffly sideways, was dragging it at a gallop towards the wicket gate of the Colonel's garden, the swimmer's essential garments still entangled in its folds. But not Jimmy's alone, unless P.C. Bond secretly indulged in underwear of silky jade-green. . . .

The fence, five feet on one side, was four on the other, and loosely piled shingle at that. As Moh scrambled up and leapt down, the slipping stones sent him sprawling, though he clutched and held an inch of coat. The dog was a quick thinker. Feeling the tug on the coat, he decided to cut his losses. Abandoning it to his pursuer, he took a fresh mouthful and tore into the gate head up, trailing a whirling wake of flannel and towelling.

And shimmering green silk.

Mr. Moh returned to fling the coat across the groyne to the young man whose wet shoulders and face of scarlet wrath were raised above the fence he himself could barely see over.

"That damned, unruly dog, I suppose?" Shiveringly he draped the chilly covering round his dripping form. "Look here, do be sporting and go and get back my pants and bags, old man! I can't go chasing all over the garden after him in this with the chance of giggling females at every window. I mean—dash it—I'm not decent!"

"Blushing modesty is highly commendable in young, pure-minded officer," Mr. Moh observed with sympathy. "But as nefarious quadruped has also removed towel I advise instant marathon to home of maternal parent, while this unworthy, but fully clothed, person retrieves nether garments from military residence."

In five days of acquaintanceship Bond had learned in a general way to detect the meaning that lay concealed within Mr. Moh's vocabulary. This advice struck him as sound.

"Go while the going's good, eh? Right ho!"

Crouching to allow his inadequate coat to cover as much as possible of his person, he made off towards the bank in a series of furtive bounds. With a delighted smile Mr. Moh watched his progress, saw him peer cautiously through the screen of grasses above to reconnoitre the road and, apparently finding the coast clear, haul himself up and disappear, and then turned back to fulfil his charitable errand.

He heard an excited bark changed swiftly to a shrill yelp of pain as he dropped to the shingle, and, smiling no longer, he made his soundless way to the gate and along a narrow path cut diagonally through thick shrubbery.

The real garden of Melita Villa was on the other side of the house and bordered the road, which there swept inland in a considerable curve to avoid the steep gradient of the Rock. The neglected strip on the seaward side was planted with a thick belt of wilted evergreen bushes to act as windscreen to an oblong of sand-defeated turf which bordered the house wall.

The path, winding through these, came out on a wider gravel path which went round the house to the front entrance, and from this rose steps to a raised loggia.

Half a minute later he was bowing, both hands outspread, palms upward, to a girl who stood tense, panting, quivering in the grip of some fierce emotion, at the top of the loggia steps.

It was scarcely quarter to seven, but she was fully dressed. At first glance she gave the impression of being smartly dressed; yet the thick dark hair, conventionally shingled, was rough, the straight tennis frock she wore with its scarlet V at the neck, its scarlet-edged breast pocket, was creased, the scarlet leather belt twisted. Cheap stockings wrinkled ungracefully on thick, ungraceful legs, whose feet were thrust into scarlet-heeled, bronze shoes.

The smouldering fury of the black eyes, the sullen temper in every line of the full red lips, connected up with the agony in the dog's yelp as eloquently as the dog-whip in her hand. The expressionless eyes of Mr. Moh swept from the towel at the girl's feet to the trail of garments that led across the four steps and floor of the loggia to the open french windows of the room behind.

A comfortably furnished room, a lounge or sitting-room, cushioned chairs scattered about, Indian rugs spread on a parquet floor, a beaten dog that crouched on one of them dejected. No jade-green in sight. When the eyes that seemed to see nothing were raised at length to the girl's face its distorting look of anger had given place to one more normal, of annoyed, haughty surprise. "What the devil have you come butting in here for?" she burst out rudely. The voice, still quivering with asperity, was deep-toned, a full contralto with a husky note in it, its musical quality, however, marred by a fatal harshness of accent, as the clear, sun-warmed tint of her full throat and firmly moulded arms just failed to disguise a coarseness of flesh.

Mr. Moh bowed again, willow-like in his humble deprecation. "Shame overwhelms me at so impertinent an intrusion, madam, but"—his hand's gesture indicated the scattered objects of his quest—"if I may be permitted to retrieve these?"

The girl looked oddly relieved, almost genial.

"Oh, sorry. You've come for these things that Carlo brought in. Carlo! Bad dog. Come here and beg pardon for your sins!"

Carlo rose and came, not boundingly as a forgiven and generously forgiving dog should come, but warily, fearful brown eyes fixed on his summoner's hand, and on the window's threshold stopped. Mr. Moh, his steps as swift as they were silent, was there to meet him at the instant of his fatal pause, stooping to caress velvety ears and feel an eager tongue lick his fingers, as a bushy tail thudded gratitude to an unexpected champion.

All the room was visible from this fresh viewpoint; chiefly, pushed back to the wall behind the heavy window curtain, a couch with tumbled cushions across which lay an embroidered silky garment of jade-green, ripped viciously from neck to hem.

A second later, P.C. Bond's unmentionable underwear clasped fondly to his breast, he was bowing profuse thanks and deprecating farewell to a frowning young woman, confused by his swiftness into uncertainty whether the dog had dared to disobey her summons or been forestalled in his obedient coming.

Outside the gate he paused to listen anxiously, and hearing no sound of punishment, guessed, relieved, that Carlo had slipped off safely into interior regions of the house.

He scrambled over the groyne and walked thoughtfully, by way of an easy pathway, up the slope towards the Bonds' cottage.

Not a nice young lady to offend, he reflected, and saw again that muscular, square-fingered hand that clasped the whip. What had there been in a dog's mischievous escapade to rouse her to such a pitch of ungoverned, destructive rage? Not the unexpected strewing of her uncle's garden with a stranger's clothes, surely. Besides, Carlo had dropped the last of them outside the window. Only the green silk thing that he knew he had bustled triumphantly indoors with, to receive that vicious slash that made him quit his hold so that she could snatch it up and tear it in two with those strong, furious fingers of hers.

But though he had got vicarious benefit of it, it was not for Carlo she had been lying in wait on that concealed couch with that dog-whip clutched in her hand.

An inviting odour of frying bacon greeted him as he approached the cottage door through a patch of garden gay with snapdragons and marigolds. Mrs. Bond opened it, and laughed when she saw the bundle he carried.

A small, neatly made woman with scarcely a silver thread in her smooth dark hair, and bright black eyes intelligent and shrewd. How she came to be the mother of a stalwart, blue-eyed young Viking like James was one of Nature's mysteries, though it had designed her to be a mother of men.

"Oh, that's kind of you, Mr. Moh! Jim's upstairs in his bedroom dressing. He told me about that dog of Colonel Rouncey making off with his clothes, the mischievous monkey! But it was as good as a play to see Jim come creeping up the path bent double in that old mac of his that he grew out of years ago, and in which he looks a comical figure at the best!"

She chuckled again as she set the bundle down on a kitchen chair, her kindly face crinkled in laughter, and over the stairs came her son's voice, reproachful, but suggestive of a responsive grin.

"That's right, Mum, laugh at me chasing all over the place dripping wet and asking for pleurisy through that dashed animal's mischief! Did you get 'em back, Mr. Moh?"

"Everything. O.K. But advise other clothes for immediate use since these after being dragged through sand will scarify tender human form."

"You bet I've put clean ones on! Look here, do stop on and have breakfast. Mum sounds beastly heartless, but she can cook. And I want to hear what happened!"

"Many ta-tas for kind invitation but I seldom consume British breakfast. And nothing happened. A dark-haired young lady permitted me to collect intimate underwear strewn over military officer's veranda in rapid transit of canine bandit, and gratefully to depart with same instanter."

"A dark young lady?" said Mrs. Bond, as her invisible son called out, "Oh well, thanks awfully," and went back into his bedroom. "That would be the Colonel's niece, the younger one, Rosalind. The other one, Lydia, is fair. I hope no one was cross with Carlo about his spree! He's a good, friendly dog really, and that devoted to his master you never see them apart. Are you sure you won't stay and share Jim's meal, Mr. Moh? I'm so glad to meet you after all Jim's talk about you."

"And I am honoured. But no, thank you, not this morning."

"Then perhaps you will come in to supper one night? We'd be very pleased. Thank you very much. Good morning."

She nodded and smiled, anxious to get back to her frying-pan, and Mr. Moh raised his bowler hat—in the dog-days he still wore, invariably, a bowler hat—and departed.

Rosalind.

Then presumably, as she would not destroy her own property, that green wrap had belonged to her sister, Lydia.

Was it also for Lydia that she was lying in wait with a dog-whip? A curious domestic situation seemed to be existent at Melita Villa. Mr. Moh went for a long walk to prolong his absence from the Clarke dwelling as far as possible, and then dallied over a roll and cup of coffee at a busmen's stall, to fortify himself for an active morning with his wife and daughter on the beach.

CHAPTER II

OVER A MIDDAY dinner which consisted of steak fried to rags shrinking beneath a mass of blackened shreds of onions, over-boiled cabbage rank with salt and potatoes in cooking which Mrs. Edward in a triumph of ineptitude had managed to combine her three chief culinary feats, since they were underdone, water-soaked, and finally burnt, a certain gloom fell on the party in the parlour behind the ironmonger's shop.

Edward thought dismally of the drop in the ironmongery trade, the bad debts on his books, and the heavy rise in the rates that the mayor's craze for town improvements must involve next spring, not connecting these thoughts with the rumblings of his outraged stomach.

Molly, used to her parent's dainty cookery, was perverse, pushed away an untouched plate and answered every rebuke in Chinese. And even her mother felt cross and wondered unhappily how long she could permit her patient husband to pay her relatives for such "board".

Only Mrs. Edward remained cheerful and burst into a hearty laugh as she put on the table a custard in which yellow lumps floated in a pale and watery liquid, and a junket which had not set. "I thought when I was dashing in the rennet that maybe it had been kept too long! But there, it'll be all the same a hundred years hence!" she remarked. "Now then, Ted, don't you sit so glum over there! What about us all going for a bit of a jaunt this afternoon to liven us up a bit? Venny can look after the shop for once in his life, the lazybones, and if we leave the dishes till tomorrow we could easily catch the two-thirty coach to the Castle! What do you say, Mary? Shall we take our tea with us, or trust to getting it there?"

"Oh, get it there—there's sure to be a refreshment place!" said Mary quickly. She had had experience of picnic food provided by Ruby Clarke. "I'd love to see the old castle, and have a ride. Wouldn't you?"

Her anxious eyes sought her husband's, and instantly she received the look he kept for her alone.

"So intensely that Molly and I will at once proceed forth and book seats on the coach!" he said with calm decision.

It was the first sentence that he had spoken, but it had the magical effect of restoring everyone's spirits. The Clarkes because it promised them a treat at someone else's expense, Mary's because she knew he would give the child a sensible meal at Baine's in the Market Square, where the coaches started, while he was waiting, and because—oh, because he was such a generous dear and always understood and forgave. "And regard it how you would," she thought, her heart aglow with an inarticulate warmth of feeling as she watched him go down the street hand in hand with his skipping daughter, *before* going back to wash up the dishes her tidy spirit revolted from leaving dirty, while her hostess titivated upstairs, "Ruby's cooking requires a lot of forgiveness."

Castle St. Roche was situated on a promontory about nine miles south of Whitesands, and was the favourite resort of tourists in a wide district. Little remained of the original stronghold save the Norman keep, the great guardroom of which contained an interesting museum, and two massive gateways of early Tudor date, but these were in a good state of preservation, and from its lofty position, dreaming above its grass-grown ramparts, the Castle commanded magnificent views of a wide stretch of country and the lower coastline of crumbling earthen cliffs which once it had most formidably defended from invaders.

In addition to paying for the coach seats, Mr. Moh obligingly provided fruit and sandwiches for consumption during the drive. It was, therefore, a full-fed and contented party for which, still paymaster, he paid the threepenny entrance fees at the lodge gate.

The cloudless sunshine had already attracted dozens of people to the Castle, and, shepherded into the latest batch of thirty or so, they were led at a brisk pace by the custodian through the Tudor gateway into the keep, first up into the museum, then up again the breakneck stone stairs on to the battlements, and finally—Sergeant Sampson sensibly kept these as a final and irresistible lure in case trippers should be inclined to waste his time by lingering unduly on the battlements—down into dungeons haunted by horrifying memories of long-ago tragedies.

Mr. Moh trotted silently in the rear of the mob, his attention chiefly fixed on the glowing face of his wife as she followed with absorbed interest the guide's capable lectures. He had not realized how secretly she must have yearned for home in the alien environment of California, where always she had seemed quietly content with her husband and child, till he had witnessed her eager response to the sights and sounds of England during the months since their return, it seemed to him that she was expanding daily in her natural environment, as dried seaweed expands when the tide lifts it back into its native element.

Personally he found this British habit of going about to stare at things in herds conducted by a guide inexpressibly wearisome, but in this instance he was grateful to the gregarious instinct, since it relieved him, for a brief space, of the undiluted companionship of Edward Clarke.

When the crowd plunged dungeon-ward he remained unobtrusively behind in the fresh air, and, though the guide gave him a keen glance as he shepherded his flock in front of him down the steps, he refrained from summoning him to follow.

The coastline lay beneath him as if it were etched on a map, every curve and indentation miraculously clear. Through his glasses he could see the town of Whitesands, its tiny harbour crowded with brown sails, and the long white ribbon of the coast road, not deserted as in the early morning hours, but crowded with cars of every type that followed one another in tireless procession. The south beach was almost hidden by the dark-green heights of the promontory, but he could pick out the Bonds' white cottage, and the trees in the garden of Melita Villa, though the house itself was invisible. Round the hedge of the garden the road swept in a sharp curve to throw off a branch road that led inland. As he gazed a small car, painted grey, suddenly insinuated itself into the moving procession close to the hedge, possibly from the gate of the Villa. It was coming towards the Castle, and presently became quite clear, for, driven with a young man's recklessness, it seemed bent on passing as many of its companions on the road as it could honourably, yet with little regard for the rule of "safety first".

But while idly he followed its course, it was the revelation of the coastline that attracted his keenest interest.

The promontory, which on the Whitesands side was curved in the shape of a sickle-blade, on this side was shown as a bare, steep green hillside lying broadside on to the sparkling waters, from which it rose sheer, crowned with dense thicket where it masked Melita Villa. But between its landward base and the unbroken line of earthen cliffs, whose crumbling nature made building a dangerous proposition and so left the whole coastline till it reached the cluster of red roofs that lay beneath the Castle rock bare of habitation, was a tiny cove with a patch of firm white sand.

From this distance that cove and patch of sand were so infinitely small that he would not have noticed it save for the gleam of sunlight on the white sand. But having discerned its existence he found the answer to a question that had been nagging at his brain all day. He had seen Lydia Torrington twice swim away round the point. Was it to this single landing-place the coast on this side afforded that she had gone again this morning when she flung her green wrap among Bond's clothes?

To a practised swimmer—and Lydia was certainly that—the distance meant little save what, even for her skill, must be a stiffish test of endurance, if a brief one, in negotiating the strong set of the currents in the actual rounding of the point; though to one with less than her intimate knowledge of the currents, both the underground drag of the water in the sickle-blade curve which she had carefully avoided and the rough bit round the point, the feat might be highly dangerous, if not impossible. Yet, if she chose to make that secluded cove her object in her morning swim as Bond made the breakwater in the opposite direction his, what was there in that seemingly innocent choice of hers to rouse the other girl to a pitch of fury well-nigh insane? . . .

A step sounded on the stair, and a friendly voice spoke. "Enjoying the view, mate? Nice bit of coast, isn't it?" The custodian stood beside him, a broad-shouldered man with the unmistakable cut of the veteran who has seen service in every part of the world, and has acquired the art, supremely difficult to the normal English citizen, of accepting men of other races on terms of easy friendliness. "Your little lot have cleared off round by the west ramparts by the cannon, but there's no hurry for you to join 'em yet, though from now on the keep will be closed for a bit . . ."

"Is it the custom then to close the door for certain hours?"

"Not half it ain't!" responded the sergeant with a broad grin. "But the fact is, a few days ago the Chief Constable—that's Major Tennant—gave me a private tip he was bringing a special party here this afternoon. The Lord Lieutenant and her ladyship with some archaeological gentlemen from London who are staying with them, besides a lot of other friends. So, though it's not strictly constitootional as you might say, and Major Tennant not so much as batted an eyelid he wanted it done, I want to keep the place a bit private for them. The Major being the type of gentleman he is, a pack of pushing trippers aren't going to be encouraged to spoil his little picnic. But that doesn't apply to you, mate, of course. You stop up here as long as you like. You won't be in the way!"

"I will not intrude my unworthy presence when honourable visitors arrive, noble V.C." An expressive gesture of his hands indicated a disposition to vanish into—if necessary—thin air on their approach. "But gratuitous permission given to remain in present position, affording brief respite from society of relatives by marriage, with whom self and family are staying, gives pleasurable relief."

"Stringy chap with a walrus moustache, and a fat party who pokes him in the ribs with her gamp, and giggles when things aren't funny—I spotted 'em. Seen 'em before, in fact. Whitesands folk aren't they? I get a lot that kind. Ignorant as blazes themselves and patronize you because you're trying to tell them facts they couldn't comprehend if you hammered it into their fat heads with a battle-axe. Though there's others, like your missus, it's a pleasure to take round! But look here, mate," he added sternly, "you stow all that about the V.C. That isn't the sort of thing one wants broadcasted. Who put you on to it, anyway?"

"P.C. James Bond informed me that distinguished soldier in charge of Castle St. Roche was a friend of his late honourable male parent, and owner of the V.C. won for incredible act of gallantry."

"Jimmy Bond wants his head smacked!" the sergeant exclaimed wrathfully. "Pity his dad didn't live long enough to trounce a bit of decent reserve into him. Now he was a great chap if you like! High up in the C.I.D. he was, if you know what that means?"

To his surprise the Chinese nodded with a beaming smile.

"I also," he declared with pride, "have a friend in it! Some great organization, the British C.I.D.!"

"You're right. Next time you meet young Jimmy you can tell him he'll hear something to his disadvantage if he happens to run up against me! See that grey Singer? That's young Robin Tennant's car. Got his young lady and her sister aboard, I bet. Miss Torringtons. Champion swimmers they are, both of them."

"Nice young ladies?"

"Mr. Robin's a nice young fellow. Hello! There's the Major's car now. So long, mate."

Mr. Moh remained where he was for a while longer, and then, true to his promise, slipped unobtrusively down the steep steps, worn to a dangerous slant by the tread of centuries.

Sergeant Sampson was standing in the doorway of the museum and apparently drinking in with both ears information that was being given in pleasantly modulated tones by the chief constable to attentive guests. He stepped back to intercept him.

"They are having their tea spread in the inner bailey," he whispered. "But you're free of the rest of the grounds. And if you look in later on I'll give you a squint at the dungeons. And show you round the layout of the defences. The Major's been explaining them a fair treat, and I've learned more than I ever knew before . . . the history and so on!"

The defensive plans of mediaeval castles, together with their history, left Mr. Moh entirely cold, but he accepted this suggestion with every appearance of profound pleasure.

He found his own party grouped on the sloping turf above the broad sea-wall eagerly discussing, not the scenery, but the distinguished visitors.

"Ruby says," Mary greeted him excitedly, "that that tall lady in grey with Major Tennant is Lady Vanburgh herself! And the Earl is here too, and Mrs. Tennant, and oh, who is that girl who looks ever so smart—look, Ruby, going round now to where the servants are setting tea behind that wall—with that nice freckled boy and another girl! Is she a Miss Vanburgh?"

"That?" Ruby was scornful. "You bet she's not! That's only Colonel Rouncey's niece Lydia, from Whitesands! That's her sister with them—not half shabby she looks beside that smart dress of Lydia's. And that boy is Robin Tennant that Rosalind's engaged to. I bet my lady feels bucked to get asked here by people like the Tennants; though of course it's only because of their young son getting mixed up with Rosalind that I suppose they felt they must ask them, and of course having them to a picnic isn't the same as a real private party at Oakleigh!"

"Is Oakleigh a big place?"

"Oh no, quite small, not more than five servants they've got, counting the chauffeur. But the Tennants are real County, and those Torringtons—why, they aren't even Town."

Mary looked mystified.

"But why? Their uncle is a colonel!"

"They're his wife's nieces, not his. He never goes anywhere now, not since the row with his nephew. They're running that Tennant boy for all they're worth, making hay while the sun shines!" Ruby exclaimed with her rumbling laugh. "And they'd better. Because Rosalind won't keep him long for herself with that Lydia about, any more than she has her other chaps. First Hervey her cousin, then Burroughs that Lydia is engaged to at this identical moment. I saw him a minute ago. . . . There he is, talking to Lydia now."

"You don't *know* Lydia had anything to do with the shindy over Hervey," put in Edward argumentatively. "All you women have got your knife into Lydia because she beats every female in the town for looks and style! A lot said young Hervey had robbed his uncle's cashbox, and the reason he cleared out so sudden was for fear of the police!"

"Louisa Martin, that was cook there at the time, told me with her own two lips that the Colonel actually caught Herman Hervey in that Lydia's bedroom at the dead of night, and the old man, who wasn't one to stand for such goings-on under his own roof, ordered him to clear out next morning or he'd set the bulls on him!"

"The Colonel couldn't have threatened him with the police if that was all he had against him!" Edward retorted. "It isn't a criminal offence, as the law of England stands, to be caught in the wrong bedroom even at dead of night! Unless the parties were married, and even then it would be a case for the Divorce Court, not the police!"

"Molly, you take your ball and go and play on the grass down there, where we can see you, my duck."

Mary Moh revelled in innocent gossip even when it concerned people she scarcely knew by sight, but not this type. But being too gentle to display her dislike of what she thought of as "nasty talk" openly, she tried to direct the conversation to less muddy channels. "Was Rosalind engaged to this Hervey, then, first?"

"Well, I don't know about actually engaged. More a sort of boy and girl affair. Living in the same house as they were, at least in the holidays when young Hervey always came and stopped with his uncle, they were about together a lot, biking and tennis and bathing together. A nice, civil-spoken young fellow he was, I must say, and keen as mustard at all water sports. Swimming and water polo and all that. You could have knocked me down with a feather when Louisa Martin told me the ins and outs of that scandal. But it's a fact, though his uncle seemed so fond of him before, he's never showed his nose in the place since, and that's over four years ago! Then, close on two years back—no, not so much—it was the winter before last—when Lydia was spending Christmas in Paris—Rosalind met and got engaged as quick as lightning to that Burroughs that had just come as junior partner to Cliffords, the solicitors. You know their office, Mary. It's almost opposite the shop."

Mary nodded, thrilled.

"I know Mr. Burroughs. A big gentleman with a solemn sort of face and black hair; but was he engaged to Rosalind first, then?"

"Yes, pore girl. But she didn't keep him long after Madam Lydia came prancing home! Not she! Lydia's one of the sly, baby-eyed kind that can't seem to keep their claws off another girl's fellow, and all so soft and innocent with it you can't sort of pin it to her how it's done. Only men are that silly."

"Silly or not," Edward ejaculated, roused, "if you ask me, Burroughs did the sensible thing when he chucked that spitfire for the other one! I shan't forget in a hurry how she pretty well raised the roof off the shop with her language last year, when I hadn't got her bike mended to the second she wanted it! A cheap, ramshackle old machine it was too, that wasn't worth the mending, as I up and told her straight! And I'd have sent it back that night as it was for someone else for her to get to tinker with it, if the Colonel hadn't happened to come in for a new collar for his dog, and when I told him about the rumpus she had made, he paid the bill with a bit extra added, and asked me to forget about it. I expect that's what she done to Mr. Burroughs—flowed out at him a few times till he up and chucked her. And plumped for the easy one. You women may crab Miss Lydia, but at least she's a lady and gives a nice smile and a word to those who serve her."

"Well, now she's got Mr. Burroughs it's to be hoped she won't go casting sheep's eyes at her sister's new young man, young Tennant. But I wouldn't put it past her to try, at any rate." Mrs. Edward heaved herself to her feet. "What about going along to the refreshment place for a nice cup of tea? My throat's as dry as a limekiln with all this sightseeing."

An hour later Mr. Moh left them still lingering over a substantial tea which had cost him a perfectly sound ten-shilling note. Major Tennant and his older guests were gone, but he noticed the two young women whom they had been discussing, each squired by her legitimate young man, but wearing very different expressions. Lydia in her smart garden-party frock was sitting on a seat on the terrace smiling up into the rather heavy face of Burroughs, who was talking earnestly, from under the lace brim of her hat.

"I am so grieved you can't stay, dearest," he heard her murmur with plaintive sweetness. "Of course I'd much prefer to drive with you—but this delicious breeze—and my poor head! And you mustn't be late for your dinner . . ."

Rosalind, perched in an ungraceful attitude on the sea-wall, looked sulky, and the slender young man leaning against the wall and staring moodily towards the terrace seemed at the moment to be at a loss for polite chat.

Sighting Mr. Moh, Sampson, genially rounding up a fresh party to take over the keep, handed his duties over to a docile little wife and joined him with alacrity.

"Come along into my private quarters, mate," he said, leading the way up to the second floor and opening a door marked "Private". "You'll join me in a cup of tea, I hope?"

But Mr. Moh, to whom he had taken an odd liking, shook his head. "With tea this unworthy worm is unfortunately replete," he murmured. "But if it were permitted to smoke a cigarette safe from the conversation of relatives by marriage while you wrap yourself round viands, everything in the garden would be lovely."

The sergeant chuckled, and shut the door of his neat kitchen on the outer world.

The oddly assorted friends sat there yarning till Mr. Moh woke regretfully to a remembrance of the return coach. But Sampson reassured him with a glance at his watch.

"It's not more than six-twenty-five now, and if you came by Skinner's coach it doesn't start till seven-thirty. Look here, I'll just go down to take a squint round and see my missus is all right. But you lie doggo here till I come back."

When he put in an appearance twenty minutes later there was a lingering touch of temper in his face.

"Sorry I've been so long, mate. But a fellow not only drove his car right up on to the terrace instead of into the park round behind the lodge, but he had the cheek to sauce me when I told him of it. Then when I'd got the other fellow to shift it right out on to the road, there was another lot wanting to see the museum, so I had to take 'em up and lend the missus a bit of a hand. She was fairly snowed under with 'em in there, but pitching the yarn like a regular oner!" The genial smile came back to the keen blue eyes. "It's been a record day, but we're keeping open till nine tonight, an hour later than usual, on account of keeping the public out this afternoon. Your little crowd are out in the grounds and look as though they're hunting about to find Father!"

"Yes, yes, this has been delicious rest, but I must go!" He stood with his fingers on the door, while the sergeant took a fresh roll of tickets from a drawer.

He caught the sound of voices above—young, angry voices. A sneering phrase in a girl's shrill tone, a scuffle, a stumble, a man's furious shout:

"Rosalind! *Cave!*"—then with melting passionate tenderness—"*Darling!* She might have killed you!"

The sergeant's broad figure bulked solidly across the stairs as from above came the voice of Mr. Moh, calm and imperturbable, "Miss is not injured, young sir."

"Don't be an idiot, Robin!" Lydia sounded less shaken by the fall that Moh's swiftness had arrested than by the young man's hopeless betrayal of feeling. "I stupidly stumbled! Don't fuss!" Scarlet-faced, Robin drew aside, his back turned to his *fiancée*, past whom he had rushed to the rescue that Mr. Moh had actually achieved. Lydia, trying to control the violent quivering of her body, smiled—though shakily—upon the little man who had caught her waist with small hands that had felt like steel.

"Thank you very much! You were very quick!"

"I am glad I was near, lady, to render service." He pressed himself upright against the wall, still holding her wrist, his glance downward on the dark well of the staircase, to let her pass him as Sampson ascended to lay a firm hand on her arm.

"Let me guide you the rest of the way, madam. The treads are dangerously worn."

Mr. Moh closed in behind her, Robin following. Neither man so much as glanced at Rosalind, left to come down behind alone.

A man standing at the museum door glanced curiously at the odd procession as it passed, but no one spoke till the sergeant, still supporting his charge, and waiting on the worn flags of the entrance gateway till the others had reached the level, said gravely to young Tennant:

"If you would like to fetch your car right up here, sir, it would save the young lady a walk to the car park."

"Right. I won't be a second."

"Sit down on this chair, madam."

"Thank you. But really it was nothing! I expect it was these silly high heels of mine! Those steps weren't built for French heels, were they!" She gave a shrill, hysterical giggle.

"No, madam."

Mr. Moh faded unobtrusively from the scene.

Next morning all Whitesands was startled by the tragic news that Lydia Torrington, Colonel Rouncey's elder niece, had been found drowned in the early hours in the waters of the Bay.

CHAPTER III

MAJOR TENNANT sat at his desk in the room at Oakleigh, which was called his office, and looked at his superintendent with eyes that betrayed little of his deep, inward perturbation.

"But what earthly grounds are there for believing it to be murder! Great Scott, man! Accidental drowning is tragic enough! And the young lady, Miss Torrington, could swim like a fish too!"

"Quite so, sir. Naturally I jumped to the conclusion that it was accident at first, myself, though it seemed a bit queer that the doctor ordered the body to be conveyed to the Cottage Hospital, near a mile off, instead of into her own home that was within a stone's throw of where she was brought ashore. But from the report he made at once to me there doesn't seem the smallest hope it was accidental. Dr. Fitz-James 'phoned to me direct from the hospital to meet him there at once, and—well, sir—from marks on the back of the neck, and bruises on the right arm above the elbow, it seems unquestionable that she was deliberately held under water by someone and drowned. When I got that, I came straight off to report the matter to you."

Tennant glanced at his watch. It was 10.35 a.m.

"Take a chair, Braice, and give me a summary of the facts up to date. Who found the poor girl's body and so on. I'd only just learned the bare fact of the death a second before you came in. But first, have you seen her uncle? Has he been informed of this latest development you have just given me?"

"Colonel Rouncey and Mr. Burroughs both interviewed me at the hospital, sir. The Colonel seemed extremely annoyed that the body had been taken there, instead of home. In fact he was fairly insulting. Called the police a pack of meddling busybodies and a lot more. Of course one made allowance for his feeling upset, but it struck me he was more angry about the publicity and scandal that must be aroused than grieved . . ."

"Losing his temper might be his way of relieving his grief. He's not young, and he'd had a bad shock."

"Well, it might be," the superintendent agreed, but dubiously. "Mr. Burroughs was quieter, but he'd got his back up too, and his manner had a nasty edge to it. In the end I simply told them that the body had been conveyed to the hospital mortuary under the doctor's orders, not ours, and when he had made out his report on the cause of death they should be communicated with. So I got rid of them both and came straight here. Colonel Rouncey said he'd have it out with Dr. Fitz-James himself, but the doctor won't give anything away. Now shall I make my report, sir?"

Major Tennant nodded.

There was a confidential touch in the superintendent's manner which he heartily disliked, which yet filled him with profound uneasiness. This was by no means the first murder case that he had handled in the twelve years during which he had held his present office, but it was the first in which he had had a personal family interest.

He had not been particularly pleased when Robin, his younger boy, had struck up an acquaintance at the beginning of the Long Vac. with Rouncey's nieces, young women whose reputation stood none too high in the county, though criticism levelled no more definite charge against either than an alleged freedom of manners. . . . Still less had he felt pleased when Robin had announced his engagement to Rosalind, the younger girl, for the very suddenness of the affair suggested the disagreeable conviction that the lad had been caught.

The single objection he had cared to voice, however, was the difference of age between them; Rosalind at twenty-seven was five years senior to the boy, but even that mild argument had turned Robin sulky.

He had trusted to luck that, with the boy's career still to make, the thing might die out of itself. And now this. . . . He hoped to heaven that Robin wasn't going to be dragged in. But from that indefinable something in Braice's manner he feared that he was going to be dragged in. . . .

His steady gaze seemed suddenly to rouse the superintendent to discomfort. He fidgeted on his chair, and hesitated as if uncertain how to begin. Major Tennant took the bull by the horns.

"Both Miss Lydia and Miss Rosalind Torrington were guests of ours at a picnic at Castle St. Roche yesterday," he said quietly. "Suppose you begin from there."

"Very good, sir." Braice sat up, relieved, as if he had got the very cue he wanted. "I understand that they remained behind till after seven at the Castle, and that Mr. Robin Tennant drove them both home. At least, he dropped Miss Lydia at the door, but her sister got out and walked part of the way home. When she arrived she went up to her sister's room, and a maid who went to call them to supper heard them quarrelling violently. The words she caught from Miss Lydia were, 'It wasn't your fault you didn't kill me on those stairs in the keep!' And the other young lady, who seemed beside herself with rage, cried out, 'And I shall kill you one day if you keep interfering with my men!' Then the maid knocked at the door, and they stopped talking, and Miss Rosalind went down to supper, but Miss Lydia stayed in her room for a bit, and later went out for a walk. She took some milk and biscuits from the dining-room up to bed with her when she came in, and that was the last time she was heard of alive by the household.

"It is the habit of both sisters to go for a swim first thing in the morning. This morning the same maid, Gladys Black, heard Miss Rosalind's door shut about six, but as it was too early for her to get up she thought nothing of it and went to sleep again. Breakfast was a bit late as the Colonel had taken his dog for a stroll, and only he and Miss Rosalind sat down to it. They were just finishing, when Sergeant Norman called to inform Colonel Rouncey that the body had been found and taken to the hospital."

"When, where, and by whom was it found?"

"By a local policeman, Bond, sir. It seems this constable, who is practising for the police water sports to be held at Harborough on August 21st, and lives in a cottage close by Melita Villa, was out for a practice swim before reporting for duty at 8 a.m. He went out at five-thirty, did his swim to the breakwater, and was returning to the south beach, when he detected something on the buoy this side of the point. He swam to it and brought the body ashore close by the Villa, where he was joined by a friend who was waiting for him on the beach. They examined it together, saw life was extinct, and then they carried it to the disused bathing-hut that you may remember there." His listener nodded. "Then Bond left his friend on guard, got his bicycle, and reported at the station."

"One moment. How came Bond, swimming, you say, from the breakwater to the south beach, to detect anything whatever of the buoy by the point which at a rough estimate must have been several hundred yards away from him at nearest? However calm the water may be, a swimmer's view is extremely circumscribed. Secondly, why did Bond not remain on guard himself, and send his friend for help?"

The superintendent paused.

"I'm no swimmer myself, sir. Never even bathed in my life. But I understood Bond to say that he saw something queer at the buoy when he stood up in the water to wade ashore. He's a tall man. Wouldn't that give him the correct viewpoint? The second point hadn't occurred to me. I'll make a note to enquire. But Bond may have wanted to put some clothes on."

"Probably that was it. Go on."

"Bond reached the station at six forty. The sergeant who was on duty rang up Dr. Fitz-James, found he had only just returned from a night call, collected him on his way, and they proceeded to the hut by the coast road at once. There is a footpath down to it from the road under shelter of the trees of Colonel Rouncey's garden. They were not therefore observed from the house. The doctor made a brief inspection of the body, which was, of course, immediately recognized by both, as it had been by P.C. Bond. The doctor then directed that the ambulance be sent, and had it conveyed to the hospital. The sergeant then returned to the station, rang up to report to me, and then went at once to inform the relatives. Dr. Fitz-James then communicated direct with me that he'd like to meet me. I went as quickly as I could from Harborough first to the station at Whitesands; then to the hospital; then, after the interviews there that I've already mentioned, I decided I'd best see you at once before any further step was taken."

"Sergeant Norman seems to have done more than inform the relatives. He interrogated the servants!" Tennant said sharply.

"Not formally, sir. He saw Colonel Rouncey, who was much upset and who went to break the news to Miss Rosalind while he waited. When he came back he said he must ring up Mr. Burroughs—to whom deceased was engaged—at once, and the sergeant left him telephoning. The maid showed him out and ran after him to open the front gate for him and his bicycle. And it was while she was doing it that she asked if it was true Miss Lydia was dead, and told him about the quarrel, and the other details I have given."

Major Tennant frowned! It sounded like an ugly and unauthorized piece of prying on the sergeant's part. However, the fat was in the fire now.

"And what, in your opinion, is the next step to be taken, Superintendent?" He spoke with rather ominous coldness, and Braice reddened.

"Well, sir, the facts seem clear. In the ordinary way I shouldn't hesitate in suggesting an arrest at once. The other young lady was on bad terms with her sister and ... and ... But, of course, though she is known to be as expert a swimmer as deceased, and was heard to leave her bedroom early, there is absolutely no proof that she was actually in the water ..."

"Still, it is not the absence of proofs that is worrying you, Braice, but the fact that the young lady is engaged to my son. Isn't that so?"

There was a pregnant silence. Braice felt angrily that he had been unfairly cornered. Neither he, nor any of his subordinates who had so far come into the case, had a shadow of doubt that Rosalind Torrington, about whom they all knew an immense amount of backstairs' gossip concerning her thwarted love-affairs, her ungovernable temper, and the cat-and-dog terms on which she had lived for years with her sister, had deliberately, and as a final act of jealous desperation, struggled with her in the water and killed her by drowning.

Still, she was, as the chief had just said, engaged to Robin Tennant and it wasn't his job to drag his superior's family affairs into an ugly scandal. He had come to Oakleigh to discover what the chief's wishes were, and here he was apparently being blamed.

Major Tennant rose slowly to his feet and lighted a cigarette from a case which he omitted to offer to the other.

"Yes." He surveyed the superintendent's disgruntled countenance with eyes in which the other could detect no expression except a slight hint of mockery. "Yes, Braice. You're quite right. That fact does complicate matters quite damnably. We shall have to discover some way out of it. Meantime, have you drawn up your report?"

"No, sir. I haven't had time yet, besides—"

"Besides, you wanted to learn how much I'd like left out. Quite so. But you'd better shove in all you've told me, including Norman's rather noxious interview with the maidservant. Suppose you take a pew here and, as our American brothers say, do it now. You will find paper and all you want, including cigarettes in that box here. I'll think things over."

He saw the man installed before his desk and walked to the door, but, with the handle in his hand, he turned.

"Was any statement obtained from Bond's friend who was left with the poor girl's body?"

The superintendent looked thoroughly taken aback.

"I—I'm sorry, sir. I forgot to ask a mortal thing about him."

"My dear Braice! You seem to have left a number of interesting threads in the air! He was in charge for, at the lowest computation, ten minutes. And the girl was wearing a bathing costume. Yet you optimistically imagine that the fact of murder is still a police secret!" On that acid note he walked out and shut the door, leaving a distinctly crestfallen subordinate to pursue his task.

In the hall his elder son, Will, a subaltern in his own old regiment, who happened to be home on a week's leave, was obviously waiting for him, and as obviously frankly worried.

"I say, Dad! This is putrid news about the murder of the Torrington girl! I knew you'd got Braice in there, and didn't like to interrupt, but it's all over the place already!"

"I thought it would be." He spoke grimly. "Has Robin come in yet?"

"Yes. He's just dashed in looking awfully peeved. I suggested his having some brekker, but he said he wanted nothing but a tub. He's in it now."

"Thank God he's home at last! He didn't say where he'd been, I suppose? No—you wouldn't question him, of course. You might keep a tactful eye on him today, Will. I've got a fairly hectic time before me. But don't stop me now. Oh, you might do something for me. Put a call through to this number." He scribbled a number on the pad that lay beside the hall telephone. "And when you've got them, give my name and rank forsooth, and ask them to connect me directly with Captain Tring, the A.C. When you're through, yell, and I'll come."

He ran upstairs and tapped on a door on the upper landing from within which came sounds of splashing water.

"Robin! It's me. Let me in. It's rather urgent."

He heard the pad of a bare foot on the floor, the shooting back of the bolt. Then a further splash as his son leapt back into the bath as he entered and rebolted the door.

The room was dim with clouds of steam. He strolled across and sat down on the edge of the bath, but he did not look at its occupant, whose rigid expectancy he clearly sensed, but at the cigarette between his fingers.

Robin's nerve broke first.

"It's true, Dad? Lydia is dead!"

Something in the low tone, the sobbing catch in the breath as he uttered her name, flashed the whole truth into his father's mind.

"It was Lydia, then? Not . . . How long have you known that?"

"Not long . . . for certain. Yesterday, really. I've been desperate ever since. And now she's—"

"Dead, yes. But, Robin, it's worse than just death. . . ."

"Then she *was* killed! Oh, my God! And I . . ." Impossible to recognize the young man's pleasant accents in that fierce, hoarse cry wrung by despairing anguish. But Major Tennant turned abruptly and stopped him with a peremptory gesture.

"She was killed certainly, by someone. But if you know any reason why she should be killed you'd better not tell me now. Look here, Robin, I'm behind you through this. Absolutely. You know that. But my superintendent is downstairs now, writing his report. And your connection with these two girls makes it rather awkward for me. As C.C., you know. You see, it's up to me, as police chief, to start the investigation. Get that?" He got up and walked to the window, his ears tense for any sound behind him. But none came, not a ripple of water, so rigidly still the bather, till a hesitating question was whispered.

"Does Braice say who . . . who . . ."

"He's full of hints of a rather virulent I-could-and-I-would type. But we can forget Braice. The point is—forgive me, lad, for being so damnably abrupt—there is bound to be an inquest, and you, almost certainly, will be called on to give evidence."

"Oh, then the police know—"

"They know nothing as yet." He walked back and stood looking down at his son. "There's been no time to collect evidence either way. At present it's a case of strong suspicion only. But though"—his tone was grave as it was kind—"suspicion is not the same thing as proof, the facts have got to be investigated."

"And it's you to do the doings!" His voice was bitterly sneering. "Devilish convenient for you. You can start on me!"

His father was silent.

Inwardly he was thinking: "This is my real job, to see this son of mine safely through, even if it means chucking up everything else. But he's cut to the heart. It's going to be touch and go."

Robin spoke again, but drearily this time, without fierceness. "Sorry, Dad. You've got to carry on, of course. It's putrid for you. What are you going to do about it?"

"As I see it, there's only one thing for me to do. Call in Scotland Yard to ensure the case being properly handled—and stand clear myself. That will free me to give—er—help where it's needed." He lighted another cigarette with a match that burnt dimly in the steamy atmosphere, and added with a quick change of subject: "You've been out half the night in that Tin Lizzie of yours, Robin. Have you had any sort of breakfast?"

"I—don't think so. I felt like a tub first. Is Mother—or any-body—downstairs?"

"No one but Will. Thank God the pack cleared off yesterday. Your mother went off to the Vanburghs just after nine. You remember she'd engaged to support Lady Vanburgh in these series of official shows they're giving. Took kit enough to last her a year instead of three nights. She left you her love."

"Thanks. I'll be down presently, then."

"Right. I'll clear off. . . ." A shout came up from the hall below.

"That's Will. He's been putting through a trunk call for me." He paused by the door. "Robin, you'll play the game by me?"

"Oh yes, Dad. I won't shirk. . . ."

Relieved for the moment by that assurance, Major Tennant went downstairs, and took the receiver from Will's hand.

"Captain Tring is there himself, sir."

"Good. Stand by and keep the hall clear. Hullo! Yes, Tennant speaking. Right. Look here, I wonder if you'd be good enough to send down a reliable fellow—someone as high up as possible—to take over the investigation of a case that's just occurred in my district. . . . No—I don't know if it's going to be complicated or not. It's the murder of a girl, and only happened early this morning. But for personal reasons I want the investigation to be handled by an outsider. . . . What? Oh, sorry, that was badly put. Let me amend the phrase. To be handled by a man who doesn't belong to my crowd. . . . No, no, I don't for a second doubt the competence of my lot, who are a thoroughly efficient and skilfully trained pack. Naturally. Being under me. But the raucous fact is that a young son of mine is engaged to the sister of the murdered girl, and might easily be subpoenaed to give evidence at the inquest, as he spent most of yesterday in the company of the two young women. You get the implication in that? . . . Good. Well, you can now grasp why I'd prefer the case to be in the hands of someone other than myself, and without personal bias. Otherwise, left to myself, I might be tempted to deflect the course of justice and so on. What? . . . Oh, thanks very much. I thought you'd catch my point. I haven't told my super yet that I'm asking your help, and he'll probably be annoyed. But we all have things happen to us that we don't like. I'm having it now, myself, and I shall quite enjoy handing on a bit of my vexation to him. But he and all his subordinates will give your man all the help he requires. Now who will you send, and when can he come? Will, look up trains from Liverpool Street to Harborough."

He turned back to the 'phone and stood listening, while Will dealt with a familiar page of the ABC.

"What? Oh, I've heard of him, of course. Absolutely the man! His rank will soothe my fellow's ruffled feelings, to say nothing of his reputation. The case is actually at Whitesands, where the girl lived. She was drowned in the Bay there, and the body recovered from the water before 6.30 a.m., within sight, practically, of her own home on the shore. Look here, I suggest he should catch the . . . one second! Got that train yet, Will?"

"There's a peach at twelve forty-five Liverpool Street reaches Harborough 2 p.m. The next is three fifteen Liverpool Street, Harborough five fifty-five."

"Can he get the twelve forty-five from Liverpool Street to Harborough 2 p.m.? The next isn't till three fifteen, Harborough five fifty-five. An infernal train service. It's eleven twenty now. . . . Can do the twelve forty-five? Cheers! I'll meet him at Harborough, and run him out to Whitesands, giving him the heads of the case on the way. Once there he can take over direct charge. Many ta's, Tring. I'm more than grateful. Good-bye."

He put down the receiver.

"Forget all you've heard, Will, old man. And now will you tell them I shall want an early lunch, twelve thirty say, and I suggest you two boys have it with me, and then fade out together somewhere. What about trying to get Robin to join you in a round of golf at Oakshott? I'll have to borrow his car, as your mother is keeping the Bentley at the Park. That reminds me; in case she's heard rumours, you might ring her up and assure her that everything is O.K. here. I'll send her a note by Wilkins before I go. But she's not to dream of cutting this afternoon's tamasha and rushing home. The less stir there is about this infernal situation the better. Tell them to send in the super a tray of food when we have ours, if he's still here. And see the Singer's filled up and in good running order, will you?"

"Quite, quite. And the next, please?"

Will grinned. "There's no next. The one bright spot in an otherwise murky hour is your presence here, Will, to look after Robin."

"I say, Dad, you don't think the old lad is really mixed up in this mess, do you?"—anxiously. "I mean, I know of course he considers himself engaged to the other one, but—"

"'Fraid he's going to be stuck in it right up to the neck," he responded with a betrayal of feeling that he did not regret when he saw Will stiffen in sudden anger.

"But good Lord, sir! That woman wasn't worth it! I mean, I'm sorry she's dead, and that, but . . . I hadn't much use for the other, the Rosalind one that Robin picked up with, but the Lydia one was a real wrong 'un! No earthly loss!"

"I advise," said Major Tennant deliberately, "that you refrain from making adverse comments on—either—girl, in Robin's hearing, old man!" And leaving his son to digest the hint as best he could, he went into his office to interrupt his superintendent's labours. Braice looked up from sheets already covered with close writing.

"I shan't be long, sir. Do you want to come here?"

"No. Braice, I've been thinking over the rather peculiar difficulty that we discussed in this case, and I've decided that there's only one possible course to take, and that is to hand over the whole conduct of the affair to Scotland Yard. I have just been on the 'phone talking to Captain Tring, the Assistant Commissioner, and he is sending down Chief Inspector Gorham this afternoon." He paused, taking no apparent notice of the expression of affronted anger that reddened the officer's face at this abrupt announcement, but a peremptory lift of one hand checked the indignant protest that sprang to his lips.

"One moment. Let me finish before you say anything," he continued in the impersonal, pleasant tone which Braice had long ago learned, unwillingly at times, to respect. "I know you have every right to think it high-handed of me to take this step without consulting you first. But I realized that in this case, considering the personal connection between the Rouncey household and mine, both you and I were up against a particularly steep proposition. You see, supposing it had been feasible to leave the investigation entirely to you, standing clean outside myself, you'd have had an uneasy feeling the whole time—if facts turned up that seemed to—well—involve Mr. Robin, or at least drag his intimate relations with the surviving sister into an unpleasant publicity—that you were somehow being disloyal to me in following them up. That's rather rhetorical, but you catch my point, don't you? The whole difficulty is a question of conflicting loyalties. Yours and mine. Our personal feelings versus our duty to our job. It seemed to me that our interests in this were really identical. We both know that the job has got to be done. But a few minutes' thought convinced me that it would save us both a lot of worry that might become acutely, intolerably awkward if I cut the Gordian knot by calling in an outsider to conduct the show, on my own sole responsibility. I need scarcely say that I explained my personal reasons fully to Captain Tring, and that he clearly understands that my action casts no reflection whatever on your competence. *Dixi*, I have spoken. Now what about it? Take a moment to think it over before you give any opinion, if you like."

He had perched himself on the other side of the broad writing-table, and now he held a match to a fresh cigarette with a hand that was as steady as a rock.

Braice, sitting back massively in his chair and glancing across at the thin, clear-cut profile, the pleasant blue eyes and sensitive lips, was conscious of two quite definite impressions: one, that he had received a severe and well-deserved reprimand for the suspicions with which he had entered the room, the other that he had been hauled, by his superior's quick intelligence, out of an impossible predicament.

"Well," the admission was made grudgingly, but with a real sense of relief, "you took the wind out of my sails for a moment, but on the whole, maybe it is the best way out. I'd have felt bound to protest a bit if you'd consulted me first, but what's done is done. And, I don't mind owning, I did feel myself what you said, that things might get a bit unpleasant. Though I'd have done my best . . ." The chief constable turned to him with a cordial smile.

"Thanks, Braice. I never really doubted that you'd see my point. But it is very decent of you to forgive my high-handedness. So that's that!"

"Quite so, sir," Braice grinned. He was no fool. He was well aware that if he had received a tacit dressing-down he was now being vigorously patted on the back to encourage him to a final concession. He made it, handsomely. "Naturally, though responsibility will rest with the chief inspector, we will give him any help he needs. . . . He won't bring his own staff, I suppose."

"Good man! I imagine he'll come alone. Tring said nothing to suggest any assistants. My idea was to meet him at Harborough. He is due by the two o'clock express. Will you join me?"

Braice thought for a moment, then, to Tennant's immense inward relief, he shook his head.

"No need for us both, sir. You can give him this report, and all the necessary facts. And if you look in at headquarters on your way to the junction I'll have all the other statements ready there for you. Then I can get through the routine work I've left standing this morning and run over to Whitesands to meet him later."

"Right. After I've dropped him at Whitesands I shall come back to headquarters myself. Now I won't interrupt you any longer." He nodded, and strolled from the room.

CHAPTER IV

HARBOROUGH railway station lies well away from the centre of the dignified, old-fashioned county town, and as, in addition to a large volume of normal traffic, it is the junction for the holiday resorts along the coast, during the tourist season it presents a scene of bustling activity which is in striking contrast to the atmosphere of leisurely quiet that prevails in the town.

Major Tennant reached the main-line platform as the express slithered to a standstill, and was in time to see swarms of long-legged children, waving buckets and other seaside impedimenta, leap gaily from every carriage in the wake of parents who wrestled distractedly with the dual problem of offspring and hand luggage, but he could detect no one remotely resembling his mental image of the detective he had come to meet.

However, a big, good-natured-looking man, who had merely paused to extract from the carriage in which he had travelled from town five children, two suitcases and numerous packages belonging to two overladen women, and to steady with a large hand an excited small boy till he was firmly balanced on his own fat legs, cast a single glance over the crowds which reviewed every male figure in sight, and promptly approached.

"Major Tennant, I believe? My name is Gorham."

"Good afternoon, Mr. Gorham. Clever of you to spot me in this riot. I was just thinking I ought to have told Captain Tring I'd be wearing a pink bow in my hair, or something of the sort, as a mark of identification!" Tennant spoke with less than his customary sangfroid, or perhaps it was that in Gorham he had met an observer who could penetrate his defences, but certainly, beneath his light manner, Gorham detected traces of anxiety and preoccupation which suggested that young Tennant's connection with this murder case was considerably less fortuitous than he had been given to understand. But he checked the thought. Any father might well feel anxious at finding a son of his involved in the smallest degree with the protagonists in a criminal charge, and when the father happened also to be chief constable, and the murder had taken place in his own district, he had a complication of reasons sufficient to account for his distress, without gratuitously imputing to him secret guilty knowledge. . . .

"Come along. Have you got any kit?"

"Always keep a bag packed for emergencies at my rooms at Chester's, in the Haymarket. Here it is. Where are we going?"

"To Whitesands—eight miles. But I've got an apology for a car outside. Had to borrow my young son's, as my wife took my own car and my man this morning when she went off to stay with friends, before we got news of this tragic affair at Whitesands. She's sending it back today, though. . . ."

They kept up the impersonal exchange of remarks common to such meetings between strangers, while Tennant threaded his way through the vehicles that blocked the station approach, then, by narrow, winding streets, emerged from the town into a country road.

"My superintendent, Braice, proposes to meet you at Whitesands later, Chief Inspector," Tennant began, and his official address marked the beginning of business relations, "but meantime he asked me to hand you his preliminary report—here it is. The individual statements it summarizes are in that case. But those you can read later?"

"Thank you." Gorham glanced through the typed sheets. "This will be very useful. But if you could run through the heads of the case as we go, Major Tennant, I'd be grateful. So far I only know the bare fact that a murder has been committed."

"Quite so. That was rather my idea in coming alone to meet you. But perhaps I'd better begin with a little local colour to give you the general background of the affair. Most of the ground about here belongs to Lord Vanburgh, though he lives at the other end of the county. Do you know Whitesands at all? No? Well, when I was a boy it was an obscure fishing village, now it is a fairly flourishing seaside resort, depending chiefly for its prosperity on holiday visitors in the summer. It possesses the usual features: hotels, boarding-houses, bungalows, and so on, bandstand gardens, and pavilion. But all very select, nothing low or vulgar being permitted by the worthy councillors, who are the more bucked with their powers that the place was only raised to the dignity of a borough two years ago. The chief developments have taken place round the northern arm of the Bay, where the sands and beach are excellent for children and bathers. On the southern curve, building was vetoed from the beginning by the estate authorities, in deference, I believe, to the wishes of an eccentric uncle of Vanburgh's, who built and inhabited the only house on the shore there, which, rather deplorably, he christened Melita Villa. This Villa was the home of Lydia Torrington, the murdered girl." He paused. "The present tenant, Colonel Rouncey, rented the house about twelve years ago, when the Admiral was removed to the family vault. The Colonel is a childless widower, fairly well off, I imagine, and the two young girls he brought with him, Lydia and Rosalind Torrington, are his wife's nieces, not his own. A nephew, Herman Hervey, his own sister's son, used to be one of the household, but he no longer shows up, I believe. My personal acquaintance with these people, barring casual encounters with Rouncey, who used to be more sociable than he appears to be of late years, dates from this summer, when my younger boy, Robin, who is in his last year at Cambridge, met the two girls at the local tennis club. They are both good at games, but Rosalind is specially hot at tennis, and, Robin being also keen, they partnered each other in a tournament, and—well, to cut a long story short, he and Rosalind became engaged."

"If it's a fair question, were you pleased with the engagement?"
Major Tennant hesitated.

"If we—his mother and I—rather regretted the step, it was chiefly on account of Robin's age and prospects," he said at length carefully. "His ambition lies in the direction of mining engineering. But he is only two-and-twenty, just completing the special course at the university, it is true, but with a long apprenticeship to serve yet before he can possibly contemplate marriage. He is a keen, ambitious youngster, too, no slacker. To the young lady's relatives—er—Colonel Rouncey—there was no objection, socially speaking, though she herself is some years older than Robin, and perhaps a trifle more—shall I say, sophisticated—than we could have wished. . . . However, though we did not venture on anything so obsolete as parental interference, the boy may have felt resentful at a slight lack of heartiness in the home atmosphere, for he has not brought Miss Torrington home much, though, of course, both sisters have dined with us, and turned up occasionally to tennis."

"You rather imagined that it might die out?"

"I suppose that was rather the idea"—ruefully. "It really seemed too much to expect that a girl of twenty-seven would waste ten years of her youth on an interminable engagement."

"And the elder sister—was she unattached?"

"No. To be frank, Lydia was far the better-looking of the two—of the blonde type—in fact, an attractive young woman, quiet, much less—Damn, comparisons drawn between sisters are always grossly unfair to one or the other. She was engaged to a fellow named Burroughs, a solicitor, who settled recently in Whitesands. A youngish chap, on the heavy side in conversation. I believe he was engaged first to Rosalind, and then changed sides. That sounds like gossip, but I warn you, Chief Inspector, you will find yourself up against an infernal quantity of gossip that contains lies, half-truths, and, possibly, a modicum of solid, bedrock fact in this case!"

"It's always so in any narrow community," Gorham agreed.

"Quite so. All I suggest is that you take local prejudice strictly for what it is worth. Including my own." A fleeting smile touched his lips. "To come down to yesterday. Mrs. Tennant and I took a party of people who'd been staying with us, and some other friends, over for a sort of picnic to Castle St. Roche, and the Torrington girls and Burroughs were, of course, included. As our guests had to leave fairly early to catch trains, the younger crowd remained behind. Both Burroughs and Robin had their own cars. It seems they lingered pretty late, and Burroughs for some inscrutable reason cleared off and left Robin to squire both girls home. Robin appears to have dropped Rosalind, no doubt by request, on the way to walk the final mile or so, but he drove Lydia right to the door of Melita Villa and left her, without going in. Rosalind got home soon after, and according to a servant's gossip—you will find details in Braice's book of the words—the two sisters had a quarrel. Lydia went out for a stroll after dark, possibly to cool off, and then went in and to bed without showing up in the family circle. That was the last time she was heard of alive, poor soul.

"This morning a young bobby named Bond, who lives with his mother quite close to Melita Villa, was returning from a longish-swim soon after six, when he discovered her body in the water, only a few hundred yards from her home. He had a friend on the beach waiting for him. He left the friend to guard the body, which they had carried to a bathing-hut built by the Admiral, but now disused, that stands beyond the garden of the Villa, and went for help. The sergeant brought the police-surgeon, who is also M.O.H. for Whitesands, and the surgeon found marks on the girl's neck and arm that pointed to her having been gripped and held under water. He then ordered the body to be conveyed for further examination to the Cottage Hospital, and later the sergeant went to inform Colonel Rouncey of his niece's death. He also seems to have taken it on himself to interrogate the servant who showed him out."

"Does suspicion point to any definite person as yet?"

Major Tennant turned and looked at him with lifted brows.

"Did I omit to mention that it was the habit of both sisters to swim together most mornings? That they were equally skilful at all water sports, and that the murder seems to have been committed near the Point, in deep water, where considerable skill was incontestably required?" he murmured politely.

"Good Lord! Was Colonel Rouncey informed of the suspicion of foul play?"

"No. Dr. Fitz-James kept that titbit of information for Braice's private ear, though the sergeant probably smelt a rat at his order re the body, and Rouncey promptly pounced on the same point. He was horribly upset, of course, and he and Burroughs leapt to the hospital and heavily strafed Braice, who was on the scene by that time, for having the body conveyed to the hospital instead of home. Braice told them nothing except that it had been ordered by Fitz-James, and left them howling for Fitz-James's blood while he came to report to me. I then rang up you people, and here you are. In fact, here we both are."

They were running down the sunny High Street of Whitesands. Gorham looked at a blue emptiness at its far end that meant the sea, and breathed in the salt tang of the air with keen apprecia-tion. This, however deplorable the cause of his coming, was a dis-tinct improvement on Whitehall pavements on a melting July day.

"I'd like to go over the medical evidence first," he said, stifling a sigh. "So far the case for murder seems to hang on the word of one doctor. Is he a reliable man?"

"Quite. But two other medicos, the leading man in Harbor-ough and the resident physician at the County Hospital there, both endorse his opinion that the bruises were inflicted before death. Their statements are with the others. However, you shall see Fitz-James for yourself. Braice promised to have the whole posse of witnesses here to meet you. Here is the police-station."

He had entered a side turning, and Gorham looked at the small spick and span building, but he sat still.

"Before I meet your people I'd like a few minutes to run through this report if it's possible to go anywhere that's quiet. What about running down on to the front, if it's not too much trouble?"

Without a word Tennant swung the car round and back into the High Street. He drove at a moderate pace between rows of shops which displayed the usual assortment of attractive rubbish for holiday-makers, gaudy-stands of postcards, spades and buck-ets, sand-shoes and bathing accessories, on to the very modest parade. Here he turned to the left, went slowly past the half-moon of hotels and boarding-houses, gay with striped awnings and hanging baskets of geraniums, past the open verandas set with chairs and tables, where waiters were already serving teas, past the pavilion and swimming baths to where the town dwindled into a colony of bungalows then back by the same route till he reached the broad approach to the breakwater. On to this he ran the car as far as vehicles were permitted, and halted.

Gorham, reading the typed sheets beside him, looked up for one appreciative glance at the expanse of sparkling water beyond the low stone wall, and returned to his study.

When he had read the last sheet, and consulted selected statements from the sheaf in the dispatch case, he ran through certain pages again as if to memorize salient points, then, his face thoughtful, he made one comment, omitting to look at the profile, tense, yet inscrutable, of the man beside him.

"This seems to give all the facts. But there are two points on which I am not clear."

"And they are?"

"The answer to the first would satisfy me, Major Tennant. Why was I brought down here?"

"My dear Chief Inspector!" Tennant twisted to look over his shoulder as he began to back the car preparatory to turning. "Be ready to leap for your life, man, if I look like landing us both in the sea. Backing cars on infernal narrow causeways like this is not my strong suit. You were brought down here to conduct the investigation into this murder. That report of Braice's—(Dash! Is that homely infant with its plain nurse safe? Good!)—is merely a preliminary assembling of surface facts. They may be wrong, or right. It is your job to test them for what they are worth." He swung the car round on to the front again. "I have been a policeman for twelve years. But I've been Robin's parent for two-and-twenty. This mess has got to be wiped up. But I felt a distinct distaste for doing it myself. Or letting Braice and his myrmidons do it. Hence you."

Gorham nodded, but he realized gravely that his question remained unanswered. Did Tennant actually intend to give him a fair field? Or had he been introduced into the affair as a figurehead to cover Tennant's official honour while, at the same time, he was preparing to thwart, deceive or mislead the stranger he had invited to take control, as he could not hope to deceive his own subordinates who knew the ground as intimately as he did himself? A sure instinct leapt to the certainty that young Tennant was linked with his *fiancée* at the dark centre of this crime far more vitally than Braice's innocuous allusions hinted at.

The chief constable's next remark, as they were running up the High Street, enhanced the high opinion he had already formed of his companion's intelligence, without dispelling his uncertainty as to the side on which it was to be employed.

"Handle my lad as lightly as you can, Gorham. He has been friendly with both these wretched girls—the one who lies murdered, and the other at whom the finger of suspicion points. You've got that now. Disguise is futile. To Robin it's tragic disaster on both counts. He won't shirk taking what's coming to him in the publicity that's inevitable. I don't mean that. Or want that. But it has shocked him in his deepest places. Torn him to bits between"— he used a phrase that had already done duty that day—"conflicting loyalties. If he can be piloted through without being irretrievably damaged, it's all I ask."

He pulled up with a jerk in front of the police-station. But Gorham waited to answer before he moved.

"I'd do that in any case, by any youngster that got caught in a case like this," he said earnestly, "whether it were your son or an errand boy. And may I say I feel for the situation it has placed you in. You can trust me to be as gentle as I can. Since I'm here, as you say, to conduct the investigation, it's my job to conduct it. Or rather"—a good-humoured smile lit his face as he hauled his bulky person out of the cramped seat—"tab along after it wherever it may lead. That's my experience of detective work. It's not so much conducting as following up."

"Quite. Well, now I'll just take you in and introduce you to my crowd, and then clear off. No doubt you will, in a friendly way, keep me in touch with the progress of your activities. But you understand that from now on you are in sole charge, and I claim no official rights whatever." A glance of the pleasant blue eyes endorsed the friendly tone. And Gorham warmed to that first real touch of his charm. "Any assistance you want Braice is perfectly ready to supply, you know. So don't hesitate to ask for what you need."

He led the way into the station—performed the formal introductions between the C.I.D. man and Norman who was waiting to receive him. And after recommending the Grand Hotel on the front as a hostelry reliable for its food and service, and requesting Norman to arrange for a car to be placed at Gorham's disposal, he took his departure.

CHAPTER V

GORHAM'S BRIEF INTERVIEW with the police-surgeon so completely satisfied his question as to Fitz-James's competence that he felt he could safely postpone his own examination of the body till he had dealt with the most pressing of the opening lines of enquiry awaiting his attention, and which had been already held up for half a day.

"I haven't heard that any attempt at resuscitation was made," he said tentatively.

"Haven't you? Well, there was, by the Oriental fellow I found in charge," Fitz-James retorted. "And I carried it on myself, not because I thought it was the faintest use, but because I guessed some fool would charge me with neglect if I didn't. Do you fellows in London waste time trying to resuscitate corpses whose heads have been under water for quarter of an hour?"

"Is that a certainty?"

"She was lying across the buoy, legs, head and shoulders submerged, when Bond spotted her. He took eight minutes to reach her. And the murderer had done the job very thoroughly before that!" was the significant reply.

Gorham nodded. Alone with Norman again his chief questions concerned the dead girl's swimming prowess. This, it seemed, was well vouched for.

"She and her sister are the best swimmers Whitesands has produced for years, bar none," Norman declared. "The place was famous six or seven years ago as being the home-town of Cyril Whittiker, the Naval Champion. His father is the local butcher, and it's chiefly owing to his exertions that the town now has swimming baths where contests can be held. But since young Whittiker went to sea, the craze for swimming that his exploits encouraged among the youngsters of the place has practically died out. We put up an absolutely rotten show last year when the Eastern Counties Swimming Clubs Association met here, and if Lydia hadn't pulled off the Ladies' Hundred Yards, and Rosalind got a third in the Lifesaving Contest—Lydia didn't compete for that, or she might have beaten her sister as she did in the Hundred Yards where Rosalind was second—we shouldn't have got so much as a Mention."

"That sounds as if these two only stood out as experts against a lot of duds!" Gorham said with a smile.

"Well, that's true. The two of them were too slack to train solidly. That's why they never achieved County form. Still, they were always fooling about in the water, got plenty of practice. You'd see them, sometimes, playing about together like a couple of dolphins. Went in every morning of their lives when the weather permitted."

"Does Colonel Rouncey swim?"

"Gosh, no! The old boy's never even been known to take a dip. The tale goes as he saw his young brother drowned before his eyes as a young man, and though he has got pretty well resigned to the girls going in, and never turned a hair when they were swimming, he used to be as nervous as a cat when his nephew Herman went in, though he was as good as the girls, if not better! Rouncey's a mild old boy, and not a bad sort. Used to play golf at Oakshott and visit a bit at certain good houses. But those nieces of his haven't made the home too comfy, by all accounts. He couldn't keep a servant a month at first with the rows that went on. Now he's got a cook-housekeeper who's been there for four years—pays her double wages and gives her a free hand, so he gets decent meals at least. But no one ever goes to the house except the girls' followers!" He winked significantly. "The fellows in the town—they dropped out of the County set years ago—find them amusing enough, but the women can't stand 'em at any price." He suddenly seemed to remember that one of these women of whom he spoke so slightingly was dead, for he added hastily: "There wasn't anything definite that I ever heard of against poor Lydia, though. If the women were a bit cattish about her, it was probably due to her being smarter and prettier than they were. It was Rosalind's fiend of a temper that everybody got a taste of that's made most of the townsfolk cut them recently."

"Quite so." He had caught that phrase from the chief constable. "But a young woman as skilful as deceased would take a lot of drowning. It would require considerable strength and even more skill in the murderer."

"Rather! The murderer would have to tread water, and keep well aside for fear of being gripped by her legs and free hand and dragged under too in the death struggle. Both hands were required, you see, to hold her head under. . . ."

Gorham nodded and rose.

"I should like to interview the constable—Bond—who recovered the body," he said. "But time is getting on, and a call on Colonel Rouncey is the first necessity."

"It's Melita Villa, along the coast road. Tell you what: Bond can run you out in his side-car. I'll release him for duty with you as long as you want him."

"Thanks. That will suit me excellently."

He liked the look of the sunburned young constable much better than he liked his sergeant. But at the motor-bicycle with its side-car he cast a dubious eye.

"Am I expected to sit in that?" he enquired of Bond.

"It's quite comfortable, sir. And quick."

"Um. I'm quick, too. That's just it. I want to stay quick, not dead." Norman missed that. But Gorham fancied he caught an unseemly chuckle as the young policeman stooped to start the engine. He fitted himself into the low seat, and they went off in a roar which precluded conversation.

On the coast road, within sight of the upper windows of the Villa, he signed to Bond to stop, and, getting out, he paused to take in the natural features of the shore.

The sands below were no longer deserted, for numbers of sightseers with the morbid callousness of their kind had come to feed their vulgar curiosity by peering about at the scene of the morning's tragedy, some even standing to stare at the drawn blinds of the house which had been the dead woman's home.

Gorham's glance went from the steep ridge of ground behind the house, covered in a dense mass of thicket and undergrowth, to the bare point of the headland which rose from its own reflection in the sea.

"Is there any path round that point?" he asked.

"No, sir. Even at low tide the water washes the cliff. It's the only place dangerous for bathing along the bay beyond the Villa there, for the bottom shelves very abruptly, and there are strong undercurrents."

Gorham nodded thoughtfully.

"There doesn't look to be any possible foothold on the side of the cliff either," he said. "I shall want you to take me round to the hut presently, and explain where you found the body. Is the hut open?"

"No, sir. The sergeant locked it. But he gave me the key in case you wished to examine it."

"Very well. Wait about here for me."

He walked along the road, and entered Colonel Rouncey's domain through a gate and gravel drive which led to the front door through an unexpectedly extensive and well-kept garden.

A shaggy brown dog limped round the angle of the house on three legs and joined him on the step, and Gorham, who liked dogs, stooped to examine the swollen paw he held up while he waited for the door to be opened.

"There, that will be all right now, old man!" he was saying encouragingly when a pretty maid presented herself on the threshold. Carlo instantly brushed past her and disappeared.

"Is Colonel Rouncey at home?"

"I believe so, but . . ."

"Please take him my card. He will see me."

She returned at once to usher him into a small room extremely untidy with its litter of books and newspapers, whose gloom was enhanced by the lowered blind.

Colonel Rouncey was still staring incredulously at the card in his hand. He was a tall, thin man in the middle sixties, and gave an impression, difficult to ascribe to any precise detail of his appearance, of a man who for years had permitted himself, physically and mentally, to run to seed.

"What does this mean?" He spoke in a tone of blustering anger, but Gorham perceived that the faded blue eyes were lined with sharp anxiety. "Are you from the police here? Perhaps you have come to apologize for the preposterous impudence, the incredible, insolent callousness, with which I have been treated today!"

Gorham shut the door.

"Not exactly to apologize, Colonel Rouncey, but certainly to explain the grave reason which made their action necessary. I am, as you can see from that card, from Scotland Yard, and now in charge of the case."

"The case? What the devil do you mean? My poor niece was drowned—"

"Unhappily she was. Won't you sit down? I'm afraid you must prepare yourself for painful news. There can be no question that the poor young lady met her death, not by accident, but by foul play."

"Foul play? You mean they do imagine that she was murdered? Oh, my God!"

He collapsed into a chair, gripping its arms with both hands, and the dog, who had been waiting at his side, instantly thumped a ponderous paw—the swollen paw—across his knee.

His bluster vanished, but the anxiety in his eyes deepened to dreadful alarm. Then, with a reassertion of long half-atrophied instincts, he suddenly pulled himself together and spoke quietly, with even a certain dignity.

"You must forgive me"—he glanced at the card he had dropped on the table—"Chief Inspector. But the shock of my niece's death, and the—the rudeness of the authorities, have shaken my nerves. They have kept me the whole day without— tidings. But this statement of yours is quite incredible. Please sit down and explain yourself."

Gorham lifted a bundle of papers from one of the chairs and took a seat, and as briefly and clearly as possible he explained the medical evidence which pointed conclusively to murder. The old man listened with riveted attention. He had succeeded by this time in his effort to conceal the alarm which had gleamed momentarily from his eyes, and his features now expressed only a natural dis- tress which was fitting, and indeed decent, in the circumstances.

His hand caressed the dog's silky ears, while Gorham spoke, in what was evidently a familiar gesture of affectionate habit.

"It still seems incredible!" he exclaimed, when Gorham had finished ending his explanation with his regret for the delay for which he was himself unintentionally responsible, as all action in the case had been suspended till his arrival.

But Rouncey brushed that aside as if he scarcely heard it. "Who could possibly have wanted to harm her here," he broke out almost querulously, "in a place where she has lived for years? Besides, she was absolutely at home in the water, up to every trick and antic. She knew every current in the Bay there as well as I know my own garden! That's why at first I couldn't believe that she was dead. I thought they were trying . . . Then I supposed she must have been seized with cramp. . . . Rosalind said it might *have* been cramp. Was anyone else known to—to be about—at the time?"

Gorham had been waiting for that feeler.

"So far the only person we know of was the young constable who found the body," he replied evenly. "No one was seen from the windows here, I suppose?"

"No one. My bedroom is on the landward side, indeed all the bedrooms are—to be sheltered from the sea winds—except Lydia's own, poor child! She chose it for herself because it was the largest in the house, and she said she liked sea views. She only changed over to sleep with her sister in the roughest winter nights."

"Her sister was in the habit of bathing early, wasn't she? Was she out this morning?"

"What? Rosalind? No. She is just as good a swimmer as her sister, but she strained her knee at tennis a week ago, she tells me, and hasn't bathed since."

"I see." This did not tally with the maid's statement to Norman but Rouncey's answer seemed to be made in good faith. "Well, can you suggest the smallest fact that might throw light on this mysterious affair?"

"Nothing whatever! Nothing what-so-ever!" The disclaimer was made with such vehemence that had Gorham been a student of Shakespeare he might have recalled Gertrude's caustic comment: "Methinks the lady doth protest too much!" As it was, he pigeonholed that impression of over-vehemence in his mind for future reference.

"Did you know of any enemies that the young lady had? Anyone who hated her—had a grudge against her?"

"Certainly not." This time his denial sounded sincere. "I don't really know what acquaintances she had in the town. But—well, in fact, I'd have said it was quite the other way. I didn't go out much with the girls. I'm a quiet sort of fellow, and nowadays young women don't need chaperonage. But it always seemed to me that men—well—flocked round her. . . . She never lacked partners and so on as some girls do. But she was engaged to be married, you know, to Harcourt Burroughs, a solicitor of Whitesands, who appears to be a respectable—er—steady fellow. He's most shockingly cut up about this!"

"Naturally. But, Colonel Rouncey, had either of your nieces ties or interests elsewhere than in Whitesands? Had they, for instance, ever thought of leaving home to start any sort of career for themselves?"

"Not that I ever heard." An odd look flitted across his face. "But in Lydia's case there was no need. My wife's aunt left her an income, about five hundred a year, and I fancy she made her sister a trifling allowance. Of course they went away for holidays occasionally. At least Lydia did. She was abroad last year. But only staying at hotels. She had no private friends with whom she ever stayed, I'm sure."

"I see. But you say she had a private income. This will now come to her sister as her natural heir?"

The Colonel sat up with a movement of genuine anger.

"I never read Miss Annabel Torrington's will," he said shortly. "It's damned indecent to be discussing the disposal of the poor child's money before she has been dead twenty-four hours."

Gorham briskly changed the subject.

"Now will you tell me when you last saw the young lady alive, Colonel? Then I shan't have to trouble you much longer. I understand she attended a picnic yesterday. Did you see her after she came home?"

"No, I don't think I did. Or only to call out good night to her on the stairs. Yes, that's it. I happened to notice at lunch that she was wearing a smart new frock, and when I admired it she laughed and said she had put it on to do honour to Rosalind's fiancé. Rosalind is engaged to a young fellow named Tennant, and it was his people who were giving this al-fresco show at Castle St. Roche. Tennant's father is rather a big-bug in the County, Chief Constable, I believe. I haven't come across him much myself. But when the girls came home only Rosalind came down to dinner with me. She said her sister had a headache. The sun, I suppose. A tray was sent up, I believe. She went out for a stroll later, and called out good night to me—this door was open—as she ran upstairs. That was about ten, I think. But that was the last I saw or heard her, poor child."

That constant phrase, used in reference to a woman whose age must have verged on thirty, struck Gorham as odd. It was as if this hesitating man who starred his speech with vague "I think—I suppose—I believe" additions, as if he lived in complete mental detachment from the relatives who shared his home, preferred to regard his dead niece still as the young girl she had been when he first settled here, ignoring the passage of changing years.

"This morning—did you go out yourself before breakfast?" He put the question gently, but instantly he noticed the worried frown that contracted the elder man's brows, though his answer was candidly given.

"I always take my dog for a run about seven." He looked down and patted Carlo as if he only then realized his presence by his knee, and a bushy tail gave a delighted thump on the floor. "This morning it was earlier. About six. It was a sweltering night and I woke at dawn and couldn't go to sleep again. But we went over the fields inland, and I saw nothing of the shore."

Gorham rose.

"Thank you, sir. Now I'll stop bothering you personally. But I'm afraid I must have a word with your niece, and also the servants." He checked an angry exclamation from Rouncey by adding with gravity: "It is my duty to collect all the information I can. And I *shall* also have to see the deceased lady's room. I will make things as little disagreeable to you as I can in the circumstances, but you will realize, I am sure, that as a police officer in charge of a criminal investigation I have wide discretion."

The Colonel shrugged his shoulders, went to the door and shouted, "Ross!" then stepped into the hall to meet the young woman who came from the opposite room, and spoke to her without attempting to mitigate the unpleasantness of his tidings, or even lowering his voice.

"Ross, my dear, there's a Scotland Yard man here. He says the police are certain now that Lydia's death wasn't an accident. They believe it was murder. He wants to see you."

"All right. I don't care."

The young woman who advanced to confront him justified, in the complete absence of any signs of human feeling or grief in her expression, the singular baldness with which her uncle had conveyed his news.

It seemed to Gorham that it was not so much a thick-set, healthy, strong and not bad-looking girl who stood before him as a rude creature of animal strength and primitive physical energy. Yet, with that unflattering thought in his mind, her first speech shocked him profoundly.

"I never for a second saw how Lydia could have got drowned by accident. But do tell me! How the devil did they find out she was murdered?"

Gorham shut the door and stood against it, surveying her from head to foot. Here was no case for tender handling.

"I am here to ask questions, not to answer them," he said brusquely. "You had a violent quarrel with your sister last night?"

She shrugged her shoulders.

"That was nothing unusual. We were always fighting. What right have you to pry into my private affairs?"

"That tone will not help you, Miss Torrington. I am a police officer sent down here to investigate your sister's murder. I have every right to question everyone whose affairs are connected with hers. When did you last see her alive?"

She stared at him with sullen eyes.

"When she came into the dining-room to fetch her milk and biscuits last thing."

"Did you speak? What time was that?"

"About ten. Of course we didn't speak. We weren't on speaking terms."

"It was the habit of you both to go out for an early swim in the summer. Did you go out this morning?"

"No."

"Be careful, Miss Torrington. You were heard to leave your room."

"Oh—by that little cat Gladys, I suppose! I went down to the beach, but I didn't go into the water."

"Did you see anyone on the shore when you were there?"

"No."

"Nor in the water?"

"No."

"The bay appeared to be quite deserted this side of the pier?"

"Yes. I saw nobody. I wasn't there more than a minute or two."

"Do you know what time it was when you went out?"

She moved uneasily.

"Do you?" he repeated.

"The hall clock struck six when I was on the stairs," she muttered.

"Colonel Rouncey informed me that he went out about six. Did you meet him either going out or coming back?"

"No. But I heard Carlo barking in the front garden, and guessed he'd gone. And his hat was gone from the hall stand."

"When was this? When you went out?"

"Yes—damn! How can I remember?" She was flustered, her eyes frightened. "No. It was when I came back."

"You are sure?"

"Yes. I noticed about the hat when I came out of the lounge."

"One moment, explain that, please. Had you not gone out by the front door?"

"Of course not. That's in front. We always cut through the french windows of the lounge to get to the beach. It's much quicker. Uncle probably went out by the glass door in the passage next to his room into the front garden. He usually does."

"I understand. Is the shore always so deserted when you go out early?"

"Yes. No one uses it before breakfast but ourselves. It is too far from the town."

"What about the policeman, Bond? He lives close by, doesn't he?"

"Oh yes, I've seen him sometimes. But his clothes weren't on the groyne this morning. Carlo dragged them off yesterday, and into our place. So that probably scared him off leaving them again, and serve him right for his damned cheek."

"You saw him yesterday when you bathed?"

"I haven't bathed for a week. I'd strained my knee."

"Then this morning you merely went to look at the water?"

"Yes."

"Did you hear your sister go out?"

"No."

"Were you in any way aware that she had gone out when you went yourself?" Gorham persisted, and her hands twisted together for an instant. He saw that her arms were disproportionately long for her height, which was five feet seven inches at a rough judgment the hands broad, with short, ugly, muscular fingers. It was this disproportionate length of arm and the shortness of her neck that gave her figure a thick-set appearance. She was wearing a sleeveless frock of green-striped washing silk, cheap in quality, faded and shrunken, open at the neck and finished with a green tie and belt.

"I didn't know anything about her when I went down. Except that the windows were unlatched, and I saw her room was empty when I came back. I went to look!" she admitted defiantly.

"Then, as you had not seen her in the water, did you not wonder what had become of her?"

"Why should I worry! She might have gone round the point, or far out. She was quite able to take care of herself!"

"She was far, this morning, from being able to take care of herself," he said gravely. "You acknowledge that you and she were on bad terms. Yet you went to a picnic together yesterday, and, according to your uncle, your sister put on a new dress to do honour to your fiancé's people—who gave the party."

"Rot! Uncle swallowed that yarn of hers, did he!" The heavy face, sullen before, flamed in sudden, scornful fury. "She put on that new flounced blue of hers that she'd just paid seven guineas for because she knew I hadn't a dress fit to be seen! And the sell was, the real bigwigs weren't smart at all! She looked beastly overdressed beside the other women, though she never cared a damn what the women thought so long as all the men made eyes at her!" She added, with cold ferocity: "I'm thankful she's dead!"

"Miss Torrington, I advise you strongly, for your own sake, not to make remarks like that!" Gorham said severely. "You don't seem to realize what I am here for. Your sister has been murdered. Do you understand? Murdered. And we are hunting for her murderer. Someone who was an expert swimmer, and who hated her. Do you get the implication of that?"

"You think I killed her!" she cried furiously. "But I tell you I wasn't in the sea at all this morning!"

"I shall get, if I can, corroborative evidence of your statement," he said with stern authority. "It was, however, fair to warn you in your own interests. Now I am going to search your sister's room, but a maid can take me up. You will kindly remain in this room till I come down. I may want you again."

He opened the door, aware that he had frightened her into cowed submission. He requested Colonel Rouncey, who was hovering anxiously about in the hall, to summon Gladys and remain with his niece while he went upstairs.

CHAPTER VI

As GORHAM FOLLOWED the maid, Gladys Black, into the long, low room which had been the bedchamber of Lydia Torrington, his attention was arrested to the exclusion of every other thought for a moment by the loveliness of the shimmering expanse of sunlit water, seen framed, as it were, in the three tall windows on one side.

"My word!" he exclaimed. "What a gorgeous view!"

He moved across to the nearest window and looked out. The house seemed to be built in a roughly triangular shape, the base sheltered under the steep heights at the back, one side, with the dining-room and hall lying straight to the garden, while this side lay at so sharp an angle to the shore as to command an uninterrupted view across the bay towards the breakwater. Looking down he could see a narrow strip of thick shrubbery, and a sloping stretch of shingle and weed-covered sand from which the tide was still receding, and on the right the formidable cliff wall of the promontory projecting far into the sea. But it was not till he leaned out that he could discern, beyond the shrubbery, the roof of the bathing-hut which had held the dead girl's body that morning while the inhabitants of her home slept peacefully, dressed themselves leisurely, and breakfasted, utterly unaware of the tragedy that had overtaken her somewhere, somehow, in that last, fatal swim.

Reluctantly he withdrew his head and turned back to survey the room and the maid, whose trimness formed a startling contrast to the scene of slovenly disorder presented by her background.

"Do you like the sea?" he genially enquired.

"The sea? Well, I'm London myself, and I thought it was heavenly when my aunt brought me over from Norwich to see the place summer before last!" she said chattily. "You see I'd had a breakdown, and at the hospital they warned me to get a seaside job if I didn't want to get T.B. And while I was stopping with Aunt she heard of this place, her being a friend of Mrs. Priest, who's cook here. And it's jolly in the summertime, when the sun's out and there's no wind. But I don't hold with a house being built right down on the shore like this one is! Why, in storms the spray gets drove right against the house sometimes, and the row of the waves booming fair gets on my nerves! And the mess it makes, soaking the carpets and curtains, and everything feeling wringing wet! And you wouldn't believe the winds we get, blowing in and slamming the doors and pitching things over! It beats me how poor Miss Lydia could stand it being such a nuisance in here sometimes, she being the only one to sleep on the sea side of the house. I'm sorry the room is so untidy, sir, but we've been so muddled today and there's been such a lot extra to do, I haven't seemed to get a minute to come up and make the bed, even!"

He noticed that she had found time to curl up the ends of her pretty hair and powder her tip-tilted nose. But he did not say so.

"Perhaps Miss Lydia generally tidied her own room."

"Miss Lydia! That she didn't, sir! Nor Miss Rosalind either! The young ladies never done a hand's turn in the house. If Miss Lydia arranged a few flowers when some of the gentlemen were coming to tea it would be all she'd do, though I will say she always hung up her own clothes, which is more than her sister does. But if she leaves them lying all over her floor I just don't take any notice, and let 'em lie."

"Was Miss Lydia the housekeeper?"

"Well—of course she was mistress-like. But Mrs. Priest orders everything and sees to the meals. . . . She's been with the master nearly five years, and knows what he likes. And he's a very easy gentleman to please, and never finds fault. I do the housework, and we have a woman in three days a week to turn out."

His shrewd glance, wandering over the room while she chattered, had observed odd characteristics which threw a certain light on its owner's tastes. When Gladys opened the doors of the large, up-to-date wardrobe smart frocks were displayed, hanging from padded shoulders. An expensive-looking brown fur coat with a satin lining was in an open cupboard; the nightdress on the bed was a pretty, flimsy affair of lace and crêpe-de-Chine. But apart from a pier-glass, a much be-mirrored dressing-table loaded with face creams and cosmetics among a jumble of soiled handkerchiefs, ribbons and discarded rubbish, bearing the dust and spilt powder of days, a comfortable easy chair, and the wardrobe, there was not a memorable object in the room.

There was not a book in the room, or a picture on the walls, and it might, for all any signs of personally chosen decorative effects betrayed, have been a bedroom in furnished lodgings in which a woman who took meticulous pains with her clothes and appearance and cared for nothing else was temporarily camping.

Yet a woman who did care for her clothes at least would scarcely have left every drawer half open, every cupboard door ajar.

"You probably know Miss Lydia's possessions well," he said slowly. "Do you notice if anything is missing from this room?"

She looked round, puzzled.

"No, sir. I don't miss anything. There's her green bathing dress gone, of course, and the green coat."

"Coat? What coat was that? She wouldn't want a coat for bathing, surely?" He knew the bathing-dress found on the body was of jade green. Gladys became suddenly wide awake, and briskly searched in drawers and cupboards.

"Well, I never! It has gone!" she exclaimed. "It was a lovely sort of silk coat, all embroidered, that went with the bathing-costume! Miss Lydia was ever so fond of it, and it did suit her fair colouring a treat! She used to slip it on to run down to the sea in, but yesterday Carlo the dog dragged it in while she was bathing, and it had a shocking tear right down it, from the neck to the hem! Well, that is a funny thing!"

"If it was torn she must have thrown it away!"

"No, she didn't, sir! She was running up the tear yesterday in this very room, when I was making the bed, and she said it would do a turn yet. It was useful because sea-water didn't cockle it up, and it dried in a minute if you spread it in the sun. But she promised to give it to me later." Her keen interest in the missing garment was explained. "She didn't want to take to her new one till there was some special occasion, and she loved the green."

"Look here, what sort of coat was it, a kind of dressing-gown?"

"No, no. A beach coat, with pyjamas to match, only Miss Lydia got the trousers so badly torn last month she did throw those away. Wait! I'll show you her other costume."

Eagerly, with fingers trembling with pleasure at the dainty beauty of the garments she was handling, she drew out from a drawer and spread on the bed an extravagant set of garments, bathing-dress, pyjamas with wide embroidered legs and front, and a long coat, all of the softest silken material.

"You see, these are peach colour, with golden embroideries! Aren't they lovely! And they don't weigh anything, and you can fold them up into nothing! The other set was jade-green all over lovely pink flowers and twirling green stalks and curling leaves, and amber butterflies. And it was better quality than this one too, Miss Lydia thought. She didn't think this would stand sea-water like the green did, so that was why she saved it, careful. Though she paid the same for both in Paris a year ago—thousands and thousands of francs she said they cost! She never minded what she paid for her clothes, Miss Lydia didn't! Look at that fur coat over there! Real mink it is, and cost two hundred pounds!"

She sighed as she folded up the things she had displayed, laying them carefully away in their tissue paper in the drawer. Gorham went over and lifted down the fur coat, glanced at it inside and out, and smoothed his hand down its soft surface. He replaced it without comment.

"It's odd where that beach-coat could have got to, though. You are sure it wasn't left on the beach, or in the house somewhere?"

"Certain! I went out to the beach for a breath of air as soon as I was dressed, only for a second, because Cook and I both overslept ourselves, but I'd have seen it if it was there. And I'm positive it isn't in the house! I tidied up every room except this."

"Thanks, Gladys. If it turns up after all be sure and let me know, will you? Now will you tell me what you all did this morning, and about last evening?"

He questioned her closely, but without eliciting any new facts.

It was obvious that neither of Colonel Rouncey's nieces was much liked or respected by the servants, though the girl's tone softened pitifully when she spoke of Lydia, with whom she had been on easy terms. Gorham had noticed the sergeant's familiar use of their Christian names.

Presently he dismissed Gladys to clear away the tea-things from the dining-room. But his swift methodical examination of the room brought to light no papers or letters which had the smallest bearing on the case. Either Lydia Torrington destroyed letters as she received them, or the searcher who had preceded him had left nothing for him to find.

He noted down while the address was fresh in his memory the name of the French shop which he had read on the tab inside the silk coat, glanced through a few receipted bills in a cash-box, the key of which was in the lock, and found that they represented only small local purchases, and finally spent five minutes in running through the pages of two pass-books lying with a cheque-book in the same receptacle. The newer one commenced in March only, and showed entries merely of cheques for small amounts drawn to "self". The completed pass-book, which covered a period of years, might, he felt, repay more detailed study than he had time at the moment to spare for it, though a hurried scrutiny revealed only that Lydia Torrington had received her income in quarterly payments of £125, paid through a London bank, and that, apart from small cheques to self which represented her personal expenditure, the great part of this yearly income had been spent on clothes, for the names of well-known London establishments—Selfridges, Evans, Barkers, etc., appeared with frequency.

He slipped the books into his pocket and went out, locking the door behind him. He glanced into the two other rooms which were on the same side of the passage, Both were small, both, once furnished as bedrooms, had evidently been used for years as dumping ground for unwanted lumber. Both were unswept and undusted, and from the window of each the view of the immediate foreshore was blocked by untrimmed, close-growing shrubbery, and from neither was the hut visible.

The wall opposite to Lydia's door was blank, the door of the bedroom it bounded opening round the corner of a passage which, after forming a landing at the head of the stairs, joined a narrow corridor on which apparently the bedrooms in the front of the house opened.

He was standing in the recessed doorway some minutes later when Gladys ran upstairs to rejoin him.

"This"—he drew the door to behind him as he spoke—"is Miss Rosalind's room, I suppose. And those others?"

"Yes, sir. Beyond the landing there"—she pointed across the head of the staircase—"is the best spare room, then the master's bathroom, and his bedroom—that door you can just see in that passage, over the dining-room it is. And my room and Cook's are down the passage beyond his, over the kitchens."

"Do you often have guests staying here?"

"Never, since I've been here!"

"If your room is right down that passage across this landing, how can you be sure you heard Miss Rosalind leave her room this morning?"

She looked at him with wide-open eyes.

"But I did, sir! It was hot, and my door was open. The door banged and that woke me, and I heard Miss Rosalind say, 'Damn!' and open it again, as if it had slammed on her towel or something."

"Does Miss Rosalind wear one of those silk coat things when she runs down to the shore?"

"Oh no, sir! She hasn't got any lovely things like what Miss Lydia has—had. Why, her bathing-dress is only a cheap old blue thing, not near so good as mine!"—with scorn. "And she doesn't bother even to put on a dressing-gown mostly. Just wraps her bath-towel round her and goes down like that."

He nodded and signed to her to precede him down the stairs. "Ask Cook to come to me in the dining-room."

He was standing thoughtfully in one of the windows that over-looked a well-kept lawn and flourishing flower-beds screened from the road by a high hedge and to the left by a grove of trees when the cook entered, a capable-looking person of middle age, neat in her appearance, and with none of the flightiness of her pretty young coadjutor.

"Good afternoon. I won't keep you a minute. But I am a police officer, come about the sad death of the young lady here this morning," he said pleasantly. "I expect you realize that there must be an inquest?"

"Yes, sir. I feel very sorry about it."

"Of course you do. But you will understand that I have to collect the necessary facts, so I'd be obliged if you would answer a few questions."

He sat down at the table and opened his notebook.

"What is your name, please?"

"Mrs. Priest. Jessie Priest. My husband was a chauffeur, and died two years after our marriage, so I went back to service."

"Quite. Have you been here long?"

"Just on five years, sir. The Colonel had had a lot of trouble with servants before that. But since then he has left the house-keeping to me, and I have given him satisfaction."

"Was Mrs. Rouncey alive when you first came?"

"Oh no, sir. The poor lady died years ago, just after they came back from India, he told me once. In London. He thought of living there with his only sister, Mrs. Hervey, but it fell through, so he came down here to Melita Villa."

"And the young ladies?"

"Miss Rosalind was still at school at first, I understand, but Miss Lydia came with him, and later on, after Mrs. Hervey died, the Colonel's nephew, Mr. Herman Hervey, used to come for his holidays. Like Miss Rosalind, till she left school. But that was long before my time. He was living here alone with the young ladies—Mrs. Rouncey's nieces they are—when I came."

"The nephew still runs down occasionally, I suppose, though?"

"No, sir. Mr. Herman has never been down since I came. I fancy," she added with a slight hesitation, "that there may have been a difference between them, because, though the Colonel never speaks of him—he isn't one to speak of his private affairs much, and naturally he wouldn't to me—I sometimes fancy he misses him still. Mrs. Hervey and him being his only real relatives, I mean," she added, as if she were annoyed to find herself discussing her employer's concerns. "Only that I've heard Mr. Herman and he used to play golf together, and chess in the evenings, and go for walks, and now—since the young gentleman went abroad—the Colonel seems a bit lonely by himself with only the dog. Though Carlo is more human than a lot of human beings."

Gorham smiled.

"They often are, dogs. Do you have many visitors here?"

"No one to stay, sir. The ladies have their friends to tea sometimes."

"What friends?"

"The gentleman Miss Lydia was engaged to, Mr. Burroughs, and Mr. Tennant, Miss Rosalind's young gentleman. I haven't heard of any others lately. But, of course, I don't wait on the drawing-room except on Gladys's day out."

"Did either of them come yesterday?"

"I heard they came to fetch the young ladies to the picnic yesterday, but I didn't see them."

"Did you see Miss Lydia when she came in?"

"I didn't see her at all, but I was picking parsley in the garden and heard her drive in with Mr. Tennant."

"How do you know it was Mr. Tennant?"

"Because I heard him say rather anxiously, 'You are sure you are going to be all right now?' And Miss Lydia laughed and said: 'Don't be a goose, Bobbin-boy, of course I am! Don't worry any more!' Mr. Tennant's name is Robin."

"Um! Rather affectionate that! To her sister's young man!"

"Miss Lydia was one for using pet names for gentlemen, sir. With her it didn't mean much. Mr. Tennant drove away then, and, being busy with dinner and washing up in the kitchen, I didn't see any of the family again till I went in to bid the Colonel good night as usual, and ask if there was anything more. He was alone in this room, winding the clock, and just going up to bed himself. About eleven that was. Then this morning, Gladys and I both overslept, and didn't wake till quarter to eight, and we had a scuffle to get breakfast ready. But the master was a bit late in from his walk, which was a mercy, for as a rule he's like clockwork, so it was on the table by eight fifteen when he came in. We didn't hear any of the coming and going at the hut, but it was the sound of a car on the grass at the top of the path that woke me. I think it must have been the ambulance. It's very rough ground there, and steep, down to the road, and I caught men's voices. But I didn't think anything of it at the time, being behind with my work."

"Weren't you surprised when you heard from Gladys that Miss Lydia wasn't down to breakfast?"

"Not surprised, sir. I told Gladys to ask if she wanted it taken up. But Miss Rosalind said she was out—not in her room. And I was vexed, thinking there'd be a second breakfast to get. You see, both of them are very inconsiderate that way, coming in at all hours and ordering meals back. It makes a lot of extra work, and one never gets one meal properly finished and out of the way before you begin preparing for the next, when the family is always doing that. But I could not guess that the poor soul was dead. . . ."

"Of course not. You didn't hear anything of the quarrel between them last night, then?"

"No, sir."

"Didn't Gladys run and tell you?"

"I thought you were asking what I heard myself!" she retorted. "What a girl like Gladys may come and chatter about is neither here nor there!"

"You think Gladys may have made a lot of it up? You know she repeated a phrase or two to the sergeant this morning. Is she in the habit of exaggerating?"

Mrs. Priest took a moment to think over her answer.

"Gladys is a truthful girl, sir," she said at last, with evident reluctance. "What she said she heard she did hear. I'm sure of that. But she only heard a bit, and when people in a family are having words, it isn't sense to take every sharp thing they say for gospel. It was wrong of Gladys to repeat it, and so I told her, not holding with gossip. She's only a young girl, sir, and thoughtless. I hope she won't get into trouble over this. I mean, have to stand up at the inquest and repeat what she said to that meddlesome sergeant, who ought to have known better than encourage her." She looked genuinely troubled, her sensible face anxious, almost pleading. "You know as well as I do that it does a girl in service no good to have it get about that she's a chatterbox, sir! There's her character to think of, and Gladys is a good, straight girl. It was the shock we all had this morning that made her lose her head a bit, and talk more than she should. So if you can keep her out—"

Gorham got up.

"I can't make promises, Mrs. Priest. She may be called as a witness at the inquest. But if she is, the best advice you can give her is to give the true answer to any question that may be asked, and not to add to or take away anything from it. If she does that she has nothing to fear. Now will you ask Miss Rosalind and the Colonel if I may see them again for a moment."

He was considering his notes when they came in together.

He looked straight at the girl.

"Miss Torrington, have you anything to add to the statement you made to me just now regarding your actions this morning?"

The old man broke in angrily:

"Look here, Chief Inspector, my niece has informed me—"

Gorham held up an authoritative hand.

"Please, Colonel Rouncey. Let Miss Torrington speak for herself. You told me," he added sternly, "that you ran down to the shore, but did not bathe. What were you wearing at the time?"

His eyes never left her face. He saw her crimson, and then turn deathly white. The reddened eyelids—she had obviously been crying—showed swollen and stained against that ominous pallor. Her very lips which tried to form a word, but failed to utter it, were colourless.

"You told me," he continued after a long pause, speaking slowly, gravely, "you told me that you had not bathed for a week, because you had strained your knee. Yet your wet towel, wrapped round your wet bathing-dress, is thrust under a heap of clothes in your wardrobe."

CHAPTER VII

GORHAM REJOINED the young constable on the road in a serious mood. Bond had parked the motor-cycle in his own garden. He glanced hesitantly from the eleven-foot drop to the beach from the grass level where they stood to the large bulk of his companion, and then remarked, with diffidence, that a hundred yards along, by the next groyne, there were planks down.

"Any by-law compelling the use of the planks?"

"Not that I've heard of, sir."

"Right. Then if you will kindly support my tottering form we will drop over here."

He landed on the shingle as neatly if with less agile grace than his junior, who grinned behind his broad back as he followed him down the slope to the sands. He was much cheered at being detailed for duty with the C.I.D. chief, who seemed to be as wide-awake as he was good-humoured.

Discreetly he waited to be questioned as they rounded the end of the groyne and walked along the wet strip of sand below Melita Villa. The thick shrubbery hid all the windows except those of the chamber which Lydia Torrington had occupied, and as Gorham jaw the angle at which the house was built to the shore he realized why—even if the shrubs had not grown so high against the two grimy windows of the disused rooms—the hut would still have been invisible. That chamber alone was projected from the house wall, by the width of the veranda roof below.

Beyond this point the ground ascended abruptly from the shore to the rough hilly spur of the promontory, which cast its shadow over the hut built on a square of artificially levelled ground well above high water mark, from which a narrow path overgrown with weeds ran inland skirting the high boundary fence of the Colonel's garden.

"You carried the body up that path?"

"To the ambulance? Yes, sir. The ambulance came along by the road and ran back as far as it could on the grass above there. It was a stiffish job to get it moving again, for the ground is rough, but—as it was—shaking didn't matter. And it was less public that way than to carry it all round by the sands, the way we have come."

Gorham nodded.

"I noticed the road curved inland from the Villa gate to avoid the hill." He was looking up at the dark green heights. "Is there no building on top there?"

"No, sir. It's private property, fenced in since a kid fell clean off the top of the cliff years ago and was drowned in the deep water below, before his mother's eyes. The ground is crumbling and dangerous above the cliff's, and there, above the Villa, as you see, it's covered with dense thicket and bramble, a stiff scramble up from the road, and nothing to reward you but scratched legs when you get there. No one ever goes there."

"Now tell me what you did this morning. What time did you come down to the shore?"

"At five-thirty, sir, the weather being favourable for an extra bit of diving practice off the breakwater. There was not a soul in sight on shore or in the bay. I looked carefully before I stripped off my mac, which I left under the groyne the other side. It being low water—"

"Wait a bit. The tide was still running out when you went in?"

"Yes, sir. The turn came at six eight a.m., so I got it both ways. It is low again at six-thirty-one this afternoon, so you can judge how much shore was uncovered. It is four fifty now."

"All right, go on."

"The sea was running strongly, so I got back in record time by my friend's watch. Six fifteen. There was no one on the beach but my friend. But as I touched bottom and stood up to wave to him, I looked round and saw there was something queer about the colour of the buoy out there by the point." He stopped.

"Well? Give me every detail you can think of."

"I thought first it was a green cap of one of the gir—young ladies from the Villa. Only it was odd she should be holding on to the buoy. But if it was some stranger who'd got caught in the currents . . . well, it didn't do any harm to go and find out if everything was O.K. When I got close—it took me about eight minutes going back against the tide—I saw it was Miss Torrington. I recognized her green suit, but she was on her face across the buoy, her head in the water. There wasn't much chance she was alive, but I towed her ashore as quick as I could—just there, below the hut, the nearest point I could reach. That would be six twenty-eight. My pal was waiting, and helped me to carry her up. The hut was his suggestion."

"Who is this pal of yours?"

"It's a visitor I've made friends with on the shore this last week, sir. He is staying in Whitesands with cousins of his wife, and he usually times me in. He's a Chinese. We both saw she was dead, but he carried on an attempt at resuscitation while I went to fetch the sergeant."

"Why didn't you notify her own people?"

For the first time Bond hesitated uncomfortably in his narrative. "If you understand, sir, I—er—was not in uniform. I didn't know what to do for the best. When Mr. Moh suggested I should proceed direct by cycle to the station to inform the sergeant while he remained with deceased in the hut, I followed his advice."

Gorham frowned down at his notebook.

"Mr. Moh? Your Chinese friend? That's odd. Do you know his address? I'd like his statement. Privately. Understand? Tell him I said so. Now give me exact times as far as you can." He noted them in his book as Bond gave them, with careful accuracy.

"I first discerned the body at six fifteen. I reached it at six twenty-three. Landed it ashore, the tide being again in my favour, six twenty-eight. These times I gauged by calculation of distances covered, sir, but Mr. Moh confirmed them by his watch. The following I noted by my own wrist-watch which I'd left with my coat. I reached the station at six forty. The sergeant heard my report, and 'phoned up the doctor, whom he picked up en route and with whom he reached the hut at six fifty-eight. The doctor then directed me to 'phone from the nearest box—we passed it as we left the town, sir—for the ambulance. And the body was removed in the ambulance at seven forty-five, sir."

"Why didn't you 'phone the station in the first place from that call box?"

"I did intend to when I started, sir. But it was engaged as I passed. A Rolls saloon, dark blue, was outside, empty. So as the remaining distance wasn't more than three minutes it was as quick to proceed in person."

"When Sergeant Norman reached the hut what happened to Moh?"

"He just bowed to the sergeant, sir, and gave him place. And while I waited outside the door I saw him walking all along by the edge of the water as if he were looking for something, and then he just seemed to fade away."

"Ah yes. Just what Mr. Moh would do. Fade away," he murmured; then, sharply: "Now one more question. And this is important, materially affecting as it does the prestige of the County Constabulary!" Bond stiffened, and tried to look as intelligent as he could. "When did you manage to get into a decent pair of trousers?" The intelligence of Bond's expression was veiled behind a healthy scarlet.

"I managed to assume certain garments when I proceeded home for my bicycle, sir, but not then being able to spare time to dress fully, the sergeant dismissed me to do so while waiting for the ambulance."

"Good." Gorham heaved a sigh of relief. They were again crossing the beach towards the road. "The thought of you careering about the countryside on that bike in wet bathing drawers was beginning to worry me. But, Bond, next time you fish a body from the sea, bathing drawers or nothing, stick by it yourself. Don't leave a stranger in charge."

"No, sir"—humbly. "But Mr. Moh, being the sort he is—"

"Quite so. By sheer luck the stranger this time was Mr. Moh. But don't rely on such a stroke of luck happening twice in a lifetime. They don't. By the way, the girl was wearing a green costume. Did you see any other green wrap on shore or in the water?"

"No, sir."

"Did you see anyone, anywhere along the shore, or showing up at the Villa—apart from yourself and Moh and the police—from start to finish of this affair?"

"Not a single soul, sir, anywhere in sight, except the young maid from the Villa as I came back from seeing the ambulance off. The doctor dropped his matchbox at the hut and sent me back down the path to find it. As I was approaching the garden I saw the maid fly out to the gate on the beach, give a quick peek round, and in again. So quick that she'd gone when I passed the gate myself. I reported same to the sergeant. That was about seven fifty-five. It had taken a few minutes to find the box, which was not in the hut but on the shingle outside."

Gorham nodded. This confirmed Gladys Black's statement.

His next visit was to the mortuary, where he stood for a moment to gaze with compassion at the marred features, before he examined the body with a thoroughness that covered it inch by inch, slowly, with minute care.

When he had finished not a shadow of doubt remained in his mind that Fitz-James was right. She had been brutally gripped by the upper part of the right arm and the neck at the base of the skull, and held under water till she drowned.

The murderer, as Fitz-James had said, had done the job thoroughly, exercising determined, cold-blooded force to control her desperate struggles till the struggles ceased with insensibility.

Two questionable points merged.

Had the murderer not realized that the body would carry its own proof of foul play?

Why had the body been thrown across the buoy?

The answer to the first seemed almost certainly to be in the negative, though it argued brutal ignorance or dense stupidity in the criminal, for apart from those bruises examined before there could be any possible doubt of their infliction before death, the question of crime would not have arisen. It would have seemed sheer accident.

The answer to the second was easier. The murderer, not content with killing Lydia Torrington, had wished the body to be recovered, and the fact of her death known at once.

But—Gorham came back to that point—it seemed unlikely that that urge would have prevailed had the murderer guessed that her death would not be accepted as due to natural misadventure only.

He scrutinized the bathing-dress carefully. It was, as Gladys had said, a jade-green edition of the one she had showed him, but showed signs of considerable wear in small mendings here and there and a certain fading of the once gay embroideries. Fresh splits in the material bore witness also to wild physical contortions with which Lydia had fought to escape that fatal grip.

He arranged for the body to be photographed, and went down to the cheerful hotel on the front which the chief constable had recommended, in search of tea. He had missed lunch, as there was no dining-car on the train that had brought him to Harborough.

Here, after engaging a first-floor room with a balcony over-looking the pier, to which he could take any person whom he preferred to interview in private rather than in the blatantly official atmosphere of the office placed at his disposal at the police-station, he deposited his bag and went downstairs to the veranda to enjoy a substantial tea.

But though it was substantial he did not linger over its despatch. And pushing back his chair he lighted his pipe, and while he seemed to be lazily watching the varied scene before him his thoughts concentrated on the case that had brought him to Whitesands.

There were several angles from which the case could be approached. The police down here, for instance, though their attitude was guarded for obvious reasons, regarded it clearly from the angle of Rosalind Torrington's certain guilt.

This line of approach appealed to him little, as he distrusted the reliability of any investigation started on an initial prejudice. An investigation which started with a definite suspect in view was apt to ignore every clue which did not point directly at its chosen quarry—to degenerate, in short, into a hunt.

The hunt should not begin till the investigation was complete, the facts collected and carefully balanced, irrelevant clues examined and discarded, the remainder sifted and tested till they ranged themselves in a solid chain of damning evidence. Every fact he had turned up so far confirmed the suggestion of the sister's guilt. She had the skill, the motive, the necessary reach of arm, strong muscular fingers, the opportunity, and—finally—there was the wet bathing-dress . . . hidden. . . .

But to get the unbiased survey that his honest mind demanded, it was necessary to put Rosalind clean out of it and approach the case from a fresh angle. The most promising line was through the character of the victim.

Lydia Torrington was twenty-nine years old, fair, with eyes of light hazel, plumpish, but well-proportioned in body, described by the chief constable, a keen observer, as an attractive young woman, quiet, much less—what word had he suppressed? Blatant? Vulgar? Either would fit Rosalind. Indolent in the home, yet liked, or at least not disliked, by the servants, and on amiable terms with her uncle. Extravagantly fond of dress, a taste not uncommon in young women, which she was able to gratify as she possessed an income of her own.

Gorham paused here. He had observed no evidence of generosity with this money to anyone but herself at the Villa. From Mrs. Priest's statement he inferred that she contributed nothing to the household, for the woman spoke of Rouncey as the paymaster. The Colonel had stated that he believed she gave her sister a small allowance.

Rosalind's clothes were, by comparison with her sister's, shabby and poor. The alleged allowance could scarcely have been a liberal one. Fierce cause for jealousy there, quite sufficient ground to explain frequent, bitter quarrels. Scarcely sufficient to explain murder.

What else had he got about her? Her sole hobby was swimming, in which she excelled from natural aptitude and constant desultory practice, but which her innate physical laziness prevented her from turning to much account.

Of placid, self-indulgent temperament then, and not above telling fibs to impress a simple-minded servant-girl.

The line of the victim's personality didn't seem to be carrying him far.

What about Colonel Rouncey?

A harmless person, apparently. Of sufficient family affection to burden himself with two young relatives of his wife, not of sufficient strength of character to give them chaperonage or guidance when they grew up. According to his servants, an easy gentleman to please, punctual as a rule, yet late that morning. That might mean nothing, of course, but a walk of two hours and a quarter with his dog before breakfast sounded rather strenuous for an elderly man who looked none too robust.

Fond of his dog. Yet he had not noticed his limp. Yet that long thorn which Gorham had extracted from an inflamed paw had been embedded there for many hours.

His earlier bluster to Braice might well be due to sudden shock and anger at treatment which he evidently regarded as a gross indignity to the dead girl and an insult to himself. He had unquestionably betrayed deep alarm when he learned that her death was regarded as murder. Did his suspicions also leap towards

Rosalind? Was inward fear that she might possibly be implicated in the tragedy the simple explanation of his secret intense pre-occupation? He pursued a lonely and detached existence in the home he shared with these two women, but he could not possibly be wholly unaware of their quarrels . . . of Rosalind's temper. Yet his subsequent behaviour when Gorham confronted the girl with his damning discovery of the wet bathing-dress and towel was no more than the normal reaction that might have been expected in such a situation, a mixture of perplexity, anxiety and rather touch-ing protective affection towards his niece, who had pushed away the arm he tried to put round her with scant courtesy.

It was odd that Moh should have cropped up in the case. He had known that he was staying along this coast somewhere, but had not received his address. But he was anxious, apart from friendly reasons, to meet him now.

The tide had swept away all traces from that strip of beach be-tween the Villa and the curve of the promontory where it dwindled to nothing beneath the steep wall of the cliff four hours before his own appearance on the scene. But though that slack fool of a ser-geant had omitted to make any search of the ground while the tide was still out, the shrewd eyes of the Chinese would certainly have missed nothing that was there to be seen.

He got up with a sigh. His next move was obviously an inter-view with Robin Tennant, who had practically been the last person to see Lydia alive. And instinct warned him that in tackling the son he was going to find himself up against a formidable antagonist in the father. Major Tennant had extricated himself with singular dexterity from his official quandary in calling in assistance from Scotland Yard. If he intended to fight the antagonist he had sum-moned into the field in defence of his boy, Gorham felt with mis-giving that in the impending battle of wits, in mental equipment at least, he was going to be badly outclassed. But, misgivings or no, he intended to put up a good fight himself. As he was leaving the hotel a page summoned him back to the telephone.

Mr. Burroughs, having learned that Mr. Gorham was investi-gating the tragic death of Miss Torrington this morning, requested an instant interview, preferably at Mr. Burroughs' office, 32 High

Street. Mr. Gorham, unfavourably impressed by the curt tone of the request, agreed to be there in five minutes.

He was standing on the step reading a brass plate which was inscribed "Clifford & Burroughs, Solicitors" in four minutes. A youth who would have looked smarter and more at home in an office-boy's uniform showed him nervously into an office, which contained furniture so brand new as to suggest, in conjunction with its owner's appearance, its acquisition on the hire-purchase system.

Harcourt Burroughs was a tall, heavily built man, already putting on flesh, though his age was probably somewhere in the middle thirties. He was dressed in clothes of severely professional cut. He was good-looking after a certain physical type, and had cultivated a slightly ponderous manner. He wore a gold signet on a square, well-manicured hand, and though his small eyes were set too close together and were dark and restless there was really no obvious detail in his sober appearance to justify Gorham's unkind, unspoken epithet: "Iky Mo!"

His greeting to Gorham was curt and barely civil, though with a wave of that over-white hand he indicated a chair.

Gorham took it, feeling grim.

"Now, Sergeant—Colonel Rouncey tells me—"

"Pardon me—Chief Inspector, Mr. Burroughs, of the Criminal Investigation Department, New Scotland Yard," interrupted Gorham sweetly.

The solicitor waved away the correction with an impatient gesture. "Forgive me, these little distinctions in police rank mean nothing to me. I know nothing about Scotland Yard!"

"You shall learn a lot more than you will like about the powers of Scotland Yard before I'm through with you," Gorham promised mentally. Aloud, he said with quiet significance,

"Knowledge is always useful."

Burroughs looked as if he controlled an ugly show of temper with an effort. He ignored the interlude and completed his interrupted sentence.

"Colonel Rouncey tells me that the police now bring a preposterous charge of foul play in regard to this tragic affair this morning, and that someone has actually had the impertinence to call you in!" The Chief Inspector maintained silence.

"Will you kindly inform me on what assumption this incredible assertion of murder is based?"

"I have nothing to add to the statement which I made this afternoon to Colonel Rouncey."

"By whom were you called in? Look here, I'd better make it clear once for all that I do not intend this sad affair—shocking enough as it is in itself—to be made the subject of a ghastly publicity campaign in the Press! As it is bound to be if some damnable crime-hound on a London paper gets wind of the fact that a Scotland Yard C.I.D. man has been dragged down to Whitesands! Sheer impudent meddling, I call it! I couldn't believe my ears when Rouncey told me! But this lady—Miss Torrington—was my promised wife! I have a perfect right to demand the full facts, and first of all I wish to know by whose authority you have been put in charge of the investigation."

"A moment's reflection must remind you, Mr. Burroughs, that you have no legal standing or right whatever in the case. I have, however, no objection to answering your last question, though it requires no answer. There is only one authority in the County which possesses the right lo request Scotland Yard to aid the County police. I was called in by the chief constable."

Burroughs stared, then suddenly an odd, vindictive light gleamed in his eyes. "Tennant! So he is responsible, is he? Then I hope he'll enjoy seeing that insolent young cub of a son of his, Robin Tennant, exposed for the dirty young cad he is. . . . I can tell you—"

"Exactly." Gorham sat up briskly and opened his notebook. "Preliminaries now being cleared away, I should like a statement from you, Mr. Burroughs. But please remember that I have no time to waste, and make your answers as brief as possible. Your full name, please?"

"Harcourt Lionel Burroughs—but I strongly object—"

"Mr. Burroughs, I am in charge of this case. Do you or do you not wish to assist in clearing up the mystery of your fiancée's death? I need scarcely remind you that no good will result from any attempt to obstruct a police officer in his conduct of a criminal investigation."

"My dear Chief Inspector, of course I want to help! I've felt absolutely stunned all day! I scarcely know what I'm doing or saying! You shouldn't make utterly unwarranted suggestions like that!"

Burroughs had learned his lesson. His bullying tone was gone, replaced by one of nervous, deprecating eagerness. "How long have you been resident in this town?"

"Two years—nearly. I invested all my little capital in this practice."

"Had you met either of the Misses Torrington before you came to Whitesands?"

"No. But I met one of the sisters within a few days of my arrival at the tennis club . . ."

"You were at once attracted to Miss Lydia Torrington?"

"Well, to be candid," he said with a sickly smile—to forestall public gossip if already the fact of his first unfortunate slip had not already reached Gorham's ears, for by this time he was terribly anxious to wipe out the bad impression he had made—"to be candid, it was Rosalind I first met! A most striking personality. Miss Torrington was abroad at the time—but when she returned I realized that I had made a—a difficult mistake. My attraction towards Rosalind, which had led us into a far too hasty engagement, was nothing to that I felt towards her sister. So naturally the only honourable thing to do was to explain. Rosalind was charmingly sensible, and at once released me from my—er—word, and, being free again, I proposed to my dear Lydia, and rejoiced to learn that she returned my affection."

"Quite," thought Gorham. "Also you had probably learned that you'd backed the wrong horse in the first place. That Lydia, not the other one, had five hundred pounds per annum."

"Since then we have been completely happy in each other," continued the solicitor emotionally, remembering rather belatedly that so far this aspect of his relations with Torrington affairs had not been stressed during the interview. "I was naturally eager for an early marriage, but my fiancée, in her sweet way, protested that she did not wish to run away from her uncle and sister too suddenly, and urged too that, as a newcomer to the district, I ought to have two years to establish my position here. Unhampered, as she laughingly put it, by the responsibility of a wife. But she had consented at last. The date was actually fixed for October, so you can guess the stunning shock this frightful news gave me this morning! My sweetest girl—dead—drowned! And then—how my lacerated feelings were repelled—revolted by this later, ghastly idea. . . ."

"Quite," said Gorham, this time aloud. "But can you perhaps, after your close intimacy with the young lady, throw any light on the cause of the tragedy? Had she, for instance, any worries?"

"Worries? Ah!" Burroughs looked distressed. "Nothing that could be connected, surely, with this appalling suggestion of foul play. But naturally my poor love confided in me—we had no secrets from each other. And, yes, she certainly was distressed at our last meeting. Only yesterday! Good God! How long ago it seems."

"Her distress was caused by—what?"

"My dear Chief Inspector! I fear I have hinted already . . . before I could fully master my feeling! But you must, I beg, regard all this as strictly confidential!" He rose and began to pace agitatedly about the room, under the sardonic gaze of the chief inspector. "God! I can't get over the shock of that suggestion of yours. That I could possibly wish to obstruct your investigation! Now that I am assured of your legitimate authority to question me, and also—as your very presence here assures me—that there are real grounds for this terrible suspicion of foul play . . ."

He wheeled in his walk and stopped abruptly by the desk to fix Gorham with a penetrating glance.

Gorham rose to his feet and spoke sharply.

"Mr. Burroughs, you are wasting my time and your own. If you have anything to relate, kindly come to the point at once. You say the lady was distressed yesterday. Had you and she quarrelled?"

"Indeed we hadn't!"—warmly. "We never had a disagreement in our lives! She was a girl of the sweetest, most equable disposition. I never saw her out of temper. Yesterday, however, as she drove with me to a picnic which the Tennants gave at Castle St. Roche, I noticed that she was extra quiet, pale, and really depressed. I pressed her to tell me if something was worrying her. At first she denied she was worried at all, but at last, when I insisted, she burst out, 'Oh, Har darling, if I tell you you mustn't pretend you know, but Rosalind was simply dreadfully cross with me about Robin!' I should explain that Rosalind has been engaged for three or four weeks to this fellow Robin Tennant. And then she went on: 'She thinks he has fallen in love with me, and suspects me of having met him this morning at the cove. And the worst of it is, it is true! He is for ever trying to waylay me!' She then told me that the young cub was forming a habit of driving down in his car to a tiny cove on the other side of the promontory, and there joining her in her early swim. She had always liked the seclusion of this little place where no one else ever went. But now it was spoiled for her by this fellow's intrusion.

"It seemed that Rosalind hadn't bathed this last week because of a stiff knee, but, the knee being all right again, Lydia was certain she would bathe as usual today, and was terrified that she would follow her round the point and meet Tennant, and be infuriated by his despicable treachery if he dared to come again! I offered to give the young man a sharp talking to, but she begged me nervously not to interfere. She said she would find some opportunity during the afternoon to speak seriously to him herself, and make him definitely understand that he must never force himself on her again. Unfortunately I had a dinner engagement with an important prospective client at Oakshott yesterday, which forced me to leave the Castle before the girls were willing to go, but as my dear girl seemed quite cheerful again when we parted, I supposed she had succeeded in her intention, though we had no chance of a private word as others were standing by. That was the last time I saw her alive."

"I see." Gorham looked thoughtful. "You have no means of knowing whether young Mr. Tennant was in the water or not this morning?"

"Certainly not. I have told you all I know about the matter."

"Do you know if he is a practised swimmer?"

"He is quite good. I've seen him several times diving and so on."

"You swim yourself, I suppose?"

"Oh yes, a little, when I can spare time."

"Did you bathe early this morning?"

"As it happens, I did. But as my rooms are in the centre of the town I always bathe from the northern beach, where there are bathing-huts and machines. I went out early today—six-fifteen or thereabouts—to get ahead of the trippers, and practically had the place to myself. The water was inviting after the sweltering night we had had, but I can't be sure how long I stopped in. All I know is that I sat down to breakfast at eight sharp, as I had a heavy day's work ahead of me. But of course, from the north beach, with the harbour breakwater in between, to say nothing of the distance, I saw nothing whatever of Miss Torrington or anyone else who may have been bathing on the south side.

"The first I heard of the tragedy was when Colonel Rouncey rang me up here at eight thirty-five, just as I arrived. I still had my hat on when I answered the 'phone. My car was outside. I ran straight out, picked him up after hearing the extraordinary story of Norman's visit, and we went together to the Cottage Hospital, where we could get no sense out of anyone and where we were kept kicking our heels till the superintendent arrived. He was very curt. The doctor, Fitz-James, equally so when we insisted on seeing him. And that is absolutely all I can tell you. Except that I have just been informed by the coroner's officer that the inquest is fixed for nine a.m. tomorrow, in the Institute near the hospital, which is generally used for such purposes."

"Thank you, Mr. Burroughs. I need detain you no further, then. You understand, of course, that what you have told me must not be repeated to any representative of the Press without specific leave." He added dryly: "Indeed, as you dislike the idea of Press publicity yourself, I suggest you discuss the affair with no one for fear of leakage . . ."

Gloom settled on the man with the word, like a thundercloud.

"Won't you—can you possibly manage to keep it from the reporters yourself?" he murmured hoarsely, with eyes grown haggard with foreboding. "A word from you . . ."

Gorham escaped without committing himself, though he smiled unkindly at that tribute to the authority of Scotland Yard as he stepped into the street.

A car, with Bond at the wheel, slithered at once to the kerb. He got in beside him, and directed him to drive slowly to Central Square, where the main roads converged, while he gave him instructions. An interview with Robin Tennant was essential without further delay, but for Bond he had other uses than those of a chauffeur.

"Bond, I want you to collect all the information available about Mr. Burroughs' movements this morning. What time he left his rooms to bathe from the north beach. When he returned. If he used his car or walked. If he took out a boat. Every detail you can get between last night and, say, eight a.m. Do you know where he lives?"

"Yes, sir. Four, Bryant Street, just off Central Square. I'm just to get the information by way of friendly talk, sir, not officially?"

"Exactly. You know the people and whom to go to. I shall want the movements of everyone who has the smallest connection with Melita Villa covered in the same way for the early hours of this morning. That is normal official routine. But begin with Burroughs. And wait for me at the station with your report. Did you do the other job?"

"Yes, sir. Mr. Moh has gone to wait for you by the call box, as you instructed. And here is the road map."

"Good. Get out here."

CHAPTER VIII

"HULLO, LI MOH! I didn't think we'd meet so soon on another job!" Gorham exclaimed, beaming, as he drew up just long enough to let the small figure of the Chinese leap nimbly into the seat beside him, before driving forward along the wide road above the bay.

"Indubitable pleasure is endured by me at beholding noble British police chief again," purred Mr. Moh. "But in this case I am merely humble observer, not highly gratified coadjutor as on former occasion of the Flying Dagger murder."

"Well, I trust you've observed something to the purpose, old man. So far as I've gone in the case I've got masses of circumstantial evidence against one person and nothing else. What I'm yearning for are a few positive facts presented by some unbiased person who hasn't some beastly private spite of his own to work off on me."

"Shall I relate what I observed? Or would you prefer to put leading points first to save loss of time by worthless irrelevances?"

"My dear chap, I haven't the remotest notion yet what is relevant and what isn't. I'm simply collecting everything I can get. The chief leading point I've got so far is that all the deceased's nearest and dearest were sporting about in the wet sea at the moment of her murder," Gorham admitted with gloomy candour. "The affair needs a dashed fish to investigate it, not a human being."

"Still, human intelligence more helpful than that of piscatorial inhabitant of the deep," Mr. Moh encouraged him. "Own intelligence, though of low grade, can supply certain facts if you can bear to lend ear to take in same. Self and family arrived in Whitesands to stay with relatives a week ago. Such relatives, excellent in character, are to this being of other race feelingly uncongenial. Therefore, desirous of gaining fresh courage daily to support such society with politely smiling countenance, I have slipped from the house about six o'clock each morning to breathe ozone on beach below now stricken Villa."

Gorham nodded. He was listening attentively.

"Twice, on Saturday and Sunday, I saw deceased, dressed in a green bathing-costume and cap, swim in a leisurely manner round the Point, soon after my arrival. I had also struck up acquaintance with P.C. Bond on the shore, who each morning, weather permitting, beats it by water from groyne beside Villa on which he deposited his clothes, to breakwater and back with earnest industry to break self record."

"And you waited to time him in. I got that. Yes?"

"Yesterday I missed departure of deceased, who must have set out earlier. But distressing incident occurred as Bond stepped ashore. Canine marauder emerged with celerity from Villa gate and energetically removed raiment of horror-stricken constable into garden of military residence."

"What? That brown tyke pinched Bond's clothes, you mean? My word!" Gorham roared with unfeeling laughter. "That must have been what Torrington referred to. Go on. What happened?"

"Pure-minded young friend registering deep shame at unhappy plight, it was up to me to retrieve lost raiment. Entering gate I heard agonized yelp from dog, and then beheld a dark young woman, the younger niece, clutching whip with a countenance distorted by evil passion, and inside a comfortably furnished apartment, the dog crouching after cruel slash. But this is the point, Chief Inspector," he went on after a significant pause. "As the dog dragged the clothes into the gate I had observed entangled with them a green silk wrap matching in colour the other's bathing-dress. The dog, it seemed to me, had also recognized it as a pretty possession of a mistress. For he had dropped Bond's underwear outside the french windows. When with swift glance I sought this green wrap inside the room, I beheld it, rent by strong and furious fingers on a couch behind the curtain where the dark girl had been lying in wait. With that whip. For whom?"

"So it was she who tore it," Gorham said, no laughter now in his eyes. "Lydia mended the rent. But the odd thing is that wrap is missing altogether today. You are quite right, Moh. She was lying in wait for her sister. Because she guessed, or knew, that Lydia had gone out to meet her own young man. But a whip! Not a nice young woman that, eh?"

"Not nice at all. A creature in the grip of murderous rage. No woman, but maddened jealousy incarnate," he assented. "I have heard much local gossip since I came. Her ungoverned temper is notorious. And her hatred of the other, who stole her lovers. Her name is on every tongue as the murderer since the fact of murder leaked out."

"Who let it out, Moh?" exploded Gorham angrily. "Not you, of course. Bond? The superintendent imagines he has kept it safely dark!"

"If he wished to"—Mr. Moh shrugged his shoulders—"he should have excised the tongue of his sergeant here, who whispers and winks, and does nothing else. But wait. I have more to relate of yesterday yet. In the afternoon at Castle St. Roche, whither self and family complete with relatives by marriage tripped by motor-coach, I, again feeling necessity to escape to congenial company, witnessed, with Sampson V.C., custodian there, who had afforded me welcome relief in his private quarters, a deliberate attempt by same young woman to murder deceased by pushing her headlong down precipitous stone stairs."

He proceeded to give a clear account of the keep incident, omitting no detail which he had witnessed, and then, with none of his usual floweriness of diction, related the result of his observations on the shore that morning.

He had reached the shore at five minutes past six when Bond was well on his way back. He had seen no one else on shore or in the water. He had noticed, but not realized the significance of, that green colour on the buoy, till the more experienced Bond had stood frowning at it before plunging across towards it.

"Neither should I have," Gorham interjected. "They paint 'em all sorts of colours, but only seamen learn what the dickens the different colours signify!"

"And I had left my binoculars at home," Moh nodded mournfully.

When, later, he had examined the beach he had found no evidence of struggle, or any prints on the wet sands but those of two sets of footsteps leaving the wicket of the Villa and leading straight into the sea. One of these sets returned. The other was single.

"You guessed a crime had been committed at once?"

"The pressure of bruising fingers on the neck made the fact indubitable. A large hand had held her under in a vice-like yoke," Mr. Moh agreed calmly. "Therefore, I advised Bond to fetch his sergeant with whom came a doctor, fortunately less fat-headed."

"Yes, I thought that was your move," Gorham said. They had reached the gate of Oakleigh, the chief constable's modest house, by this time. "Look here, Moh, I'd be grateful for your help. I'm staying at the Grand—which is less grand than its name. But I suggest that, till after the inquest at least, we keep our connection dark. What you've told me practically clinches the guilt of R.T. But . . . Well, my next job is to interview young Robin Tennant, who is certainly in the thick of this mess somewhere. Will you wait here till I come out, then we could run out and interview this Sampson fellow together? As he saw practically all you did yourself I'd sooner use his evidence than yours at the inquest if it's necessary. What sort of witness will he be?"

"Truthful. But not willing to volunteer evidence likely to distress Major Tennant, for whom he cherishes deep respect. But humbly suggest you should see him alone. I shall be in the bandstand garden this evening. But I now prefer to trot back on flat feet to Whitesands, where uneatable supper is awaiting me. A message to Clarkes, Ironmongers, will bring me to your side with celerity of lightning flash."

Before Gorham grasped his intention he had opened the door, slipped out and vanished.

Gorham turned the car into the drive and presently was shown by a maid into Major Tennant's office.

"Well, Chief Inspector! Had a busy afternoon?" Tennant greeted him with friendly informality. "Thank God this is your job, not mine. I know the boring grind an investigation of this sort entails. I hope my crowd are treating you decently?"

"Very decently. But so far I have done no more than follow up the facts supplied by the superintendent, whom I am meeting for a conference this evening. As you say, there's so much to be crammed into the first few hours that I'd be greatly obliged if you would let me postpone my report to you till after the inquest tomorrow morning. And just let me ask your son a few questions now."

"I don't ask for any report during this stage of the proceedings. You would, of course, notify me if an arrest were to be made." He strolled over to the fireplace and rang the bell. "But I should like to ask—you have interviewed poor Rouncey, no doubt—if you have collected any evidence which tends to—er—widen the scope of the enquiry?"

"Nothing whatever. Quite the other way about, in fact."

He thought he caught the sound of a quick breath from Tennant, but the tone in which he bade the servant who answered his summons request Mr. Robin to come for a few minutes was as imperturbable as ever.

"By the way, Gorham," he added briskly while they awaited the young man's arrival, "I forgot to mention that the borough coroner or Whitesands was only appointed a week or so ago, and this will be his first experience in office. Have you seen him yet?"

"Not yet. But I understood from Norman that he was till fairly recently medical officer of health there, and quite a sound man."

"Oh, quite, an excellent little chap. Only resigned in favour of Fitz-James for private reasons. Felt the nervous strain. He's one of the oldest inhabitants, and very zealous for the town's best interests, and so on. But you may find a certain amount of gentle tact necessary."

The door opened and Robin Tennant walked into the room.

"Ah, here you are, Robin. My son, Chief Inspector Gorham of the C.I.D. The chief inspector wants to ask you a few questions, Robin. About the Whitesands tragedy, of course. Would you prefer me to stay? Or go?"

The young man shrugged his shoulders.

"Oh, stay by all means, sir." He turned his brown eyes—hard, unsmiling eyes—on Gorham.

"Well, Chief Inspector?"

"The most wretched aspect of a policeman's life is that he so often has to ask questions that sound impertinent, Mr. Tennant," Gorham began with a frank and good-humoured attempt to lessen the boy's hostility. "So perhaps you would tell me in your own fashion whether you noticed yesterday anything, any event or change of mood, or even an odd word, connected with Miss Torrington which might throw light on her death."

"Miss Torrington seemed in quite good spirits during the afternoon, and when I parted from her at her door," he replied in even tones.

"You were with her the whole time?"

"I saw very little of her during the earlier part of the afternoon—you are referring to the picnic at the Castle, I suppose?—since I was on duty among my parent's guests. And Mr. Burroughs, who was engaged to Miss Torrington, was present to look after her. When he left, somewhere about six, half an hour or so after all the others had gone, Miss Torrington joined her sister and myself on the ramparts. Personally"—he was speaking with a sort of careful deliberation, as if selecting the briefest phrases in which to embody his statement, to shirk nothing except the annoyance of repetition, standing stiff as a ramrod by his father's desk—"personally, I found the trippers everywhere tiresome. And her sister, becoming impatient of the crowds, wished to leave. But Miss Torrington seemed to enjoy watching them, commenting on their dresses and hats. Also she had been interested in something she had heard my father say about some ancient jewellery in a case in the museum. You remember, sir?" He turned to the silent auditor, who stood, shoulder turned, on the hearthrug. Tennant wheeled round, his keen eyes lighted up in an amused smile.

"Certainly I remember delivering an instructive lecture in the museum," he said lightly. "It is news to me that anyone found it interesting. But pleasant news, of course."

"At the time she hadn't been able to get near the case. So we went back into the keep to have a final glance at the view from the battlements, and she went into the museum on the way up. I waited for her on the landing. Then, when we had seen the view, we all came down and drove home."

"At what time did you leave the Castle, Mr. Tennant?"

"After seven—a quarter past, at a guess. It was just after the half-hour when I put her down at the door of the Villa. Her sister drove most of the way with us, but elected to get out and walk the last mile."

"Then it was really Miss Torrington who caused you to linger so long at this Castle?"

"Put like that, yes. She found the people amusing. But I was in no special hurry myself. It was hot, and there was a breeze there."

"There appeared to be no special reason for her wish to linger except the pleasantness of the place generally? She did not, for instance, appear to be looking out for an acquaintance in the crowds? Meet anyone she knew? Or exchange even a casual word with anyone?"

"She was just enjoying herself, as I said." An impatient note crept into the dry tones. "She certainly knew no one there, and spoke to no one, unless you count as speaking a murmur of apology she made to a brawny fellow who came behind her as she was bending over the jewel-case. She simply moved aside to give him room, and smiled at him. Then she saw me waiting in the doorway and came straight across."

"I see. A casual encounter. You didn't happen to notice the man specially?"

"No, except that he was a big fellow, and the tweeds he wore—reddish brown—struck an incongruous note among the worthy citizens Sampson was lecturing with a fair imitation of my father's instructive methods. He leaned over the jewels and I did not see his face."

"Did anything occur after you both left the museum that you wish to mention?"

"I have nothing further to say. In mentioning what I have done I have consulted your wishes, not my own, Chief Inspector," he added in dry comment.

"Then it only remains to ask what you were doing at six o'clock this morning, at the time of the fatality." Gorham spoke with undiminished good temper. "Were you at home here, in bed?"

Robin's reply was a staggering one.

"No. I did not go to bed all night."

"You did not? But you were in someone's company at that special hour, Mr. Tennant?"

Robin stared at him with hard, defiant eyes.

"I was in my car—driving or not—alone all night. All I remember is that at six or thereabouts I was at the Cove under the Rock. . . ."

His unconscious use of the local name for the promontory stopped Gorham for a second, though instantly a guess flashed the truth into his mind. But this was no moment for either guesses or betrayal of ignorance. The expurgated narrative he had already received was not going to be followed by one equally misleading, of which he could not check the omissions by private knowledge.

"One moment, please. Will you kindly be more explicit, Mr. Tennant? Do you mean you were driving late and met with an accident? Were unconscious, perhaps? If your father has already heard your story do you prefer that he should explain?"

"I can see no earthly reason for my bothering my father since I am perfectly ready to repeat to you what I told him an hour ago!" he retorted brusquely, and Gorham shot a quick glance at the man by the fireplace.

In height Major Tennant had the advantage of the younger man by a couple of inches, for Robin was compactly built, slender and light. He was standing upright, his head slightly turned, his expression inscrutable, but in the eyes that rested on his son's face hovered the hint of a smile that was touched with tender pride.

Gorham thought: "I was completely wrong about him. He said the boy would not shirk. He isn't shirking anything himself!"

Aloud he said quietly:

"Will you begin from last evening, then? And give me all the details you can, whether they seem important or not."

"I spent the evening here, with my people, and went, in due course, to bed," Robin began, with the icy self-control he had employed from the beginning. But now his jerky sentences seemed freer from hesitation. "At least, I went to my room. But as I happened to be thinking over a private matter and also felt distinctly off colour, after a bit, as I hadn't undressed, I decided to go for a run out of doors. I went downstairs somewhere about one, as you're keen on times. I filled up the old tank and headed southward, letting her all out, and just attending enough to the road ahead to steer clear of accidents. One does, you know. I soon lost my bearings altogether, but at the moment the fact did not perturb me. If I had any target at all it was London, but after an hour or so the idea palled. Besides I'd kept off the main roads from choice, and English by-roads aren't designed for travel as the crow flies. What Johnny was it who said the rolling English drunkard made the rolling English road? Whoever he was, he was right. After some more time it occurred to me I'd somehow doubled on my tracks when I struck what seemed to be the same common for the second time. And at that point my radiator started smoking like the devil, and I realized I'd run out of water. So I pulled up. And went to sleep. When I woke it was broad daylight. There was plenty of common all round me that looked like Bramwood Heath, but not a part I knew. Bramwood Heath is a fairly massive tract of land and practically devoid of inhabitants, but I found, by luck, I was close to a cottage with a pigsty on one side. My watch had stopped. While I paused for thought an old dame tottered out of the door with a piglet wrapped in her shawl. I asked her for water, and she said there was a bucket in her kitchen where she'd been sitting up all night nursing the pig. She looked the part, and wept as she showed it me. It was limp and appeared to be passing out. The old dame seemed stricken with grief, so, as I'd got some whisky in a flask in the car, I suggested shoving some of it down its throat. We did so, and the treatment appeared to restore it to life. I left her the flask in case it should succumb again, drank a cup of tea that she made to celebrate its revival, set my watch by her clock, and left at five twenty. By the by, it was your flask, Father. The silver one. Did I mention this bit to you? I forget.

"In the thrill of seeing the animal restored to animation, it was in fact completely whiffled, I forgot to ask her name or the way. But it didn't matter, because after exploring for a bit I spotted Castle St. Roche in the distance, and a few more turns brought me on to the coast road, which I followed, skirting the Castle rock. I stopped the car when I reached the promontory and went down to the Cove for a bathe. No one was about. I stayed down there for a time; then, as the thought of bathing no longer appealed, I went back to the car."

"Did you notice the times?"

"Oh lord, yes! I forgot. I stopped on the sand from five thirty-eight to six-six." He responded with sarcastic promptness. "Anything else? No? Well, I then turned inland towards Harborough, stopping at this gate. But the car was all in—and I decided to go straight on to the garage on the Harborough road. I got there just after eight. The fellow there said he could put it right in an hour. He must have been nearer two, because it was nearly ten-thirty when I came home. And that is that. My father has already asked me if I met anyone or saw anything on the coast road. The answer to both questions is in the negative. That, I think, completes my statement, sir."

He looked at his father, who nodded his dismissal.

"Quite, old man. Thanks very much."

There was silence in the room till the door had closed behind him.

It was broken by a quiet remark from Major Tennant.

"In the light of that revelation I seem to have been even more honourable than I knew in calling you in. Eh?"

"You knew he had been out all night, I suppose," Gorham said slowly. "And you must have seen from his manner last night that something had happened to upset him badly."

"Last night? Before the murder?" Tennant spoke with unwonted sharpness. "Do you know what it was?"

"Yes. He witnessed an attempt by Rosalind Torrington to kill her sister by throwing her down a stone staircase at the Castle!"

"Good God! How did you get that?"

"From one of the two men who caught the girl and saved her life. The second is Sampson, the caretaker."

At that moment, after a brisk rap on the door, the head of Will Tennant appeared round it with a suggestion of urgency that arrested the chief constable's exclamation of annoyance.

"Sorry to interrupt, sir. But can you speak to me for a moment?" Tennant walked into the hall and shut the door behind him. When he returned, after the briefest interval, his expression was grim, and he handed the paper he carried to Gorham.

"Quick work! The *Harborough Evening News*, nine thirty edition."

WHITESANDS TRAGEDY
ASTOUNDING REVELATION OF ALLEGED PREVIOUS ATTEMPT TO MURDER LYDIA TORRINGTON

A correspondent has come forward with a remarkable story which throws a sinister light over the discovery of the body of Miss Lydia Torrington in Whitesands Bay at an early hour this morning.

As was reported in our mid-day edition, the body of this young lady, a well-known resident of the popular watering place, and first winner of the Champion Cup presented to the Whitesands Swimming Club last July by Mr. Ebenezer Smith-Levison, Charter-Mayor of Whitesands, was recovered from the bay by Police Constable James Bond, before seven a.m. And deep sympathy was then expressed for the family of the young lady, her sister, Miss Rosalind Torrington, whose prowess in swimming exercises equals that of deceased, and Colonel George Rouncey, late of the — Rifles, uncle, with whom the Misses Torrington made their home at Melita Villa, Whitesands.

The tragedy was at first believed to be caused by cramp, due to the chill of the sea at the early hour. But as the morning passed, dark rumours began to permeate the public mind that our able police entertained suspicions that death was not due to natural causes. Not desiring, however, to cause unnecessary pain to the bereaved relatives, or to hamper the activities of the police, we loyally refrained from referring to this sinister rumour, or voicing these public suspicions, which seemed to receive grave confirmation when Chief Inspector Gorham of the C.I.D., New Scotland

Yard, arrived in Harborough early this afternoon and proceeded straight to Whitesands.

In the interests of justice we can, however, not withhold the astounding story submitted by our correspondent, which we give in full, but without comment or prejudice to ourselves.

This gentleman was examining the interesting treasures in the Museum of Castle St. Roche at seven p.m. last evening, when his attention was attracted by sounds of a violent female voice on the stairs above, followed by a scuffle, and a sharp protest, "Rosalind!" from a man.

A second later he saw Miss Lydia Torrington being supported in a half fainting condition down the stairs by Sergeant Sampson, V.C., the stalwart custodian of the Castle. Behind the sergeant came Miss Rosalind Torrington, and her fiancé, Mr. Robert Tennant, younger son of the chief constable of the county, both in a state of violent excitement. The inference drawn by this gentleman from what he heard and saw was that an attempt had been made—to the horror of Mr. Tennant—to kill Miss Lydia Torrington by brutally thrusting her down the almost perpendicular stone staircase, and that the murderous attack had only been foiled by the promptitude of Sergeant Sampson, V.C.

Sergeant Sampson has refused to make any comment on this story. But our informant states that while he had kept the matter to himself last evening, on reading of the mysterious death of Miss Torrington this morning he decided that he could no longer withhold publication of this previous (alleged) attempt on the life of the unfortunate young lady.

We publish his story on his sole responsibility, without accepting ourselves the smallest responsibility for its truth or falsehood.

Gorham dropped the paper.

"I'll make that editor sorry he was born!" he said grimly. "I must get back to see the coroner at once, and Braice. I take it you will be responsible for the production of your son in court, Major Tennant?"

Tennant nodded, his eyes bitter.

"What about the girl—when she sees this?"

"The A.C. directed me to bring an assistant with me, sir, in case of just such a contingency as this. I felt it best the search of the Villa should not be done by a local man. He has been stationed inside the house since five p.m."

CHAPTER IX

IT WAS OBVIOUS to Gorham from the first that the elderly and inexperienced coroner would prove unequal to the task of keeping his court in order.

From an early hour the large room where the inquest was to be held was besieged by pressmen and members of the public, clamorous for admission.

The town was in an uproar. The roadway outside the Institute and every street leading to it were thronged by seething crowds in a state of ugly excitement which threatened on the smallest provocation to burst into violent demonstrations.

When cars containing the witnesses began to arrive, the extra body of police drafted to the town from divisional headquarters had to exert force to clear a passage for them, and to prevent their occupants being mobbed by the crowd, which cheered wildly, or booed, as each well-known face was recognized.

With the insensate sentimentality of mob psychology, Burroughs, the bereaved fiancé of the dead girl, received a deafening ovation.

"'Pon my soul, being murdered seems to have turned Lydia—whom they hadn't a good word for alive—into a pure and popular heroine!" murmured Fitz-James to Gorham in sarcastic comment on the scene.

"It isn't so much that they love Lydia as they hate Rosalind. They are out for her blood. Have been since dawn!"

"Nasty position for poor old Ferrers holding his first inquest! Show ought to have been shifted to Harborough to get any hope of an unbiased jury. They'll be with this rabble to a man."

Fitz-James had scarcely disappeared into the police-guarded doorway before the chief constable drove up, with his superintendent at his side.

One glance about him gave him the state of affairs. He gave a direction to Braice, who leapt back into the car, which turned and went back the way it had come; then, heedless of the looks, half respectful, half hostile, of the populace, he stood nonchalantly in the lane formed by policemen to the door of the Institute and greeted Gorham with whimsically lifted brows.

"Quite an attractive little local circus, eh?"

"They started the game by smashing most of the Colonel's windows this morning, yelling, 'Murderess!' Listen, they think this is she now!"

The distant shouts and cat-calls of the crowd had suddenly deepened into a single low, menacing roar, which swelled in volume as its object approached, as the waves of cheering rise and swell as a popular procession passes on its way. This was not cheering. As the chief constable distinguished the ugly syllables that formed the burden of the roar his thin features sharpened in an expression of acute disgust.

"Pah! It makes one sick!"

"When a mob is carried away it is always governed by its lowest elements," Gorham said philosophically. "It is only the two servants. Under a uniformed police guard to give the crowd something to look at. When Braice and I saw how things were working up we shifted the young lady and the Colonel to Dr. Fitz-James' house first thing. And after giving them breakfast he drove them round to the back door of the Institute via the hospital grounds. They have been waiting inside for half an hour."

He went forward to meet Mrs. Priest and Gladys as, the former stiffly indignant, the latter in frightened tears, they stepped out of the car in the wake of a constable and Sergeant Norman.

"Cheer up, my dear!" He patted Gladys's shoulder. "Nothing to cry about! You did that splendidly, and all the mugs here were sweetly had!"

"Oh, it was dreadful!" she sobbed. "They shrieked and pointed—"

"Don't be silly, Gladys," snapped Mrs. Priest. "And don't take up the gentleman's time! They wouldn't have looked twice if they'd known it was only you, and what's it matter what a bunch of low, ignorant gorms like them do anyway!"

She swept the girl inside.

But if public feeling ran high outside, inside, as the coroner took his place and proceedings opened, there was a grim atmosphere of determined expectancy, which warned Gorham and those others who were sufficiently experienced in such scenes that the case was already prejudged.

The coroner tried manfully to adhere to the programme carefully mapped out. After he had made a brief and quite unbiased statement of the facts, the first witnesses were called. Colonel Rouncey formally stated that he identified the body as that of his niece by marriage, Lydia Annabel Torrington. James Bond testified to the finding of the body, and Mr. Li Moh corroborated.

It was on Mr. Moh that one of the jury decided to try his prentice hand at interrogation.

"You say you were on the shore at six five a.m., and saw nobody. Did you, when you had seen the body, form the opinion that deceased had been a victim of foul play?"

"My unworthy opinions being of too lowly nature to interest court engaged on stern siftment of facts only, I refrain," said Mr. Moh with beaming suavity, "from rude intrusion of same."

"A perfectly proper answer," interposed the coroner sharply. And the juryman sat down with abruptness, and the witness retired amidst suppressed titters.

The police and medical evidence was heard without interruption till the end; then another juryman rose.

"Do the nature of the injuries indicate that they were inflicted by a man or a woman?"

"They gave no indication either way."

"You mean that they might have been inflicted by either a man or a woman?"

"The question is one for a natatorial expert to answer rather than a medical man. Given the necessary physical qualifications of length of arm and strong wrists, together with the required natatory knowledge and skill, the murderer might be a member of either sex."

The juryman sat down with a satisfied air.

Colonel Rouncey, recalled, said that his niece had seemed in excellent spirits at luncheon the day before. He understood that

Mr. Burroughs had called to drive her to an al-fresco party given by Major and Mrs. Tennant at the Castle, but he had not seen him. She had returned in the early evening, and had not appeared at dinner. He understood that she had gone to lie down because the sun had given her a headache. Later she had gone out for a stroll, and the only time he actually saw her during the evening was when she was running upstairs again to bed. She had then called out, "Good night, Nunky." He called back to ask if the head was better. She said, "Quite, thanks, dear," very cheerfully.

He had risen early himself, after a restless night, and had taken his dog for a walk across the meadows towards Harborough. He went out at six, by the gate of his garden which led directly on to the road, and had seen nothing on the shore, which indeed his own house blocked from view. He had sat down to breakfast at eight fifteen directly on his return. He had thought nothing of Lydia's absence, as she was frequently unpunctual at meals.

Gladys Black, housemaid, deposed to having carried up Miss Lydia's dinner-tray to her room. Miss Lydia ate a good dinner and seemed cheerful. At quarter past ten, on her own way to bed, she had taken in two slices of madeira cake, which Miss Lydia liked to eat before she went out bathing. She was then in bed eating her biscuits. She had not heard Miss Lydia go out next morning. She had wakened at six because Miss Rosalind's door banged, and she heard her open it again saying a word. She heard the Colonel whistling for Carlo in the garden, but nothing after, because she turned over and went to sleep again, it being too early to get up. Next thing she knew, Cook was shaking her and saying it was a quarter to eight. They both heard sounds of a car and men's voices at the top of the path while they were dressing, but they were that scuffled they took no notice. She ran out and just looked at the sea when she was dressed, but not above a second, as the dining-room had to be dusted. She hadn't seen or heard anything funny any time.

She then, looking flushed and pretty, returned to Mrs. Priest, surprised but relieved that the old gentleman's questions had not referred to the quarrel she had overheard, and had all been so easy to answer.

Rosalind Torrington was then called.

What pretence to good looks she possessed was temporarily lost beneath the heavy sullenness of her expression, the blotchiness of her complexion, the roughness of her thick, dark hair, and the carelessness of her dress.

The cynosure of every eye in the room, she stood a clumsy figure, and cast cowed yet smoulderingly resentful glances furtively from under her black lashes about her.

In a voice scarcely audible she answered the coroner's questions. She knew her sister to be an expert swimmer, skilled in diving, swimming under water, and so on?

"Yes."

"You are practised in the water yourself, have often bathed with her?"

"Yes."

"It was your habit to go out for swimming practice together most mornings?"

"We went for a swim most mornings. Not necessarily together."

"When did you last see deceased alive?"

"That last night, when she came into the dining-room to fetch her milk and biscuits."

"Did she then appear to be in her usual health and spirits?"

"I suppose so. She didn't say anything about feeling ill, or anything else for that matter"—sulkily.

"Your room is close to that occupied by deceased. Did you hear her leave her room yesterday morning?"

"No."

"Were you asleep when she went out?"

"I suppose I must have been. I'd probably have heard her otherwise."

"You did not bathe yourself on Tuesday morning?"

"No."

"Why was that, if it was your usual practice?"

"I slipped on the tennis-court last week and strained my knee. I haven't bathed since, because it was stiff."

"Did you mention this strain to anyone? A doctor, for instance?"

"No. It wasn't bad enough. Lydia knew. We were playing together."

"Miss Torrington, you understand that it is important to discover the exact time, if it be possible, at which deceased left her room. At what time did you wake yourself?"

"About half past five, but I didn't get up then."

"Will you tell us what you did do, after you woke?"

"I stopped in bed for a bit," she muttered. "Then I got up and—and—" She stopped, with a hunted look in the eyes that suddenly glared round the room.

"And then you dressed." It was more an assertion than a question, but if he intended her to accept it as such, her sullen stupidity missed her cue. She pointed to Gorham.

"No, I didn't!" she burst out furiously, "That beastly nosy parker of a policeman went spying in my room, so he knows perfectly well what I did! I put on my bathing-dress and went out and tried the water. But when I knelt, my knee hurt like the devil. So I went back again, and into bed. I wasn't in the water above a minute. And I went straight back. But he found my wet bathing things. So I had to tell you. And that's all."

The jury whispered together, but she was permitted to leave the witness-box without interposition from them, though the impression she had left on the court was anything but favourable.

The coroner breathed again, imagining that he had steered the inquiry safely past the worst danger point. Gorham, from wide experience, and the chief constable from intuitive perception of deepening tension in the atmosphere about him, did not share his confidence.

Harcourt Burroughs was the next witness.

He had had time to collect himself during the night, and had assumed, together with the sombre and correct trappings of woe, which included a band of crepe round the arm, the touching part of the bereaved lover.

After the first formal questions which, with the tedium common to such legal inquisitions, elicited what every person in the chamber knew already, his name, status in the town, and the relation in which he stood to the dead girl, he proceeded to give a succinct account of the conversation with Lydia on Monday afternoon, which he had already repeated to the chief inspector.

He described her preoccupation during the drive to the Castle as "amounting to mental distress", then made a dramatic pause.

Gorham realized that, his urgent desire for secrecy having been totally defeated, he intended to vent his spleen on Robin Tennant.

The pressmen sat up with pens poised, sensing sensational disclosures.

The jury also sat up with the air of terriers at a hole who at last smelt the rat they were alert to snap at.

"Did deceased relate any reason for her mental distress?"

Uncomfortably the coroner put the inevitable question.

Burroughs cleared his throat.

"She did," he replied, his deep tones betraying strong emotion. "Seeing my earnest desire to learn the cause of her distress in a very natural wish if possible to allay it, she at length admitted to me that a situation of extraordinary difficulty had arisen between herself and her sister that morning, which threatened the disruption of her sister's engagement. She dreaded that, unless the gentleman, Mr. Robin Tennant, to whom her sister had recently become engaged could be induced to cease from trying to meet her privately, joining in her morning swim in Rosalind's absence, and so on, terrible unhappiness to her sister must ensue. I offered to speak to Mr. Tennant myself, and request him to abstain from pressing his company on my fiancée unless her sister was also present. Miss Torrington thanked me for my suggestion, but said that, shaken as she felt by the scene Rosalind had already made that morning, it would make less fuss perhaps if she could find an opportunity during the afternoon to speak seriously to the young man himself.

"When we reached the Castle there was little further chance of private conversation between us. But when I bade her good-bye just after six she seemed so entirely to have recovered her usual tranquil spirits that I supposed she had succeeded in carrying out her intention to her satisfaction, and my anxiety on her behalf was entirely allayed. When I learned next morning from Colonel Rouncey, who 'phoned to me just as I reached my office, that my fiancée was dead, I was absolutely stunned. . . ."

"The deepest sympathy must naturally be extended to you, Mr. Burroughs, in the sad circumstances," murmured the coroner, trying to take in the gist of a note which had been handed to him and talk at the same time. "Er—you did not leave the Castle till after six? May I ask why you did not drive Miss Torrington home yourself, instead of leaving her to come with Mr. Tennant in the embarrassing situation you have mentioned?"

"I had a—an important dinner engagement at seven thirty, and had to change," he replied, looking slightly deflated. "I did suggest, even urge, her to come then, but she said the breeze there was delightful—she mentioned a touch of headache. The air was very refreshing. So I had to leave her—little thinking I was never to see her again alive!"

"Have you ever joined the bathing parties you have referred to?"

"Several times. But not recently. The pressure of business compelled me to take my dip early, if at all."

"Did you bathe yesterday morning?"

"As a matter of fact, I did. I am a heavy sleeper as a rule, but the night before last was so stiflingly hot that I woke early, and decided to have a bathe before breakfast to freshen me up for the day's work. But I went in, as usual, from the north beach, which, as you are, of course, aware, is on the other side of the harbour and nearly a mile from the scene of the tragedy, so I knew nothing of the events there."

"Thank you, Mr. Burroughs. That is all, I think, unless any member of the jury wishes to put a question?" He looked nervously at the jury as a man who did not understand the nature of explosives might look at a barrel of gunpowder to which he was compelled to hold a tentative match.

At once the juryman who had tackled Mr. Moh, and who had been brooding angrily on his rebuff ever since, sprang to his feet. "You was engaged to deceased's sister, wasn't you, first, before you took up with her?"

"Really!" broke in the coroner, annoyed. "I can't allow that question. It is not relevant."

"It's relevant this way," the juror argued doggedly, "as showing Rosalind has had reason to 'arbour a jealous grudge against deceased for years. If she saw the new young man she'd got going the same way it 'ud be the last straw."

"Kindly sit down at once, sir! I cannot permit such gross remarks in the court!" commanded the coroner, roused to such determined show of authority that the man obeyed. "You may go," he added to Burroughs. But the match was set to the gunpowder, and from then on he fought desperately to control the resultant blaze.

Robin Tennant, the last person to converse with Lydia Torrington outside her home circle, gave his evidence amidst a storm of heckling from the jury.

With haggard eyes, but jaw grimly set, he stood up to the fire. He had known Miss Lydia Torrington since the end of June, when he had become engaged to her sister. He had bathed with both sisters frequently since. Twice this week he had had an early swim with Miss Torrington alone. He was not aware on either occasion that Miss Rosalind Torrington was not to be of the party. He had not heard of the injury to her knee. He had not bathed on the morning of the tragedy. He had heard nothing at the picnic party of the alleged difference between the sisters mentioned by Mr. Burroughs. Miss Torrington (he doggedly refused to accept the term "deceased" from first to last, and invariably amended the coroner's phrase when he used it) had said nothing to him of her sister's alleged jealousy. She had seemed in gay spirits. Had kept on making comments on the crowds, which she found amusement in watching. She had insisted on exploring the keep a second time before she would consent to go home. He had seen the local papers, but had nothing to say about the outrageous statement they had had the audacity to print, except that the person said to be responsible for it had been quite wise to remain anonymous. Miss Torrington was not injured on the stairs of the keep. As she had come down—the anonymous person had apparently missed that bit—she had joked with Sampson about her high French heels not being fitted for the worn steps. He had driven both sisters home, and Miss Torrington had parted from him quite cheerfully at the door of Melita Villa."

"You have heard it insinuated that you were in love with deceased." This from a juryman, of course. "Is that true?"

"You have also heard me state about forty times, what every man-jack of you knows already, that I am engaged to Miss Rosalind Torrington!" he retorted, with blazing eyes. "And if you want further information to back that fact, I will inform you that I desire our marriage to take place as soon as she will consent to become my wife!"

On that desperately reckless declaration he was at last permitted to go.

After the high-strung tension of this scene, the matter-of-fact evidence of Chief Inspector Gorham came as an anti-climax.

He gave a resume of the result of his investigations with an impartial frankness which concealed nothing except the points which he did not wish to disclose, and revealed nothing which had not been openly stated by previous witnesses.

His official rank overawed the jury, and it was with diffidence that a quiet little man with kind eyes and a weak mouth, who had not yet spoken, rose to put a question.

"Have you ascertained the whereabouts of every member of the household from roughly before five-thirty, when, according to her sister's evidence, deceased must already have quitted the house, till after the discovery of the body by Constable Bond?"

Gorham replied to him with flattering readiness.

"It isn't, in normal circumstances, easy to check the alibi of anyone at an hour when most people are in bed and asleep," he said. "But in this case, as you have heard, both the servants were in their rooms, from which no view is obtainable over the shore. They each corroborate the other's evidence on this point, and the truth of their testimony is borne out by minor facts with which there is no need to detain the hearing. Colonel Rouncey himself went out at six. The maid, Gladys Black, heard him whistling his dog in the front garden, and his niece, Rosalind Torrington, heard the dog's responsive barking at approximately the same moment. He certainly did not appear on the shore thereafter, so we may accept his own statement that he went inland.

"As for the remaining member of the household, you have heard the evidence of the young lady herself, which is confirmed by the maid Gladys Black, who was wakened by hearing her bang her bedroom door and make an exclamation at six o'clock. The body," he added with significant emphasis, "was sighted by Bond, who took eight minutes to reach it from the shore, at six fifteen."

"You mean she could not possibly have gone out and returned in the time. Is there anything to prove that when the maid heard her bang her door, at six o'clock, she was not then *returning*?"

"Nothing but the young lady's own statement."

"Did the maid hear her run downstairs after she had exclaimed?"

"No. But that proves nothing. She was wearing sandals with rubber soles which are soundless both on the stairs and tiles of the hall. I tested the fact by experiment. Superintendent Braice and I waited in the maid's bedroom last night while the girl Gladys, wearing these same sandals, walked from the bedroom of Rosalind Torrington downstairs and across the hall under observation of Sergeant Norman. And we heard no footstep. The result of the experiment was, so far, entirely negative. But it seems probable that the young lady was leaving her bedroom when the door banged, since she must unquestionably have been standing on the landing outside it when the maid caught her exclamation."

He waited for the man to remind him that after it had banged the maid had heard the door reopened. But he merely said, "Thank you," with an odd smile, and sat down again without exposing the fallacy on which the argument had riskily been based.

Gorham breathed again. "The beggar saw it too, and knew I saw it," he thought, "but he wasn't going to hound the girl. . . ."

"Re those wet bathing things, why did you go and search the sister's bedroom at all?"

Sir Aggression was on his feet again.

"Why did I do what?" The chief inspector turned to him with puzzled blandness, and then grinned with amusement. "Oh, I see. It is the normal routine in such cases as this to run through the house for papers and so on, belonging to deceased, which may be helpful to the investigation. Not the young lady's room alone, but every room in the house has been submitted to examination. The search was a customary formality, and, I need scarcely say, was conducted with the full permission of Colonel Rouncey."

"Thank you, Chief Inspector. I think we need not detain you any longer."

Gorham bowed and briskly availed himself of the coroner's dismissal to join Braice at the back of the room.

The coroner gathered his strength for the supreme effort of the summing up. His statement was a masterpiece of fairness. He directed the jury to clear from their minds all prejudice possibly engendered by any rumours they had heard or read outside and to base their verdict solely on such proven facts as they had had presented to them by reliable witnesses in this room. That the deceased had met her death from foul play was incontestable from the medical evidence laid before them, but . . . His voice took on an almost pleading note as he reached the familiar phrase in the directing formula that suggested the recording of a verdict of "Murder by some person or persons unknown."

As he began his address, the chief constable rose from his seat and, making his way quietly to the side of Rouncey, bent and touched him on the arm. At the touch the old man, who had been staring vacantly before him, started, and raised to his eyes full of anguished bewildered distress.

"Come, Rouncey, and you too," to Rosalind sitting beyond her uncle, Tennant whispered with urgency. "No need to wait for the verdict here. There's a private room at the back. Come, Rosalind!" His sons had followed him. From a back bench Will on the far side literally hauled the girl to her feet, and Robin, smiling at her as she turned, as Rouncey rose obediently to Tennant's guiding hand, tried to slip his fingers through her arm.

"Come along, let's clear off, dear."

She tore herself from their touch with a shrill, hysterical shriek of fury that was utterly regardless of spectators, and struck Robin across the face with a resounding slap.

"Take that! You dirty cad! I'll see you in hell before I marry you. I'll—" A large figure joined the group. Gorham thrust the helpless young men aside. With one hand across her mouth to stifle her torrent of screamed abuse, he picked her up as if she had been a baby, and a second later, almost before people had. comprehended what was happening, had removed her from the hall and deposited her on a bench in a room at the back, of which Bond smartly held open the door.

"Now, young lady, you can yell as much as you like," he said. But apparently, he had once more cowed her, for her frantic screaming subsided into tempestuous, hysterical sobs.

Gorham mopped his brow and glanced at the chief constable, who stood, grim-faced, his back to the door. Will Tennant, near his brother, watched the scene with a fair imitation of his father's insouciant manner. Robin, stiffly upright, with blind eyes, only a red streak vivid across his livid face, seemed stricken into immobility.

Rouncey, amidst them all, looked with helpless bewilderment from the two constables who guarded the outer door with impassive stolidity to Tennant.

"Braice will let us know," the chief constable said briefly.

"What—know what? Tennant! I don't understand! What are we waiting for?"

"The verdict, man!"

"But—but we all know already she was drowned—poor soul, poor soul. They said it over and over again in there!"

"Yes, yes, but—" Impatiently, then, as he saw the twitching face, which seemed to have grown old in a few hours, he added more gently,

"Don't you understand, Rouncey?"

"No, no! Oh, Rosalind, *do* stop that distracting crying . . ."

Braice thrust open the door and came in. His rapid aside to his chief was heard by them all.

"Didn't even leave their seats, sir. Unanimous verdict. Murder . . . against Rosalind Torrington. . . . Committed for trial. . . ."

Quick as he was, Major Tennant was just not in time to catch Colonel Rouncey's swaying figure as, with an inarticulate cry, he crashed full-length on to the floor.

Part II
THE MURDERER
CUR? A QUO?

CHAPTER X

GORHAM WENT UP to town on the 10.45 express from Whitesands, the single through train of the day, and when he had sent in his notes, and a verbatim report of the inquest, to the Assistant Commissioner, he waited with considerable impatience for the expected summons to his office.

When it came, he found Captain Tring still studying his notes.

"Hullo, Gorham. So the sister did do the murder! The fact seems to have been obvious from the start, or Tennant wouldn't have wanted you down to wipe away the mess! Nasty jar for him, poor chap! What was your personal conclusion? I gather you included all the facts in this report of yours?"

"Yes. I completed it on the way up. I'm sorry I hadn't time to get the final part typed, sir, but I was keen to get your opinion on the case quick."

"Isn't the case finished?"

"Well, if you agree, sir, I'd like to return there at once to clear up a lot of little points that I hadn't a moment to go into properly."

"What points?"

Gorham hesitated.

"Well, I hadn't time to search that Cove the other side of the promontory, sir, for one thing. And another is that green beach-coat," he said at last. "It was odd the way it disappeared. While the household was at the inquest I had Manning search every foot of the Villa, but he did not come across a trace of it. Yet the girl was in the habit of using it with the bathing-dress it matched. And she had mended it, too. I inferred from the look of her clothes that mending wasn't a hobby of hers either. So it looked as if she intended to wear it again. . . ."

"You say she generally dropped it on the shore, where Moh spotted it the day before when the dog retrieved it with Bond's pants."

He grinned. Gorham had incorporated the episode in his notes in weighty official terms. "By the way, I fancy young Bond must be a son of James Jeffson Bond who was detective-inspector of the Department. He was before your time here. Killed in an opium dive in Whitechapel about fifteen years ago. J.J. was one of the smartest fellows we ever had. The widow was given a grant as well as a special pension. But I'm certain there was a small kid."

"I've heard of J.J. of course. I'll look into it. This young man is very keen, and smart too. But he is no longer small. Anything but. But about that wrap, sir?"

"If you and Manning can guarantee that it wasn't purloined by the girl Gladys, it may have been washed into the sea. In fact it must have been. Moh swore there were no other footprints on the sand but those of the two young women, and it can't have walked by itself."

"The tide was going out when Lydia started. If she dropped it there it's more likely it would have been left high and dry. What I wondered was"—he offered the suggestion dubiously—"whether the girl took it with her, to keep it safe from Rosalind's clutches. And with the idea of using it. It was very light, and practically waterproof. And dried in a few minutes. She could have carried it easily rolled up and slung on a ribbon round her neck. Her dressing-table was heaped with soiled ribbons—as if she'd been rummaging for a length. That's sheer conjecture, of course," he added quickly, "but she may have intended to land somewhere."

"But she had not taken it other mornings!"

"No. But she mayn't have been willing to risk damaging it other mornings, even if she still intended to land. She was the plump type that fancy themselves lying about with next to nothing on. Specially with men about. This time it was already ruined by the rent. But if she did take it, it must have got torn off in the struggle and be at the bottom of the sea by this time."

Captain Tring was studying a coloured map of Whitesands Bay and its neighbourhood, issued to tourists at a cost of twopence, which Gorham had included with his papers.

"What you're trying to get at is that its disappearance points to a clear intention on her part to land and meet someone," he said. "This map makes out that landing anywhere is impossible till you get right round the promontory. Practically from the hut onwards it is charted 'Dangerous for bathing'. 'Dangerous currents'. 'Dangerous cliffs'." He pushed the map aside and looked up. "The first possible landing-place, according to this, is the Cove where young Tennant says he was! Was it he she went to meet?"

"I don't believe it was, sir. On Tuesday. Burroughs was out to make mischief for young Tennant, whom he obviously detested, but his account of that conversation rang true. And she wouldn't have chosen Burroughs to confide in if she wished to meet Tennant again."

The Assistant Commissioner ruffled the papers on his desk, then rapidly scanned the report of Robin Tennant's evidence for the second time.

"I see he admits meeting Lydia twice when she was ostensibly bathing, but doesn't mention where their rendezvous was. And there's no reference at all here to that night ride of his. Someone managed that omission quite cleverly, Gorham. Was it you? Or the young man's father?"

"In the list of questions I submitted to the coroner I omitted any likely to raise the point. And as Burroughs obviously hadn't an inkling of it it wasn't dragged out," Gorham acknowledged. "All Burroughs did succeed in doing in his attempt to score off the boy was to show him up in the invidious light of the latest bone of contention between the sisters. Incidentally, he supplied an overwhelming motive that clinched the verdict against Rosalind."

Captain Tring sat back in his chair, frowning.

"I don't like it. Gorham. It was the suppression of a piece of evidence that might have told vitally in the girl's favour had proofs of her guilt not been so strong. But for the affair at the Castle the previous day, I mean. You knew that previous attempt at murder to be a fact, though to the jury it was merely a canard they ought to have disregarded completely. But for that, aware as you were that young Tennant was at that Cove at the actual hour of the crime, it would have been your plain duty to ask for an adjournment pending enquiries." He paused. "As it is," he went on presently, as Gorham remained silent, "though you'd have preferred an open verdict to give you more time to complete the investigation, I infer you were satisfied she was guilty. That wet bathing-dress taken with the skill she possessed in the water, and the previous day's unsuccessful attempt to kill her sister, leaves no loophole for doubt."

"There was no doubt she tried to shove Lydia down those stone stairs the previous day, and," said the chief inspector, sighing, "if Moh hadn't saved the young woman's life so quick then, I'd be happier in my mind now than I am about the correctness of the verdict."

"My dear Gorham, I do wish you would try to cure yourself of your exasperating habit of talking round a subject, instead of making your point promptly and rationally, so that a plain man like myself can grasp what you are getting at," cried Tring with irritation. "And don't introduce extraneous subjects such as your happiness into this interview. It means nothing to me. I am not here to promote sweetness and light in the lives of my subordinates, but to induce them to carry through their jobs with a modicum of the intelligence that one might confidently expect from the average child of ten!"

"Yes, sir."

"And don't sit there wasting my time and your own grinning and saying, 'Yes, sir!' like an infernal parrot when I'm waiting to learn what you mean about the correctness of the verdict! I gather it was one of those beastly popular verdicts, where the whole neighbourhood, including the local idiots sworn in on the jury, condemned the wretched girl before proceedings opened. Chiefly on the Press disclosures. But apart from the inquest, on your personal report, I can't see that there's the slightest ground for regarding the case against her as inconclusive."

"She was accepted by everyone as the obvious criminal before news of the previous attempt came out. On the grounds of her ungoverned temper and her jealousy of Lydia. Both were notorious. But when I took over the enquiry I tried to get outside this cloud of local prejudice, for it seemed like a case of giving a dog a bad name and hanging him. Yet every fact I turned up told dead against her. She had threatened to kill Lydia in a violent quarrel the night before. She had been in the water and lied about it. She had been robbed of her former lover Burroughs by Lydia. She saw the thing happening over again with young Tennant. The deadly jealousy she felt for Lydia had been fed for years by every incident of their joint lives. She could swim as well as Lydia, but in any public contest it appears that Lydia always just managed to pull off the prize. Lydia had plenty of cash, and fashionable clothes. Rosalind had to eke out a slender allowance, and her clothes are cheap and shabby. The one sister outshone the other perpetually, and, from certain hints I got, did it with deliberate malice. For instance, she got herself up to kill for this picnic party, while Rosalind, whose young man's people were actually giving the show, and before whom, and the swells they had as guests, she must have wanted to shine, had only an old frock to wear. Call it a small point, sir, but to a young woman in Rosalind's mood, smarting under a sense of petty humiliation, it might well have been the final straw."

"That caused the assault on the stairs?"

Gorham assented.

"Your idea is that the stairs attack was made in a moment of rage after an afternoon of pin-prick exasperations, perhaps brought to a head by her catching some glance between Tennant and Lydia," Tring said thoughtfully. "While the actual murder displayed a different technique, was a cold-blooded, well-planned affair."

But it was Gorham's turn to look perplexed.

"All I meant was that every item that pointed to Rosalind having been the underdog between the two for years only told against her now," he acknowledged with his usual honesty. "But do you consider the two attacks show essential points of difference, sir?"

"Do you?"

"Well, now you suggest it—it is worth considering them—as possibly representing opposite types of crime." He frowned over this fresh lead, then set it aside for future consideration. "I had taken the murder to be a result of momentary murderous impulse like the other. She had this crazy, jealous hatred of Lydia—she guessed she was going to another secret meeting with her own young man—she followed, grabbed her in the water and held her under long enough to drown her, and then, getting the wind up at seeing her dead, bolted back home and into bed. She had certainly been in the water.

"Her towel as well as her bathing-dress had been wet enough to damp all the woodwork in its corner. When I confronted her with it she said she had dropped it in the water. It was certainly gritty with sand. And she also swore that she had not concealed it till after Norman's call at the house. Because she didn't want to own up she had even been down to the shore then. Exactly the sort of stupid thing a dense young woman would do in a blind instinct of self-preservation."

"Or panic at discovery of the crime. Like every other point, it cuts both ways, Gorham. It is obvious that the criminal never gave a thought to those tell-tale bruises left on the body. The thing was staged to look like accident. But look here, cutting the girl out of it, who else was there, unless you suspect young Tennant of participation in the crime, who could have murdered Lydia? It isn't as though there were a fleet of possible murderers sporting in the Bay at the moment, like a school of porpoises."

"That's the deadliest fact against the girl that there is. Tennant is an unknown factor as yet—but, as Moh guarantees the shore clear of all other footprints, it stands to reason that any stranger approaching the spot must either have swum a fairish distance, from the coast beyond the promontory, or used a boat. The latter hypothesis is unlikely because the boat itself implies a second man."

"I'd have requested an adjournment of course, had a single fact turned up that complicated the case against the girl."

"Yet, sir, when I stood in that court and witnessed the dead set everyone made at her it made me uneasy! I felt it was too obvious, that somehow I'd managed to overlook some essential clue that might alter the values of the whole case against her, if I could lay my hands on it and stick it in its proper place. That was why I wanted to go over it with you. I thought that perhaps you might detect some point in the evidence that I'd missed."

"Not a hope, Gorham!" His chief regarded his troubled face with genuine kindliness. "What you miss, even my intelligence, which, as an official formality, we must accept as peculiarly keen and penetrating, is unlikely to detect. But, my dear fellow, frankly, I can't see what is worrying you. You hadn't an earthly fact on which to base a request for adjournment. And the chances are that if you had got the open verdict you played for the young woman would have cut and run. As it is, she is safe under lock and key and from all you tell me of her a brief time for cool reflection won't hurt her. Do her a lot of good, in fact. After all, a coroner's verdict isn't a hanging matter. The case for the defence has still to be prepared before it goes for trial. What about the men in her family circle, Burroughs and the uncle?"

Inwardly he was curious to trace the cause of Gorham's evident dissatisfaction with himself. Either it sprang from undefined intuition roused by contact with the actors in the case, or, as Tring was inclined to believe in view of the cast-iron array of facts against Rosalind Torrington, simply from a decent instinct to defend from any miscarriage of justice a young woman whom her little world united to condemn, and whom he himself heartily disliked.

That latter point alone, if he knew anything about Gorham, would be sufficient to spur his scrupulous sense of fair play.

"Burroughs is a self-seeking bounder. He bathed that morning, but from a beach nearly a mile away, though approximately at the right time. But he had no motive. His one interest was to keep the girl alive, as he stood to gain £10,000 on his marriage to her. I also surmised pretty clearly from his dread of her death being broadcast in the papers that he'd secretly been borrowing on the prospect, besides, and was terrified of his creditors dropping on him as soon as it became known. As for the uncle"—he paused—"there is no record he ever was in the sea in his life except when it flooded his own study. But his manner was queer. As if he knew more than he intended to tell. Otherwise, I got the impression that he was liked. He seemed well-meaning, if ineffectual, attached—well, perhaps less by affection than sheer habit—to the Torringtons, whom he practically adopted after his wife's death. And he was horribly upset."

"My dear Gorham, so might you or I be if we found our family circle suddenly replete with victim *and* murderer!" Tring retorted. "As for his knowing more, probably he does! Families always do. There's nothing in that. The young woman was shifted to Harborough, I suppose? How did she take her arrest?"

"There was a brutal scene. She started the racket by smacking young Robin across the face when the C.C. went to convey them from the Court during the summing up. He saw what was coming and wanted to spare Rouncey, as well as the girl. She turned on the boy like a tiger-cat. She was screaming Billingsgate at the pitch of her voice, when I came up and removed her to a room at the back. She dropped down into noisy sobbing once there. Rouncey looked completely dazed and kept asking Tennant what it was all about. His right cheek was twitching badly. When Braice came in to report results Rouncey collapsed on the floor, and the doctors had to be summoned hastily to attend to him at one end of the room, while Braice attended to the girl. Tennant ordered his two sons to leave the place. His eldest was present, too, a taking youngster, shadowing his junior. But Robin went up to the girl and stood with his hand on her shoulder while the charge was read. The mob outside were yelling the roof off. She listened to Braice, stupidly, like an ox. But when the two constables laid hold of her, pandemonium broke out! She screamed and fought, scratched and kicked till she was gripped by force. The elder Tennant lad tried hard to get his brother away, but he stuck by her mulishly, till suddenly he was violently sick. His hand was pouring blood. She'd bitten it through, her teeth meeting in his hand. He went then to the cloak-room. One of the constables had blood pouring down his face from her scratches, and the other's hands were bleeding. Braice didn't show any undue tenderness in hustling her into the van, and my sympathies were with him. But Tennant called him to order sharply. It was the only time he looked annoyed. You would never have guessed from his cool manner that he had any personal stake in the show. Burroughs had slunk away without even having the decency to wait for poor Rouncey and the care of him fell entirely to the chief constable. He had had a slight stroke, and was utterly helpless. Tennant arranged that he should be taken to a private room at the hospital in Harborough, where he would be away from all reminders of recent events, and he waited to see the start. He also interviewed the Villa servants to enquire if they were frightened to go back there alone. A number of windows had been smashed. The cook was a sensible person, and declared they'd be all right, but she was clearly grateful when Tennant arranged for a constable to spend the night there in case of another demonstration. I had a word with him before I left, and he enquired if I were returning. I said that remained with you to decide. But if you consent, sir, I'd be glad to get back at once."

"As you like, Gorham. I should have thought that Manning or one of the others would have done as well to complete the case, but the truth is you hanker after a seaside holiday and put in for it under the heading of duty."

"That's it, sir." He rose, beaming. "I'm not sure Manning couldn't have taken it over if it had happened in a black-country slum. As it is, I feel I ought to complete the investigation myself. Manning was doing a job for me after I left. But I'll send him back at once. You'd be surprised how like the seaside is to the posters, sir. All yellow and blue, and flowering shrubs up against the sky on that promontory." He stopped. Then added in a different tone. "You have no special lead to suggest, then?"

"None you haven't thought of for yourself, man. The disposition of deceased's property, and, of course, young Tennant's activities. Don't hurry away while Major Tennant wants to retain you—if he wants to retain you! That lad of his doesn't funk his fences, whatever his other shortcomings may be. And if you see Bond's mother and she turns out to be J.J.'s widow, tell her I inquired after her. But J.J.'s son ought to be beating a London pavement with a view to the special branch, not wasting his time under a country fool who hadn't the gumption to search his own shore before the tide covered it."

"I propose to hint strongly at Norman's offences to the C.C. before I leave, sir. But not till then, to avoid unpleasantness," Gorham responded, grinning, and departed.

But before he left the building, after setting certain enquiries afoot, he sought out Chief Inspector Gray, whose lifelong study of botanical subjects combined with his mild good nature caused him to be used as a ready reference by ill-informed colleagues in quest of immediate enlightenment on the nature of plant or tree. Before him he laid a small object.

"Would you say that that thorn came from a bramble, Gray?"

"The thorns on most species of bramble are wide at the base, and hooked, like those on a rose, though others have sharp, spine-like prickles closely protecting the stem. This might be one of the latter, but if so it is of very uncommon length," said Gray with a dubious shake of the head. "Where did you come across it? Is it important?"

"In a dog's foot. I don't know whether it is important or not. If it gives away the nature of the country where the dog picked it up it would clear up a useful point."

"The bramble is common throughout the country in copses and hedgerows, and waste grounds and neglected gardens, since it grows in any sort of soil," was the discouraging reply. "But"— Gray was examining the specimen through a magnifying glass—"I cannot believe that this came from any bramble. It is a true spine such as terminate the branches of Blackthorn, *Primus Spinosa*. The Blackthorns are as ubiquitous as the Brambles. They grow on sandy soil as well as on chalk. But in my opinion this spine came from Buckthorn. Belong to the family Rhamnaceas, you know."

"I didn't," said Gorham flatly. "But take it this spine comes from the family what's-his-name, does that give any indication of the sort of ground my dog must have walked on to pick it up?"

"The true Buckthorn, the only wild specimen which produces a spine, I mean, grows mostly in chalky districts, in copses and woods. That is *Rhamnus catharticus*. It is a shrub, grows about ten feet in height, and the ends of the branches often harden into a spine. The alder-leaved buckthorn, *Rhamnus frangula*, grows everywhere, in hedges and so on, but as it does not produce spines we may disregard it. There is also Sea Buckthorn. *Hippophae Rhamnoides*. A very thorny, low-growing plant, from three to eight feet in height, perhaps, but of drooping habit, that grows wild on sea-shores and cliffs from Yorkshire or Sussex. On the South Coast, in seaside towns, they plant it in public gardens, and under cultivation its height is increased."

"That last sounds as if it would suit my book all right. Does it grow in East Anglia?"

"Oh yes. I have often seen it growing wild on the earthen cliffs near Cromer, and it occurs sporadically along the whole of the East Coast. It is a pretty shrub with a silvery sort of appearance, and when the flowering season ends in July it is covered with bright orange berries. Very pretty indeed. But mind you, though

I feel sure this is a spine from a buckthorn plant, I can't say for certain whether it is from *Rhamnus catharticus*, the inland growing species, or Sea Buckthorn, which is variously known as Sallow Thorn and Willow Thorn. It is quite a distinct plant, you know."

"Thanks very much, old man!" Gorham regarded his colleague with fond reverence while he put his specimen back into its envelope in his pocket-book. "You have given me just what I wanted. Now I know what to look for!" He scribbled down notes of the details he had received, got Gray to check them, and set off again on his journey to Whitesands, this time driving himself in his own car.

CHAPTER XI

IT WAS CLOSE upon four thirty when Gorham, after a swift drive through the long, tranquil highways of Essex and Suffolk, drew up before the police-station in Market Square, Harborough. He had omitted luncheon from the programme of his crowded hour in London and he was firmly resolved to repair that omission at once at the "Golden Crown", the ancient posting-house across the Square, whose reputation for savoury pies stood unrivalled in the three counties. He cast a loving look at the high-peaked gables and mellow red-brick of the inn beyond the grey austerity of the Gothic market cross, then entered the police-station to report his return and pick up any messages that might be awaiting him.

He was informed by the station sergeant that a man who refused to give his name had rung up three times within the last hour, urgently requesting to be informed if Chief Inspector Gorham intended to return to Suffolk that night.

"If he rings up again before five tell him he'll find me at the 'Golden Crown', opposite. After that I shall be at Whitesands." Relieved that there was nothing that need delay his meal further, he hurried out and across the Square, and sat down in the long, panelled, and oak-beamed coffee-room to a magnificent high tea. Twenty minutes later he pushed back the chair beside one of the latticed windows and lighted his pipe in a mood of placid content. The cold roast duck had been as perfect as the ham and crisp salad, the crusty home-made bread, the butter, the honey, the cream and tea.

Seated in one of the capacious wooden armchairs which had served stout Suffolk farmers when they flocked into Harborough on market days for a couple of centuries, he might easily have been himself one of the sturdy race who bought and sold cattle in the Square outside on Tuesdays, when the place was alive with a bustling throng of men and beasts, and not, as it was today, sleepy and deserted in the hot sunshine.

The door at the end of the dim brown room opened and two young men came in. As Gorham recognized them with a nod and smile, they strolled up to join him, and he understood that the second act in the Whitesands drama had opened.

Both wore Fair Isle jumpers and golden brown plus fours, and both were hatless, but with their clothes the likeness between them ended. Robin's freckled face was unsmiling, the thin lips, across which a darkening bruise contrasted with the bloodless pallor of his cheeks, immobile and grim as his out-thrust jaw and hard eyes. The tall young soldier's brown eyes smiled engagingly, especially as their glance rested for a second on the heterogeneous remnants of the chief inspector's meal.

"Good afternoon, Mr. Gorham; hope we haven't interrupted your—er—tea!" he said. "But my brother and I rather yearned to meet you, you know, and they told me we might find you here with luck."

"So it was you who rang up? No, I've finished my tea. But can I order anything for you?"

"Thanks, no. We had some while we were waiting for some halfwit at the station to discover if you were returning or not. One of those indifferent sort of fellows who know nothing and care less. Still, tackled for the fourth time, he eventually came across with the tidings that you were on view here for a strictly limited period. Hence our arrival in force."

"He doesn't deserve censure," Gorham said with a smile. "I didn't know myself till I had obtained leave to return. But there were a number of small points that I had not had time to go into owing to the abrupt termination of this morning's proceedings."

"Then you don't consider that the—er—verdict, and so on, this morning, closes the investigation?"

"What do you mean? The fact that the prisoner is committed to stand her trial closes the preliminaries as far as she is concerned."

"But if so, may I ask why you still think it worth your while to keep on carrying on?" Will urged. "I mean, that's what your return rather indicates, doesn't it?"

"I'm still in charge of the police investigation, if that is what you want to know. In the very brief time I had at my disposal before the inquest this morning I had to leave a good deal of work unfinished, but my return to carry on means no more, I'm afraid, than a preference for finishing a job myself that I have begun."

"You considered that verdict justified, then, yourself?"

"My dear Mr. Tennant, that is a serious question to answer. I consider the verdict precipitate, because it was based on prejudice, and insufficient evidence. The police naturally prefer, before an arrest is made, to have their case tested and complete, unless of course the criminal is caught *in flagrante delicto*. In this case, the evidence was circumstantial only, and even so, as you know, there was a good deal that did not come out in court."

Will exchanged a swift glance with his brother, and received in response a barely perceptible nod.

"Quite so. And that rather brings us to the reason of our coming to you. My brother felt—I mean—well, that it was rather up to him to roll up with more details of his personal share in this miserable affair than he was called on to give this morning. Not that they throw any fresh light on it, unhappily. But—well—we have chatted over the thing a bit between ourselves, and, as he naturally wishes to pull his full weight in this poisonous situation, we decided to find out if you were still in charge, and if so, to roll up and give you all the information he possesses. That's the general scheme, eh, Robin?"

"Scarcely." The boy's voice was as hard as his eyes. "What my brother is really trying to explain is that it bores me to shelter any longer behind Miss Torrington's skirts and leave her to bear the whole brunt of blame since it is quite as much mine as hers. A fact she was perfectly justified in emphasizing when she smacked my face this morning."

"Oh, I say, Robin, old man, draw it mild," Will protested. But Gorham interrupted with considerable sharpness.

"Blame for what?"

"For that damned fracas at the Castle, that those infernal fools on the jury were prejudiced by!"

"You mean that her jealousy of your relations with her sister was justified? But that point was thrashed out this morning. Didn't you realize that it was the jury's belief it was justified that clinched the case against her by supplying a damning motive?"

The white face flushed crimson, but if he were taken aback he showed no signs of flinching.

"What I realize is that it's up to me to take my share," he retorted doggedly. "And kindly correct that beastly phrase you used. I had no 'relations' whatever with—with her sister. Whatever idiocy there was, was entirely on my side. She knew nothing whatever—"

"Did you discredit Burroughs' evidence, then?"

"Burroughs is an impossible swine. He deserves kicking! In my opinion he made the whole story up to gain kudos for himself. But even supposing that some of what he said was true it only showed that if—if it had been hinted to her that Monday that I— that her sister was worried, she wasn't standing for it for a single second! She said nothing whatever to me about it. She was just friendly—and so was Rosalind, till she started snapping at me to be quick and stop mooning on the stairs, and then she caught me looking at—at her sister. . . . Oh, fatuously, I suppose . . . the light was on her hair . . ." His voice broke on a strangled sob.

Gorham's back was turned as he leaned out of the window to knock out his pipe. He stayed so for a moment thoughtfully, and when he drew in his shoulders and resumed his seat he slipped his pipe into his pocket and produced his notebook.

"The single point about that fracas, as you call it, that matters," he said quietly, "is the cause of Miss Lydia's stumble. Whether it was due to an inadvertent movement on the part of the person behind her, or to a deliberate push. If you take my advice, Mr. Tennant, you will leave it at that, for the present, at any rate. The *Gazette* correspondent is not, you must remember, the only person who was cognizant of that stumble. There were also the man who arrested her fall and Sampson. Both reliable witnesses, one of whom certainly, and the other probably—I have not as yet taken his statement—heard your exclamation of protest which virtually gave the show away at the time. So far as I understand it, you have come to me with a desire to help the prisoner. No. Wait a minute. I want you to be clear over what you are doing. I don't intend to question you at all over that previous affair. The evidence of Mr. Moh and Sampson is enough so far as I'm concerned, because it isn't that, but the actual crime of Tuesday morning that I am here to investigate. I suggest that you keep all the palliating circumstances you can bring forward with regard to that previous alleged assault for the ear of counsel for the defence. And meantime leave the subject alone. The case for the defence has yet to be worked up, and you can rest assured that the trial, wherever it takes place, will be conducted in a very different spirit from that wretched show this morning. Now that is common sense, and I'm sure your father will endorse it. Does he know you have come to me, by the by?"

"For God's sake leave my father out of it! I am of age. And ready to answer any questions you can put to me. But kindly oblige me by refraining from dragging my unfortunate family into an affair which is mine alone!"

"But look here, Robin, old man, I do. rather get Mr. Gorham's idea!" put in Will, in pacific yet urgent accents. "What my brother is very keen to make clear, sir," he added to Gorham with a nice touch of dignity in his pleasant tone and manner, "is that my father—since he deliberately handed over the conduct of this case to you—has no official standing in it at all. And I need scarcely assure you—since you have yourself met my father—that his sole intention in calling for your help was to give you an entirely free hand."

"I was thinking of Major Tennant as a very competent, unofficial adviser—not as chief constable. But as you object to that question, let's get on to the next. Where were you in the habit of meeting deceased, and at what times, when you bathed together?"

He caught the flicker of the lad's eyes at the word, but his answer was given in level, impersonal tones.

"When there was a party of us we bathed from the south beach, below the Villa, any time from ten o'clock to noon, as the tide served."

"And latterly, on the occasions when you met her alone?"

"From the cove the other side of the promontory. At about seven. It was nearer for me as I had to get home to breakfast at eight-thirty."

"Were you aware, when you went to this cove, that she would be alone?"

"Not the first time, on Saturday. The second time, on Sunday, I wasn't sure. Nothing had been arranged. The meetings were quite casual."

"You wouldn't have been surprised, then, either time, if both sisters had joined you?"

"Naturally not. In fact both times we kept looking out towards the point more or less expecting her—my—the younger Miss Torrington—to appear. But she was never so keen on that cove as—as her sister was. She preferred the Bay itself."

"Can you give me any idea how long it would take a reasonably good swimmer to reach the cove from the southern beach? It is a fairly stiff pull, I take it?"

"That's awfully difficult to say. You see, in sea swimming weather conditions vary every day. In the first place he would have to take a fair detour in order to avoid first the currents under the cliff and under the face of the Point, though from there towards the cove it is plain sailing for the water is quite shallow. It defeated me absolutely every time I tried. But the girls could do it without turning a hair. Under decent weather conditions, I mean, of course. They were both marvellous in the water, though they had never gone in for speed or long endurance tests."

"You mean a Channel swimmer, say—or one of that type of expert—would think nothing of this trifling trip. I quite understand that. But, taking it from the sheer ordinary amateur's point of view, the class these two really belong to, I infer, can't you give me an idea how long it took Miss Torrington to cover the distance one of these mornings, for instance?"

"Well, the sea was like a millpond. Probably twenty minutes, easy going, across the Bay, and through the stiffer bit out round the Point, and well under ten to the cove. But as I went out to meet her, and we fooled about in the water for a bit, I can't vouch for it to a minute."

"No, I see that." Gorham dropped the question. He realized that he would have to go into this baffling estimate of the time required to negotiate these strips of water where conditions seemed to vary every fifty yards or so with some expert who understood the factors that must be reckoned with. But already he dimly sensed a vital discrepancy that looked like opening up a fresh field of enquiry, though for the moment he put it aside. "Then your last bathe together was on the morning of the picnic, Monday?"

"No, Sunday," came the quick correction. "She told me that swimming in the early morning always made her feel sleepy in the afternoon, so on Monday neither of them would be out, as they wanted to look their best at the picnic."

"You bathed alone at the cove on Monday, then?"

"I didn't bathe at all, or go near the coast."

"You are sure of that, Mr. Tennant?"

"Of course I'm sure"—impatiently.

"You did not leave your home before breakfast at all that day?"

"I didn't say that. I said I didn't run down to the sea. I went out for a stroll. Smoked a cigarette on a stile, and so on, then went in for a tub and change before breakfast."

"Did you meet anyone you knew?"

"Not a soul, which was quite a relief, as the house happened to be packed with guests who looked for a considerable amount of chat at brekker—which personally I find wearing."

"Well, to come to Tuesday morning." He took out his map and spread it on his knee. "Here is Bramwood Heath, four miles of it or more roughly. The northern edge of it reaching nearly to a parallel line drawn east from Castle St. Roche. You had penetrated well into the heath after approaching it from the south, I understand. Can you point out approximately where you halted?"

Robin bent over and traced the line of the western boundary with his finger.

"The old dame's cottage must have been somewhere round here. I can't show the exact spot because it was right off any road, a mere apology for a footpath, and I never remember to have been in that part of the heath before. But it must have been in this direction, because I headed more or less east when I left her as a cursory glimpse of the castle through breaks in the trees gave me my bearings, and I came out on to the main coastal road here, passed under the castle and along to the cove. From there, as I told you, I turned inland by this road"—the slim brown finger continued to follow his route—"past our own gate, then on to White's garage on the Oakshott-Harborough road. I left the old lady's cottage at five twenty, and as I went all out down the coast road, nine miles of clear run, it must have been five thirty-eight to five forty when I reached the cove. I told you all this last night."

"I know, but it makes it clearer to check the distances on the map. At what time did you reach White's garage?"

"Just after eight. Ten past, to be exact. The chap looked over the engine while I had a cigarette, several in fact. All I had on me. I strolled along the road and fished a packet of gaspers out of a slot machine, then later on had some coffee at a busmen's stall. And fooled about generally till the car was ready, and tooled home."

"You say you covered the distance—nine miles—from the cottage to the cove in about eighteen minutes, yet it seems to have taken you over two hours to reach the garage from the cove, a distance of eight miles."

"Seven and a half. White's is half a mile out of Harborough on the Oakshott road."

"How do you account for this discrepancy?"

"Am I expected to account for it? I seem to have mentioned that the car was running infernally. I got out and tinkered with it twice. Running is the wrong word. It crawled. And when it wasn't crawling I'd stopped it and sat inside and cursed. At first the engine trouble didn't perturb me much. Gave me leisure for thought, and so on. But I own before I reached White's I was thoroughly fed up, because I thought I must have damaged the radiator irreparably, and that would have meant shoving it into dock for weeks."

"And you met no one, either before or after you went down on to the beach at the cove, who could confirm these times you give?"

"No one. I had a couple of cigarettes on the sands. I was there exactly twenty-six minutes. I looked at my watch when I started the car. It was six six. The main road was entirely deserted at that unearthly hour. The bus went with a bang till I'd run about half a mile up Oakleigh lane, then it started playing the deuce. That, as you know, is a secondary road and carries little traffic at its brightest moments. Not so much as a hen passed me till I turned out into the Oakshott-Harborough road. Sorry, Mr. Gorham, but you will have to accept my unsupported word. Or not. As you like."

Gorham rose. Standing, his large frame seemed to loom over the small figure of young Robin Tennant with a suggestion of ominous impressiveness.

"Mr. Tennant, why did you go down to that cove where twice before you had met Lydia Torrington at that hour?"

Robin closed his eyes. If he had been pale before, the skin stretched over his cheekbones now showed deathly white, and across that rigid mask the blackening bruise across his tightly compressed lips leapt into arresting prominence, scoring an angry mark across its livid pallor.

For a second he was silent, then with a sudden movement he flung around, and with the gesture broke the tenseness of that pause.

"Oh, just that . . . Because I'd met her there, of course!" he cried, his voice quivering, high and unnatural in tone. But his back was turned now to Gorham, only the sleek, close-cropped hair showing.

"And you met her again?"

"You fool!" He turned with blazing eyes. "I didn't meet her! She had gone already into the water where she died!"

"She'd gone? Then you learned somehow that she had been there? Take care what you say, young man! You've never hinted this before!"

"That's no tone to use, Chief Inspector!" sharply exclaimed Will Tennant. "Robin, old man . . ."

But his interference was ignored by both men, though it afforded Robin breathing space in which to get a grip on himself.

"She'd told me not to come again, because it wasn't playing the game if Rosalind was jealous. Before we parted, I'd promised I wouldn't. On the sands I saw no sign of her. I got it she had kept her side of the bargain if I hadn't. Then, when I'd gone up on to the top again I saw her green coat spread out to dry. On a boulder that wasn't visible from where I'd been below. I saw she meant to come back. The tide was coming in. I kidded myself I'd better go back and fetch the coat up higher, in case it got wet again before she came. I went a step or two. But damn it, I didn't go. I started the car instead and bolted off. Round the corner towards home. It was that spurt that finished the engine. It went all out for half a mile or so, then slithered to a standstill, smoking like hell. I didn't care if the damned thing burned and me in it. But it was something to do, so I got out presently and opened the bonnet to cool off and fooled about. I crawled on later to our gate, and stopped again. But I couldn't stick the thought of going indoors. So I went on. The rest you know. What are you going to do now? Arrest me for murdering her, perhaps. If not, and if you've quite finished making me rake over my private affairs, I suggest we go, eh, Will?"

He marched towards the door, and Gorham let him go. He realized that he would gain nothing by detaining him in his present mood. Will followed without a word, but when he reached the door through which his junior had disappeared he came back, his eyes wide with anxiety.

"Look here, sir, you surely don't imagine—"

"I don't imagine anything," Gorham interrupted roughly. "I wanted the facts. And I've got them, or some of them. But let me give you a word of advice. Don't let that boy get his hands on your revolver just now. He's in a mood to blow his brains out, and yours too, unless you handle him tactfully."

"I know. That's why I'm getting him to come up to my cousin's house. They will help. That she-devil drove him absolutely desperate! But"—his passionate earnestness contrasted oddly with his ludicrous phrase—"do grip hold with limbs *and* tail, sir . . . young Robin is *straight*!"

He shot out of the room.

Gorham remained standing in deep thought for a good five minutes before he too left the coffee-room, paid his bill, and walked out into the sunshine of the Square. The Singer was gone. But he saw a Bentley drive up to the police-station opposite, and the tall upright figure of the chief constable mount the steps with something less than his habitual litheness.

But though he hesitated for a moment, he finally entered his own car without crossing the Square.

On the high road outside the town he stopped for petrol at a large garage fenced in behind a row of brilliant blue-and red-painted pumps, which a notice board proclaimed in scarlet lettering "WHITE'S."

"You ought to call yourselves 'The Union Jack'," he chuckled to the mechanic in oil-stained overalls who came to attend to his wants. "Red, white and blue, eh? Shove in a couple of gallons, please. By the way, is young Mr. Tennant's car still laid up here? He told me he nearly bust it up yesterday morning."

"I don't think so. . . . Hi, Bill, here's a gent asking if Mr. Robin's Singer's still here? You attended to her when he brought her in yesterday, didn't you?"

Bill, who appeared to be passing a pleasant hour breathing the fresh air at leisure, strolled across.

"Friend of Mr. Robin's, sir?" He touched his cap with a grin that attested young Tennant's popularity here, at any rate.

"He told me about your place, if I want anything done while I'm here," Gorham returned with his genial smile. "Happen to remember what time he turned up here yesterday? He thought it was soon after eight."

"Eight?" Bill looked puzzled. "I'd have said it was a good bit later than that. More like after nine. It took me near an hour after she'd cooled off to overhaul the engine and put her ship-shape again. He'd run his radiator dry and he thought he'd fair burned her guts out, but there wasn't any leakage anywhere. But he'd got the exhaust valve fairly choked and his carburettor hadn't been cleaned in a month of Sundays. But he waited while I done the job, and took her away hisself."

"Oh, good. That sounds like quick work! But what makes you think it was so late when he brought her in? He said she was running dead slow and it took him nearly an hour to get here from his own gate, and he'd left there round seven. . . ."

"That's right about her running slow. It's a wonder he didn't have to walk behind her and shove! He'd practically run himself out of water for a second time, for one thing. And even then the engine was all hotted up, so I had to let her cool off before I could touch her. But he must have been mistook about the time he left, or been longer than he'd thought for, because it was nearer nine than eight by a long chalk before he brought her in. For one thing I'd had me breakfast at the shelter along there at eight thirty, and stopped for a bit of a chat with some of the chaps off of the eight thirty and eight forty buses that halt there for ten minutes. And finished up a job what I'd bin on the night before on a Wolseley, ready for the gentleman—Mr. Marchmont it was—to call for on his way out to golf at Oakshott at nine like it had been promised, before Mr. Robin turns up. Thanks, sir. You ask him again, sir, and you'll see, if he thinks a bit, he'll tell you the same. Afternoon, sir. Nice day!"

"So that's the first link in young Robin's alibi gone west!" thought Gorham grimly as he drove on. "Not that this end of it matters so much, of course. For the girl was dead by six ten at latest. But on his own showing she'd been in that cove. He owned he saw her wrap, though he hadn't intended to let that out. But supposing he did meet her—and swam out round the point . . . from the cove. I'll have to go into the question of those infernal currents, and work out times and distances out there with some expert. Perkins ought to have been put on to this job—not a thick-headed landsman like myself. But that has got to be my next job. I'll 'phone Bond to have the police-boat at the pier. . . . Say Robin saw that girl murdered . . . or did it himself . . . or helped . . . or tried to rescue her out of that hell-cat's claws and failed . . . and made himself an accessory by screening the said h-c. . . . what would he do next? Come straight back to the cove, dress in the car and bunk away? Anywhere . . . so he could get out of sight quick, and hide while he pulled his wits together? His nerves are shot to pieces. No doubt about that. But he's the quiet, high-strung type that go all out when they're desperate. Bill said his engine was hot. But could it have been so hot if he'd been running dead slow? That first mad sprint—and then lack of water might do it. But he said the old dame gave him a bucketful. What size of bucket and how much water? Everything hangs on the time of that tide. . . ."

He had sighted a call-box, but the complicated fashion in which, trying to pull up in its own length, a manoeuvre for which his car was perfectly adapted, he executed a spirited war-dance all over the road and path before bringing her to a standstill, was due not to lack of skill, but to shock, as a remembered phrase shot into his consciousness.

"The tide was coming in!" The tide had not turned till six eight. Two minutes after he swore he had left the cove. In that single phrase he had given the game clean away. Had his story been true, the tide would have been on the turn, maybe—supposing his watch wasn't accurate to a minute. But it was incredible that he had remained long enough on the sand to smoke a couple of cigarettes and still be unaware of the tide's movement.

That inadvertent phrase showed that he had been aware of it, as conclusively as it proved that he had left the shore much later than he said. He had admitted himself that the passage from the point back to shore could be done with ease in ten minutes. . . . He broke off his speculations abruptly to call up Norman, who undertook that Bond and a boat with a reliable sailor should be awaiting him in ten minutes, at the pier.

But when he had completed his conversation with the Whitesands sergeant and had paused for a minute, he rang up the station at Harborough.

"Hullo, yes? The chief constable? Yes, sir . . . he's here now . . ." And then a different voice. "That you, Gorham? So you are back? May I regard your return as—er—personally encouraging?"

"I'm afraid not. Specially since I've had a more detailed edition of the story I got in your presence last evening."

"That sounds portentous! Am I to share these ominous revelations?"

"Your elder son was present. Ask him about it. You won't require my inferences to supplement yours. You are letting him go up to town?"

"Yes, to my sister, Lady ffinch-Heriott, Cheniston Gardens. It occurred to me that the society of her quite nice youngsters might help to restore a more normal outlook on life. Any objection?"

"None whatever. Only—this is the immediate point, Major Tennant—if he were my lad, I'd take very considerable care that he wasn't left to his own devices for a single second, just at present. It is your affair, of course. But I thought I'd just mention it."

"Ah, er—thanks. Not a flavouring of official anxiety behind your hint, is there?"

"When I want to safeguard anyone officially I have official resources—and use them." He spoke shortly. He had every intention of sending Manning to town on the heels of Robin Tennant with instructions that he was to be kept under close observation till further orders. "But I understood you hadn't seen much of the boy today, and I'm presenting you gratis with the impression his manner made on me, to act on as you think fit. Good-bye."

CHAPTER XII

THE CIRCLE OF green chairs in the enclosure round the bandstand was sparsely occupied when Gorham drove along the front to leave his car in the official park, and he had no difficulty in picking out a small, immobile figure on one of them, who listened with Oriental patience to the nauseating strains of the Happy Song from *Sunshine Susie*.

After a brief interview with Manning, who was waiting for him in his hotel, he crossed the parade, bought a day ticket, and strolled into the enclosure.

In front of Mr. Moh's chair he paused to glance across the crowded beach towards the water, while he counted his change.

"Join me on the breakwater, Moh," he murmured in a low voice. "I'm going to view the scene of the crime in a boat. I'd like your company."

He walked on through the other exit, along the parade and out on to the pier, at the far end of which Moh, who had made his way thither by the beach and a flight of steps, joined him with unruffled calm.

"You got my message all right last night? I was awfully sorry to cut our meeting, but with the publication of that Castle yarn in the local rag I had a crowded evening."

"Aware such must be," said Mr. Moh, "when I read it, the grease being bung in the conflagration, I took immediate family and relatives by marriage to the pictures."

Gorham chuckled.

"I wish you'd join us at the Department, old man! A pleasant time would be had by all. Specially me. Bond is waiting here with a boat to take us out to the point. Do you know anything about sea-swimming and currents?"

"Not on your life!" said Mr. Moh with candour.

"Well, I've got to work out an accurate schedule of distances, and the approximate time it took or might have taken half the population of Suffolk to cover them, swimming at different rates of speed according to their several capacities," Gorham murmured with a sigh. "So if you pine for more of that band this evening you had better not come with us."

"Eternity is around us," Mr. Moh assured him cheerfully. "Every moment snatched from the clangour of that saxophone to listen to the music of a friend's voice is doubly sweet. And family are out to tea and supper at neighbours, from whom absence of this unworthy one is unmitigated pleasure to all concerned."

Bond, looking young and stalwart if a little shy, in flannels and a blue jersey, saluted Gorham at the landing stage.

"You directed me to come in rough, plain clothes, sir. I hope these suit."

Gorham looked him over critically.

"Quite, so far as I'm a judge. That blue suits your eyes nicely. This the police-boat?"

"No, sir. We don't possess an official launch, sir," Bond explained, blushing hotly. "This is hired from Charles Weston the boat-owner here, and on receiving your orders I proceeded to secure Weston's brother-in-law, William Smith, sir. He's a retired coastguard, has lived here for twelve years and knows every inch of the coast." He led the way down the splashed steps.

"Good." Gorham nodded pleasantly to the grizzled man who stood to steady the boat against the stone wall as they climbed in. "You understand what I want, Smith. To go over the scene of yesterday's crime, and learn all I can about the conditions under which it was committed. I'm a landsman myself, so that is where you come in. But you understand that everything that passes between us is strictly confidential?"

"Ay, ay, sir," was the laconic reply.

They shot out beyond the breakwater and Gorham turned to scan the whole curve of the Bay, with the little town lying behind its sheltered harbour, and with its wide strip of beach along which a fringe of gaily painted bathing-huts and machines under the lee of the parade was backed by the frontage of hotels, the casino, and swimming-baths, and at the extreme end a cheerful colony of bungalows, occupying two thirds of the curve, from its centre to the northern extremity, where the promenade became a mere gravel path.

On the other side of the pier, where the High Street debouched on to the parade, was a short row of private hotels overlooking the bandstand gardens, then buildings abruptly ceased, and the narrow sandy strip of the southern beach swept round towards the forbidding heights of the promontory, with a tranquil background of pastoral country. He could discern a faint blue trail of smoke rising from the chimney of Bond's invisible cottage, and a constant procession of motor vehicles passing along the coast road, but beyond these no sign of human activities, for Melita Villa, crouched under the steep hill against its dark groves of trees, showed no signs of life.

Out here, on the blue water, with the rushing breeze their speed created full in their faces, it was extraordinarily pleasant, but the pleasure was equally brief.

Under the promontory Smith shut off his engine and looked round enquiringly. He was a shy person and rarely wasted words.

His glance said: "Here you are. Now what?"

Gorham sat up and opened his notebook and chart, on which, Bond's keenly interested eyes noticed, were points marked with certain pencilled ciphers.

He pointed to the small buoy near the cliff and fifty yards in an oblique line from its farthest point.

"That is where you found the body. Run through your statement again, Bond." He checked off each item with his eyes on the coast, and by the chart, and by his previous notes, while Smith sat with his hand on the wheel and listened.

When he had finished with Bond, whose account tallied in every detail with that he had already given, the chief inspector turned to the boatman.

"The cliffs all along this coast are earthen, given to dangerous landslides. Why is this bit of water under the sickle curve of that cliff, which is overhanging, and looks as if it might slip into the sea below any minute, dangerous? One would have expected it to be shallow, silted up."

"That's right, sir, about the general run of cliffs along here. But the appearance of that one is deceptive. You scratch off an inch or two off of the surface and you'll find it solid rock. It's a freakish outcrop of rock like that of Castle St. Roche. The base shelves steeply down under water to three fathom in places, so the landfall, instead of silting up, slips clean down on to the ocean bed out there for dispersal. That's one reason. But another is the presence of underground springs that spurt up, they believe, through fissures in the rock and, while they help to wash the rock shelf clear, form a strong current underneath that sort of drags down a swimmer. You'll find the same sort of thing at Scarborough. Stretches of the coast safe enough for a child to play about in; then, close under the rocks, a strong sucking undercurrent that'll drag a chap in before you can say knife. They lost a lot of men from the coastal training camps that way, during the war. And this place is the same, only the suction here isn't near so strong."

"Where does the line of safety run, then?"

"Well, sir, draw a line from this buoy to that little hut yonder, and keep outside it, and you've got a widish margin of safety."

Gorham nodded. The significance of this critical patch of water that immediately lapped the whole length of the Whitesands side of the promontory with regard to this case lay in the fact that it precluded the possibility of anyone entering or leaving the bay by the cliffs.

They moved gently forward to the extreme point of the promontory, and here Gorham found that, looked at from the open sea, the word point was a misnomer, for the cliff face stretched for a width of from twenty to thirty feet.

A light wind had sprung up and their ears were filled with the musical rhythm of the surf which plashed against its face, as the ripple of each successive wave broke to fall back in a froth of white foam.

"Is the water deep here?" he asked.

"Yes, sir. Three to four fathom along from here back to the buoy. S'utherd the sea bottom rises again, and round the other side of the point it ain't more than a fathom and a half maybe."

"Look here, in this position alone, with that face of cliff shutting out the view on either side, could the crime have been com-

mitted without the smallest danger of being overlooked by someone on shore? Do you know any reason that makes it impossible it
could have been done here, close in under the cliff?"

"No, sir. There ain't no reason that I know of, the prisoner
being as she is, a powerful strong swimmer—"

Gorham interrupted.

"Don't answer with any preconceived opinion as to who did
the thing, man. Put the prisoner out of your head. Just think of
it this way. . . . Lydia Torrington was drowned—certainly not far
from that buoy, as her body had to be towed there later—by someone unknown. Call it a man if you like. Picture it to yourself. How
and where do you suppose it could have been done? From my—
the detective's—point of view, the first thing the man would want
to make sure of would be that no one could see the struggle. This
stretch of thirty feet or so of water close under the shelter of that
cliff would give him that essential privacy. Now what is your view
as a seaman with close knowledge of this coast?"

Smith pondered the matter with corrugated brow.

"Well, sir. The tide runs strong here, but there ain't nothing
to prevent it happening here like you said," he said at length, "but
mind you this here chap of yours would have to be a powerful
swimmer, what had plenty of practice in his leg strokes to keep
himself up against the wash of the tide while he used his hands
for the job. With the tide running in he'd run the danger of being
bashed against the rock, or round with the shore drift into the Bay.
. . . In rough weather he'd have had to swim right out and give the
cliff-point a wide berth. . . ."

"Yes. I should imagine it would be impossible to negotiate a passage round the point at all," said Gorham patiently, "in rough seas."

"That's right, sir. The breakers dash right up against that
point with a bit of a gale blowing. . . . He'd be knocked insensible
in no time."

"Quite so. But we are dealing with a given crime committed
at a given moment, six a.m. yesterday, with five minutes' margin
either way. Now what about it?"

"Yes, sir. Yesterday morning there wasn't as much wind as'd fill
a pocket-handkerchief. There wouldn't have been hardly a ripple,
not near as much as you see now. And the tide was still running

out. A strong swimmer could have done it easy along here, sir; he'd only got to keep himself afloat and prevent himself being dragged under while the struggle went on. . . . Three minutes—or a few seconds more—for the pore young woman would know how to hold her breath, and take longer than most to be choked into insensibility, though the very fact that she was struggling would shorten her time. . . . I take it, what he done was to grip her sudden like—before she could take a long breath—and then—if she didn't manage to get her head up again—well, it would be over pretty quick . . . two minute."

"She'd be insensible, you mean. What would he do next?"

"I take it," the man said slowly, pitifully, "he'd do that first to stop her struggles, then finish up his job easy-like, then, him being, like we agreed, a good swimmer, he'd swim under water to that buoy—the tide, you remember, sir, being in his favour for that, balancing the shore drift—it would be a matter of half a minute or more, carrying her in front of him. Then after taking a bit of a prospect round, to fill his lungs, and make it sure it was O.K., he'd hoist her up, and go under again. That's how I make it out it could be done, sir."

"Absolutely, Smith. Given all the facts we know, that's how it must have been done, since it was done."

While he listened he had transcribed the man's slow speech verbatim in shorthand in his notebook.

Now he closed the book and stared upwards, frowning, at the bulging front of the cliff that overhung its clear reflection in the water. It might be possible to leap or fall from the upper surface of that curved cliff face into the sea beneath, though its height must be between forty and fifty feet, he judged. But nothing short of a creature endowed with wings could have ascended to the top from below.

The other men waited in silence, the thoughts of each engaged with that tragic struggle that was vividly present in all their minds which, so recently, had made this spot, so tranquil, so serenely indifferent, so beautiful in its changing lights and hues, a scene of foul murder.

"It doesn't seem possible a woman could have had the grim nerve to do it!" Bond burst out.

Gorham brought his glance down sharply.

"Now round to the cove," he ordered Smith. "Slow as you can, and keep as close inshore as possible."

He saw at once as they cleared the corner that the promontory at the landward end was much wider than be had supposed, roughly triangular in shape, with the base of the triangle scarcely inferior in width to its sides. On the Whitesands side it curved in the form of a sickle-blade, but here it lay broadside on to the sea, its smooth steep hillside rising towards the skyline, clothed almost to the water's edge with short grass, and low-growing shrubs, now in the season between blossom and fruit, clothed in foliage of varying greens.

From the rock onward, except for a narrow break at the point of the cove, where, as he saw a charabanc pass, he realized that the road must give a clear view over the sea, the coastline was much steeper and more picturesque, Castle St. Roche standing up finely in the distance. But except for a white patch of sand strewn with boulders in the cove, which was merely a tiny indentation in the coast and scarcely worthy of so distinctive a title, the shore at the foot of the cliffs seemed to consist simply of rocks and shingle, narrow, and no doubt extremely uncomfortable for walking. The crest of the green slope was crowned with dense thicket, which crept down in a tangle of green shrubbery to the level of the cove.

"The water here looks shallow enough to wade in, almost. Hello! that looks as if someone had scrambled up there pretty recently! Stop, Smith, and shove her nose in."

The boatman obeyed, and while he held her steady, across a yard or so of transparent water they surveyed with keen interest faint yet unmistakable signs above high-water mark that someone recently had climbed up the hillside, had slipped and scrambled up on hands and knees, clutching at and uprooting tufts of grass that now hung withering, scoring a scratched path in the thin soil, and above catching at branches of shrubs more than one of which had snapped under his weight and, like the dying, bent grass, hung drooping on the parent bushes treacherously to betray his line of passage.

Gorham looked from the tell-tale marks in the hillside towards the cove. Only the extreme southern corner was visible. Given the extra feet of water that separated them from that scored pathway made by someone who had climbed up out of the water and the gentle swell of the hillside beyond, the climber would be wholly invisible from the cove and road above it.

Only just invisible. But supposing a swimmer had come round the point of the headland as they had come, and spotting a spectator on that bit of road, and urgently needing to lie doggo for a time till the coast was clear, wouldn't he have done just this? Desperately have scrambled up this almost sheer hillside, forcing the soft earth to yield him precarious foot- or knee-hold, till he was high enough to crouch hidden among the shrubs? Rather than swim straight back to the beach he had set out from? To be reported later coming, at the fatal moment at which a murder had been committed, direct from the scene of the crime?

According to Robin Tennant, Lydia Torrington, a steady, practised swimmer, could cover this course of shining water to the cove in under ten minutes.

Had the criminal then followed the direct and simple route home by water for exactly that space of time he would have been exposed to chance observation from the shore.

Thorough as ever, however, he put Robin's statement to the test of Smith's and Bond's experience, by patient questioning which tended in the end to confirm the young man's estimate of Lydia's speed. But this questioning had one enlightening result. It brought out the fact that Smith had often accompanied the Torrington girls in a boat when they first came to live at Whitesands with their uncle.

"But did they learn to swim here, then?" he enquired, puzzled. "Somehow I had got the impression they were already practised swimmers at that time!"

"So they were, sir. They'd learned as little kids where they lived before, Swansea, sir. It wasn't them Colonel Rouncey engaged me to go out regular with, but his nephew, Mr. Herman, when he come down to the Villa to stop with his uncle. The Colonel never seemed to give it a thought when the girls were out. I suppose he was so used to them being in the water he didn't trouble. But when Mr. Herman came down, and took to sea-swimming like a fish as you might say, his uncle didn't seem able to contain his anxiety for his safety. So he came down and engaged me to stand by regularly. He told me once he felt nervous about anyone dear to him being in the sea ever since he'd seen his young brother drownded before his eyes as a boy off Dartmouth. And Mr. Herman being the only blood-kin he'd got left, it brought it all back."

"Didn't Herman jib at being mollycoddled like that?"

"Not he, he only laughed. Him and his uncle was rare fond of each other, and Mr. Herman was an easy, good-tempered one. But the fact was, he was a natural born swimmer from the first. Everything came easy to him. Except young Whittiker he was far and away the best swimmer that I ever saw on this coast. But he never would show off, and always kept it pretty dark on account of worrying his uncle. Down here, at any rate. He taught his young cousin Rosalind a lot more than she ever knew before, but neither of them was in his class really. His form was professional, theirs amateurs at best. It was easy money for me, of course, but after a bit I went and told the Colonel it was waste of good cash. So he dropped it, him being set at rest about his nephew being drownded."

"Do you know Robin Tennant or his brother? Sons of the chief constable? They used to come out with the Torringtons often, didn't they?"

"Mr. Robin did this summer. I never saw Mr. Will with 'em. Don't believe he liked 'em."

Smith found this great London detective a much more friendly person than he had expected, and, thawed by his easy-going method of asking questions, he was talking now with refreshing candour.

"Why? Did he say so?"

"This being in confidence sir, it cuts both ways, eh?"

Gorham laughed.

"Of course. Covers you as well as me," he said.

"Well, both the young gents often come out with me or my brother-in-law Charlie, what owns most of the boats here. For years they have. Before Mr. Robin took up with the Villa bits of skirt. But this summer, in June it was, both being home, they'd been out twice, diving off the boat and so on. And the second time it being we were out again, when Mr. Robin he spots the girls and Burroughs bathing off shore, and he says, 'Look here, Will,' he says, 'let's tool over and join the girls,' he says. But Mr. Will, he answers, 'I'm not going near those infernal girls, and you won't either unless you're a damn' fool, young Robin.' And Mr. Robin fires up, 'I'll mix with whom I please, and damn fool yourself,' says he. And Mr. Will, he says, 'I'll be hard up for company,' he says, 'when I find myself messing about with Lydia Torrington and the town riff-raff she picks up with.' Then he adds, grinning like, 'Sorry, old man, I apol' and that for damn' fool.' So they drops it and dives overboard. And left the other lot alone. They've not been out with me again, and next time I see Mr. Robin he was with the Villa lot. But from that I dedooces that Mr. Will he hadn't any use for Lyddy Torrington."

"Quite a fair deduction, too," Gorham agreed. "But what sort of swimmer is Mr. Robin—above the average?"

"Not bad, and he's had a bit of practice with them girls this month that may have done him a bit of good. But I wouldn't say he was up to much. Nothing to get certifilicates on. Nothing what you'd call scientific about Mr. Robin's style. Just out to amuse himself. Just a dive in and a bit of a splash round, and a lie up in the sun was about his mark."

Gorham looked again at the scar on the hill-face. Did this account supply another reason for a swimmer who had been in the water already over half an hour, and was feeling the strain of exhaustion, to climb ashore at the first point where he saw a chance of foothold, besides desire to escape observation?

Robin might be no expert in the water, yet be as active as a cat on land.

"All right," he said reluctantly. "I suppose we'd better stop patrolling this spot and get on to the cove to make sure that track wasn't left by some mischievous kid climbing about where he was strictly forbidden to be. I'll have to pick it up from above as I'm too heavy to play at being a cat burglar, and you too, Bond. What about you, Li Moh?"

Mr. Moh had not contributed a single remark to the discussion so far, and Smith, whom his unobtrusive presence in their midst had intensely puzzled, turned round and surveyed him with curiosity.

"Climb presents no difficulty even to non-feline honest person who has knowledge of slight knack required," Mr. Moh murmured. "If noble Chief Inspector desires tracks discerned by his keen glance to be traced upwards it can be done, if no dismay is felt at removal of outer garments first. Such," he added with a fond glance at his blue serge reach-me-downs, "being my party suit."

Gorham chuckled.

"Go ahead, Moh! Don't mind us! I can bear anything but seeing you drowned before my eyes."

"No jeopardy of drowning attaches to simple, fly-like feat." Like lightning he stripped off coat, trousers, boots and socks, and clad in a chic creation of shantung silk which appeared to combine the offices of vest, shirt and pants, stepped off the boat, which Smith steadied against the bank, and in a second was swarming up the hillside to the left of the other tracks, with, as he had said, the ease of a fly walking up a wall.

Bond looked at the chief inspector, shamed.

"Please, sir, I'd like to have a shot—"

"Ever done it before?"

"No, sir. But if Mr. Moh can, I can."

"When you can do a tenth of what Moh can you'll be the smartest man in the County Constabulary, and that isn't saying much," came the crashing retort. "Stay where you are. This isn't practice for an Alpine expedition."

"Seen that gentleman about," observed Smith, his tone one of keen appreciation. "Is he a sailor, sir?"

"May have been. There's nothing he can't do!"

"Ah, Chinks are like that sometimes. Clever as monkeys. Though there's others . . ." He shook his head.

In a surprisingly brief space of time the climber reappeared above and came down, more slowly, but with the same deftness, choosing the footholds he had made in his ascent. Bond and Gorham leaned across and lifted him dry-foot into the rocking boat.

"Well?" said the chief inspector eagerly.

"He ascended here. Above is deep-cut track of wet bare feet in soft ground. No child, Gorham. A footprint measuring twelve inches in length. He lay flat on ground overlooking open sea and bay for considerable time. The soil is sandy, but deeply indented. Then he rose and walked some yards away from point towards the land. Then turned, and as I think, ran back to the extreme point. There the footprints end."

"End? Do you mean the ground records no more?"

"The ground records no more because he leapt into the sea." Gorham stared at him in complete bewilderment.

"Do you mean he dived off over the top of that curving cliff that we looked at just now, clean into the water, man? But such an act would be sheer suicide!"

Mr. Moh, who was rapidly assuming his neat garments over the silk creation slightly less chic than it had been before his climb, shrugged his shoulders.

"It may be he did suicide. All the prints tell is that he leapt. The stance was one of extreme delicacy, but the height, forty-five feet maybe, presents no insuperable difficulty to a diver of practised skill. In Honolulu, where I tripped once on police duty from 'Frisco, I have seen such feats done as easy as falling off a log."

"Have you?" said Gorham doubtfully. "It seems dashed high to me. What do you say, Smith?"

"Why, it's right what he says, sir! I've seen 'em myself in the South Seas do things in the water that might make a sea lion sit up and take notice, but then the populations being what they call properly amphibious from infancy, blacks and whites, they don't hardly count. But the point about a dive isn't so much the height, as the take-off, and the depth of water below, sir."

"But look here, you're not going to tell me that any ordinary, common or garden swimmer like the people we've been talking about, these Torringtons, young Tennant, or Bond here, could get away with a dive of forty-five feet?"

"No, sir, I'm not. There ain't no facilities for high-diving practice in Whitesands—except the twelve-foot dive off the breakwater. And I never heard of them girls using even that, nor Mr. Robin either. Though Bond here does. But they are amatures, sir. But if it come to a real expert like Whittiker, why, he wouldn't think much of a height of fifty feet. With a corresponding depth below and a clean manner of taking off any fair diver could do it. But when it come to diving in off that headland, the take-off ain't clean. There's near four fathom of water below on the corner round by the Bay, like I told you when you passed remarks there. Whittiker did it two or three times as a lad, before he went to sea. But no one else I ever heard of, with success. In fact," he added simply, "two tried, but one of them bashed his skull in, and the other was alive when they fished him out of the sea, but he went barmy."

"Well, it couldn't have been Whittiker this time, since he is with his ship in the Mediterranean," Gorham said rather shortly. "The cove, Smith. I must fling a cordon round that place without loss of time. I was told it was well fenced in, after the fatal accidents they had there, but it is obviously accessible."

He wrote rapidly on a page of his notebook under the chug-chug of the engine, and before wading ashore he handed it to Bond. "Bring all that back with you at once. Smith will land you at the nearest point to the High Street. Don't waste a second. Casts of those prints must be taken by daylight. If I'm not here, look for us above. And Smith, buck up, and wait afterwards here to take us off again. Got all that?"

"Look here, Moh," Gorham said, worried, as the boat shot away, "this introduces an absolutely new factor into the case!"

"But you were seeking traces of someone who climbed up all round the face of that cliff! Your eyes never left it!"

"That was sheer routine. Besides, I'm tracing Robin Tennant's movements yesterday morning. But he couldn't have left your tracks. And you heard what Smith said of his swimming form. He is a smallish boy, takes nines in shoes, I should say, with small, neat hands and feet. You measured those prints by your own?"

Mr. Moh nodded calmly.

"Mine are eight inches in length. These are half as long again. You believe young Tennant was in this murder?"

"He was here, on this very spot, by his own statement, at five forty that morning. He'd met deceased twice before, alone here. He lied to me about the time he reached a garage later in the morning. Put it back an hour at least. And has three hours, from five forty to eight forty, absolutely unaccounted for. And under questioning he let out he had seen the girl's green coat on a boulder here spread to dry when the tide was *coming in*, though previously he had sworn that he left this place at six six! How does all that strike you?"

"He saw that green coat—after six eight—and it disappeared after! That is an essential clue. A key-piece of the mystery. But the rest, with regard to young Tennant, is scarlet herrings, my dear Gorham, if I may humbly give opinions, wildly, without data to go on."

"You will in any case. And they couldn't be wilder than my own at the moment," said Gorham crossly. "Why are you so certain he is guiltless? The size of his hands cuts him out as principal. It required a hand with a reach as large as mine to inflict those bruises round the neck and arm. Rosalind's could just have done it. Robin's is too small. But why discount him even as accessory?"

"Because the wrong woman was murdered in that case," Mr. Moh said with simplicity. "The dead one he loved. It is the survivor he hates. On those stairs on Monday, shock rent all disguise from his soul. At one sister he looked with passionate worshipfulness. From the other he recoiled with shrinking disgust, as a person whose stomach somersaults inside at contact with a loathly grub!"

"Then how the dickens do you account for his behaviour at the inquest?" Gorham demanded. "Why bellow an offer of marriage at a person you regard as a loathly grub? He stuck by her afterwards, too, as you'd expect a decent lover to do, till she bit his hand."

But Moh refused to be convinced, for deprecatingly, but with unaltered firmness, he flatly dissented.

"I heard him in court, and his motive highly defeats me. But the truth is as I said. When you see primitive truth—if only in a lightning flash—it cannot be mistaken."

"Then, if you are right, and he found he'd fallen in love with Lydia after getting engaged to her sister, did it strike you that Lydia returned it? I mean, did she love him back, or was she playing him up, or actually trying to fence him off?"

"She turned on him—whoof! sharply, as a woman slaps a child who blabs a secret—absently—a hasty slap—so, as to a tiresome child. I cannot speak with certainty of the woman, Gorham. She babbled and laughed to Sampson as we descended the stairs, but with a tongue divorced from her mind. Only this I felt, while the boy and the tiger-girl were obsessed with feeling, she was engaged only with secret thought as one who looked backwards and forwards over some private plan that might need readjustment . . .

because the boy in his folly had exposed a link of it? I don't know. But certainly it was not the assault that bothered her. It was something connected with what had led to it. They were excited, but she was cool, calculating . . . a secretive woman, with smooth, round cheeks, but experienced eyes."

"Robin had pledged his word to the other girl, at any rate," Gorham muttered thoughtfully. "His conduct this morning—and later to me—might be simply a desperate attempt to keep his word to her. My chief remarked that he didn't seem to be shirking his fences. Perhaps that was what he meant." He was pacing the ground, his eyes scrutinizing the sand and shingle for confirmation, however slight—of Tennant's statement. "Those are big boulders there—that group the tide is lapping at now. He said he stood and smoked a couple of cigarettes where he couldn't see the coat. Only spotted it from above. About here that might be true." He went across and spread out a newspaper on one of the rocks, putting stones on it to keep it in place, then tested its invisibility from other parts.

"Hullo!" He stooped and picked up the stub of a cigarette.

"Egyptian. Mel . . . presumably Melachrino. An expensive brand. Possibly chucked here by some chance passer-by, of course. His brother smokes Navy Cut and his father Osbornes. He said he bought gaspers at the garage, so probably he uses them habitually. Nothing else here." He put the stub away in an old envelope, however, for future reference. "Collect that paper, Moh, and come along. Let's try and find a reasonable path up on to that hill. Bond ought to be back soon with the plaster."

CHAPTER XIII

THE CLOSEST SCRUTINY of the footprints on the extreme point of the promontory added nothing to the clear account of them given by Mr. Moh.

That a tall man had ascended the hill-side, crouched flat on the ground where, invisible himself, he could, with head cautiously raised, survey the entire panorama of the Bay and open sea spread out beneath, had some time later risen and walked back about twenty yards towards the green growth of shrubs and stunt-ed trees which increased in density and height as it approached the landward end of the plateau, and thence, running back, had taken a clean header from almost the highest part of the cliff, whose bulging face Gorham had studied from the boat, into the deep water beneath, was plainly written in the thin layer of soft soil which clothed the rock. For in spite of most of the outlines being blurred by winds that had blown its sandy particles about, sufficient shape remained to make the direction of the footsteps indubitable. Where the shelter of an isolated furze bush had pro-tected it from the mischievous play of the breeze, Gorham was able to take a single perfect cast of the right foot, and during the tedious process of hardening, he drew a careful diagram of the di-rection of the remaining impressions, then walked with Moh and Bond to halt beside the last footmarks which faced the land.

"Did he come back here simply to get extra momentum before taking that tremendous spring? What do you think, Moh?"

The gaze of the Chinese detective was on the dense greenery ahead. "I think no," he said finally.

"You think he heard someone in that undergrowth, and chose the danger of that dive rather than the danger of being seen up here? Seems to me that's the only adequate reason for the fright-ful risk he took—unless, of course, he doesn't enter into our busi-ness at all, in which case it was probably a genuine case of suicide. What's your opinion, Bond?"

The young policeman flushed with pleasure at being referred to. "It occurred to me, sir," he stammered, with becoming diffi-dence, "that it must have been a chap who knew this coast well, because he chose deep water to dive off into. If he'd gone off into the Bay, it is deep water all right, but then he'd have been up against the currents."

"And courted the publicity which we assume it was his object to avoid," Gorham added dryly. "But yes, go on."

"Yes, sir. But to the right of that place where he climbed up—over there—there's a much easier take-off, the face of the cliff is flatter, and it's less in height by twelve feet. But the rock floor of the sea slants upward there and the depth rises from twenty feet to barely six. It was there the casualty happened that Smith mentioned; the man's head was smashed to pulp. If this diver had gone in from there, just choosing the place from the look of it, not knowledge, he'd have crashed too."

Gorham nodded approvingly.

"Quite a good point, Bond. One that should narrow down our search. This place has 'trespasser' notices all round it in addition to a six-foot paling. How many points are there that afford entrance?"

"The rocky path up from the cove, sir, and another by a break in the fence above the road, and the easiest from that path that skirts the Villa garden, where it is only wired, sir. And I noticed yesterday morning that two of the posts are down. But the brambles have run so wild all over the ground there are no paths inside, and there's no easy walking, though some bits are easier than others."

They spent a strenuous half-hour peering about in the wilderness of bushes and trees, among which brambles of every variety had twined their formidably armed trailers, and found little to reward their exploration but lacerated hands and ankles.

Mr. Moh, regardful of his party suit, politely withdrew from the search, and sat down on his outspread pocket handkerchief to watch the translucent, changing hues that heralded sunset refracted in shining tracts of light from the skies behind him across the darkening surface of the sea.

From this aesthetic enjoyment he glanced up with a bland smile when Gorham rejoined him, plucking a thorn from the back of a much scratched hand.

"That was a job that required gauntlets," he said ruefully. "Yes, there's plenty of evidence that people have been in there recently, and one spot, close by that path among the rocks that we came up by, where someone cached his clothes. Several threads of gent's underwear, summer weight, were caught on a thorn of the bush that covered the ditch he used." He exhibited the fragment before placing it lovingly in his pocket-book. "But as so far there is no indication of the time at which those prints of yours, or the tramplings in that thicket, were made, otherwise we have got nothing definite whatever, except"—he added severely, as Bond, dishevelled, and bleeding from vicious scratches on hands and arms, yet looking intensely cheered, appeared bearing a large cricket-bag—"the disgusting ignorance of young Jimmy Bond here, who, though he is the son of J. J. Bond, one of the smartest detective officers the Yard ever had, has actually never heard of *Hippophae Rhamnoides!*"

Mr. Moh looked horror-stricken.

"Can you beat it!" he ejaculated.

"You can't. I led that six-foot specimen of brawn and brain-lessness up to an eight-foot high bush with pretty, silvery sort of leaves all over it, and covering roughly ten foot of ground where there was grass instead of bramble, and said, just to test him, mind you, 'Is that *Hippophae Rhamnoides?*' And he said he'd never heard!"

"I'm sorry, sir, but it's a fact I hadn't. It is covered with bright orange berries in autumn, but I've never heard its name. But the Vicar would know!"

"What the Vicar knows is neither here nor there. It is the gross ignorance of J.J.'s offspring that I regret."

He knelt down and, after carefully extracting the dry cast from its mould of earth, packed it in the open bag in a nest of crumpled newspaper. "Now carry that down to the boat," he ordered, "and if you so much as get it chipped I'll make you sorry you were born. Also," he added without a trace of the good-humoured raillery with which he had hitherto treated the young man, to soften the severity of his warning, "you have been trained so far in a bad school for discretion, young man. Keep a still tongue in your head from now on, for if you don't, I'll break you, understand?"

"Yes, sir."

"Then go ahead. And don't mention even the ground you've covered with me beyond my hearing."

"Your search really revealed nothing?" Moh asked as they followed the stalwart figure of the constable through the fringe of the undergrowth.

"Nothing except that thorn-bush," was the cryptic response. "There seem to have been at least three men inside this enclosure since the last rains, judging by the trampling of those infernal trailers. One—the diver—came up from the cove first to cache his clothes, then to collect them. Someone else had got in through the broken fencing from the bank above the road. And one may have both entered and gone out by that path that runs by the Villa garden. But it was impossible to get any footprints. In the mud of that path—the only possible surface that would retain them—the trampling of the police when they conveyed the body from the hut to the ambulance has obliterated all earlier impressions."

"The naked man," said Mr. Moh thoughtfully, "having survived his dive, swam round to the cove, climbed up and dressed again, and then—"

"Probably waded along the shore carrying his boots and socks till he thought it safe to put them on, and either stroll on along the shingle, or climb up and strike off across country."

"If he survived," said Mr. Moh again. "If he died, another might have collected his clothes."

"Quite so. It's all conjectural so far."

He sat in impenetrable silence after putting on the shoes he had removed to wade through the shallow water to the boat, during the quick run to the pier. But, allowing the others to precede him up the steps, he lingered for a word with Smith.

"Look here, Smith. I want certain enquiries put through among the sailors and boatmen down here. Are you game to take on the job?"

"Glad to, sir. Anything I can."

"Well, first I want to learn if anyone connected with the waterside here has ever come across any swimmer—bar Whittiker, of course—capable of diving off that point. Anyone whatsoever. That dive may have no connection whatever with the recent murder, you know. If so, the sooner it is eliminated from the case the better. You have never heard of anyone but Whittiker. But someone else might have heard gossip that you missed. Get that? Secondly, I want a list of everyone who took out or brought in any boat between, say, six p.m. Monday and ten a.m. Tuesday. Visitors, trippers, residents, anyone, for whatever purpose."

"I can get that easy enough, sir. My brother-in-law is the biggest chap in the boat-hiring business hereabouts and nothing much goes on along shore that he doesn't know. The tally of anyone what hired craft or reported with same. And any notions regarding diving-birds I can pick up. Where shall I report?"

"I'll be along the breakwater wall about ten thirty. Wait for me. But, mind, not a hint of that latest dive from the point must be allowed to get abroad—or any suggestion that we have been searching up there!"

"Ay, ay, sir. Ikorna."

Gorham had had a quick bath and a still quicker dinner, and was finishing his coffee in the dining-room of the Grand Hotel, when he was informed that two gentlemen were waiting to see him in the private sitting-room which the manager, glad to have the London detective as a guest, yet anxious to keep police business from disturbing the cheerful holiday atmosphere of his hotel, had now placed at his disposal.

The chief inspector, who expected to be confronted with reporters, was agreeably surprised to find instead two elderly gentlemen whose appearance suggested the legal profession, but who obviously belonged to a class and type very far remote from those of Harcourt Burroughs, the last solicitor he had interviewed.

Mr. Henry Assheton—the spokesman gave his name at once—was a man of prepossessing countenance in which the constant exercise of a keen intellect, a life's experience in the extravagances and foibles of human nature, and the discipline in intricate and occasionally petty legal detail had not vanquished, had indeed enhanced the unmistakable signs of broadminded and cultured intelligence and kindly humour.

"This is my cousin and professional colleague—Mr. George Assheton, from London. And as you can guess, our business with you has reference to the tragedy yesterday morning," he said, when the brief preliminary interchanges were concluded, coming to the point with a promptness that increased the favourable impression his appearance had created in the chief inspector's mind.

"If it tends to throw light on the investigation I shall be grateful for anything that you can tell me, and so far as possible, I need not assure you that any communication you make will be treated as confidential," Gorham replied.

Mr. Assheton smiled. Mr. George Assheton, who appeared to hold merely a watching brief, nodded grave acknowledgment.

"The facts I have to communicate are bound to come out to the persons concerned within a few days at most. I am not, therefore, in any sense violating professional confidence, though, in view of the curious circumstances, I am anticipating their publication by a few hours, and shall be obliged if, so far, you will regard my statement as confidential."

"You must realize that if it bears on the actual murder I can't bind myself," Gorham said with honest hesitation. "You understand as well as I do that fresh facts that turn up in a criminal enquiry have to be investigated—and possibly published—at once, or they are apt to lose their value. With that reservation, as I said, you may rely on my discretion."

"Thank you. The facts I have to relate have, so far as I am aware, no direct bearing on the murder whatever, so my confidence is safe.

"But first I must explain how my cousin and I come to be associated in this affair. The legal firm of which I am now senior partner in Harborough was founded by our great-grandfather in 1790, and has since descended from father to son in the direct line. My father's twin brother, however, a man of extraordinary brilliance, preferred London to the more restricted sphere of a county practice, settled there, and made a great reputation and—er—fortune, which unhappily he did not live long to enjoy. When he died—he was a widower—my cousin, then a boy, returned to my father's house, and we were brought up together as brothers, and though in due course he entered the legal firm in Chancery Lane, and I was articled to my father, we have remained in close touch with each other, both in our personal relations and also in the interchange of a certain amount of business. Now for the point. In April last I received a communication from a Mr. Harcourt Burroughs of Whitesands, introducing a friend of his, Miss Lydia Torrington, who desired to make her will. To my chief clerk, who interviewed her on her first visit to the office, Miss Torrington submitted an already written note of her testamentary wishes, and it was immediately obvious why Mr. Burroughs preferred that she should employ our professional services rather than those of his own firm, for after payment of two trifling legacies of fifty pounds each to a sister and uncle, Mr. Burroughs was named as residuary legatee." He paused, and Gorham sat up in his chair. But Mr. Assheton held up his hand.

"One moment. I have not yet reached the extraordinary part of this affair. The document was drawn up in accordance with her instructions, which were quite definite. But on the occasion of her second visit, when she came to append her signature, as she and her family were entirely unknown to me, I made it my business to interview her myself, in order to satisfy myself that she fully understood what she was doing."

"Did it strike you that she was being coerced?"

"There was no suggestion of coercion whatever," was the dry response. "The young woman came by herself on each occasion, and she impressed both Mr. Gray and myself as a person of singularly acute business instincts and determined character. However, her note of instructions, which was in her own handwriting, contained certain phrases which suggested possible dictation, and, in the slightly unusual circumstances, I talked the matter over with her.

"Her manner was perfectly frank. She assured me that her personal estate was small, derived from a legacy inherited from a Miss Annabel Torrington, an aunt of her father, that her sister and uncle, her only living relatives, were persons of ample means, and needed no further provision, the small legacies being merely in the nature of tokens of good will. That she was engaged to Mr. Burroughs, but for private reasons which, I gathered, were connected with his professional career, the marriage could not take place till the late autumn, and she wished to make temporary provision in his favour meantime. With that she signed the document, which she left in our charge, and I heard nothing more of the matter till this afternoon."

"You read of her death yesterday morning?"

"Certainly. I was in the act of communicating by letter with Colonel George Rouncey, who, I omitted to state, was appointed executor under her will, when the afternoon edition of the *Harborough Gazette* came out with a definite statement of foul play, and the startling news that a representative of Scotland Yard had come down to take over the investigation. I decided to await the finding of the inquest which Mr. Gray attended on my behalf, with directions to arrange an immediate interview with Colonel Rouncey on its conclusion. This he was unable to do, as you will understand, and he returned with word of Colonel Rouncey's grave illness. I telephoned the County Hospital and learned that he was still unconscious, and would be incapable of business for some time. As it thus appeared likely that I might have to take preliminary action, as an initial step I 'phoned to Mr. George Assheton to send me particulars of Miss Annabel Torrington's will."

"In order to form some idea of the amount of the estate?"

"Exactly. My cousin instantly informed me that Miss Annabel Torrington had been a client of his firm, and, as he deemed the matter important, he would come down at once in person."

"I had seen a suggestion in *The Times* that the younger sister, Rosalind, was under suspicion. It was that that brought me down," said Mr. George Assheton, speaking for the first time. "But I'll mention that later. Go on, Henry, finish your side first."

"My cousin arrived early in the afternoon, but I was engaged, and we had not exchanged two words when Mr. Burroughs called on me and demanded to see Miss Lydia Torrington's will."

"You were right in believing that he knew its terms, then."

"Certainly he knew, or guessed, its terms." Mr. Assheton's tone grew formal. "I wish to make it quite clear, Chief Inspector, that I know nothing to the detriment of Mr. Burroughs. His conduct in regard to this matter of the will—one of the very few transactions in which we have come into contact—was professionally correct, though his manner during our brief interview today did not attract my admiration. My cousin was present in my office when Mr. Burroughs was shown in and made his singular demand.

"He became extremely brusque when I reminded him of my inability to disclose the contents of Miss Torrington's will in the absence of instructions from the executor, and before the formalities attendant on her death were fully complied with. He reproached me for treating him with unwarranted distrust, and inquired how long I proposed to hang up the settlement of the estate.

"I replied that I proposed to do nothing till the legal formalities arising from the inquest, and regarding the funeral, and the difficulties caused by the temporary incapacity of the executor to apply for probate, were first settled. I allowed him, in short, to realize that I was out of sympathy with the indecent haste he was displaying. He retorted that he was as well informed as I on the legal aspect of the case, but that no harm could possibly come of my giving him the confirmation—verbally—that he wanted, that he was residuary legatee, since Miss Torrington had herself told him that her estate was, roughly, £10,000. My reply was to ring and have him shown out. I will not disguise from you, Chief Inspector, that my temper was ruffled by the man's impertinence, but the really extraordinary point of the interview lay in that final statement of his. As soon as we had got rid of him I explained to my cousin, who had been a silent auditor of the discussion, about the young woman's previous visit, and he at once observed that she must have deliberately misled Burroughs, because her income of £500 was an annual charge upon Miss Annabel Torrington's estate, and the capital sum which it represented reverted on her death, as a matter of course, to her great-aunt's heirs."

"But what on earth could have been her object in trying to mislead you, Mr. Assheton?" Gorham exclaimed. "Burroughs—well, there are several explanations that might cover a deception in the case of Burroughs, but why had she tried to leave you with much the same impression, as I understand she did? Could she have misunderstood the facts of the case herself? Some women are hopeless muddlers when it comes to financial questions!"

"The young woman did not belong to the muddle-headed type," said Mr. Assheton dryly. "But she certainly conveyed the impression to me—I have since referred to the notes which I jotted down, according to my habit, immediately after our interview—that her fortune was at her own disposal, though she cleverly avoided making any definite statement of the actual sums involved, which, of course, at that time, was not a matter of interest to me. But my cousin will assure you that several letters received by him at the time of her great-aunt's death, seven years ago, make her knowledge indubitable."

"Quite," said Mr. George Assheton.

Gorham looked from one to the other, and then, with some hesitation, ventured on a leading question.

"Mr. Assheton," he addressed the London solicitor, "would you have any objection to explaining the reason for your interest in Rosalind Torrington? You said just now that it was on her account that you are down here."

"My interest is simply a sort of moral responsibility that I feel for the unfortunate girl, Mr. Gorham. I know nothing whatever about her part in this deplorable crime, but the long connection of my firm with the affairs of her family urged me to come down to see what could be done for her, that is, to discover if she were in need of help which I should be glad to give. But I felt that, to help effectively, I had best get in touch with you first and learn whether her situation is really as desperate as it would appear from the finding of the jury this morning. I have never met you before, but your reputation is not"—he smiled—"unknown to me, and it was a relief to find you in charge of the investigation."

"The evidence against her is serious," Gorham said frankly, "but my greatest difficulty so far is that Colonel Rouncey's breakdown has deprived me of my chief source of information about these two sisters. They seem to have lived here without forming any intimate acquaintance, and so far I have got nothing but gossip of a very unreliable type to go on."

"Do you mean that you doubt the justness of this morning's verdict?" Mr. Assheton asked with genuine anxiety, but Gorham hesitated.

"I can't say that. The evidence against her covered the facts so far as they are known. But the evidence is circumstantial only. It often is in cases of murder, of course. But, as you know yourself, a case built up on circumstantial evidence alone may appear absolutely safe and complete, as this one did to the jury, yet its very plausibility may veil some vital point that tears the whole theoretical case to pieces once it is detected and tested. At present I'm simply going over the whole surface of the case and checking up the constituent details, a job I'd much have preferred to complete before any arrest was made. But there our hand was forced. As I said, my difficulty is to get information about Lydia Torrington's past life. Enquiries are being pursued in various directions, but it is slow work with the small amount of data we have to go on. But if you would oblige me with any information you possess about the history and personality of these Torringtons, Colonel Rouncey— anyone connected with them, in fact—it would be of immense help. Did you, for instance, see these sisters or Colonel Rouncey yourself at any time?"

"The girls, no. Colonel Rouncey, yes, at the time of his wife's death, frequently."

"That was the time when he took these nieces of hers to live with him. Can you tell me how all that came about?"

"I had better begin at the beginning, with Miss Annabel Torrington, who was a client of ours for forty years," began Mr. George Assheton. "My personal acquaintance with her was slight because she had always been in the habit of consulting my father's partner, Mr. Williams, and regarded me, when I became a member of the firm, as an irresponsible youth entirely unworthy of trust in grave affairs. This opinion the passage of five and twenty years did nothing to eradicate, and when, on Mr. Williams' death, I inevitably became her rather diffident adviser"—a twinkle of humour lighted up his face—"she continued to treat me with severe and condescending reserve. In her way she was a fine old lady. She came of a long line of soldiers and had great pride in her ancestry. She was practically the last of her race, and centred her affections on the two children of her brother who was killed in Afghanistan, whom she adopted and brought up. Annie, the girl, married George Rouncey, a distant cousin, at the age of eighteen, and spent most of her life afterwards in India. The boy, Ralph, was naturally the object of his aunt's most passionate pride, but his career was tragic. A lad with a brilliant future before him, he entered the Army, and almost immediately contracted a reckless marriage with a Miss Price, a governess in his colonel's family whom he met in Malta. She was a pretty and attractive person, but unhappily of very unstable character. From the first there were money difficulties, for the young woman was wildly extravagant, and Ralph was dependent on his aunt. When his regiment was ordered to South Africa he sent her home with her baby, Lydia, and a year later rejoined her, a physical wreck from enteric. They lived together in an obscure village in Wales, but, well, there was a second child by that time—and before his year's sick leave was up Ralph shot himself. Miss Torrington never recovered from the shock of her nephew's death. She refused implacably to hold any communication with the widow, whose conduct it was, as she believed, that had driven him to his disgraceful end. She went abroad for some years, and finally took up her residence in Torquay, where she passed the latter years of her life in strict retirement."

"What happened to the widow?"

"As my client refused to continue the liberal allowance she had made to her nephew, she was left practically penniless, and, I'm afraid, resorted to the most dubious means to keep herself going. The Rounceys, however, who had no children of their own, were consistently kind, though they were not rich, and sent home frequent cheques, which were seldom applied, I fear, for the benefit of the children as they were intended to be. Mrs. Torrington acquired the habit of begging money on her sister-in-law's account from Mr. Williams, and more than once he settled her debts. But she refused to part with the children when he urged that they should be placed at a reputable school, well aware that with them she would lose her only hold on the Rounceys. To cut a long and sordid story short, after various deplorable connections with men she married a second time, and was again widowed. Her own death occurred shortly before the Rounceys' final return to England, and it is at this point, on the death of Mr. Williams, that my personal acquaintance with them began, close on thirteen years ago. Mrs. Rouncey was in an advanced stage of cancer when they arrived. Her illness was the immediate cause, indeed, of their return, but during the voyage the disease made rapid strides, and though they took up their residence at first in rooms in Lancaster Gate which had been found and prepared for them by Mrs. Hervey, the Colonel's sister, the poor lady was soon removed to a nursing-home in Wigmore Street, where, some weeks later, she died.

"When her husband first called on me he was in a state of bewildered grief over her condition. There were various business matters to be carried through with regard to his wife's money affairs, which we had always managed since we had arranged her marriage settlement, but his chief preoccupation was about these girls about whom his poor wife was fretting deeply. She had been devoted to her brother, and the pitiful fate of the two children was constantly in her mind. He said that nothing would satisfy her but that he should go down to Swansea, where they had been living for some years in a lodging-house kept by people named Bull, to discover their circumstances for himself.

"Some days later I called in Lancaster Gate and was shocked to learn from the Colonel, who had just returned from the nursing-home, that a medical examination which had taken place that morning had revealed that no operation was possible, and that the end was a matter of weeks only. To distract his thoughts from his absorbing grief I remained with him and questioned him about the Welsh journey.

"He gave me an appalling account of the girls' forlorn condition. It seemed that they had frequently been left for months at a time in the charge of these Bulls. Bull himself was an ex-prize-fighter, a coarse but fairly decent fellow according to his lights, but the woman was a hopeless drunkard, and he was also having trouble with a son who lived at home, but whom Rouncey did not see. Lydia was seventeen, her sister a few years younger. Both were supposed to be attending a cheap school in the town, but actually they were running absolutely wild. The lodging-house was dingy and empty, and Bull, between worry over his son, whom he described in forcible but unrepeatable terms, and helplessness to control the girls, whom he had simply kept under his roof from good-nature, was at his wits' end. His one desire was to get them off his hands once for all. He told Rouncey frankly that he'd be thankful to be rid of them, money or no money, and the upshot was that Rouncey brought them away with him then and there. His wife was in no condition to be troubled, so he took them to his sister. Mrs. Hervey took them in, though with extreme reluctance. She was the widow of a doctor, in straitened circumstances, I understood, but her profound objection to accepting charge of these girls arose from her dislike of bringing them into contact with her own boy, a nice lad of twelve. However, she kept them for a month, and presently persuaded the head-mistress of a reputable school in Essex to take them as pupils. Eventually Rouncey, who had no ties in England, and who disliked London, took a lease of Melita Villa, and apparently gave them a home there."

Gorham nodded.

"That makes it very clear, and bears out everything I have been able to get myself. But now to come back to the money question. Did Miss Annabel Torrington take notice of them after the death of the objectionable mother?"

"Miss Annabel Torrington came up from Torquay during Mrs. Rouncey's illness, and it was then that she made her will. She utterly refused to notice the existence of the younger girl, but on rather strong representation being made to her that the expenses for school fees and so on were likely to fall heavily on Rouncey, who really had no duty towards them at all, and who accepted the burden of their maintenance simply out of affection for his wife, she consented to allow Lydia, Ralph's actual daughter, £100 a year. But the terms of her will were strict. After her great-aunt's death, Lydia was to be paid an annual allowance of £500 as a charge on her estate. In the event of Lydia marrying this income was to be continued to her, and to be carried on to her eldest legitimate child until such child attained the age of twenty-one, on which the trust was to be wound up and capital and interest to pass absolutely to the child. In the event of Lydia dying without legitimate issue the trust was again to be wound up and capital and interest to pass absolutely to Colonel George Rouncey, or, failing him, to his nephew, George Herman Hervey. Is that clear?"

"But this situation has now arisen, and, my word, it is the Colonel, not Rosalind, who benefits by Lydia's death!"

"Exactly. Miss Annabel Torrington was an old lady of rigid moral views. From hints she let drop to me when I tried to argue the matter and persuade her into making some provision for the unfortunate younger child, she certainly ascribed her nephew's suicide directly to the scandal of its birth, and bitterly resented the fact that it was permitted to bear his surname. I believe she even quarrelled with Rouncey before they finally parted after his wife's funeral, because he refused to make any open difference between the two sisters. Whether the younger girl is aware of the facts of her birth I don't know, but—to return to the immediate object of our call this evening—I can definitely vouch for the fact that Lydia was perfectly well aware that she possessed only a life-interest in her income when she drew up that farcical will in favour of this fellow Burroughs. I resent quite as strongly as my cousin does her attempt to make Mr. Henry Assheton a party to the deception."

"She could not guess that she was to be murdered."

"No. But by coming to me," intervened Mr. Henry Assheton, "she made me an innocent participant in the deception which she was practising on Burroughs. For he was obviously satisfied by her action, though I grant on very flimsy premises, that the promise she had made of the reversion of her estate should her death intervene before their marriage was consummated was a substantial one. The affair, which, at the time, seemed a perfectly normal piece of business, takes on an extremely fishy aspect in the light of the young woman's knowledge of her financial position. But for Colonel Rouncey's illness I should at once have placed the document in his hands and washed my hands of the affair. In the present circumstances, in view of the incapacity of the responsible executor, George and I agreed that my plain duty was to place such information as I possessed before the police-officer in charge of the murder investigation."

He rose to take leave, but the London solicitor detained him for a final word.

"Mr. Gorham, I can rely on you not to publish any of the details I have given you of Rosalind's early circumstances, can't I?" he said, his face softening compassionately, as it had done with every reference to her. "I knew, of course, that you were certain to ferret them out eventually for yourself. That is true, is it not?"

"Naturally I am having all possible enquiries made—in Swansea and elsewhere," Gorham admitted, with a slight smile. "I quite understood that you were—well—just taking the bull by the horns—in being so frank."

"The fact is she is one of those unfortunates to whom society has never given a fair chance. Think of her, a neglected little child left to coarse, vulgar people like the Bulls during her earliest, most sensitive years, and owing her rescue from such degraded surroundings to the fortuitous charity of Rouncey! I learn that it is her undisciplined temper which is now the most telling point against her. But when was she ever given a chance to learn decent habits, or self-restraint, poor child! And now, in this terrible situation that has arisen, owing to poor Rouncey's illness, she is left utterly forlorn and alone! I cannot but feel that such a forlorn creature demands the championship of every decent citizen whom a safe and assured position in society has prevented from personally experiencing her temptations."

"I wish the members of the jury this morning had held your views on citizenship," Gorham said grimly. "But rest assured, nothing you have told me will be used against her. As for her defence, the chief constable, Major Tennant, is arranging for it, and I suggest you should settle things with him."

"Tennant? He hasn't much cause to love that connection. But how exactly like him to step into the breach! Yes, yes, I'll see him at once—if only to congratulate him on the gallant way that lad of his played up this morning! A fine boy, a thoroughly fine boy!" His pleasant face glowed with warm feeling as he went out.

When they were gone, Gorham stood perfectly still, and exclaimed, "Damn' fool!" very loudly, causing a waiter who was entering to start nervously, whereon Gorham laughed and kindly explained that he didn't refer either to his late visitors or to the waiter, but to himself.

The waiter said, "Yessir."

CHAPTER XIV

AT SIX O'CLOCK on Thursday morning, Major Tennant, who had been at work half the night, was sweating in a troubled dream. He was searching desperately through innumerable pitch-dark corridors in some strange house to find Robin before he shot himself, always hearing him running and sobbing ahead, and never able to catch up with him. . . .

The telephone by his bedside shrilled suddenly in his ear. He sat up, his heart missing a beat, and grabbed the instrument with his thoughts racing forward to meet disaster.

"He's done it! I was crazy to let him out of my sight! This is poor Will to tell me. How can I ever face his mother?"

But it was not Will. It was Chief Inspector Gorham.

"Yes? The chief constable speaking? Great Scott, man! Why at this deathly hour?"

His tone was light, but his face was chalk-white still, though his thumping pulses slowed down to something nearer normal as he listened.

"Sorry to disturb you so early, but I've got a crowded day before me. Besides, it's the rule in this case for everyone to rise at dawn, and I've caught the infection. I'm going out now to that cottage on Bramwood Heath. It occurred to me that you would like to come."

"You mean you want to be certain I don't suborn your damned witnesses against my lad behind your back!" thought Tennant. But aloud he said casually, "You've traced the cottage then? Well, as you have finally wrecked my slumbers I don't mind if I do."

"Good, sir. I'll be at your gate in five minutes."

"Detective Inspector Manning, who came down on my train on Tuesday, located this cottage for me yesterday, but he did no more," Gorham explained when they met. Heavy rain had fallen in the night, and the morning was grey with lowering clouds and a northeast wind. "But I had to send Manning back to town last night, to follow up a job there."

Tennant suppressed a flicker of anger that common sense told him was as futile as it was unjustified. In Gorham's place he must have tested every link of Robin's damningly inconclusive story, and kept him tailed, too, which, he supposed, was Manning's present job. But to discuss Robin was more than he could bring himself to do.

He sat in hostile silence till the castle-crowned mass of St. Roche emerged into view, grim and massive against an ominous sky.

"Hasn't it occurred to you," he said, flicking one hand upward towards the towering rock, "that that fracas there really tells in favour of that miserable girl?"

Gorham nodded, his eyes on the ribbon of road ahead.

"That it is assuming incredible stupidity on the part of a criminal to suppose that first assault should have been followed up at once with a second? Yes, that struck me. But as a plea, it tells against the prisoner, sir. She has displayed abnormal stupidity all through. Take her conduct at the inquest yesterday. Could anything have been more densely stupid? She was in a blind funk, of course, and it came out in tearing and biting the very people who wanted to stand by her. But after a display like that in public no argument that was based on the natural caution of a normal, reasonable woman or man would hold water for a second. No, if a case is to be built up which is to clear her it will have to be done without her help."

"God knows where the material is to come from, then."

"I'm taking the line that promises most—the life of the victim herself. People aren't murdered without some cause. Putting the sister arbitrarily aside, who else connected with her had both the motive and the necessary chance? I've got a mass of new material to work on at least, and I'd like to go over the whole case with you later and hear your views. But let us get on with this present job first."

Tennant relapsed into sombre thought again. The last two days had revised his first impression of Gorham as the typical London policeman promoted to higher rank, big, good-natured, sensible. That first slightly contemptuous conception was giving way before a realization of solid strength in the man. He was no fool, patient, inexorably persevering . . . indefatigable in pursuit.

Forty-eight hours of sleeplessness and anxious, wearing un-certainty had strained his nerves, and suddenly he felt a threat of panicky fear. Was he to see this bulky juggernaut of a fellow pulverizing the slender bones of his lad's body, crushing it out of its bright semblance of vitality—breaking it? . . .

They turned from the coast road on to the heath and, without pause or hesitation, Gorham followed the twists and turns of various paths till, on the edge of a wood of dark Scotch firs, he drew up before a cottage.

"This must be the place, I think. There's the pig-sty on one side."

A little, bent old woman came to the door before they reached it and peered up at them with birdlike eagerness which, when she saw strangers, was quenched in disappointment.

"Morning, mother. Were you expecting someone?" Gorham asked.

"Hearing a car I just stepped out thinking it might be a young gentleman. Were you wanting something, sir?" She looked at him shrewdly. "Water for the engine, maybe?!"

Gorham chuckled. "You are well up in mechanics, aren't you?" She laughed with a touch of pride. "I know now they want water, though I did think it was only petrol they used up. But a young gentleman that come along Tuesday, he asked me for a drop of water, so now I know different. You lives and learns, and I was always one for learning."

"Was that the night you sat up with your pig?"

The bright eyes in her wrinkled old face lit up with excite-ment. "Then you know that young gentleman, and he telled you about Rupert!" she cried. "Come in, sirs, come in! Is he coming himself?" They followed her into the tiny, low-ceilinged kitchen, which Gorham's bulky figure seemed to fill up.

"Yes, I heard about young Rupert. Hullo, is that he?"

But the diminutive black piglet who occupied the patchwork mat by the hearth did not stay to be admired. With a whisk of his curly tail he dived between Tennant's legs into the outer world.

"He's not used to strangers, sir," the old lady said with an apologetic look at each which deprecated the infant's abrupt withdrawal from their midst. "But it's balm to me to see him so brisk, so you must kindly excuse him!"

"He certainly seems pretty spry now!"

"And he is, thanks to the young gentleman!" she cried. "But if you'd seen him Monday night! All the hours I sat with him in my lap dozing and jerking awake, and wondering if he'd last till morning! And I see the young gentleman's car out there by the wood all in among the bracken, at sunrise, and yet I was that dejected I scarce gave it a look, never guessing how he would act by me, and when he come up and asked for water he took and looked at the mite I had for warmth wrapped up in my skirt. And he says, 'Grannie,' he says, 'poor old Rupert looks a bit passy, what about trying him with a drop of whisky?' and with that he goes back and fetches his flask, and, 'I don't suppose he's a teetotaller,' he says. And with me holding his little head all limp-like so it brought tears to my face to see one so perky reduced to this, and he pours a drop down his throat and a quiver runs through his frame and he splutters and opens his eyes, and the young gentleman, he says, 'Go it, young 'un, this is the stuff to give the troops!' And he pours down some more and the little one he stirs so brisk it was a joy, and we wraps him in my shawl in the wood box, and I makes a cup of tea, and the young gentleman takes my bucket to his car, and he didn't use all the water either, because of me having to fetch it from the pump at Bramwood Corners, him being so thoughtful it was an example. And before he goes he says, 'Good-bye, Grannie, and don't you go howling any more over Rupert; he'll live to be a stout fellow yet. And thanks for the tea!'"

The delighted joyous play of expression by which with gnarled hands and wrinkled features and twinkling eyes she lent dramatic intensity to the narrative so breathlessly poured out touched and held both men, for her confiding trust in their sympathy was childlike. Then she added, grieved: "I wish he hadn't went so quick. But it's to visit his brothers and sisters. And they are as fine a litter as you'd see anywhere in the land, and it's my son-in-law that says that, and he's a travelled man, that's been as far as Germany and Stowmarket! But it is nursing the one that I call Rupert after the name the young gentleman gave that makes it dear to me. When you watch a young one sick or in trouble, whether it be child or pigling, you feel that sort of aching yearning. . . . Is the young gentleman coming back to fetch his flask, sir? I've kept it very careful."

She opened a drawer in the dresser and brought out a bundle of clean, soft shawl from which she tenderly unwrapped a silver flask that the chief constable instantly recognized as his own. But though he nodded his recognition, he made no attempt to take it. Instead he opened his pocket case and, scrupulously avoiding meeting Gorham's eyes, took out an unmounted photograph and held it towards her.

She took it with a cry of pleasure.

"Why, it's the young gentleman himself! But it would be taken years ago, when he was gay and laughing, sir! But I'd know it for him anywhere still, with his head so sleek, and the way he holds it!"

"You saw his car out there at sunrise, you say. That would be some time before he came in?" Gorham put the question briskly.

Tennant had turned abruptly on his heel and was staring out across the hollyhocks in the patch of garden to green uplands of bracken that he could not see. He had taken that snapshot of Robin in the grounds of Oakleigh a bare week before. But the old dame was right. A week had robbed the lad of youth and gaiety and laughter. And his heart was aching over him with that helpless yearning she spoke of.

"Damn it, I must be falling into my dotage to sentimentalize with an old woman who sobs over a pig!" he thought savagely.

"Ay, the sun comes up early summer mornings, and he hadn't risen when I sees the car out there." She spoke absently, absorbed in the snapshot, then, obviously feeling that she was being impolite to her visitor, she looked up and glanced at the clock on the chimney-piece. "Just after four, sunrise is."

Gorham stared at his wrist-watch, then at the cheap clock, and back.

"Does your clock keep good time, Granny?"

"Never a minute out!" she replied proudly. "And my son-in-law, he says so too."

"But I see you don't hold with summer time," he said gently, "What does your son-in-law say to that!"

"The beasts keep God's time, and living here alone with them I does the same, sir. Gwennie, my daughter, laughs at me for being an old-fashioned one, but my son-in-law, he says it's best to do as I've always done, and he can make allowances."

"Well, well, it's lucky for me you do, or perhaps you'd have been in bed when I came, and we'd have missed this chat!" said Gorham good-humouredly. "But if your day begins an hour earlier than mine, mine lasts an hour longer, so we're quits. And, tell you what. You give me that gentleman's flask for him, and keep that photo instead, till he calls for it himself."

Tennant came slowly back, his glance travelling from the clock to Gorham's beaming face. He put five shillings down on the table, and smiled down into the wrinkled, sweet old face.

"Yes, keep it. I'd like you to. And good luck to young Rupert!"

"But aren't you going to peek at them all?" she cried, disappointed.

"Not this time," Gorham called over his shoulder. "But give them all my love, Granny!"

"I never thought I'd feel so indebted to a mortal pig outside a pork pie!" he added to Tennant as they walked towards his car. "But after this I'll feel it's sacrilege to eat one! Here is your flask, sir. No need to examine the tracks now. That clock lets your son out of the case altogether."

"You definitely believed he was in it, then?"

"Look here, Major Tennant, how far did your own suspicions extend?"

"I did not, for one single, asinine second, imagine that he had any part in the commission of that brutal crime!" he retorted.

"Guilty knowledge of Rosalind's intentions, or actual movements—accessory after the fact, eh, something more like that?"

"Well . . ."

"Exactly, sir. But if you heard that second edition of his story yesterday in detail, you must have got the suspicious discrepancies in it as clearly as I did. He could not possibly have been or communicated with Rosalind after seven o'clock, when a police watch was put on the Villa, and we know she was inside. Till, in fact, he saw her at the inquest twenty-six hours later. But from five forty onwards, when he stated he spent half an hour at that cove, where on two previous occasions, Saturday and Sunday, he had met deceased by arrangement, he could not give any account of his time. But there were two glaring discrepancies in his statement. He said he reached White's at eight ten. When according to Bill, the fellow who attended to him, it was after nine—"

"Yes, I got that from White's myself." Grimly: "They told me you'd been enquiring. But what was the other discrepancy?"

"The state of the tide. He said he spotted that green wrap on the boulder when he was quitting the cove at six five, when the tide was coming in. The tide wasn't due to turn till six eight. It left a narrow margin, of course, for sheer mistake. But if the water was noticeably advancing on shore so as to threaten to wash away the wrap it was obvious that he had remained at the cove at a later time than he had said. It gave me my first clue. Either he was lying without due care to details—and on that possibility I had to reckon—or he was mistaken either in the state of the tide or the time at which he was on the shore."

"This is quite interesting. Go on."

"I'd spent over half an hour on the south beach on Tuesday evening and noticed that, without definitely measuring the growing distance between the water's edge and one of the groynes—it was then going out—I'd hardly have discovered which way it was going. But when I spent ten minutes at the cove last evening I saw that the case there was different. The shore was strewn with rocks which each formed a tide mark in itself. Even if you weren't thinking about it, you couldn't help noticing the encroachment of the tide as it crept up round one after the other. Your eye took it in unconsciously. Well then, it followed that if he was right about the tide he was wrong about the time, and that fitted in with the fact that he was wrong again in the time he arrived at White's, an hour later than he imagined or, at least, stated. There remained a chance that he was speaking the truth in both cases, and the fault lay in the clock at the cottage by which he had set his watch."

"And you asked me to accompany you when you cleared up the point! Candidly, Gorham, did you guess the true explanation lay in the hour's difference between normal and summer time?"

The chief inspector shook his head with a broad smile. "Sorry I can't claim to be as bright as that. All I hoped was that I'd find the old lady's timepiece dead slow. Two days later it wouldn't cut much ice as evidence, perhaps, but it would show up her clock as entirely unreliable. What we did get was sheer luck. But luck that cuts the boy out of the case entirely. Because he did not reach the cove till the body had been brought ashore by Bond, and he couldn't possibly have communicated at any time afterwards with Rosalind. So that is that. Moh is perfectly right. That green wrap looks like being the essential clue. Robin was evidently used as a sheer cat's-paw."

"Damn it all, Gorham, I was just beginning to breathe freely again! What the devil do you mean now?"

"Why, look at the points for yourself!" Gorham, still beaming, halted at the Castle entrance. "On Saturday and Sunday, Lydia met him at the cove by arrangement, knowing her sister wasn't coming, but not telling him that, though she let Rosalind guess somehow that it was her young man she was going there to meet. Monday she went again. But he didn't. My idea is he stayed away because of some scruple he felt. But did Lydia tell Rosalind she'd been alone that morning? Not she. She wanted the girl to believe it was Robin she was constantly meeting round the corner. And they had a blazing row. But when it came to Tuesday morning Lydia wasn't leaving anything to chance scruples on his part. She extracted a definite promise from him that he would keep away from the cove. But she went herself, much earlier than usual, and I am ready to bet that she didn't mention his promise to Rosalind."

"But, Gorham, this is to cast a foul insinuation against that poor dead woman! Are you deliberately suggesting that she fanned her sister's jealousy of my boy's folly over her to screen an intrigue with someone else?"

"You may take it from me, she didn't go out at dawn on Tuesday morning to enjoy the pretty landscape from that cove by herself, sir. She certainly reached the cove, for she left her coat behind when she went out for her final, fatal swim. As I said, she used your boy as a cat's-paw. But that is as far as I've got. Whether the person she went there to meet came, and, if so, whether he committed the crime when they swam out together, there is no evidence to show either way. And now, I hope you are not hungry for breakfast, because I want to put a few questions to the custodian here before I run you home."

"Oh, my dear Gorham, don't mind me!" Tennant said airily as, finding the wicket open, they mounted the steep path of the glacis to the massive gateway where the oaken door stood already ajar.

"I begin to feel as if all those years when I imagined myself a singularly astute and able policeman were a mere dream. I am a child in your hands."

At the clang of the bell, Sampson came down the stairs, and behind his large figure trotted a small man who smiled radiantly at Gorham.

"Good morning, sir. You're an early visitor!"

"Don't blame me, Sergeant." The chief constable responded with his pleasant smile. "It is Inspector Gorham who is responsible."

"Morning, Mr. Moh! How came you here?"

"Having been invited to breakfast by Sergeant Sampson, latest and deeply cherished friend," Mr. Moh murmured, bowing. "I was transported hither on bike of Jimmy Bond, further winged by self's urgent longing to escape meal provided by relatives by marriage. But, Jimmy having to report for duty, I must return to Whitesands on flat feet, or 'bus."

"Don't keep the poor devils long, Gorham." Tennant was conscious of an appetizing odour that floated down from the sergeant's quarters. "That bacon of theirs will be ruined."

"Would you care to take something, sir?"

"No, thanks, I'm due home, and Gorham is coming with me. But he wants to ask you a question or two first."

"Among the visitors you had last Monday, do you remember a tall man in reddish-brown tweeds—rather loud in pattern—who came in rather late, after six, that is?" Gorham asked as Sampson turned to him. And Major Tennant, who had expected some reference to the now famous stairs episode, listened in surprise.

"You mean a fellow who came in a blue Rolls just on six thirty? Yes, I remember him right enough. He brought his car right up to the terrace there, and was insolent when I requested him to remove it to the car park. Told me if I was so b—y particular I could ask his pal in the car to shift it myself. And I did too. Made him take it right out on to the road again, so his lordship had to go and look for it when he left."

"Did he stop long in the museum?"

Sampson stared.

"Funny you should ask that! He only stood a second on that terrace giving a general glance round, and then went straight up. Most people look at the sea view there first. Being engaged with ordering away the car I didn't follow at once, but he was in the museum when I took the next party up, and I left him there. But he wasn't in the place above half an hour all told, I should say, because when I went down to the gate, after Mr. Robin left, the Rolls had gone."

"Can you give me any description of him?"

"Nothing more than I've just told Mr. Moh here. He was in my quarters when the row happened, and I mentioned it to him at the time. A big muscular-looking fellow, in his late-ish thirties. Hazel eyes set a bit too close together, pasty skin, square features and big jaw. Nasty brute to come up against in a free-for-all, I'd say. Expensive clothes and a wedding ring. Six feet, and putting on weight. Not bad-looking if you like 'em fleshy, but not a gentleman born. Spoke too well for that."

"That's a nasty one," Tennant murmured. "Do I speak too well to be a gentleman, Sergeant?"

Sampson chuckled, but stood to his guns.

"Wasn't casting aspersions, sir. You talk as if you'd never had to think about how you sounded, sir, it coming natural to you in the nursery, so to speak. That's what I meant. This chap spoke as if he'd had to listen to himself to make sure his vowels came out right. Like the announcers on the wireless. One got a lot of officers like that in the Kitchener armies."

"'Correspondence Course in English, Temp. Gents and Etoni-
ans specially invited,'" Tennant commented, his eyes twinkling,
"'by an Old Contemptible.' Now all Gorham wants to hear is the
type of underwear this fellow was sporting, then you can go back
to breakfast. Isn't that so, Gorham?"

"He didn't miss much!" the chief inspector responded, grinning. "Did you see this fellow speak to Miss Torrington—the one
who is dead—in the museum, Sergeant?"

"I did not see them speak, sir. When I took my new lot in, the
room was full already. She was looking at the jewel-case, and he
was looking at the weapons on the wall, and then strolling from
case to case. He was by the jewel-case, and she was worming her
way through the crowd to join Mr. Robin in the doorway, when
I cleared off to go back to Mr. Moh, who was waiting for me in
my quarters."

"Don't you ever allow people to look round by themselves?"

"Not in the museum, sir. There's too much portable property
there that I'm responsible for. But my missus was there all the
time. But she was busy and didn't notice this fellow in brown plus
fours to speak of. I saw him over all their heads, being annoyed at
his rudeness."

"I see. Now, what was the man in the car like?"

"Oh, he was an obliging sort of chap. He shifted at once when
I told him to, and said, 'Sorry, Sergeant, I didn't know you'd got a
car park here!' I didn't get much of his personal appearance except
that he'd got an odd sort of squint that gave him a comical look.
He was wearing plain grey, and didn't look tall, but then he was
stooping over the wheel. He was clean-shaven and much younger
than the other. The funny thing was his face seemed familiar, as
if I'd seen him before somewhere. But we get thousands of visitors here every year, and as I told Mr. Moh, I couldn't place him
beyond being pretty certain I hadn't seen him lately."

"It sounded as if he knew you too, though!"

"There's nothing in that. The sergeant's name figures in all
the guide-books. In fact," explained Tennant with malicious calm
while the custodian's bronzed countenance took on a rich crimson, "he is the prize exhibit of the place himself. Parents point
him out—Sergeant Sampson, V.C.—to their little children, and the

infants go away thinking he is the original hero who carried off the gates of Gaza."

"If the man was ever at the Castle before," Sampson said, pointedly ignoring the chief constable's chaff, "it's likely it was over three years ago. Before the car park was marked out. The place was altered a lot down behind the lodge where the gardener lives when the grounds were extended."

"Probably. Did you happen to notice the car's number?"

For the first time Sampson hesitated.

"I did read it, and I think it was XY903581," he said. "The car was a saloon, dark blue, but it looked as if it had seen years of service. Sorry I can't do better than that."

"You have been great! I wish there were a few more people about who observed details as you do! You ought to hear the vague descriptions we have to deal with generally! I've a hope that one of these fellows may give us a bit of useful information if I can run across them, but there's no need to tell anyone I am trying to trace them. You would be able to identify the man who cheeked you, I suppose?"

"Sure. And the one in the car, too, most likely, if I saw him again. Thanks, Chief Inspector! Glad to meet you. Used to know J. J. Bond of the C.I.D. well. A great chap he was!"

"Rather! Before my time at the Yard, unfortunately. But the Assistant Commissioner was talking of him yesterday. Now, Li Moh, what about coming along with me? I want to know," he added sternly, "what you think you are doing here at all."

"Am about to devour admirable bacon with sergeant and lady."

"Sorry to disappoint you, but you are not. You are coming with me!"

"You are coming to Oakleigh yourself, Gorham! Bring Moh along, too if you must, but for goodness' sake be quick about it! Our bacon is possibly quite as good as Sampson's, but the deuce of it is that it is ten miles further off! 'Morning, Sergeant! Sorry to rob you of your guest, but your loss is my gain."

The chief constable had suddenly become peremptory. He laid a firm hand on Gorham's arm, including Moh in the party with a nod that put an end to the argument. After a hurried word to Sampson, Li Moh trotted away at Gorham's heels.

Major Tennant, sitting alone during the swift drive to Oak-leigh, was thankful for the brief respite it gave him in which to sort out his tumultuous thoughts.

The personal problem of Robin remained one that time alone would heal. It was sheer unmitigated misfortune that a young man, cool-headed and self-sufficient, should owe the arousing of his emotional side to a vulgar young woman like Rosalind Tor-rington. But it was Lydia who had made use of the vague awak-ening of emotional susceptibility to quicken his feelings, appar-ently for her own calculating, cold-blooded purposes, into a blaze of fierce passion. The boy was crazy with shock at present, but it remained to be seen, when the first intensity of his youthful tragic passion had spent itself, how far the sterling grit in his character would reassert itself to give him back his normal balance.

"Work will be his best cure," Tennant thought. "I'll arrange to take him to Germany next week for a few weeks, and then settle him to start his apprenticeship at once. Meantime he is safe with Jessica in Cheniston Gardens. Her youngsters are as wholesome an antidote to those poisonous nieces of poor Rouncey's as you could well find. And now I can tackle Gorham and Braice on the official side of this infernal investigation without feeling green with funk as to what new idiocy of the lad their next report is going to disclose!"

"I am a grass-widower at the moment," he explained cheerfully to his oddly assorted guests as he led them into the hall at Oakleigh. "And my sons, as you know, are up in town at their aunt's house. So I suggest we have a quick breakfast and then get down to business. If you propose to take a general survey of the case, Gorham, what about ringing up Braice and requesting him to join us?"

"Just what I was going to suggest myself, Chief!" said Gorham genially. "His local knowledge would be very useful, and, besides, I want to ask him to set on foot enquiries regarding that Rolls."

"Good. There's the 'phone. Talk to him yourself while I go and change into something neater in gent's suitings than happened to me this morning when I leapt out of bed at your call."

CHAPTER XV

THE CHIEF CONSTABLE was inwardly amused to observe, when they adjourned to the office where Braice was awaiting them, that Gorham and his superintendent were already on easy terms. While he himself produced cigarettes, Gorham presented the Chinese, at whom Braice had glanced on his entrance with surprise.

"This is Mr. Li Moh, late of the Californian Police, who was present at the finding of the body, Super. He has been keen to meet you ever since the inquest yesterday."

"Tactful handling of rough crowds made deep impression!" Mr. Moh bowed reverently and Braice melted.

"There were only a few real toughs among them!" he said tolerantly. "We arrested three of the lads who smashed the Villa windows. One got seven days, and the others were let off with a fine. But with the prisoner's removal to Harborough the town has quite calmed down again." He turned to Major Tennant. "Mr. Mayhew is seeing her this morning, sir. They report her behaviour as very difficult, but Matron is doing her best."

"What's the latest of poor Rouncey?"

"I called at the hospital on the way here. He is still unconscious, but his pulse is steadier, and the house physician is hopeful he may definitely improve in a day or two. His own solicitor, Mr. George Assheton, is in Harborough, and he is settling the defence with Mr. Mayhew."

"Good. But the longer Rouncey is out of it the better for his own sake, poor chap. He has had a rough deal."

"I've put out a general enquiry for the car you spoke about this morning, Chief Inspector," Braice continued, "and as you said, there isn't much doubt it is the same Bond saw empty on the coast road at six thirty-seven a.m. Tuesday. Dark blue saloon, Rolls. But the number you gave me as reported by Sampson was XY903581, while in Bond's report it figures as XY903587. But he simply memorized it in passing."

"Probably Bond's is the correct figure. It struck me as smart of your constable to memorize it at all in the circumstances," Gorham said. "It was a piece of gratuitous observation that may be highly useful in connection with a statement obtained from Sampson this morning. By the way, with regard to that early leakage of information of which you spoke last night—"

"I've checked it. Sergeant Blackman is temporarily in charge at Whitesands police-station and is perfectly discreet. But all enquiries for the Rolls are proceeding from headquarters."

"Quite. If the car has any significance in the case it is wise not to give the occupants warning beforehand." He hurried away from the awkward subject of Norman's misbehaviour, which was a matter strictly for private discussion between Braice and his chief later. Fortunately the suspicions of the superintendent, who was on his mettle to establish his personal efficiency and that of his subordinates before the man from Scotland Yard who, whatever his reputation, was inferior to himself in official rank, had promptly alighted on Norman as the garrulous offender, without any hint from himself. "But, as I told you last night over the 'phone, certain fresh facts came to light last evening when I went over the scene of the crime that may, if they are relevant, give the investigation a new direction."

He proceeded to give a concise account of the discoveries on the promontory, to which the superintendent and Major Tennant gave keen attention.

"But, mind you, the connection of these footprints with the murder on Tuesday is at present only conjectural," he finished. "It is self-evident that that spectacular dive must have taken place in the early hours of the morning to have escaped observation, as apparently it did. But we did not examine the prints till Wednesday evening, and though their direction was clear, the outlines in every case but one where a bush had acted as windscreen were blurred. I could not swear that they had not been made on Wednesday morning, not Tuesday. Could you, Li Moh?"

He shrugged his shoulders.

"There had been no rain. But slight breeze had sported cheerfully with sandy soil. Twelve hours or thirty-six? The earlier date is probably the correct one, but the later is also possible."

"Exactly. But probability is not proof though it gives us a new and suggestive lead in the case."

"Highly suggestive, I should say," the chief constable observed with a smile. "I like your caution, Gorham. But have you any objection to giving Braice and me a review of the successive aspects under which this case has presented itself to you? I don't ask for any details that you may prefer to keep to yourself for the present, of course, but personally I am still back at that first view of it which culminated at the inquest yesterday morning, and I doubt if Braice is much forrader. Are you, Braice?"

"Well, no, sir, I'm not," he admitted frankly. "The circumstantial evidence against the prisoner seems to me complete still, and I can't see how these footprints work in the case. But," he added, "I'd very much like to hear."

Gorham frowned in thought for a moment.

"Well, take it this way," he said at length. "Coming to the case at first it seemed as clear as daylight that, as there was no one else, if you except young Bond, but the sister who was in the water at the time, she must have committed the murder. She had a strong motive, and the necessary skill in swimming, with the physical points of abnormal length of arm and large, muscular hands. But as an outsider, two points struck me from the first as queer. Why had the body been placed across the buoy? And why had the victim risen at dawn to swim round to that cove? It was the second question I concentrated on. In answer to numerous enquiries I found that, though she had often swum round the point before, it had rarely been so early. It had generally happened when a party of them were in the water together between breakfast and lunch. Yet this week, on Saturday and Sunday, she made this trip before breakfast, according to the statement of Mr. Robin Tennant, who bathed on those days from the cove. On Monday she went again, but was back in good time to dress for eight o'clock breakfast, apparently just doing the swim there and back. But on Tuesday she not only went for the fourth morning in succession, but she started while it was still fairly dark, before five fifteen, and took her green coat with her as if she intended to stay at the cove long enough to make it worth while to dry it, and wear it. The coat was seen by a reliable witness on a boulder there after her death. The only explanation was that she hoped to meet someone on Tuesday morning at the cove, but, wanting to keep this meeting secret, had gone out on the previous mornings to make the Tuesday trip seem quite normal to her family. But, her sister being the only person likely to take much interest in her doings, as a further precaution, she gave Rosalind to understand it was still Mr. Tennant that she was meeting."

"You mean she wanted to screen the identity of the real man under the name of Mr. Tennant!" said Braice eagerly.

"That was what it looked like to me. And that was as far as I got till yesterday evening when I saw those footprints. Simply the suggestion of an unknown man in the background of the affair whose presence was entirely unsuspected at the time.

"Examination of the scene of the murder disclosed other details. She had gone round to the cove, and left her coat there spread out to dry, and then swum out again. The murder was unquestionably committed under cover of the extreme point of the headland, because there alone the crime could have taken place without danger of her struggles and possible cries being noticed from the shore on either side. When she was dead, or at least insensible, the murderer swam with the body, probably under water, to the buoy, and hoisted it across it. So far it is fact, and, except for the disposal of the body with the motive of immediate discovery, does not contradict the early theory that Rosalind followed her in a rage, met her under the cliff, struggled with, and so drowned her." He paused. "I cannot think what earthly reason the girl would have, though, for wishing her death to be immediately known. Also, in my opinion, the defence might make a strong point out of the physical strength and skilful manoeuvring required for that last job. However, now we come to the evidence of the cliff face, always supposing that the tracks were made on Tuesday morning. The murderer, having deposited the body where it will be soonest found, swims back again under the water to regain his clothes cached in a well-hidden spot above the cove. He rounds the point and sees someone at the point of the shore he is making for. He is caught between two possible fires. Rescuers coming out to fetch the body on one side of the headland, an observer on the other. He can't be caught in the water, so he shins up the cliff. He lies doggo, and then, when he has got up and is making off towards his clothes, he gets another shock. He hears voices in among the trees. He races clean back to the point and dives off into the sea. This time he is able to swim back to the cove unobserved. He dresses and finds his car, a Rolls."

"Have you the smallest notion who your hypothetical murderer is, Gorham?" Major Tennant asked slowly, as he stopped.

Gorham shook his head.

"Don't forget, sir, it's all pure conjecture. The footprints indicate a tall man, the murder itself postulates uncommon strength and exceptional skill in swimming and diving. But Lydia had received no letters lately—she rarely had any. And though there is a telephone at the Villa she had not been heard using it. The girl, Gladys flies to the 'phone whenever she hears it because she has various pals who ring her up. Manning made certain of that when he was in the house. But Lydia knew ten days ago that she was going to your party at the Castle on Monday. Easy enough to arrange a casual encounter with her man there among the crowds of trippers. Was that why she made her companions linger there after everyone else? She was certainly ready to go immediately after she had exchanged a casual word with Sampson's brawny fellow in brown plus fours, who came with his pal in the Rolls that was seen next day on the road to Whitesands at the right time." He frowned. "But it is very thin!" He turned suddenly, with sternness, on Mr. Moh. "Look here, Moh! You weren't at the Castle this morning for sheer pleasure! You've obviously got a working theory of your own. Suppose you trot it out!"

"Listening," said Mr. Moh calmly, "to incessant babble of relatives by marriage, it is revealed that deceased's life is like large woodland after powerful gale which fells trees like ninepins. Back through career of deceased are lovers, felled to earth . . . back and back and back, felled lovers."

"She collected them chiefly from her sister. . . . Burroughs first—"

"Not first. Herman Hervey. Friend of Rosalind with whom he hiked and tennised. But being found by uncle in Lydia's bedroom one night he was turned out neck and scruff."

The chief constable frowned annoyance on this gratuitous resurrection of a five-year-old scandal, but Braice corrected the statement. "It was the other young lady who was generally blamed for that quarrel!"

Mr. Moh nodded gravely.

"Rosalind was left to hold the baby. It was in her sister's room that he was discovered."

Gorham met the eyes of Mr. Moh.

"What were you doing up there with the V.C. this morning? I mean what about it?"

"Conversation of V.C. sergeant deeply attractive as he spoke of Hankow, which I left with revered parents at early age of five. Also, to leap swiftly to present from remote past, it seemed possible that deceased had encountered one of series of felled lovers there, and made a date for the cove rendezvous, Tuesday."

"And working your own line you got my fellow in plus fours too! I got at him by a different means. Money. But what defeats me is how they originally got into touch with each other, and made the appointment for the Castle, if they neither wrote nor 'phoned!"

"I dwell in earnest thought on high convenience of telephone box on coast road," returned Mr. Moh quietly, "for person who did not wish members of family to listen in to private conversation. How easy to have definite time arranged for lady to call up given number from same!"

"By Jove, you've got it! But why then a meeting at the Castle at all? It looks as if I'd been wasting my time over that!"

But the Chinese gently dissented.

"Idea occurs to me that while general plan of early meeting was settled, a last-minute word was required—say about progress of sister's injury which they reckoned on to prevent her interrupting them. Yet for some reason a telephone call at a given moment, which must necessarily be a fixed time when a public call box is used, could not be managed."

"So they settled to meet at the Castle for the final word; yes, that covered the difficulty." Gorham turned back to the chief constable, who raised sceptical eyebrows.

"All this would make an ingenious plot for detective fiction, but aren't we soaring rather far away from our facts?" Tennant remarked with politeness. "A possibly entirely fortuitous one-second encounter in a crowded museum, and the presence of the

Rolls half a mile from the Villa at six thirty-five a.m. on Tuesday, seems to me slender foundation on which to build a charge of murder! A really damning case could be made out against Bond now! He actually knew the young woman by sight. He was known to be in the bay at the correct time. You have only to invent a plausible motive . . ."

Gorham grinned appreciatively.

"Enquiries have already eliminated Bond, sir. The skipper of the trawler *Sally Ann*, which is in harbour for repairs, had a half-crown with another sportsman on Bond covering the course from the south beach to the breakwater in six minutes. So he watched him from the breakwater from start to finish through his glasses. Incidentally he makes it certain that deceased went out before five ten, when he took up his station, because otherwise he couldn't have failed to see her. Unluckily, Bond took seven minutes, so the skipper lost further interest in him and went home with the pal who had lifted his cash, taking his glasses with him. If that skipper had remained he must have seen the crime committed through his binoculars, there'd have been no chance of mistake, and I shouldn't be here. Still, his evidence and that of Moh, who watched his return from the breakwater, clears Bond in one." His grin faded. "But you are right, sir. The main fact we've got so far is that the murder was done by an expert swimmer. And the Torringtons themselves are the best that Whitesands has produced for years."

Braice nodded.

"The Whitesands lot are sheer rabbits. But according to the secretary of the East Anglian Association of Swimming Clubs, whom I interviewed after our conversation last night, the Association shows a pretty poor average over the last five years, both for speed records and long distance tests."

"It's endurance rather than speed we are looking for."

"He said there were a number of promising youngsters coming along from the schools who are likely to hit up the speed events within the next two years when they compete in the adult classes, as they have been trained in the later trudgeon and crawl strokes from childhood, but last year's show was a complete frost. I'm having the lists he furnished me with of the club's membership checked up individually, as you wanted, but I don't fancy they will yield much."

"How about divers?"

"Nothing doing at all down on this part of the coast. If you believe it was a local man who plunged off that promontory, from what he said of the general form about here, you can put it out of your head. The only great name he could mention was young Whittiker, now an international champion . . ."

"Yes, yes. . . . I know about Whittiker. You can't be five minutes in Whitesands without hearing about him!"

"Don't grudge us our only celebrity, Gorham! His diving exploits off that very promontory covered the paternal butchery with glory and caused us endless vexation till we had the whole place strongly fenced in. There were two fatal accidents to young fools who thought what Whittiker, who was the hero of all the youngsters about, could do, they could do. But don't centre your hopes on Whittiker, my dear Gorham. He is the only fellow in living memory known to have pulled off that plunge successfully, but he is a Jack Tar, serving on board the cruiser *Achilles* in the Mediterranean Squadron, and though he spends his spare time collecting pots for high diving with his superiors' full approval, they would not grant him special leave to come home to commit our local murders."

"Whittiker isn't the only man who dived successfully off that point, Chief," Gorham said soberly. "Nor the only fine swimmer Whitesands has produced either. Smith, the ex-coastguard who took us out in a boat round there, told me that Colonel Rouncey's nephew, young Hervey, was the most expert swimmer he ever saw, though for private reasons he never even joined the local club. And last night, making enquiries for me in the local pubs, he found out that Hervey once did that actual dive."

"Good lord! But I don't believe it," Tennant said sharply. "We'd have been bound to hear of it! I tell you, after Whittiker's pyrotechnic show we had to make stringent regulations! On whose authority does this yarn rest?"

"On that of young Whittiker himself. According to Smith's account, Hervey, who was a few years older, was a devout admirer of his, and was always hanging about to watch him at practice—"

"That's right!" Braice nodded. "The boys followed him about in shoals. He was a good-natured lad, and never above giving them a bit of instruction."

"So Smith said. But when he got fed up and wanted real practice, he'd go out early, before the fry was about. And one morning Hervey met him and said he intended to try that dive. So while young Whittiker stayed on guard in the water to rescue him if necessary, he went up and shot in off the headland like a bird. Then he swore the other boy to secrecy, explaining that his uncle would worry himself to death if he heard of it, and there was no need that the old man should be fretted, as he never intended to do it again, once being as much as he ever wanted. So Whittiker didn't give him away. Till one evening during his last leave, in May, when a lot of fools were pestering him with praise. Then, when one chap kept harping on his great local feat, saying he was the only man alive who had accomplished it, he suddenly rounded on them all and gave them the facts about Hervey."

"Oh, well, if young Whittiker vouched for it it is true," Major Tennant said with singular reluctance. "He is a thoroughly decent young sportsman, exactly the type to repudiate kudos he wasn't entitled to. And no doubt he'd be a trifle ashamed of the fuss his home crowd still make over an exploit that seems small beer to himself now. Look here, Gorham, this may seem significant to you, because in Herman Hervey you get your necessary skill in sea-swimming combined with a connecting link with the Villa household. But he cleared out of the neighbourhood about five years ago and, so far as I have heard, has never been seen here since."

"No. I got that. The housekeeper at the Villa has been there four years, and has never seen him, and there is no photo of him there either. It looks as if the break with his uncle was pretty complete. Still, as you said, those two points taken together are significant. And apparently deceased was the cause of the row."

"Dash it, Gorham"—Tennant looked genuinely annoyed—"surely it is unnecessary to rake up the unsavoury details of a five-year old scandal of which"—he glanced severely at Mr. Moh—"nothing definite was ever really known. The young man had a perfectly good reputation in the county, where he visited quite a number of houses when he was spending his vacs with his uncle. I never met him myself, but the fact that he was accepted as a member at Oakshott to a certain extent speaks for itself. His uncle and he played there together quite a lot. The general opinion was that they were much attached, and certainly Rouncey practically dropped out of the social ken after the quarrel. My personal feeling is that poor Rouncey has had a sufficiently rough time over this tragedy with his wife's nieces, without the police starting to ferret out irrelevant scandals about a young relative of his own. An innocent and entirely absent nephew who was a perfectly decent, quiet, well-bred and unassuming fellow when he was at home, and who besides is probably planting quite useful tea in Assam at this moment!"

Gorham laughed at his heat.

"Quite so, sir," he said easily. "If deceased went to meet anyone at all at the cove it is fairly obvious that it must have been someone from outside her normal circle. She had a holiday in Paris last year, for instance. It might be someone she met there. But as I started by saying, though I'm sure she went out with the intention of meeting someone, we have no proof that he actually turned up. In that case we are back where we started."

"And if the footprints clue fizzles to nothing you will be satisfied that the prisoner we hold now is guilty."

Gorham nodded, closed his notebook and rose.

"You've got it exactly, Super. The only test of circumstantial evidence is elimination of every other suspicious pointer." His tone was quite gentle, but while he said a final, friendly word to Braice Major Tennant was suddenly conscious of a new and startling conviction.

"He is not only certain of that wretched woman's innocence, but he guesses who committed the murder!" he thought. "But he isn't giving his theory away till he's had time to test his facts!"

He followed his guest into the hall. Gorham gave him a rapid confidence. "For yourself alone. Lydia's will, dated April, names Burroughs residuary legatee. Good morning, sir, and thanks for that breakfast," he added aloud, and Major Tennant, ignoring the murmur, caught his cue.

"It occurs to me that I owe you more than breakfast, Gorham. You have eliminated—good word, eliminated—my son and young

Bond, I infer, from your list of possible suspects, but if I can supply any substitutes from my family or subordinates," he murmured, "myself, for instance, or Braice . . . By the way, I propose giving Braice an unvarnished account of the pig episode, to clear away any doubts that may yet linger in his mind as to my son's criminal aptitudes. Any objection?"

"None whatever. The truth is due to him, specially as it can only do good," Gorham chuckled. The telephone bell shrilled, and Major Tennant answered it.

Gorham went back into the office to fetch the chart which he had left behind. Mr. Moh had already proceeded forth to the car. When he returned he realized from a chance phrase to whom Tennant was talking. He went over.

"Is that Mr. Will, Chief? Might I have a word with him?"

Tennant lifted his eyebrows, but handed over the receiver.

"All serene, he says."

"Good. That you, Mr. Tennant? No, this is Gorham speaking. I say, when you said 'she-devil' yesterday, who did you mean? What? Yes, I thought so. Thanks. That's all. Good-bye."

He nodded to the chief constable and ran down the steps to join Mr. Moh sitting patiently in the car. But his good-humoured face was full of grim satisfaction, for Will's reply had been: "My dear, good soul, surely you have tumbled to the sort she was by this time! Lydia, of course."

CHAPTER XVI

"QUICK OF YOU to get on to Herman Hervey!" Gorham said as they sped towards Whitesands, but Mr. Moh waved away praise with speaking hands.

"After hearing you question Smith yesterday I merely leapt along broad trail already blazed by you. But it is true, from further babble let fall by relatives by marriage after insinuating questions last night, he has not been seen in Whitesands since the bust-up. They know everything, these babblers, but the single fact one wants—what Hervey looks like! For years these townsfolk saw him frequently, but all they can say is that he was tallish, and had straight, pleasant eyes!" He sighed.

"They all emphasize the fact that his uncle and he were fond of each other," Gorham said thoughtfully. "Have you heard any gossip about Burroughs' financial position, by the by?"

"No. He is not liked. But he settles his bills quarterly, and is gathering a low-class practice together. He has the reputation of being a skinflint."

"He doesn't know where to turn for a copper, in my opinion. Lydia was his one hope alive or dead. No, no, he had no hand in her murder, though he expected to benefit by it largely. All the time he was bathing he was under observation of the boatman's boy, young Charlie. . . . Take an interest in Norman churches, Moh? No? Well, I do." He pulled up the car by the low stone wall of the churchyard, and walked up the path towards the ancient building with its typical Suffolk tower. "They built them big in those days. Before the Black Death came along and swept off two-thirds of the population, I'm told. There's the parson coming out now." He stopped and pointed out the beauty of the flower-covered graves to a mystified but obliging companion, who murmured appreciation, till the little vicar approached.

He caught the glance of innocent eyes that obviously recognized him with curiosity as the London detective in charge of the case that had suddenly covered Whitesands with unenviable notoriety, and the vicar was guilelessly gratified when Gorham raised his hat and commented on the prettiness of the churchyard.

"Yes, yes, the people take a pride in keeping their graves well. But we could do with more rain still. The grass was growing very scorched."

"It looks like clearing up again. The weather has been marvellous this week. I thought it had broken for good this morning, and I hope to get time to explore the country a bit before I leave. It strikes me as wonderfully green in spite of the drought. Even on the cliffs, and up on the headland. By the way, someone mentioned that you were a great botanist, sir. Would you mind telling me where I'm most likely to find buckthorn growing hereabouts?"

"Buckthorn? Why, almost anywhere in the lanes."

"Is that so?" Gorham looked puzzled. "A colleague of mine, who makes a study of these things, told me it was not much use to look for buckthorn—*Rhamnus catharticus*—he called it, down here because it liked a chalky soil. I shouldn't have thought there was much chalk in this district."

"Neither there is. Your friend was right so far. I do not know a single specimen of *Rhamnus catharticus* growing nearer than Oakshott woods, seven miles away. But there are several varieties of buckthorn, you know. *Rhamnus frangula* is quite common here. Here is a bush growing in the hedge of my own garden."

"I wish I knew more about these things," Gorham said ruefully, and with perfect truth, as he contemplated a singularly uninteresting-looking bush indicated by the vicar's hand and hoped that he was looking at the right shrub. "But why call that buckthorn, sir! It doesn't seem to have any thorns!"

The vicar laughed.

"The common name is a little misleading, perhaps. That kind—the alder-leaved buckthorn—doesn't produce thorns—or rather spines! But if your friend told you to look out for a thorny specimen here, he probably mentioned the sea buckthorn, of which there are several fine examples up on the promontory—but nowhere else in the immediate neighbourhood."

Gorham, looking suddenly intelligent, turned to Mr. Moh.

"Do you remember that pretty, silvery sort of bush up there that I pointed out to you? That Bond couldn't tell me the name of? I wonder if that was the thing Gray meant!"

Moh nodded, but before he could speak the little parson broke into a chuckle.

"It was, my dear Chief Inspector! Yes, yes. Of course I recognized you at once! My verger, who is a keen student of crime, pointed you out to me in the street yesterday. You could not remain incognito in a little town like Whitesands for a second, you know. But about the sea buckthorn. Bond, the local policeman, a very respectable young man, called at the Vicarage this morning with a twig. He was very hot and ashamed because he ought to have known it for *Hippophae Rhamnoides* himself, and he was bursting to redeem his fault! He borrowed a student's manual on botany from me and intends to study the subject in earnest."

Gorham's eyes twinkled.

"Good for him. I like zeal in a young man, and knowledge is always useful. They didn't do nature study in London Elementary Schools when I was a boy, or I might not be so ignorant myself now. But thanks to you, sir, if Bond has the audacity to hand me any information about any of the buckthorns that grow about here I'll be able to take a firm line. Did you say that the promontory is the only spot where sea buckthorn grows?"

"Within three miles or so. After that you will find it occurring sporadically on the cliffs both north and south."

They had reached the private gate into the Vicarage garden, and the vicar, still chuckling, nodded and passed into his own domain. Gorham walked briskly back to his car.

"Sudden burning interest in local flora throws romantic light on noble friend's character," murmured a plaintive voice at his side. "But is reason for same secret?"

"Not from you, old man. Rouncey swore he took that dog inland for his run on Tuesday morning. But when I called at the Villa in the afternoon the poor brute met me with a swollen paw in which a spine of sea buckthorn had been embedded for hours. Did the dog pick it up on the promontory on some private ramble, or when he was out with his master? Rouncey was so preoccupied he hadn't even noticed the dog's limp. Yet they seemed inseparable."

"They are. Colonel is never seen unless complete with dog."

"Exactly. It struck me as extraordinary proof of Rouncey's mental worry that he hadn't spotted that swollen paw. I bet Carlo had tried to rouse him to it too. After I'd extracted the thorn he bustled in ahead of me and planked his paw straight on his master's knee to show him it was all right again. But even then Rouncey only played with his ears and noticed nothing."

"He had had a shock."

"Yes. But I'm certain it wasn't either the dead niece or the living one that he was worrying over. He had to sort of drag his thoughts up to attend to what I was saying about them. Look here, Moh, it's incredible that he felt a spark of affection for two young women who had made his home wretched for twelve years! They'd become a sort of deadly habit, that was all. But—this is strictly for your ear alone—it is he, and after him his nephew Herman Hervey, who inherits the dead girl's money."

"Ah! You think money is the motive of this crime?"

"It is the motive of nine out of ten in my experience."

"And in mine." Moh looked grave. "So that was what you meant when you spoke of money being your guiding clue! You have an odd assortment of clues, my Gorham—a footprint—the green wrap—a thorn in a dog's foot."

"I'll add two more that seem to cancel each other out," said Gorham grimly. "The Colonel's collapse when he realized that Rosalind was really for it, and the last item you have just supplied yourself—the straight pleasant eyes of Herman Hervey! I'm going to collect my mail at the police-station, Moh. This is where you get off."

Mr. Moh beamed with maddening calm.

"When did you first guess who murdered Lydia Torrington, Gorham?"

The chief inspector looked at him soberly.

"You don't miss much, do you, like Sampson. When I studied her pass-book, after seeing her fur coat."

"And the motive was money? Or is this the tenth crime?"

"Run home to your relatives by marriage, Li Moh, I'm busy."

His morning mail, though it contained a summary of the will of the late Miss Annabel Torrington, gave him no fresh facts, but a brief conversation with Manning informed him that Captain Tring, on receiving his report of the Assheton statement that morning, had decided to handle the Swansea end of the enquiry himself.

"He didn't mention what he expected the poor fish down there to pick up for him after a lapse of twelve years," Manning growled, "but they've got a softer job than mine, which is to produce a dossier of this heir presumptive of old Torrington, George Herman Hervey. Can you give me a description of him, Chief?"

"Not a hope. He vanished from here years ago without leaving his photograph behind. Swimming and diving were his star accomplishments. He was, I rather gather, at a public school, but his mother was a widow, and poor. Try St. Paul's for a long shot. And the passport office for photos. It could be. He would be about twenty-five now, for he was still at college when he was here. They speak of his vac's. . . . What college? . . . Find that out, Manning. Aren't you paid to be a detective? His father was a doctor. If you can trace him in any twenty-year-old medical directory it may tell you his university. George Herman possibly followed in Daddy's footsteps. But look here, old man, bend to it and use your brains. If any fellow can pull this off it's you, and it means a lot to me."

Having thus stimulated his subordinate by a judicious mixture of jeers and flattery, he left the telephone and the police-station and went down to the branch of — Bank in the High Street, at which Lydia Torrington had kept her account.

The manager, a Mr. Watson, who had been warned of his visit, received him at once in his private room, and, staring eagerly at Gorham, who bore an immense tome with him, began an inquisitive and entirely vain attempt to extract news of the activities of the police in the Whitesands murder.

Gorham was good-humoured, but a little short.

"I have two pass-books of the late Miss Lydia Torrington which cover a term of nearly four years," he said, coming to business much more quickly than the manager wished. "But I should be obliged if you could let me see her account during the whole time she was a client of the bank."

"It is an unusual request." Watson hummed and hawed a little to enhance his own importance, but eventually the chief inspector sat down to a prolonged and detailed study of the dead woman's account.

The credit side yielded nothing more than he had obtained from Mr. George Assheton. Till seven years before, presumably the date of Miss Annabel Torrington's death, Lydia had received an allowance of £100 a year, paid in half-yearly instalments of £50 through Barclay's Bank. From then on the allowance, paid quarterly through the same means, figured as £500 per annum. No other items whatever appeared on the credit side.

This swiftly verified, he turned to a laborious examination of expenditure.

It was immediately obvious that the recipient had never attempted to save or invest any part of this liberal income, or to benefit any friend or relative. After a careful comparison of the dates of cheques drawn to "self" Gorham realized, with real surprise, that she had not even contributed her quota towards household expenses, so far as could be traced. And as a meagre five pounds paid quarterly to Rosalind was set down without disguise, he could not believe she had concealed payment for board and lodging from motives of delicacy, or for any reason at all, except that she had made none.

She lived on her uncle, and spent £500 a year on annual holidays, and clothes to sport in a one-horse place like Whitesands? "Query!" He thought grimly, "Mr. Assheton was right. A very cool-headed and astute woman, Lydia. Not giving anything away. No."

He began methodically to analyse her expenditure for each year apart from the cheques drawn to "self". This at first appeared to be a task of extreme simplicity, for the London shops with which she had mainly dealt—presumably by post—bore well-known names—Selfridges, Barkers. . . . These he disregarded, though when he came to any name unknown to him he methodically traced it in the trade directory he had brought with him, and when it proved to be some smaller establishment dealing in any article of wearing apparel he crossed it off the list he had made out. But when he came to add up the totals figuring under the names Evans, Barkers, Selfridges, Freeman, Hardy & Willis, and Prichard's of Harborough, a startling fact appeared. For every pound spent among the other shops during the last six years, ten had been paid to Evans. In other words, her annual expenditure fell roughly into three classes.

Personal—in which he included amounts drawn for holidays—£200. The well-known shops—£50—slightly more or less.

Evans—£250, until the current year, when the account dropped to £5. In the pass-book the name, which at first sight, seeing it neighboured by Selfridges and Barkers he had accepted as that of the Oxford Street shop, appeared simply as "Evans". In the bankbooks it was more accurately noted. But here a fresh discrepancy instantly appeared. In a few small instances the full name was entered, "D. H. Evans & Co., Ltd.", in the large remainder, "D. Evans" only.

The Bank manager, under cover of his own avocations, had watched his proceedings with puzzled interest, but at the end of an hour, when Gorham had completed his task and was filling a page in his notebook with a precis of results inscribed in his odd shorthand, an inkling of the chief inspector's object had dawned on him, and he came across to the table.

"If you have been trying to trace any friends of the late Miss Torrington through her accounts," he observed, in slightly patronizing accents, "I could have warned you that it was labour wasted."

"Could you? Why?"

"Well, you see, I happened to know Miss Torrington very well indeed. She often came in here for a friendly little chat. A really charming young lady! And sometimes she would laugh and almost apologize for what she called her disgraceful extravagance in spending all her money on dress! 'Really, Mr. Watson! I feel quite ashamed you should know how much I waste every year!' she said to me once, though naturally I hastened to assure her that it was none of my business."

Gorham looked speculatively at his neatly dated lists, and up at the manager's face. Its intelligence, he felt, was not emphasized by the self-conscious smile which lifted the waxed tips of a yellow moustache.

"Was that after some special extravagance?" he asked casually.

"Two hundred for a fur coat last autumn bought through Evans—yes! And I am bound to admit she made a charming picture in it! Mink, you know, an exquisite soft brown fur that suited her fair complexion to a tee! But costly enough for a duchess. Though when I chaffingly told her, when she displayed herself in it to me, that she was wearing the year's living of a working-class family on her back, she protested that it wasn't really so extravagant because it would last her a lifetime!"

"Wonderful how women will fall for clothes, isn't it! She seems to have bought largely from these people—D. Evans."

"Yes. One of those agencies that give a big discount, you know. Some friend of hers introduced her to them, and"—he shrugged his shoulders—"you know what the ladies are, Chief Inspector, when they think they are on to a bargain deal! She owned she used to get positively intoxicated with the marvellous cheapness of frocks and hats and dainty lingerie she could get through them, and then was rather alarmed by the total they mounted up to!"

Gorham nodded, smiling, as he put his papers together.

"Still, she never seems actually to have outrun the constable; she always seems to have left a trifling margin each year. She never thought of adding to her income by investment?"

"Always rejected any suggestion of it! Said she didn't love money for itself, only for the pleasures it gave. She had plenty for her needs, and why scrimp to make more!"

"Quite! As you say, it was her own money, if she did do herself pretty well in clothes and annual holidays abroad. The couple of fifties she withdrew last July represent holiday expenditure, I take it?"

"Yes, she had an incorrigible habit of carrying her money with her in notes, though I wanted her to do the thing in the usual way by letters of credit. She stayed in Paris and elsewhere, and said her method of carrying ready money with her left her free to move about when she liked. But though she was abroad for a month I don't doubt that frillies from the Paris shops accounted for a good deal more of that hundred than hotel bills, or travelling expenses."

"Quite so. Probably, as I see she has two hundred standing to her credit now—she was planning another foreign trip this autumn?"

"I believe she was"—vaguely. "Yes, she certainly mentioned a possible visit to the Riviera soon—though no definite plans were made. I remember now! She said she might go off in the end at almost a moment's notice! You know, Chief Inspector, her murder is the most ghastly thing that ever happened in my experience! A pretty, taking, innocent creature like that, suddenly done to death by that raging demon of a sister that she had been kindness itself to! Do you imagine that all those frocks and things she bought were for herself only? Not a bit of it! And when one realizes what she must have had to put up with daily in her home, living with a maniacal, murderous vixen like that! She, the gentlest and sweetest of women! Yet she never breathed a word against her sister. Always had some excuse to make for her tempers, praising her tennis and swimming, and that! By Jove, I'm not a vindictive man! Far from it! I'm dead against all blood-sports, and so on. But when I heard that that foul-mouthed devil had committed that wanton, unprovoked, wicked and cruel crime, I said to my wife that if there was any justice in England, she would be hanged sky-high!"

There was a gleam of severity in Gorham's eyes, a grimness about his mouth, that Watson, holding open the door, failed to see. His answer was noncommittal, though grave.

"The—er—arrangements are quite efficient, if not sky-high, Mr. Watson. And I think you may rest assured that the person at present under arrest will receive just treatment.

"More than she's ever had yet!" he added to himself as he started the car. "Upon my soul, if I meet many more fatuous fools like Watson in the course of this job I shall begin positively to like that black-eyed termagant!"

His next call, which was at the office of Harcourt Burroughs, drew a blank, for he was informed by the loutish clerk that his master had gone up to town the night before, without leaving any address. A firmly authoritative manner, however, produced the name of a dingy hotel in Covent Garden at which Burroughs had stayed in the spring, and Gorham, calling at the police station once more, held a second long conversation with Manning on the 'phone.

"Burroughs has gone up to consult old Miss Torrington's will, of course," he ended. "And when he realizes how he has been had, he may bolt—so keep him well tabbed. If necessary, detain him. I'll be up myself, as I said, some time this evening, but meantime, if you want me, call up Harborough. That's my headquarters from now on. I'm going to interview the secretary of Oakshott Golf Club now to see what I can pick up about Hervey, who was a member there. So long."

CHAPTER XVII

CAPTAIN BRYAN, the secretary, turned out to be a pleasant-mannered man in the early thirties, who looked too young to have fought in the War, though the empty left sleeve of his coat told its own tale.

He took Gorham at once to his own charmingly furnished sitting-room which commanded a wide prospect, did the honours with drinks, and then raised inquisitive brows as his glance scanned his visitor.

"I say, I hope you haven't come to tell me that one of our members has so far fallen from grace as to attract your official attention!" he said. "You know we pride ourselves on our intense exclusiveness. Only the most respectable in the land admitted, and every name jealously scrutinized by a committee whose twin gods are Burke and Debrett."

"No, no! Nothing known as yet against your stainless reputation," Gorham chuckled. "Your members are as virtuous as they are aristocratic, for all I know to the contrary. But I should be immensely obliged if you could give me any information you can about a man who was a member some years ago—Mr. Herman Hervey. You remember him? Well, you will see the point at once. His uncle, Colonel Rouncey is, between ourselves, very seriously ill. And it seems strongly advisable in the circumstances that we should get in touch with Mr. Hervey, who seems to be his only male relative."

"Is it as bad as that with old Rouncey?" Captain Bryan exclaimed, startled. "My word! I'd heard rumours that he was ill, but I'd no idea it was anything really serious—worse, I mean, than one might have expected after the appalling show in his family this week. Those two young women have put it across him properly ever since he was fool enough to saddle himself with them, but even he could scarcely have expected them to end up by bumping each other off!"

"Those two? I understood it was only Rosalind who was disliked!"

"Hullo! Am I being by any chance—"

Gorham met the questioning grin in a pair of amused and quite intelligent blue eyes, and laughed.

"Pumped? No. Begged for the smallest scrap of light that you can throw on that queer household—yes. Colonel Rouncey's illness has cut off my single source of information. And candidly, Captain Bryan, I've been so overwhelmed with the bitterly prejudiced views I've met everywhere so far that I'd give anything for a fair and unbiased opinion that might give me a chance to get the whole group into proper focus. I came down to Whitesands on Tuesday, a stranger of course, and so far Lydia Torrington has been represented to me as an angel of sweetness, her sister as a raging shrew, Hervey as an unscrupulous Don Juan, and Colonel Rouncey as a dark horse. Do you endorse those labels?"

"Certainly I don't," replied Bryan with warmth, "as regards Rouncey and Hervey at any rate, and I feel strongly inclined to query Lydia's claim to any angelic qualities too," he added, frowning. He paused and lighted a cigarette.

"I see the difficulties you are up against, Mr. Gorham," he resumed, when he had thrown the match out of the window. "I've heard the tone of the gossip the murder has roused myself. I haven't the smallest objection to telling you what I know of these people, but frankly it isn't much."

"It's not so much facts as some sort of trustworthy idea of their real character that I want," Gorham said. "Major Tennant, the chief constable, who placed the investigation in my hands, is absolutely the only fair-minded informant I have had, so far, and, unfortunately, he did not know them personally till quite lately."

Bryan nodded.

"I knew and liked Rouncey practically from the first moment he turned up in our midst," he said. "He had just lost his wife, and he struck me as one of those guileless, helpless sort of beggars who are absolutely dependent on affection, yet are apt to concentrate on one or two people. Shorn at one fell swoop of his profession and his wife, the two things that had, so to speak, anchored him in life, he seemed to me to be feeling utterly lost, groping about to look for something to link himself up with again, and never finding it. He'd been in India during the War, and one night, when a crowd here had been swopping yarns, and he'd been listening with a sort of lost look as if he felt himself a complete back number, I—well—I asked if I might join him at dinner. Rather cheek, of course, from a mere youngster, but he didn't take it that way, and he became, for him, quite expansive. I asked him why he had planked himself down with a house in a remote spot like Whitesands, and he said the girls—his wife's nieces—he always spoke of them like that— needed a home. One place was as remote as another to him, and he'd been brought up by the sea. His father was a naval captain. He had wanted his only sister, Mrs. Hervey, to come and keep house for him, but she refused on account of her boy. He was at St. Paul's, and she didn't wish to disturb him and so on. He positively cheered up into real animation when he talked of his sisters and young Herman. And later on, when Herman came to spend his vacs with him after his mother's death, he livened up quite considerably. In some ways they were rather alike, Rouncey and his nephew, I mean. Herman Hervey was a very likeable lad, quiet, and almost as shy as his uncle, yet with plenty of fun in him if you got him going in a congenial crowd. Both men were quite popular in the neighbourhood, but the trouble was that by the time Hervey joined the circus, hostesses were already beginning to fight shy of the girls. After—er—I mean, later on, when Hervey left the place, they were absolutely barred, and since then Rouncey has become a mere memory, socially speaking."

"Before we touch on that scandal—oh yes, you needn't be discreet, I've heard all about it—Hervey found in his cousin's room and the subsequent row—was it both the nieces who were disliked, or only Rosalind?"

Bryan looked a trifle worried.

"Look here, Gorham, you must understand that while in my position here I'm bound to listen to everybody's views on every mortal subject. I may be the recipient of tons of gossip that it would be grossly tactless to repeat aloud in the common ear. Still, to give you the gist of it, without mentioning names—a haughty dame once announced to me that that impossible girl with the lovely Shakespearean name possessed the manners of a barmaid. But when she went on to quote the type of way she had behaved at a garden-party where she had been a guest, and the language she had used, I pointed out that the comparison struck me as rough on barmaids, with whom my informant had only what you might describe as an academic acquaintance. But while the reasons for Rosalind's unpopularity were quotable and public, about the other there were really ugly rumours, yet nothing overt that could be taken hold of."

"You mean that these ladies—hostesses—used the excuse given by Rosalind's vulgarities to get rid of them both—but specially Lydia?"

"I do mean exactly that. None of them had any real use for Rosalind, of course, but they would chat freely over the latest enormity she had committed. But mention Lydia, and they'd shut up like oysters. It was Lydia they could not stick."

"Did it ever strike you that the uncle regarded these two young women from much the same angle as these ladies?" asked Gorham, after a pause.

"I had nothing to go on. I never met either of them in person, by the way. There would have been an unholy riot if anyone had suggested introducing them through our sacred portals, but naturally no one ever did. Rouncey never mentioned them except in the most casual way, but—mind you this is my impression only for what it is worth—he was, as I said, fond of his nephew, quietly bucked, you know, when the boy was with him, and that. Well, he didn't interfere or show the slightest worry while Herman Hervey was by way of being chums with Rosalind. They played tennis, and biked all over the place together and so on. But when the old boy somehow discovered that Herman was mixing himself up with Lydia he roused himself and booted him out instanter."

"Your inference being?"

"One you can draw yourself. That he cleared the lad out for his own sake. Just as I'd pack off my own tyke there, Gladstone, into safety if the cook's dog started mange. Yes, old man, I mentioned you"—as his handsome terrier raised his head from his paws and glanced round—"but nothing in praise, so you needn't look so cheered. It is only inference, of course. Rouncey never came near the Club again afterwards, though he has never dropped his sub. But one day, months after, I ran across him at the junction, and noticed he had got all his old look of depression back, but when I asked him, cheerily, what news of Hervey—ignoring the late fracas with my well-known tact—he brightened up, same as before, and said he was in France, mugging up the lingo.

"As a matter of fact, I've had several cards myself at various times from France, and Germany and Italy. But I haven't heard from him now for a couple of years, and he never favoured me with an address."

"Then you have no idea where he is now?"

"Not the remotest notion."

"And you can't put me on to anyone through whom I might be able to trace him?"

"Not a hope. He kept up with no one here." He paused, and added, with doubtful reluctance. "The only outside word I ever got of him was, I'm afraid, a complete frost. A cousin of mine who had met him here several times that last summer, swore to me that when she went to see her fat-headed kid snoop a prize at his prep, school near Aldeburgh last year, she spotted Hervey, as large as life, on the sports ground, and her infant phenomenon said he was a new master. But I can't believe he'd be so close without running over to look up his uncle or me. Lucy had only seen him at a distance here, and four years before at that, and, though she has quick eyes, her kid hasn't. He is short-sighted and wears goggles, and probably got the chap she pointed out wrong. To be beautifully candid, too, I took a chance and dropped him a line at the school, Montgomery House—but I got no answer."

"Was the letter returned?"

"No. But that implied nothing. It is quite a common name. Probably it was handed to some blinking young ass called Hervey who had not the gumption to do anything about it when he spotted it wasn't meant for him."

"Yes, that's quite probable. Still, it might be worth looking into on the off-chance," Gorham said thoughtfully. "Well, I'm much obliged, Captain Bryan. By the way, I noticed you seemed sure that Lydia, not Rosalind, was the cause of his quitting home. May I ask how you got that? The general tale gives the younger girl the benefit of it, you know."

Bryan looked thoroughly vexed.

"I know it does. It has often made me sick that I couldn't contradict it. But the fact was, a couple of days before it happened Herman himself dropped a hint that he was up to his neck in some worry on Lydia. He was bothered, and we really were rather pals, you know, but then he got hot and asked me to forget it. So naturally I have," he added with dry significance. "When I heard of the rotten show I simply put two and two together. That is absolutely the lot."

"Quite. I'm very grateful, as I said. Now only one more question and I will go. Can you give me a personal description of Mr. Hervey?"

"What was he like to look at, you mean? Dash it—I don't know! An ordinary sort of fellow with the full complement of features I suppose. I'd have noticed if he was an ear short, or broken-beaked"—dubiously—"he'd got rather nice eyes, I remember—looked straight at you when he talked. Brownish, I fancy, or they might have been hazel, or blue."

"Or grey, or pink!"

"No, I'd have known if they were pink," he chuckled. "Sorry, Mr. Gorham. All I can swear to is that while he was on the thin side he was about my height—five nine—and had flat shoulders and, yes, well-cut, sensitive sort of hands. I notice hands. I'd know him anywhere, of course. He'd a nice shy smile that you noticed because it was rare."

"I may take it, then," said Gorham, rising, with a smile, "that while he was neither a hulking brute, nor a film star for manly beauty, he hadn't any actual deformity, a club foot, or a squint, say."

"You may, absolutely," Bryan assured him. "He was an ordinary-looking, well-bred, quiet-mannered young fella of the normal public-school type. You won't stop and have a spot of luncheon with me? No? Well, if you should happen to run across Hervey tell him from me he's properly for it when we meet for cutting me dead all this time. Good-bye. Decent weather we're having, aren't we?"

From the nearest telephone-box Gorham got in touch with Braice at Harborough police-station, and from the superintendent's cheered accents grasped at once that he had news.

"That car, Gorham! It has been traced. Two fellows answering your description arrived in a Rolls saloon, No. XY903587—Bond's number was correct—at the Royal Martyr Hotel at Winslope—that's a small village between Bramwood and Oakshott—soon after seven Monday evening. Dined and had a smoke in the garden and turned in at nine-thirty, ordering a breakfast hamper to be prepared for them and coffee at four-thirty, as they wished to leave at dawn. They also paid their reckoning overnight. The older man, who appeared to own the car, gave the Boots, who got up to prepare the coffee, a tanner tip. The other man, whom he called, 'the squinting gentleman', who had a drooping eyelid, slipped him a couple of pound notes. The Boots didn't hear much talk, but he did get an impression that the 'gentleman' was a bit fed up with the big man. They left the inn as soon as they'd swallowed their coffee. About four forty a.m. But at six thirty-five or so, the Boots, who hadn't bothered to go back to bed and was cleaning the passage, answered a telephone call. He swears it was the 'squinting gentleman's' voice, and he asked if his friend had returned to the inn. The man said no, and the 'gentleman' said 'he didn't think he could have in the time'. And that's the last they heard of either of them."

"That's Bond's telephone call accounted for," said Gorham, pleased. "Has the car been picked up since?"

"Once. By an A. A. man, at Whorley Cross—that's eleven miles south of Whitesands on the London road—at seven forty-five a.m. Tuesday."

"Good enough! Heading for London, obviously."

"I've got a police call out, and the chief suggests—if you agree—an advert in the local papers for all pedestrians or motorists on the roads between Winslope—Whitesands and Whorley Cross to report any cars they met between the hours of four forty—seven forty-five a.m. Tuesday, with five pounds reward for the right information."

"Excellent. Carry on with the adverts and reward. Publicity will help now. That early start from Winslope, and Bond's smart bit of work in picking up that number at the call-box, indicate a definite link with that footprint. But we want to fill in all the details possible. Look here, Braice, I'm off to Aldeburgh on a clue that may end in smoke, but may not. I'll return to Harborough as quick as I can, about four, with any luck. Then I must head straight for London. Could you manage to collect Li Moh to come with me, and also Bond with all the doings left at Whitesands police-station—the casts, and my attaché-case! If the Chief would care to accompany me to London I'd be gratified. But if this clue I'm after now falls down, the enquiries in town may take a bit of time, so he must do as he thinks best on the report I shall bring. Cheerio, old man. Congrats on your smart work."

"One second. You said Aldeburgh, didn't you? Among the reports from swimming clubs, the Aldeburgh list includes a man named Harvey. Spelt with an 'a' though, and Christian name George. So far the local sergeant has been unable to identify him—trace him at all, in fact. But I thought I'd mention it."

"Thanks very much. It may mean something, or may not—like my own pointer. But I've a hunch we're getting warm, Super. That all? Right, so long,"

As the chief inspector drove through extensive and perfectly kept gardens to the imposing entrance of Montgomery House his memory recalled a bare East End playground of his own early days, and he thought of the white-faced children in overcrowded slums whose only playing-fields are reclaimed graveyards, paved over, but drearily adorned round the walls with tombstones of forgotten dead.

The headmaster, who presently received him in his study, looked like an epitome of all the headmasters he had ever dreamed of, tall, intellectual, severe-looking in clerical clothes, a man of authority and weight—especially, thought Gorham, feeling frail and shadowy before this giant champion of the Church—weight.

"Heaven help the kids he swishes!" he thought with awe, his heart filled with compassion for these unfortunates whom a moment before he had been inclined to disparage for the luxurious places in which their lot was cast.

Aloud, he apologized for disturbing Dr. Normanby without an appointment, promised to be brief, and stated that he had come to seek information about a certain Mr. Hervey—spelt with an "e"—whom he believed to be at Montgomery House.

"Certainly a Mr. Hervey has been a member of the staff here for the last year." (Gorham drew a deep inward breath of satisfaction.) "Unfortunately he is not in residence at present."

But even this addition to the headmaster's previous confirmation of his purely tentative statement of belief only slightly damped his spirits.

"Can you furnish me with his present address, sir?"

"I could. I should prefer to learn the nature of your business with him before I do so."

"That is natural. But first it would be well to make certain that we are referring to the same gentleman, sir. The information which led me here was far from complete, and Hervey is not an uncommon name. My Mr. Hervey was educated at St. Paul's; he is about twenty-six years of age, five feet ten in height, is a fine swimmer, a man of quiet and pleasant manner, and his Christian name is Herman."

"Your description fits my assistant-master exactly, with the exception of the name. He uses the signature 'George H.' I am unable to say whether the H. stands for Herman."

"Herman is the name by which he was known in his home circle. It is not improbable that he preferred a more formal signature for his professional life. You are quite certain about his swimming accomplishments, sir?"

"Quite."

"Did he leave here quite recently?"

"Pardon me, the reason for your visit is still unknown to me," came the quietly significant reminder.

"The reason is official, sir, and, I am afraid, private. I believe Mr. Hervey is in possession of important information which may have a vital bearing on an investigation in which I am engaged. Beyond that admission I fear I cannot go."

"Then I regret that our interview must end. You must realize for yourself that it is impossible for me to discuss the private affairs of Mr. Hervey with a stranger, without first obtaining his sanction."

"I am a detective-officer, sir." He paused. The impassive expression of the headmaster's face did not relax, though the hint of an ironical smile touched the severe lips.

"So your card informed me. That scarcely alters my position."

"Doctor Normanby, let me state mine frankly. When you realize the gravity of the case I cannot believe you will continue to obstruct my enquiry. Have you heard of the Whitesands murder?"

"Yes, vaguely. I remember no details. Someone was drowned."

"A woman. At the inquest a verdict of murder was recorded against her sister. She is now in Harborough gaol awaiting her trial on a capital charge. When I was called in to take over the investigation the evidence of her guilt seemed conclusive. I believe her to be innocent, though the case against her is damning. My theory depends entirely for corroboration on evidence which I believe Mr. Hervey can supply. And every minute lost is of essential value. It is a matter of life and death to the prisoner. The true murderer has had two days already in which to efface his tracks under cover of the general assumption of this young woman's guilt. Now, sir, do you still urge that a private scruple should weigh against her desperate need?" Dr. Normanby frowned.

"No. But before I give you Mr. Hervey's address I should like you to be more explicit with regard to his personal status in this affair. I object strongly to acting in the dark. Can you assure me, for instance, that he will be willing to supply this information that you require?"

"Willingly or not, he must give it. It is his duty as a citizen to aid justice in protecting the innocent and punishing the guilty."

"As it is mine now?"

"I am not impertinent enough to say so, sir. The point is not likely to have escaped you now that you know why I am here."

The uncompromising reply did not appear to offend Dr. Normanby. He sat still, a formidable figure in his high-backed chair, in profound thought, and Gorham, waiting in silence for his decision, was conscious of the dark, penetrating glance that rested on himself.

"I must give way, of course."

He turned to his desk and wrote a couple of lines on a card. But his hand remained over the address he had written, and when he raised his head his impassive expression had given place to one of troubled earnestness.

"Mr. Gorham, you have not relieved my anxiety on Mr. Hervey's account, or given me the reassurance"—the deep voice was oddly moving in its betrayal of controlled feeling—"that I had hoped that this affair is not to involve my young friend in any personal trouble. Yet I should be deeply grateful if you could do so. Mr. Hervey is a young man for whom I have the highest regard, and, more than that, he has laid me under a debt of gratitude which I can never hope to repay."

"Gratitude, sir? Indeed?" Gorham was genuinely surprised. Every generous impulse in his nature urged him to respond to an appeal which, from such a person, was, in truth, astounding. Yet official caution prevailed.

His theory of the Whitesands murder was complete. But it had yet to pass the final, irrefragable test of substantial proof. Till it had passed that test he could not, in sheer honesty, guarantee Herman Hervey's immunity from guilt.

His theory covered the motive for the crime, and every sinister detail of its committal, but it did not include the name of the murderer.

"Doctor Normanby, I cannot promise you that Mr. Hervey may not be faced with a difficult situation," he went on gravely, after a scarcely perceptible pause. "All I can say is that the information which I want to obtain from him should lead to the arrest of the real murderer, and the release of the present prisoner. But if you would care to tell me anything that you know about him I should be greatly obliged. I have never met him myself, and the descriptions his friends have given me are vague, and old at that. None of them had seen him for over four years. And it was sheer chance that put me on to the fact that he was a master here."

"Everything I know about him is highly to his credit."

"Exactly, sir"—eagerly. "Was he here last Monday night?"

"No. He left the school on Easter Saturday. I cannot state his movements during the last month with any certainty, though I have heard from him twice."

"Oh. You see, so far as I can make out he practically disappeared four or five years ago."

"Five years ago he left Cambridge to begin his career, if that is what you mean." Dr. Normanby spoke sharply, and with a glow of inward satisfaction Gorham realized that at last he had succeeded in annoying him into filling in the details of Herman Hervey's lost years. Ten minutes spent now in picking up what might later prove to be of immense value, should his theory break down, could easily be recovered on the road to Harborough.

"The suggestion of 'disappearance' with regard to Mr. Hervey is sheer nonsense," the headmaster said firmly. "His career has been perfectly open, and if he did not care to keep in touch with such acquaintance as you have come across, no doubt his reasons were adequate." He paused. "You may be aware that in swimming records England lags far behind other nations." He had decided, apparently, that frankness was the best service he could render to his assistant-master, and, logically, he began his story at the beginning of his personal association with him. "I was anxious that my boys should be instructed in the latest Continental methods, and therefore advertised for an instructor in various French, German, and Italian scholastic papers. This was nearly two years ago. I received numerous replies, among them one from Mr. Hervey, then teaching in a school near Bordeaux. His references were highly satisfactory. He is a qualified instructor in swimming, speaks French and Spanish fluently, and both of his former headmasters spoke enthusiastically of his character and excellent discipline. He also referred me to his tutor at Cambridge, who happens to be an old college friend of my own, and his reply clinched the engagement. Mr. Hervey joined us at the beginning of the summer term last year." He paused again. "He is a shy young man, and had been abroad for so long—ever since he left Cambridge—that at first his colleagues found him a trifle reserved. But he had quite settled down among us, and had earned the liking of the whole staff—the boys had capitulated from the first—even before the terrible experience of last Good Friday, when only his pluck and determination averted an appalling catastrophe, the drowning of six boys."

He drew a deep breath.

"My word, sir. What happened?"

"Easter fell early this year, you remember, ten days before school broke up. After morning chapel, and dinner, the boys were given till tea-time to amuse themselves as they chose. Some went out with parents, others played football, tennis and so on. Three were down with measles in the infirmary. Two of the staff were away with influenza. The others were kept fully occupied in an informal sort of oversight. I was engaged in taking the Three Hours' Service in a village church close by. I mention these details to explain how the absence of six boys was not at first noticed."

Gorham nodded.

"Easy enough to understand seeing the acreage of the grounds," he said. "Everyone would believe they were with someone else."

"Exactly. No one could possibly be blamed. On my return, however, I found their housemaster already growing anxious.

When he made sure from me that they had obtained no special leave of absence that they had forgotten to report, he became definitely alarmed, his thoughts turning to the shore half a mile away, which is, I need scarcely say, strictly out of bounds.

"But by that time it would have been already too late to save the children if Hervey had not discovered them.

"Four little lads had requested him to take them down to the bathing cove about three o'clock. It was fine, but there was a strong wind blowing and the sea was rough. The boats were all drawn up to the upper beach. He noticed at once, however, that a small boat always kept handy for emergencies was out on the water. He saw it was tossing a good deal, as if the rowers were in difficulties, and through his binoculars he saw it was filled with our boys, and actually saw it capsize. He did not hesitate for a second. Shouting to his charges to race for a boatman to fetch help, he flung off his blazer and plunged straight to their rescue. The little boys kept their heads, but they had difficulty in finding the men, who had gone home in view of the weather. Fortunately the other lads were all older, and managed to keep afloat till he reached them. He collected them first and cheerfully directed them how to hold on to the upturned boat, and then, two and two, he brought them ashore. Thanks to his training, they trusted and obeyed him perfectly.

"We reached the shore ourselves to find the boatmen bringing in the last boy, and Hervey himself completely exhausted with his incredible exertions and the buffeting he had received.

"The boys were little the worse, though we kept them in bed for a couple of days. Hervey soon recovered, and protested against being put to bed—I had him in my own house. But I insisted, and later the doctor looked grave and suggested that he had strained his heart. On Saturday a consultant came out from Ipswich and advised his instant removal to hospital for examination and possibly an operation. He had sustained some injury to the spine, and the immediate dread was paralysis. I wanted the operation to be performed here, but the necessary apparatus could not be brought—X-rays, electrical treatment afterwards, and other things only available in a hospital. He was conveyed to Ipswich at once, the operation was performed with complete success, and he remained there till he was sufficiently recovered in health to come away to Wales with my wife and myself. On the commencement of term, when I was compelled to return here, his health was almost restored, but as rest was still advisable, rather against his will he consented to prolong his vacation till the end of the summer holidays, and when we parted he crossed at once to Brittany to revisit some of his old haunts."

"And he is still abroad!" Gorham exclaimed, seeing his theory vanishing at the word into thin air.

"No. He returned to London recently. He has been wandering about, but he gave me this address of a friend's flat where letters would always reach him."

He handed across the card, and rose to indicate that the interview was at an end. "Now, Mr. Gorham, though I cannot conceive how he can possibly be connected with your case, you will understand that if he is involved in any difficulty, great or small, I am prepared to back him to the fullest extent of my capacity."

"Quite so, sir. I must urgently request that you will not communicate with him for twenty-four hours. May I rely on that? In return I promise to let you know at once if he needs your help."

"Very well."

"Mr. Hervey was not facially marked in any way by his experience?"

"Certainly not." He led the way, dismissively, into the hall, but there paused before a large school group which hung framed, among many others that lined the staircase, on the wall. "That is he." His finger pointed to a standing figure in the second row, whose pleasant eyes looked straight out at the photographer. "These"—the finger moved lower to a row of jolly youngsters squatting on the grass—"are the boys whose lives he saved."

"I venture to hope that they got off with the scare they must have had, sir. You must have felt ready to hug them simply for being alive."

The headmaster's face softened into a faint smile.

"My private feelings," he responded dryly, "did not deter me, when it was certain that they were unharmed, from punishing them severely for breaking bounds. *Pour encourager les autres.* Good afternoon."

"Good afternoon, sir. And thank you for giving me so much of your time." The servant handed Gorham his hat and showed him out. Five minutes later he cleared the lodge gates and was speeding along the road to Harborough.

CHAPTER XVIII

IT WAS A GORHAM new to Major Tennant's experience, determined, resolute, and impatient of interruption, who walked into Harborough police-station a few minutes before four, to find awaiting him the chief constable, Braice, Bond in the charge room on guard over an attaché-case and gladstone bag trying to look smaller than he was, and Mr. Moh effacing himself practically to the point of invisibility in a corner.

"My case is complete, or it is a complete fiasco, sir," he said brusquely to Tennant. "In either alternative the final proof lies in London. I must 'phone my A.C. at once. Then we must start. Meantime will you be so good as to inform the hospital that I must have a word with Colonel Rouncey if he has recovered consciousness."

"He has. But he is very weak. They are not letting anyone in."

"They've got to let me. Tell them I shan't hurt him."

He walked into Brake's private office and shut the door behind him.

The chief constable smiled at his superintendent, and shrugged his shoulders.

"This," he remarked lightly, "is evidently where Scotland Yard takes the floor and we senior officials jump to it. See there's food handy, Braice, in case he wants it. I believe the fellow lives on air when he's on the war-path."

He ran down the steps, crossed the square, and entered the grounds of the County Hospital, the stone gates of which flanked the tea-garden entrance of the Golden Crown.

He must have performed his allotted task effectually, for when Gorham reached the building a professionally disapproving though interested house physician met and conducted him at once to the private room on the ground floor where the patient lay.

"You understand he must not be agitated. And you must not stay more than five minutes," he said on the threshold.

"I shan't damage him, and three will be plenty."

He went to the bed beside the open window through which, beneath the lowered sunblind, a strip of turf showed pleasantly green. He bent over, gently pressed the weak hand on the sheet, and smiled down into the perturbed eyes.

"You know me, sir? Don't worry any more. I've got the whole thing straightened out, I believe. All about your meeting that morning."

"It was Carlo. He barked . . . and led me into the copse . . . from the path. He was there—"

"When you first went out? Yes, I thought so. He was fully dressed?"

"Of course—without a hat. Smoking. He was passing with a friend."

"Did you see the friend?"

"No. He was waiting for him, hanging about—so he just went up to look at the house."

"I know. You can see it below, through the trees there. Then you chatted?"

"For a few minutes, not long. Then we walked down to the lane to Oakleigh where he had left a car. And parted. He urged me to go. He didn't want it known he'd—"

"I know what he didn't want," Gorham murmured, to soothe the worried fear that leapt into the sick man's eyes. "How did you come out of the copse—by the path again? Yes? And when you parted where did you go?"

"Over the stile across the fields. Not far. But I was upset. I didn't want—ever—to go home again. Sick to death of it—years and years. No peace."

His breath came in a heavy sigh. Then, with weary compassion: "Poor miserable child . . . goaded. . . . But Tennant is seeing to her. Good fellow, Tennant. Can't be pleasant for him—his decent lad."

Gorham, alarmed at his mounting flush, pressed the electric bell on the table by the bedside and stooped down to add a hurried word.

"Don't worry your head about her any more, sir. She didn't do it. No, no, no. No need to fret about anything. It's all right." Rather dubiously, to the doctor who entered and pushed him unceremoniously aside to touch his patient's wrist: "I don't think I've hurt him."

The pulse was apparently reassuring, but the physician spoke firmly.

"Talked quite enough for the present, Colonel. This chap must clear out. What?" He stepped back and signalled to Gorham to bend over to catch a whisper.

"No, no, don't worry any more. Would you like him to come?"

"Not yet . . . no . . . not to—not to drag him in."

"All right. I'll be seeing him soon, so I'll just give him your love, eh?"

"Yes, just love. And be kind to the poor little thing."

"Yes, yes, we're seeing after her all right, sir. Our job now, not yours any more!" He gave him a cheerful glance, and left the room, passing a nurse in the doorway.

Back at the station his rougher manner returned.

He barked at Bond.

"Put all that in my car. I'll want you too. Fill her up and don't be all night about it."

Then a grateful gleam lit his eyes as they shifted from a thick slab of veal pie on the superintendent's table to the cup of steaming tea that flanked it.

"My word, Braice, that's the stuff to give the troops! You're a great man!"

"The chief, really." But Braice looked pleased. "You want me to carry on here? The Rolls, of course, but what about the swimming club reports?"

"Carry on with everything, old man," he spoke thickly, his mouth full of pie. "Aldeburgh gave me a lot, but there's still a chance I'm dead wrong. But if so you can drop everything, for the footprint clue is eliminated, and your prisoner is guilty. I'll give you the dope as soon as I've got it myself."

"You won't drop a hint?"

"Sorry. Well, this one. Lydia has been blackmailed to the tune of two-fifty a year ever since she came into her money. And I can't say how much, but she succeeded in lifting a tidy sum out of Burroughs probably for the same purpose, or I'm imagining things. And I couldn't," said Gorham positively, pausing to finish his tea, and banging the cup down to emphasize his statement—"imagine as much as all that. I haven't got the imagination. I'm damned, Braice! There's both your cup and saucer come in two! Must be made of eggshell china!"

"What did you think they were made of, iron?" Braice retorted. "We have 'em to drink out of, not for use as clubs! But have you an earthly what's happened to Burroughs? He's absconded."

"No, he hasn't. He's planked in an hotel in Bedford street, with a chap of mine sitting on his head to stop him off the poison bottle, old man. I want his yarn before he takes his sweet life, see? I'll send that along to you with the rest of the goods. If"—with a sudden relapse into profound gloom—"there are any."

Tennant, sitting by Gorham's side in front in the car, and, slightly nettled by his arbitrary silence, determined to ask no questions, had time to regret his vow, for they had run through the crowded narrow streets of Colchester before the chief inspector spoke.

"The way I read it, sir, is that deceased was blackmailed for years under cover of buying clothes through a commission agent called Evans. Her pass-book looked suspicious when I examined it on Tuesday. The figures for clothes were too high. In a place like Whitesands even an extravagant person doesn't spend £300 on dress. And Lydia was frugal. But the name was Evans. And the only cancelled cheque in that name in the pass-book pocket was for five pounds ten, to D. H. Evans, the Oxford Street shop. When I saw her account, dating back to her aunt's death, at the bank, it became a certainty. She gave out to the bank manager that she'd bought a fur coat—mink—for £200 last autumn. The entry for £200 was there right enough. But why go out of her way to comment on it to the manager? He let out she generally made some laughing apology for her extravagance when these entries appeared, but when it was a bona-fide purchase from D. H. Evans or any other ordinary shops she didn't bother."

"She knew herself it needed explanation if the manager did not?" Gorham nodded.

"Same thing with the servant at home. On Tuesday the girl showed me a second beach-suit, fellow of the green one she was drowned in, both bought from Perron et Cie, Rue Cambon, Paris. She had given out that she had paid an extravagant sum for them. But at the Galeries Lafayette they showed me on Wednesday the identical thing priced six pounds. And Perron's, being referred to, quoted the same price. And I saw the fur coat, soft brown fur, said to be mink, with a D. H. Evans label *sewed into the lining by Lydia herself*. And if it cost a penny more than fifteen pounds I'll raise my hat to the next marmot I meet at the Zoo. I'd got as much as that by Wednesday when I came back. But the bank account gave me something more. She'd paid several cheques for small amounts—including that to D. H. Evans—to ordinary shops this year, but for the first time not a quid to this D. Evans. The most feasible explanation of that is that somehow she had wangled it that Burroughs should be her paymaster instead."

"This defeats me altogether! You mean it offers an explanation of that will business? By the way, what did you mean by that sinister communication of yours about Lydia making Burroughs her heir? Did she leave any money?"

"A couple of hundred, no more. But she had given Burroughs to understand that her income was derived from capital that was hers absolutely, though in actual fact she held merely a life-interest in it. I can't tell you more than that, because the information reached me through a confidential source. But she signed the will last April."

"But what the devil did she make the will at all for, man! She couldn't know she was going to die within four months!"

"No. But Burroughs imagined they were going to be married next October. But"—grimly—"if he had handed out a big sum to forward some enterprises of his young lady's, he wasn't taking any chances on accidents intervening beforehand. Hence his idea of the will. Astute business chap, Burroughs. But not quarter astute enough to cope with his little woman!"

"This sounds like pure moonshine! That common, silly, brainless—"

"Not brainless, sir. She took you in as well as Mr. Robin. But not his brother. Odd, that. He must have tripped over her some time. That's the lot, so far." He added abruptly, "We are going to Burroughs first to get the truth out of him about this money deal."

"Look here, Chief Inspector"—Major Tennant spoke with definite impatience—"I begin to find these sudden shifts and changes of yours more than a little tiresome. I understand that Burroughs, whatever underhand pecuniary dealings he may have had with this dead woman, is not of major importance in your case. And the deal itself appears to be conjectural on your part, wanting confirmation you hope to obtain from the fellow himself. The result may certainly substantiate the unfavourable view you take of her character and career, but it can have no bearing whatever on the actual murder. Who committed the murder? Certainly not Burroughs. Then have you really obtained definite proof against someone else that lets the sister out? If so, I confess I'd be grateful for a frank statement of, at least, the murderer's name. Without wishing to seem unduly inquisitive I'd like to remind you that I have an official right to claim your confidence."

"If you are dissatisfied with my conduct of the case, sir, the remedy is in your own hands. You have only to lay your complaint before my official superiors, and request them to withdraw me from the case."

"Don't be a fool, Gorham. It's not your conduct of the case that I'm complaining about, but your conduct towards me. Damn it man, I've been a policeman myself for thirteen years! I'm not a child! You must have the common sense to realize that I find this dashed Baby-wait-a-little-longer, Mother-knows-best attitude of yours, infernally exasperating, as you would yourself in my place. Still"—the note of nervous irritation in his voice was abruptly checked, and the smile that gleamed in his tired eyes was suddenly friendly again—"I know by the terms of my own bargain I have no earthly right to demand any explanation till you're ready to give it. I handed the job to you, and it is yours to carry through by what methods you think best."

"Look here, sir," Gorham spoke with worried earnestness, "it's not that I'm out to make mysteries in order to pull off a spectacular alone-I-did-it stunt at the finish. You asked if I had obtained definite proof against someone else which clears Rosalind Torrington of guilt. The answer is, no. What I have got is a case built up on two solid, separate chains of fact which refuse, so far, to be linked together. I have spent most of this afternoon trying to think out a way to reconcile the contradictory statements of two absolutely reliable witnesses, and have failed. The only person who might have given me the answer one way or the other was Rouncey, and just when I was leading up to the question he showed symptoms of threatening another seizure, so I had to stop. Both my chains of fact are fool-proof as far as they go, but they both break off at the same point. The problem is these two conflicting statements."

"What are the two chains of fact?"

"One leading up out of the past, Lydia's past; the second covering the circumstances of the crime," was the troubled reply. "You know the questions in every crime—where, when, and the rest . . ."

"*Quis? Quid? Ubi? Quando?* Those are answered in this case. We know who was the victim; that the crime was murder; and when and where it was committed. But I get your point. At last!"

The chief constable grew alert, a sparkle of keen intelligence banishing the lines of fatigue from his blue eyes.

"It is a missing connection between the final questions—*Cur* and *a quo*—why and by whom—that's worrying you. You've got sound answers to both separately, but unless you can make them tally—fit your answer to the 'why', the motive, in other words, on to the answer you have got to the 'by whom' which is covered by your reconstruction of the circumstances of the crime—both answers are useless."

"You have hit it exactly, sir. Both my chains of evidence are true in fact. But unless they can be fitted into each other they can have no bearing on the murder. And so far these two conflicting statements separate them. If I fail to get the missing link that reconciles them my case falls to the ground."

"And the murderer gets off without a stain on his character."

"Oh no, Chief. The failure of my attempt to bring home a charge of murder to the person who dived off that point will, by eliminating every other possible suspect from the case, establish the guilt of Rosalind Torrington."

Tennant's face grew haggard.

"My God—yes, it must, of course. You've somehow inspired me with such faith in your ability to clear obstacles that look insuperable that I'd lost sight of what your failure must mean to that miserable girl."

"We needn't worry about failure till it happens," said Gorham philosophically. "All I've said was simply to explain that I can only tackle the job in my own way. One thing after another. All neat and methodical. My next job, for instance, is to finish this piece of pie." He produced an uninviting newspaper parcel from his pocket and regarded it with affection. "Then I collect Burroughs' evidence—he's at the 'Wentworth' in Bedford Street—and get a report from Inspector Manning, who's been handling the London end of the enquiry today. He will be at the 'Wentworth' too. That will take about an hour. All that is normal routine, sir, and if you want to cut out of it I can either pick you up later, or, if you prefer, submit my written report of the completed case tomorrow morning, in my office. At headquarters."

The chief constable turned and stared, then suddenly broke into a shout of laughter.

"Gorham, I'm inclined to envy your superiors at the Yard. They must find you quite an entertaining fellow to work with, far more amusing than Braice ever is. Certainly I shall leave you to tackle your routine job alone. I don't yearn to renew my acquaintance with Burroughs. You can have that item of your programme to yourself with pleasure. But if you attempt to exclude me from the later, more exciting items, and foist me off with a written report, I shall be hurt. And if you think I intend to risk my valuable life sitting here beside you while you drive through Whitechapel and eat pie, you can correct your impression of my foolhardiness. I'm brave, of course, but not d—d brave. So pull up, please, and change places."

"Right, sir. I'll look in here first, though."

He drew to the kerb outside Bow police-station, and was absent for ten minutes. When he returned he took Tennant's vacated seat with a brief, "O.K. so far," and relapsed into silence till they were running through the Strand.

Tennant refrained from interrupting his thoughts. His mind, piecing the scattered fragments of the case together, formed a picture of what might have happened on the coast that tragic morning. That green-clad figure slipping from her home in the twilight of a summer's morning to meet Someone at the cove. She and Someone meeting and swimming out again, leisurely, she certainly unsuspicious of danger. Then, suddenly, in the open sea, under cover of the point of the promontory, a swift, determined grip on the nape of a white neck, a deathly struggle while she, choking, fought for her life. Then the murderer's swift appraisement of his situation as he held the limp, still thing, the few strong strokes that would bring into view the chimneys of Melita Villa, the upper windows reflecting the sun's slanting rays, the dash for the buoy where the body would be discovered from the shore of her home, far, at any rate, from the cove his guilty conscience connected with himself. Before Moh came on to the beach, of course, but perhaps not more than a minute before. Then back again still under water, to the shelter of the point to peer round the farther side. And a nasty jolt. Some spectator was it, on the road above the cove? Essential he should not be seen in the water with that buoy asking for discovery of its secret—so—a swift ascent of the hill-side where the convex formation of the earth-covered rock concealed him from view of anyone on shore. A wait up there lying flat, then—well, what then? Why had he not slipped down again at the place he had ascended, or crossed the wilderness and descended by the path to the cove? Was someone still watching there? By Jove, it might well have been Robin! So—that dive. And the rest silence.

How much of all that had Gorham got chapter and verse for?

The whole reconstruction was imaginary apart from those footprints in the sand. And the date of those was problematical.

Braice's case required no imaginary aid to fill out an array of damning facts. A young woman whipped to murderous jealousy by certainty that Lydia had gone again to meet her lover follows to confront her with her gross betrayal. Meets her at the point and drowns her in a desperate struggle in which her fury lends her just that advantage of strength that their equal skill in the water demands. Then, the deed done, her swift return—heard by the servant, the stripping off and hiding her wet bathing-dress and the towel. The lies, the mixture of brazen effrontery and cowardly terror—just what might be expected. . . .

"Here we are, sir," came Gorham's voice. "You leave us here. I have only one call to make after this, in a turning off Edgware

Road. If you wish to be present I'll pick you up outside Marble Arch tube at eight-thirty."

"Right. I'll be there."

He opened the door and slipped out on to the pavement as Gorham slid into the driving-seat. But suddenly, as the car swung round into Bedford Street and he was left alone, the optimistic mood which Gorham's personality had aroused in him vanished, and he felt dispirited and weary.

The fellow was after all an able and practical police officer only. Not a worker of miracles. He had never claimed to be engaged on more than the sound and necessary work of elimination of every possible suspect but Rosalind Torrington from the case. It was certainly not his fault that his robust and vigorous character had influenced him, Tennant, into leaping at a belief that he was capable of a miraculous clearing up of the mess against his own reason and common sense.

He had intended to spend his vacant hour in looking up his sister's household. But on the instant he changed his mind. He had despatched Robin to Jessica's charge to give him a chance to pull himself together in an entirely fresh atmosphere, and it was useless to disturb the lad till he had final news to give him. He would just make sure that he was all right, though.

He rang up his sister, and regretted he couldn't turn up to dinner as he had wired he would do.

"Detained—you know the lyric about the policeman's life, Jessica," he added mendaciously.

"I thought it was you who detained people, not people you," came Jessica's voice, jeering at the flimsy excuse, and he chuckled, feeling better.

"I'll blow in later . . . and stop the night if I may."

"Do! But don't worry your poor, weak head, dear, about your nursery! Yes, they are both here, but my nursery is behaving quite nicely as hosts. Edwin and May—but especially May—rallying round the stricken heart with intense earnestness, and rather showing the clumsy parent the lifted eyebrow, keep-off-the-sacred-grass sign. But I'm inclined to believe that a pleasant time is being had by all, for the furrows on Will's brow are coming distinctly unstuck. So leave it to Jeeves!"

"Bless the child!" he said heartily, picturing a shingled Jeeves blue-eyed with curling lashes and a serious but most kissable mouth.

Relieved by this conversation, he sat down to dinner in highly welcome solitude, at Watteau's, where the head waiter knew his tastes.

Meantime, after a brief conversation with Detective-Inspector Manning, who, after reporting his own progress and receiving certain orders, delivered a sealed note from the Assistant Commissioner, Gorham consigned his passengers to his charge and entered the dingy passage of the private hotel. He directed the equally dingy factotum who doubled the parts of porter and odd man to lead him at once to the room of Mr. Burroughs.

A shilling having removed all scruples as to omitted courtesies from the mind of the factotum, he obliged by thrusting him into the solicitor's presence with the single utterance "Genlemn-syou-sir", and promptly withdrawing.

The chief inspector stepped into the disordered bedroom and closed the door behind him, and as the man, starting up from the suitcase he was feverishly packing, wheeled round and realized the identity of his visitor, he drew himself up and attempted to carry off the situation with a haughty exclamation of anger at the intrusion.

But Gorham cut him short with an authoritative gesture.

"Mr. Burroughs! No bluster, please. The time for that sort of bluff is past," he said with severity. "You must be aware that you have placed yourself in a very serious position by running away from Whitesands like this. And I see I'm only just in time to prevent you from trying to run further!" he added with a significant glance at the half-filled suitcase on the bed.

"What the hell do you mean! I came up to town on business—"

"Business that included getting your passport renewed—eh?" He watched the sickly pallor overspread the man's unshaven face. "Come, come, we know all about the business that brought you up last night. But you didn't mention to your clerk or your landlady you contemplated a trip across the Channel, did you? . . . Odd time to choose for it, too, with your fiancée lying unburied. Did you really suppose I'd let an important person in this murder investigation I'm conducting slip through my hands without taking the common precaution to have you watched?"

"Look here, you've got it wrong, absolutely wrong! I had to come to London on urgent private business! Nothing whatever to do with the murder!"

"Had it nothing to do with the will you persuaded deceased to make in your favour?" Gorham retorted.

Burroughs looked desperate.

"She didn't leave anything. She'd nothing to leave."

Gorham sat down on the bed and, planting his two hands on his knees, leaned forward.

"You only learned that today. At Somerset House. Mr. Burroughs, by your own statement to me, at the very moment that Lydia Torrington was murdered you were bathing in the sea and at that moment, you *believed* yourself to be her heir! Now. Wait a minute. Think! Mind you, I am not actually charging you with the murder. Had I come here with the intention of arresting you, it would have been my duty to give you the preliminary warning. As it is, I am pointing out that your conduct from first to last has been highly suspicious. The single fact that I have detected you now preparing to bolt out of the country would justify my taking immediate action."

Burroughs groaned, and collapsed on to a chair almost whimpering. It was obvious that he was completely unnerved.

"I had nothing whatever to do with the murder!" he protested. "Nothing! I was on the north beach the whole time! I didn't know a thing about it till Rouncey rang me up. And then I nearly fainted with the shock. I told you all that before!"

"What I want," said Gorham brutally, "are facts—solid facts that I can test and verify, not a pack of assertions and fairy-tales such as you entertained me with during our interview at your office. If you have any explanation to give of your relations with the murdered woman which can possibly explain the damning fact that you persuaded her to name you her residuary legatee, and your astounding subsequent conduct, I am prepared to listen to it, but if you haven't . . ."

He shrugged his shoulders.

The wretched man looked at him with hunted eyes.

"Are you asking me to clear myself of complicity in the murder?" he muttered. His bluster was gone, but sharp cunning gleamed for a second in his bloodshot eyes as he glanced up from between the hands in which his face was half hidden at the indomitable figure of the chief inspector.

"I am asking you to come across with the plain story of your relations with the deceased," barked Gorham sternly. "And don't attempt to lay traps for me. I can only regard your reluctance to speak out honestly as highly prejudicial to your best interests, but if you refuse . . ."

"I don't refuse." Burroughs straightened his shoulders and tried with small success to recapture his dignity as a man and a lawyer which his initial collapse had distinctly impaired. "I am perfectly ready to answer any questions you like provided you put them with common civility! When I left Whitesands last evening I had every intention of returning this morning. Your suggestion that I either ran away in the first instance, or have been in hiding since, is entirely unwarranted. This is the hotel at which I generally put up when I come to town, and I have made no attempt to conceal my presence here. My business was purely private, and had nothing to do with that ghastly murder."

"It had everything to do with the will which you persuaded your fiancée to make in your favour," was the sharp retort. "Your first action this morning was to consult the will of Miss Annabel Torrington to discover the amount of Lydia's estate."

"And what I did discover was that I'd been had!" Burroughs was stung to a bitter snarl. "I didn't persuade her to make that will either! She offered to. We were to have been married in October. It was only a temporary arrangement to safeguard me from total loss of a sum she got me to pay out. Eight hundred pounds she and her damned pal Evans had out of me . . . and now she's dead, and her will isn't worth the paper it's written on, and I'm faced with ruin! Instead of following me about, your b—y cops would have been better employed catching Evans, though I bet he's cleared out already—gone while the going was good. His office in Greek Street has been empty for a fortnight. But the neighbours seemed to know nothing about him there in any case. I bet the office itself was a sheer blind! Hired for a few weeks, probably, just to put up a show! And you have never heard of Evans, I suppose!"

"Don't worry about Evans. He never had an office of his own. Just used that place in Greek Street that belonged to a perfectly decent little milliner for a consideration when he wanted it. We're looking after Evans all right. It's your part in these money transactions I'm out to get hold of at the moment. Suppose you start at the beginning. When did you first meet Evans?"

"Last March." Burroughs looked startled, and not a little intimidated by the detective's display of knowledge. Gorham's air of official omniscience did not betray that it was recently acquired, the fruit of two days' indefatigable exertions on the part of Manning and his assistants, who had worked out a dossier of Evans to which the A.C.'s sealed note had added the crowning touch. "But Lydia first mentioned him when she came back from France last year. She was away for three weeks with an old school-friend, staying mostly in Paris. One day when she was talking about her trip she told me she had run across a man there who used to be awfully in love with her. She said I needn't feel jealous because it was only a boy-and-girl affair—when she was a romantic little girl—and chiefly on his side, at that. And he was a boy living with his parents. And they had completely lost sight of each other. But since then he had made a fortune. Had got a flourishing business in Paris with a branch in London—"

"Did she say what the business was?"

"Yes. A dress-importing business. Buying frocks, coats, etcetera, at trade prices from French wholesale houses—last year's models and that—and selling them at ten per cent profit here and abroad, Australia chiefly. He had made a jolly good thing of it for years, and was obviously awfully prosperous. He had taken her and her friend about a lot in a swell car he sported, and treated them to several expensive entertainments. . . . Shouldn't be surprised if that friend turned out to be sheer bunk like all the rest! . . ."

"Did she ever bring Evans home?"

"You bet she didn't! But she'd got a convincing yarn to cover all that too. Mind you, she scarcely ever told you anything in so many words . . . it was what she let you infer. . . . One day she looked worried when I admired a very chic fur coat she was wearing, and owned up that it was a present from Evans. 'But, darling, honestly, I don't know what to do about it!' she said. 'It was awfully nice of him to send it me, and I don't suppose he paid anything like as much as one would have to do in the shops, but it is mink—dreadfully expensive fur—and I know uncle would be awfully annoyed at me accepting expensive presents. . . . He's awfully old-fashioned in his ideas, and I haven't even liked to tell him about meeting Mr. Evans again.' Naturally I took the hint and didn't mention him either at the Villa. Not that the Colonel ever talked to me if he could help it. He never had a word to throw to a dog. Just fidgeted about and cleared off as soon as he could when anyone was there. Later on Lydia told me she'd after all insisted on paying for the coat—I'm bound to say at the time I admired her for being so damned scrupulous—but she said Evans was a bit hurt. Well, then, after a bit of coolness between them she heard from him again at Christmas . . ."

"Did you see any of his letters?"

"No. I'm only telling you what she said . . . the way things sort of leaked out about Evans. I gathered he'd forgiven her for being so fussy about accepting the coat by Christmas, and in January she told me that he had written saying he was turning his business into a company, and laughingly suggesting if she wanted ten per cent interest for any loose cash she had lying by, now was the time. She didn't bother about it, because her money was invested in Government stock, and as she didn't know anything about investments it was best to leave it so. But it set me thinking. It happened I'd made a few hundreds in a lucky hit, but I was terribly pressed. I'd had to buy out Mr. Clifford. . . . the last payment is made now, but it has been a frightful pull to scrape the instalments together. And I'd got other debts. I'd gone the pace rather as a student, and I've been struggling under a millstone of entanglements ever since, never able to get ahead of embarrassment. These few hundreds by themselves would have simply been a drop in the ocean— but with Clifford paid off and the practice freed at last from that drain, I thought if I could find a lucrative and private investment for this little nest-egg—"

"I quite understand, Mr. Burroughs," Gorham interrupted with dry impatience. "You've been in the hands of moneylenders for years, and what you wanted was a private cache for the results of your last and luckiest ticket in the Irish Sweep that wouldn't have to appear among your assets if your creditors got the wind up and turned nasty. Don't worry. It was a normal part of my routine work to look up your financial status, but all that is your own affair. It is the Lydia-Evans combination that interests me. How did they work the ramp?"

Burroughs winced.

"It never for a second occurred to me that it was a ramp! Look here, if you'd known Lydia you'd never have guessed it either. I ran up to town last March, and she was up too at the same time, to visit the dentist. She mentioned she was meeting Evans for tea at the Savoy. I don't know which of us suggested I should join them. At any rate I did. We had a jolly party. Evans struck me as a darned good sort. He chipped her about turning down his offer of a share in his company—said she'd missed the chance of a lifetime and so on. But not as if he cared a rap for the cash side, only sorry not to do her a good turn. They were friendly together, but his manner to her was just that of an old friend, nothing more. He said he was glad to meet me, congratulated us both, asked when the wedding was to be. Well, after we'd seen her into her train at Charing Cross—he drove us both in his car, a Rolls, mind you—he offered me a further lift, and dropped in at a very prosperous-looking dress and millinery establishment in Greek Street on the way. They were just closing, but I saw there was a big staff, though he took me straight up to his private office, and we spoke to no one but the manageress, whom we passed on the stairs. She only smiled, and said, 'Good evening, Mr. Evans.' But somehow she impressed me favourably at once. Rather on the dowdy side, but sensible, and trustworthy. Well, he stood me dinner at the Troc and, to cut it short, I suggested taking up shares in his show. Offered to make it a cash transaction, and gave him the money next morning in notes. He gave me an acceptance, but I haven't a scrap of written evidence that the transfer of my cash was anything more than, say, payment of a debt. At the time I hadn't a doubt it was perfectly O.K. And dash it, even now I'm not dead certain he tricked me! The Greek Street place was shut up this morning when I went there, but a fellow told me the business was moving to bigger premises—"

"In Leicester Square. Quite true. But nothing to do with Evans. Go on."

"Well, a few days later I mentioned the thing to Lydia. She was a bit flustered, asked me questions: Did I think I'd been wise? Was my money quite safe? She had always liked Evans, knew he was a thoroughly good sort, and, of course, he had the real Midas touch, but suppose anything happened to him—like a street accident— before all this dreadful business that she didn't understand, about the forming of the company, was finished? She felt responsible because he was her friend, and she had introduced us. Of course she knew I was really safe because when we married I should have all her money, but suppose anything happened to her before our wedding! . . . I chipped her with having got accidents on the brain, but she looked serious and kissed me. . . . Pah! Well that night she rang me up to say she'd got a bright idea, and next day she asked me to draw up her will. I sent her to Assheton's of Harborough. I didn't persuade her to make that will at all. Though I acknowledge I felt an immense weight had been lifted off my mind when it was done. When we were married I knew I could clear off all my liabilities at once and make an absolutely fresh start. My practice, once it is clear of debt, is a sound if small one, and it is capable of being worked up. Then came her death. And the same day a peremptory refusal to renew a heavy bill fallen due. I went to Assheton and he refused to give me any satisfaction. He thought I was being indecently previous, the smug swine. I rang up Evans' private number, and was told he was out of town. I began to smell something fishy behind the will business, and rushed up to town to look up the aunt's will at Somerset House, as, if I hadn't been a b—y fool, I'd have done in the first place. You know what I discovered. It was useless to try to retrieve my credit. I haven't ten quid of ready cash today that I can lay hands on, and between them they'd lifted the only liquid money I had, and all I can possibly hope for is whatever balance she may have left in her account to meet liabilities that a thousand would scarcely cover!"

Gorham rose.

"I'm sorry for you, Mr. Burroughs. Seems to me that in trying to cope with this astute lady you met a good deal more than your match in brains. But I advise you to pull yourself together and face the situation with common sense. Absconding abroad isn't going to help. It means abandoning your profession and living on your wits for the rest of your life. I suggest that you face your creditors with the frank truth, that as you are not worth shot and shell if they bankrupt you, they lose everything. Whereas, if they give you time to go back to Whitesands and get on with your job there, your practice is your one solid asset. They will fight shy of legal proceedings as much as you do. Public examination of their books is a thing that sort of bird avoids if he can. Too much is apt to be dragged into daylight, and the law is a two-edged weapon. You've got to stop in any case to give evidence at the trial. Better make a virtue of necessity and gather in all the local sympathy you can collect as the bereaved fiancé, eh? The publicity may do your business a lot of good, give it quite a fillip! We shan't give away any private sidelights that don't concern the case—unless you play the fool and force us to. As for the young woman's balance, don't bank on that. It just covers the two legacies you made her insert to save your face, with a hundred or so to the good."

"Good G—d! And my eight hundred!"

"Take my tip and don't whine to anyone about that lost eight hundred. It won't enhance the respect they have for your business acumen in the town. You were played for a sucker by the hoariest confidence trick in creation, the guileless feminine sweetheart and the bluff, honest pal, Put a little horse-sense into yourself, man! Go home and carry off the situation with the bunting all out! Now I've got to go. But look here, Burroughs, I accept your tale as true, because most of it squares with information I've got already. But don't start anything with us now. See?"

"No, no. Honestly, I've told you the stark truth, nothing else. I believe you are right. I've been crazy with panic all day thinking of the cursed hole I'm in. Are you sure nothing has leaked out in the town?"

"Quite. Can you see Mr. Assheton letting out professional secrets? No one else has anything on you that I know of. Probably they think you came to town to choose a crêpe hatband to act chief mourner at the funeral. Mr. Assheton has got the funeral arrangements in hand. It is to take place at two p.m. tomorrow but you'd better wire him about the time. You will be the hero of the hour in a nice black suit. And no one will guess that you're mourning the loss of eight hundred quid a damned sight more than your sweet young lady."

"Oh, keep your cursed sarcasm to yourself!" the man shouted, turning on him with blazing anger. "I know I've been had for a mug, but she *did* like me at first. I hadn't a bean when we got engaged . . . if she hadn't liked me she could have turned me down when she saw I was in love. . . . It was after I told her about winning that cash she must have . . . must have . . ."

"Probably," Gorham said, and departed.

CHAPTER XIX

MAJOR TENNANT waited with growing impatience at the appointed spot, scanning Oxford Street as closely as incessantly moving crowds along the pavement, and interminable chains of buses halting to block out the view, would permit for the approach of the police car. He was a man accustomed by training to acting on his own initiative, and the suspense of the last two days, during which he had compelled himself to accept a subordinate role and hang about inactively while the Scotland Yard man took the lead and doled out meagre scraps of information which seemed as pointless as they were disconnected, had had a wearing effect on his sensitive temperament, and, it must be confessed, on his temper. Dinner had revived his fortitude, but not his optimism.

"I was a fool to come on this senseless expedition," he thought irritably. "It's simply a case of gambling on the hundredth chance, and tomorrow I'll be back where we were on Tuesday morning, getting down to the real job, and preparing Robin to face the infernal publicity of that vixen's trial." He glanced at his watch for the second time in five minutes.

"Sorry I've kept you waiting."

Gorham had come out of the station exit behind him, and Tennant raised questioning eyebrows.

"Hello! Where's the rest of your little touring party?"

"Manning has it in charge, sir. He will be along in a moment."

"But I'm still to be conducted round the sights by the chief guide? I'm privileged, my dear fellow! Where do we go now, the Chamber of Horrors to meet your elusive murderer? Or is it still a case of the blind leading the blind?"

"I'm not so blind I don't see you think I'm making mysteries for the sheer pleasure of being dramatic, sir." Gorham's good humour was proof against the other's sarcasm. "But talking of drama, a thing I heard a fellow say in a play once—one of Shakespeare's it was—stuck in my head. This chap said to his wife: 'Thou canst not utter what thou dost not know!' Put like that it sounds obvious. But it's true of me now. I can't utter what I don't know. When I've seen one of the two men we are going to call on now I'll know who did the murder. And if you come with me you will know as soon as I do."

"Good enough! Lead on, Macduff! Hadn't we better agree on some secret sign by which you will communicate the sinister revelation to me?"

"You won't remain long in doubt, Major Tennant," was the sober reply. "If he is the criminal you will witness his arrest."

Tennant's irritation finally vanished. He felt remorseful. By his own deliberate act he had called Gorham to take control of the investigation, and now, when he was bracing himself to face the gravest duty a police-officer must perform, the act which must place a fellow human being on trial for his life, instead of giving him the loyal support that common decency demanded, he was pettishly baiting him as an outlet for irritated temper with the true cause of which the chief inspector's conduct of the case had nothing to do.

"Sorry, Gorham," he murmured with a little smile. "Afraid I've sounded rather boorish. But I appreciate your difficulties. Did the interview with Burroughs yield anything?"

"It confirmed my theory so far. Lydia and Evans, the blackmailer to whom she paid regular hush-money, rooked him of eight hundred pounds last March by the bogus share trick. A trick you'd imagine couldn't take in a modern baby in arms, if we didn't get proof positive that the con men pull it off every week, specially on victims of Burroughs' conceited type. The will business was done by Lydia to allay any belated misgivings he might have developed later. And it served their turn perfectly. He hadn't the smallest suspicion that Lydia was not, as she asserted, in control of the capital from which her income was derived till today, when, driven by private financial pressure to ascertain how he stood, he turned up the aunt's will at Somerset House. This mustn't go beyond ourselves. It would not be fair to Burroughs' reputation in Whitesands."

"Quite. But what the dickens was her object in grossly swindling the fellow she intended to marry? The thing defeats me altogether!"

"She wasn't going to marry him. Yes, I know it was given out that the marriage was to come off in October. But in my view she had made quite different plans for October. Her engagement to Burroughs and the will business, and even her semi-*sub rosa* love-making to her sister's young man, were all designed to one object, to jolly the whole lot of them, her sister included, along till she had bullied or persuaded or threatened Evans into agreeing to the plan she had determined on for October. . . . Hullo, Manning!"

"Yes, sir. The young man has turned up at last." The voice of the tall man who had hurried to join them sounded breathless. "I hadn't to summon him. He came of his own accord. Evans is inside. He hasn't quitted the flat since his return on Tuesday. I've got the search-warrant for the premises, and Sergeant Prout is there on guard. And Moh. I gave Prout your instructions that if you summoned him by name he was to take the man to the station and keep him till you arrived, if not, he was to let him go."

"Right. I've an idea that the A.C. intends to turn up himself, but I'm not sure. But in that case Prout will get his orders from him when he reaches the station. You are sure Evans doesn't guess we're coming?"

"Don't see how he can. We've been careful. This way, sir. A first-floor flat. Over a greengrocer's. Convenient, that, as the lower premises are closed at night. But I've got the keys."

They hurried through a court behind the Regal Cinema, and round a couple of corners till they reached a dark and empty street at the end of which Tennant saw the lights and traffic of Edgware Road. He was suddenly infected with a spirit of excitement in which minor doubts and threads of thought were forgotten. He lost his half-unconscious sense of official superiority. He might be chief constable in Harborough and fancy himself great and good at his job of keeping order in a sleepy country district, but these fellows of the C.I.D. put in as much experience of criminal hunting in a week as he spread over a year.

He'd been right to call in Gorham, and right, dead right, to trust him, dead wrong to lose confidence in him because he brought an easy-going, matter-of-fact manner to an intricate job and always said less than he knew. His easiness was the ease of the expert with absolute mastery of the technique of his work.

He was ashamed of his very excitement now since, in spite of his titular rank, it stamped him in his own sight as an amateur.

Gorham only spoke once as Manning slipped ahead into a shuttered doorway.

"You understand, sir—unless I get that connecting link here, this means nothing."

Tennant nodded. They slipped, noiseless shadows, round the half-open door, which was instantly closed behind them, shutting them in the inky blackness of a narrow passage in which were to be felt large bodies squeezed flat against a wall to let them pass.

"Moh's gone up," came breathed information that did not reach the volume of a whisper, and a circle of light from a torch illuminated the lower steps of a flight of stairs that terminated the passage.

They went up.

A second, shorter flight, consisting of four stairs only, appeared less impenetrably dark, for a chink of light came through a door ajar on the second landing from which, as they sighted it, the small figure of Mr. Moh stepped soundlessly back.

The intuition of the chief constable leapt to a possibility of connection between this presence of Mr. Moh on the upper landing and that sudden chink of light. But . . . his not to reason why. . . . Gorham, who would not have lent his approval to any nefarious tampering with a lock by an official subordinate of his own, accepted blandly, without probing for causes, the lucky chance that the door was open.

Across the darkness of a tiny lobby they looked into a large room furnished as a sitting-room, in which were two men, one sprawling in an armchair behind a table on which stood glasses, a water-jug and two whisky bottles, one empty, the other full, from which the younger man had apparently just unscrewed the stopper, for he had banged it in again none too gently as they reached their post of observation. The angry voices, raised in dispute, reached them clearly.

"Pour out that drink and stop talking like a b—y fool! It hurts me like hell to move!" came in a menacing growl from the man in the chair. But the younger, who was facing his companion, his back to the doorway, appeared to be in a mood of indignant revolt.

"Shut up, Evans! You're doing yourself no earthly good lounging there soaking whisky. This wretched room looks as if you'd been planted there since I saw you last night. You haven't even shaved. If you're ill you'd better go to bed and let me fetch a doctor—"

"Damn doctors . . ."

"Well, I'm not coming again! I've absolutely finished with you. I'd never have interfered at all if I hadn't hoped you and your wife were going to get things finally settled between you at last. Now all that is taken out of our hands. So that's that. Still, you do look frightfully ghastly tonight. Honestly, I don't like leaving you alone if you're really dicky . . ." His tone was filled with a reluctant anxiety that the oddly blotchy, yet pale and haggard face of the man in the chair justified. His tousled appearance—he was clad over his underclothes in a dingy dressing-gown—added to the two-days' growth that darkened his fleshy jowl, sunken features and heavy-lidded, bloodshot eyes, combined to give him a sufficiently ghastly aspect. Turning to glance frowningly at the bottle, which obviously he connected with the fellow's stupid condition, a sound behind him attracted the younger man's attention, and he wheeled round to confront Gorham.

The chief inspector spoke.

"Mr. Herman Hervey, I believe . . . of Doctor Normanby's staff?"

Tennant saw the pleasant face, which a second before had looked resentful and anxious, flush up in hot surprise.

He came forward at once.

"Yes. But . . . what . . . I mean . . . is the Head here?"

He looked at Gorham frankly, yet with a touch of uneasiness, that made the more pronounced a flickering pulse in the drooping right eyelid, and an intermittent throbbing of the facial nerve.

"No. But will you be good enough to explain why you wrote from here instead of your hotel, to Dr. Normanby? Deliberately misleading him as to your address?"

"I didn't mislead him!" Hervey retorted hotly. "At least I gave him this address, which I told him was that of a friend's flat, instead of the Mandville in Russell Square where I'm staying because—well simply because he'd said something about running up to town to choose prizes in July, and I didn't want him to know about this beastly tic!" He rubbed his face. "He had been so awfully decent to me, you know, and when this started I didn't want him to drop in on me unexpectedly. I say, do explain . . . Are you a friend of his?"

"Not exactly. To be candid. I'm a police-officer engaged on the Whitesands crime, and I've been trying to trace you on account of Colonel Rouncey—"

"My uncle? What? Does he want me to run down?"

"I'll tell you about him in a minute. Finish your own explanation first, will you? I saw the headmaster this afternoon, and he informed me of your illness and its cause, but assured me that when you parted from him after your Welsh holiday your health was quite restored."

"So it was. But I managed to get a cold in the head in Brittany, and then neuralgia started, and all this." Again he rubbed his cheek and drooping eyelid. "The doctor I've been consulting here says it's a sort of aftermath—weakened nerves and that, simply temporary, and nothing to worry about. But after the Head's most awful decency to me in the spring—no one could have been kinder to anyone than he and Mrs. Normanby both were—I didn't want to worry him about it. But if he'd dropped into the Mandviile when he was in town, of course he must have spotted it instanter. So, as I had run across Mr. Evans in Oxford Street the very morning I first wrote, I gave his address instead of the hotel. Three weeks ago that was, and the beastly thing was much worse than it is now."

"Hadn't you seen Mr. Evans before that morning?"

"No. Before we met in the street I hadn't seen him for nearly five years. And then only twice. It was rather cool, I own, but when I came round and told him he didn't mind, did you, Evans?"

"Mind? Why should I? I thought you were fibbing and it was some wench you expected letters from, but I'm not one to disoblige a pal."

Evans had not shifted his position. His heavy eyes surveyed the group by the door with an indifference that went better with his drawling tones and the physical inertness of his big body than a hint of tense waiting for what might happen next that his wary stillness suggested. "Don't mind your asking all your little pals to come in and make themselves at home, come to that. What about offering everybody a spot . . . me as well?"

Manning, at whom the chief inspector suddenly glanced while ignoring this genial invitation on his own account, obligingly walked round the table, splashed a small drink into the tumbler and handed it to the passive host.

Evans drank it greedily at a gulp.

"Felt I could do with that, old sport," he murmured to the detective, who remained beside his chair, and permitted him to replace the glass on the table.

"Thank you, Mr. Hervey, that explains what looked a little odd at first, about the address. But now, about this tragedy at Whitesands. You must have seen the papers! Why did you not go down at once to your uncle's help?"

Hervey stared.

"Look here, I thought you said you came from my uncle! Surely he told you that he wrote himself to urge me to do nothing of the sort?"

"Had he this address too, then?" Gorham asked sharply.

"My dear fellow! I'd told him I was at the Mandville. He wrote there, of course! I got the letter Wednesday morning. He told me the ghastly thing that had happened and the frightful time they were having with a 'bobbie' planted on them in the house, and Rosalind absolutely demented, and he said it would be absolutely the final straw if I dashed down and got mixed up in it too. He begged me not even to write! If ever anybody had had a foul time it was Uncle George! But still, if that was how he felt about it I felt the only thing for me to do was to stop away till he summoned me. Has he sent you to fetch me now?"

"Not exactly. He had a slight stroke after the inquest and has been in hospital at Harborough since. But certainly before you race off down there I must explain his wishes more fully but"—he looked at Evans slouched back in his chair between Manning upright on one side and on the other the small figure of Mr. Moh, who had flitted round the table so silently during the preceding conversation that even Gorham was not certain at what moment he had made the movement, then back at the young man's twitching face—"it had best be in private. I suggest you go to my quarters, where I can give you full details of everything." He opened the door and with a firm hand on his arm drew him out on to the landing. "Prout . . . are you there? Good! Show this gentleman the way, will you? If Captain Tring is there he will explain the whole situation to you, Mr. Hervey. If not, make yourself comfortable till I come. You can amuse yourself looking up trains to Harborough," he added with a smile to Hervey, "because we will probably go down together tomorrow. Go ahead with Prout now. I shan't be long."

His final words had been inaudible in the room.

He re-entered slowly, closed the door and, with his back against it, drew two papers from his pocket and glanced through them.

A flat sense of the fatuity of the proceedings had invaded the mind of Major Tennant during the interrogation of Hervey which culminated in blank disappointment with his abrupt dismissal, but now, suddenly recognizing the nature of the forms in his hand, he realized that somehow—somewhere—in that apparently unilluminating interchange the chief inspector had got his missing clue.

He stiffened with a thrill of excitement, yet completely bewildered. Then, as his eye fell on Mr. Moh on guard by the left side of Evans' chair, light poured on his mind.

"I ought to be kicked for passing it to a Chink!" he thought with extreme self-disgust.

Gorham advanced to the table and began to read. . . .

"Samuel Bull, *alias* David Evans, I arrest you on the charge of murder by drowning on Tuesday, July 28th, 193—, in Whitesands Bay, of Lydia Annabel Bull, née Torrington, your lawful wife.

And it is my duty to warn you that anything you say may be used against you at your trial."

At the first phrase Evans struggled to his feet and stood with staring eyeballs and purple countenance apparently unheeding the iron grip that seized his wrists on either side. But as the name of his wife rolled out he let out a bellow of frenzied rage that drowned Gorham's voice as he uttered the customary warning. And as he realized his situation, as he flung his twelve stone of weight bodily on Manning, the police-officer staggered back. Gorham dropped his papers and sprang to Manning's assistance. Li Moh, hanging like a limpet on to the wrist as he held, was whirled clean off his feet and dashed down against the table. For half a minute extraordinary and harsh things happened to everybody, for the man fought his captors with the blind ferocious strength of the beast from which he was appropriately named, and the muscular training of his father who at one time had been heavy-weight champion of England.

It took the four men all their strength to overcome his desperate resistance, but the end came with unexpected swiftness, for suddenly, with no more warning than an agonized groan, his struggles ceased and he collapsed.

"Don't touch me! God! Don't touch me!"

In the act of snapping the second handcuff, Manning looked, frowning, at his chief.

"Now what!" he muttered. "Gosh, that whisky couldn't have been poisoned, sir?"

It looked for a moment as if the prisoner were rolling in his death agonies. Sweat poured from his face, his congested features witnessed to unaffected physical sufferings of alarming violence. His head bent double over his manacled hands, and the groans he controlled were more poignantly veracious evidence of his agony than the loudest screams could have been.

"Couldn't be. We know Hervey opened the bottle," Gorham murmured. He picked up the bottle and smelt it, even poured out a spoonful and drank it. Then he shook his head, the perplexity clearing from his face "Nothing wrong with that, Manning. He must have damaged himself inside somehow when he dived off that cliff. Ring up Dr. Willoughby. We'd better have him medically examined before we attempt to shift him."

While his subordinate went to the 'phone, which was in the lobby, the others stood over the prisoner. Evans seemed oblivious of their presence, of everything but his physical condition.

But after a minute he raised his haggard face, dawning of returning sense in his eyes.

"Could you . . . lift me . . . on that sofa? Better perhaps . . . lying down. . . . It was that struggle."

"Better wait till the doctor comes," Tennant responded gently.

"That's it. He won't be long," Gorham added. "How long have you been like this?"

"Wasn't so bad at first. . . . Got a twist. Felt like a sprain inside. . . . All right while I didn't move . . . but getting worse. Sat here since last night . . . couldn't sleep with it. And that rough house just about finished it. Here, damn you, let me see that name in the warrant myself. . . ."

Gorham did not move.

"Don't worry, Bull. The warrant's O.K. You are charged with murder in any case. . . . Oh, the woman's name you mean? The registration of your marriage to Lydia Torrington is dated twelve years ago when she was living in your father's house in Swansea. We know you and she met at Castle St. Roche on Monday, and again at the cove on Tuesday morning to discuss what you were going to do."

"How the—do you know all that?"

"You were seen together at the Castle. And your movements on Tuesday morning have been traced from the pub at Winslope where you slept the night to the cove, and that dive of yours off the promontory."

"We agreed to meet for a swim. Like old times! It was me that taught those two kids to swim. Always about after me she was. But my old dad knew a thing or two about women. 'You keep off that young female, Sam!' he'd say. 'She's like her ma, a wrong 'un born!' It was after he'd given me the strap when we'd been out after midnight together on her seventeenth birthday that I was ruddy fool enough to get married to her to stop her jeering at me for letting myself be given a hiding at nineteen. And the old man was right. That damn-fool act of defiance that I hadn't even the nerve to acknowledge to him after has been a halter round my neck ever since!"

Gorham roughly interrupted. He saw that, while the man was sane enough in the ordinary sense of the word, he was talking now chiefly to distract his thoughts from his bodily state.

"Look here, Bull or Evans, or whatever you prefer to call yourself, you'd better think twice before you speak. If you want to come across with a statement later on, well and good. But you got the formal warning? Anything you say now may be used against you at your trial."

The ghost of a grin appeared on the twisted features.

"I got it all right. But my number is up anyway. Let me talk. I'm not telling you anything you don't know already, am I? It was that damned dive did it. It was a devil of a take-off, and after an initial slip I had to take a twist in the flight to lengthen the angle . . . that's when I ricked myself . . . He added a few candid details about the internal injuries he had sustained which it is as unnecessary to transcribe as it is to repeat the adjectives with which he adorned his remarks. That thin veneer of refinement which Sampson had noticed had sloughed from him like a shrivelled and outworn skin, leaving the original Sam Bull, the coarse, unruly, brutal son of the old prizefighter bare of disguise. But if he was brutal it was at least with a brutality untinged by fear, or any weak instinct to whine against fate.

"Besides," he added, "I wasn't as young as I used to be when I first took Lyddy out with me in the water. Funny thing was, my old dad couldn't learn to swim a yard. Yes, it was the worst day's work I ever did—that five minutes with Lyddy before the registrar. It gave her a stranglehold on me that she's never quit using since! I thought I was well rid of her when that barmy old uncle took her and Rosie away from Swansea. Gee, they said he sent her to a ladies' school!" His chuckle ended in a groan. "Lyddy! I bet she taught the flappers there a thing or two! I'd almost forgotten her when she ferreted me out a few years after, soon as she was free to act on her own! I'd started in business on my own by then with the cash my old dad left, and was doing pretty well. I didn't mind taking her round a bit for a week or two at a time, when she dropped on me in Paris, but I was flat I wouldn't live with her again. That was what she wanted, and once Lyddy wanted a thing she'd work for it by hook and crook. She was the sort never to let go of a bloke till she'd got the last ounce out of him . . ."

"You blackmailed her pretty persistently yourself."

"Blackmail? Damn it, if she insisted on claiming me for a husband I'd a right to my wife's money, hadn't I? I made her pay and she paid because she thought it kept me on her string. But I'd have paid twice as much to be quit of her for ever. Why, five years ago I slunk down to Harborough and got hold of that young idiot Hervey to induce her to agree to a divorce! I was prepared to make it well worth her while! But not she! She wanted more than money. So she trapped him into a row with the old man and got him kicked out instead."

"So this time you went yourself," Gorham said grimly. "But what was your great idea in taking Hervey?"

"What d'you suppose it was?" Bull spoke sullenly, yet with a sardonic humour that seemed to derive a sort of amusement from probing the shallows of his captors' knowledge. But Gorham's knowledge was not shallow.

"You needed a second to ensure your getaway," he said promptly. "To drive off with the car and bring it back to pick you up when you were ready. You chose Hervey first because you could bank on his loyalty to his uncle, because if he was recognized his presence would cover yours, and because you realized his local knowledge of the coast there would be useful. And it was, since while you were questioning him about the currents round the headland he let out the story of his own dive. You remembered that when you heard men's voices among the trees when you'd just decided to make for your cached clothes after lying doggo up there. So you took a header into the deep, and missed the bus badly. But you needn't have risked the jump at all. It was only Hervey and his uncle talking! Not the cops as you imagined. . . . Look here, Bull, you played a dirty trick on Hervey when you inveigled him into playing a blind hand in your game. You know he hasn't an idea what your real object was in meeting Lydia! Why not come across with a statement that lets him out decently?"

The man moved in his chair.

"Keen on putting that young mug clear, are you? Well, if I do, what about giving me a spot of relief in return?"

"Don't be a fool, man! I'm not bargaining," Gorham exclaimed sharply.

"Manning"—as he re-entered the room—"you and Li Moh search the premises. Li Moh, it's up to you to produce your essential clue!" he added with a grin.

Blandly the Chinese bowed and departed with Manning on his errand.

"Shall I go, too, Chief Inspector?"

Gorham shook his head, but the glance with which he met the veiled smile in the eyes of Major Tennant was significant.

"No, sir. This gentleman," he turned to Bull, sagging forward in his seat, grey-faced, haggard, the dews of death gathering on his face that was brutally grim yet somehow, for the first time, pleadingly, almost pitifully anxious, "this gentleman is the chief constable of Harborough. He is with me in this case. He and I know perfectly well that Hervey only consented to join you on that expedition to Whitesands because he thought it afforded a chance at last to free his uncle from the miserable burden of that woman which has crushed him for years. Lydia imagined she had cajoled you into agreeing to acknowledge her openly as your wife—in October she was to leave the Villa and join you. You told Hervey that, didn't you?"

Bull nodded, but he did not speak. He seemed to be waiting.

"You put him off with some tale when you rejoined him somewhere along the coast road when he brought back the car. You felt ill, and he was so annoyed you hadn't settled things at once that probably you had a blazing row and he dropped you here, and left you. When he came round with the news of her death you saw he'd jumped to the conclusion, like most other people, that her sister had met her and fought with and killed her, and you let him believe that. But the fatal flaw in that story was clear to me from the first. Rosalind might perhaps have drowned her sister, but she would never have put the body on that buoy."

He paused. The only sound in the room was the man's choked breathing. It came in gasps. But the eyes never left Gorham's face.

"The man who killed his wife had first offered divorce. His wife refused to divorce him, and ferreted out the reason he wanted it. It wasn't enough, you see, since she refused to give him his freedom in any other way, that she should die. Her death had to be known as incontestably certain. So he placed the body where it must be discovered at once. He forgot, or did not know, that the body would betray marks of his rough handling; his idea was it would look like an accident—an attack of cramp, say, that made her cling to the buoy and fall across it insensible and drown there before help could reach her. Wait a minute, Bull. Let me finish before you say anything. The point of the buoy was that Lydia was not only dead, but known to be dead. The man whom she would not divorce was free to marry again—marry someone who he knew would not accept him on any other terms. That led us, after a time, to Greek Street, where there was a milliner, an honest, sensible, good little woman, from whom the husband had rented an office. . . . All we got there was that they had been friends. The man had shown her many kindnesses, had helped her in her earlier struggles to put the business on a sound footing. But only in the way of decent friendliness. Nothing whatever else. The little woman's character—she was a plain person, not young—made any other suggestion impossible. Except to such a mentality as Lydia's. The night before she died, determined to clinch her demand for open acknowledgment of her marriage with her husband when they met next morning, she went out after dark and posted a letter to Greek Street."

"What? She taunted me with that. But I didn't believe her. Yet—"

"Yet you've been wondering since, haven't you?"

"I—I couldn't get out—to find out."

"We found out all right. By an odd chance—since the business is shifting its premises—the place was empty, and the letterbox hadn't been opened for two days when the police removed the contents for examination. It only contained a few circulars and one letter addressed to Miss Annie Green. This it was officially necessary to open, as the handwriting was at once recognized. This is the letter—you see it is unsigned, but quite to the point."

He held it out. It was a half-sheet of thin French paper, scrawled with a single line of venomous writing:

You shan't have my husband. I want him myself.

"Hasn't . . . she . . . seen it?"

"She? Miss Green, you mean? No."

"Do you mean to show it her?"

Gorham looked thoughtful.

"It is anonymous. My position is difficult," he admitted.

"Mine," said Major Tennant, "isn't. May I see it?"

He took the letter and held it in one hand while he extracted a cigarette from his case and lighted it.

"Write out what you've said about Hervey, and everything else. It's all true," Evans muttered. "I'll sign it. Hervey only came as a friend. He thinks Rosie did it. He doesn't know a thing about what happened from first to last."

"Good enough!" the chief constable said cordially. "Very sensible to make that clear at once. I dislike intensely the unnecessary annoyance to outsiders of involving them in police investigations with which they have nothing to do. Sorry, Gorham! Forgive my carelessness. I oughtn't to be trusted with matches."

He dropped the flaming scrap of paper on the floor and extinguished the blaze with a deliberate foot.

"Really, sir! That makes it impossible even to approach Miss Green on the matter."

"I'm afraid," agreed Tennant with blatant remorse, "that it does. It would never do to let a blameless lady learn that an English policeman could tamper with private correspondence. We shall have to rely on the witnesses we have already got and leave her out."

The door opened and Mr. Moh, gliding to the table, laid across it a crumpled coat of jade-green silk.

"The essential clue," he said, "stuffed into the suitcase he carried in the car. That, with the cast of the footprint on the promontory, completes your case, noble Chief Inspector!"

The prisoner's snarl ended in a groan that flecked his lips with bloodstained foam.

"Lyddy's case ended when she wouldn't let me go," he muttered. "If it hadn't been for that old fool sheltering her like he did I'd have made her toe the line years ago."

He relapsed into sullen silence and remained still till the doctors came.

"Gorham," said Tennant, when at last they finally quitted the house together, "what defeats me is how in that utterly futile conversation you had with the guileless Herman you got that missing link that clinched your case against Evans."

"That! Oh yes, but it wasn't anything Herman said, sir. I knew Evans—or Bull—was our man as soon as I got into the room."

"Quite so." The chief constable's voice was patient, even kind. "So did Li Moh apparently. To judge by the judicious way he sidled round to the side of that unfortunate devil's pew. What I am humbly explaining is that I didn't then, and don't even now, understand the first thing about it."

"It was perfectly simple, sir. Moh probably followed out some hunch of his own, but my case hung on that drooping eyelid of Herman Hervey's. Everyone I interviewed about Hervey—up to Doctor Normanby, his headmaster, whom I saw today, and who only parted from him last May—denied that he had any facial defect. But Sampson swore that the man with Evans had a squint. If the man with Evans wasn't Hervey, from whom alone he could have got the intimate local knowledge of the coast that all his actions showed, it followed that Evans, though I guessed and finally got for certain his shady connection with deceased—it is to the Chief and Manning that all the credit is due for the brisk way they followed up and pieced together the details of Evans' dossier—had no connection with the actual murder.

"Sampson and the people at the Royal Martyr at Winslope all swore to Braice that Evans' companion had a squint. But the man with the squint had got to be Rouncey's nephew or my two chains of evidence wouldn't join. And my case for murder based on Lydia's money transactions with Evans fell down. See? When I saw Hervey and realized he had developed his squinting look since he parted from Doctor Normanby, there it was, all tidy and clear."

"It is far from clear to me. Though I must take your word for it till"—he grinned—"I read your full, nicely composed report which may reveal the points now dark to my keen intelligence. As for it being tidy . . . Do you grasp that this denouement of yours releases our charming Rosalind to become my daughter-in-law?"

"I shouldn't let that fear keep you awake tonight, or what's left of it, Major Tennant." Gorham shook his head with a chuckle. "The young man's offer struck me as being strictly for—so to speak—the duration. When he finds that her life is no longer in jeopardy I imagine he will regard that smack she gave him at the inquest, not to mention the bite she followed it up with, as a strictly honourable release from his engagement."

"Perhaps you are right. You have an uncanny knack of being right, man. I should distrust it if you were a subordinate of mine. But I shall do my damnedest to pry poor old Rouncey loose from that girl. If ever a man paid with his life for an act of pure, gratuitous Christian benevolence, he has!"

"I agree. But it was Lydia who was the real curse. Probably the younger one, away from the hourly fridging of Lydia's malice, won't be half so bad. She's had a scare, too, that ought to sober her temper down. And she's honest. Give her some stiff physical job somewhere that she likes, on the land, say, and she may turn into a decent citizen yet."

"That's an idea! Healing influence of the great wide spaces, and Mother Earth, eh what? In some remote part of Australia. The remoter the better for poor old Rouncey, who can then set up housekeeping with his beloved nephew, and embark on an old age of sparkling gaiety unimpaired by the raucous presence of what Moh would call relatives by marriage. Hello . . . what are you doing?"

Gorham had stopped under an electric standard. He fished an envelope out of his pocket and, after reading the address on it, carefully held it in the flame of his lighter till it was consumed.

"Wiping out the last evidence of your crime over that letter, sir."

Tennant chuckled. "Night, night, Gorham. You are a real sport," he said. "But if I hadn't taken the bull by the horns and burned that letter, that poor devil would have been robbed of his last bit of peace in this world."

"Willoughby is certain he'll be quit of this world before forty-eight hours are over," he murmured soberly. "But it was my peace you preserved, sir, not his. I'd never have been able to forgive myself for such a breach of official discipline if I'd had to destroy it myself. Good night. Thanks to you I shall sleep like a little child."

THE END

Printed in Great Britain
by Amazon